SKULLS AND STITCHES

A Dark Suspense Romance

N.J. Weeks

Cover Designer: Pia with Crimsonsdesigns
Editor: Stevi Mager, SML Editorial
Proofreader: Taylor Robinson, Taylored Text

Ebook ISBN: 979-8-9871626-0-6
Paperback ISBN: 979-8-9871626-1-3
Hardcover ISBN: 979-8-9871626-2-0

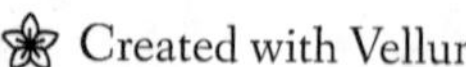 Created with Vellum

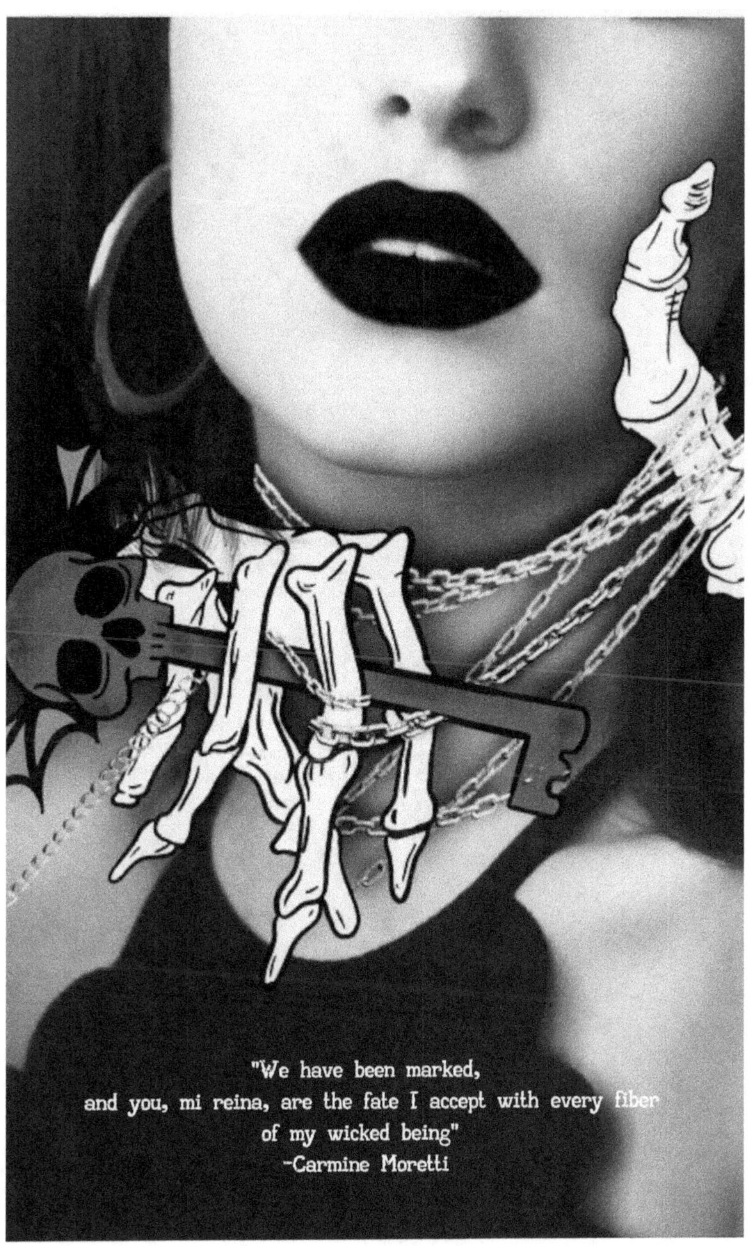

"We have been marked,
and you, mi reina, are the fate I accept with every fiber
of my wicked being"
-Carmine Moretti

AUTHOR'S NOTE

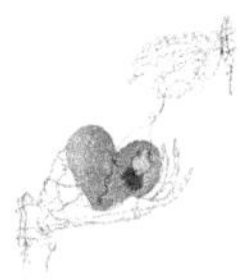

Skulls and Stitches is a dark, suspense, romance novel that contains explicit content not intended for readers under the 18 years of age.

This content includes:
Explicit sex scenes, graphic violence, grief, loss of a parent, loss of child, alcohol use, drug use references, death and profanity...lots and lots of it.

To my daughters,
Love yourself enough to do what your heart tells you to, even if it feels scary. Never underestimate your worth. Never dim your unique light to appease others. Pursue your passions fiercely, because sometimes our dreams are what saves us when nothing else can.

To my readers,
If you wish spooky season lasted year-round, prefer your romances dark/mysterious with a healthy dose of spice and Jack Skellington was your first animated crush...this book is for you.

# Skulls and Stitches
Playlist

01:30   04:03

bad decisions - Bad Omens
Come Undone- Bad Omens
Just Pretend- Bad Omens
I Miss You- blink-182
The Night We Met- Lord Huron
Iris- DIAMANTE & Breaking Benjamin
Come Undone- Bad Omens
This Is Halloween- izzy reign
Someday -Nickelback
Sally's Song- Amy Lee
How You Remind Me- Nickelback
CONCRETE JUNGLE- Bad Omens
Rag Doll - Aerosmith
Limits- Bad Omens
Why Can't I?- Liz Phair
Dial Tone - Catch Your Breath
Nowhere To Go- Bad Omens
Home- Nickelback
Here's to the Night- Eve 6
Without You- Our Last Night
THE DEATH OF PEACE OF MIND- Bad Omens
The Moment I Said It- Imogen Heap
Hemorrhage (In My Hands) - Fuel
Scars - I Prevail
I Will Follow You Into the Dark - Death Cab for Cutie
Another Life- Motionless In White
Him & I - G-Eazy & Halsey
Wonder - Megan McCauley
I'll Wait- Kygo & Sasha Sloan
Fine Again- Seether
Beggin For Thread- BANKS
Broken (feat. Amy Lee)- Seether
Slow Dancing In a Burning Room- John Mayer
Bring Me to Life- Evanescence
Change (In the House of Flies) - Deftones
LA NOCHE DE ANOCHE - Bad Bunny & ROSALIA
Far Away- Nickelback
Home- Edith Whiskers

Phrases
TO KNOW

Sienna and Carmine both are of Puerto Rican and Italian descent. There are cultural references made throughout the book as well as some phrases/words spoken in Spanish. Like the main characters of this story, I also am of Puerto Rican and Italian descent. With that being said, I am not a native Spanish speaker. Keep in mind that some of the phrases/words used may be a rough translation. For that I apologize, you can blame my mother (as I do) for not fully passing on her beautiful native language to me! (I'm kidding mommy, I love you!)

Reina : Queen
Mi hija : My daughter
Siempre: Always
El que tiene las respuestas: The one with the answers
Muerte: Death
Mi Amor: My love
Scheletro: Skeleton (Italian)
La Casa De La Espiral: The house of the spiral

"Believe nothing you hear,
and only one half that you see"

- Edgar Allen Poe

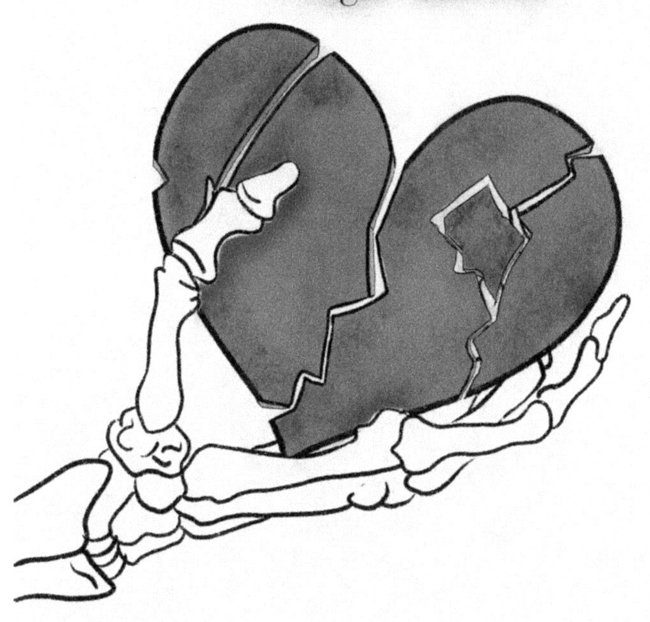

Prologue

Carmine

Alone with my thoughts—an arguably dangerous place to be —I sit at my desk, feening for a cigarette. Thankfully, I spot a half-empty pack of Parliaments near my computer. I reach for the pack as I feel for the lighter that I keep in the pocket of my black and white pinstriped suit. Wasting no time, I take a smoke out, gliding the filter along my lips, wetting it slightly as I light the end.

The crackling flames of the fireplace echo in the study as I lean back in my chair, taking a long, much needed drag. With each puff of smoke that I breathe in comes a brief ping of relief. Though, I've learned relief through vices that aren't *her* are fleeting. Every high fades just as quickly as it comes. It's simply a band-aid on my damned soul.

The bittersweet sting of obsession has poisoned my bloodstream. Visions of her taunt me, permeating my bleak heart. My living flesh betrays me, because inside, I am already dead. I have money, power, endless connections, but

I crave more ... *I crave her*. All I want is for her to know I exist.

The man who still holds her heart hostage is a weak fool. In time, she will see that her shattered soul is best suited as my prisoner, not his. I may be a stranger to her now, but I am confident I can corrupt her just enough to convince her it is me, Carmine Moretti, that she belongs to.

As I exhale, I watch the smoke ominously gather in the direction of the black box sitting on the bookshelf. It's a haunting reminder of what was risked in order to be where she is today ... *alive*. If she only knew what is inside that box, she would, no doubt, see me as the monster I am. Although, I hold on to the hope—delusional as it may be—that in time, she will find solace in the shadows that define my existence.

I have always considered myself to be a man of few words. Yet, lately, I am overwhelmed by the incessant urge to put onto paper the thoughts that consume my mind. It's unsettling for my dimmed conscience to feel as though it is being jolted back to life by this peculiar combination of guilt laced with desire. This unfamiliar concoction of emotions is taking over me. It grabs hold of any free space my mind allows me to have, when it isn't obsessing over the moment, I can be a shadow lurking in the dark no longer.

The cigarette dangles from my mouth as I twirl the crimson ink pen in my hand, trying to conjure up the words to say. The idea of me writing anything is comical. I write checks, not poetry. Words have never been my thing, *violence* is. But I fear that if I do not release these words into existence, I will embark on a vicious rampage that I may not be able to come back from. As I impatiently wait for the moment that I can claim the one my aching soul yearns to call *mi reina*, I will settle for pen and paper.

I must write a letter to the one my soul has been knocking at my flesh to join. Here comes a poem for the broken-hearted. An anthem for the lover who lost the battle but is determined to win the war ahead. A letter to the one I desire, with every fiber of my wicked being. I will make her mine, even if it's the last thing I do, because every breath I take without her next to me is a burden I can no longer bear.

Fuck it. Here goes nothing.

Mi Reina,

Life without you is purgatory. My heart is a ticking time bomb, locked in a holding cell with bated breath, anticipating the moment my tattered hands will have the privilege of touching your flesh. Life with you will be like a game of Russian roulette: unpredictable and impulsive. Together, we will live on the edge of greatness that our broken souls know nothing of, but desire immensely. Through pain, grief, flames, and dust, it's plain to see that you and I are meant to be.

El que tiene las respuestas

I drop the pen, holding the letter in my now trembling hand. Adrenaline filling my veins. She is the one I need to stand by my side, sharing this grey area of life I reside in with. Maybe then our demons can be acquainted, as we spend the rest of our days dancing in a burning room, while the world spins on past us. *What a wonderful nightmare that would be.*

The path to her will be tricky, for revenge is on the horizon. There is no telling the bridges I will burn, the risks I will take, the countless lives I may need to steal to get to her.

She is a perplexing *rag doll*, scarred and broken. I want nothing more than to mend all her broken pieces and revel in the masterpiece that is her fractured beauty. Soon, she will have no choice but to succumb to her fate and realize that to truly live is to die in my *skeletal* grip.

Chapter 1

Sienna

12 YEARS AGO

October 30th. Devil's Night.

I admire the dark October night sky as I walk amongst the rows of headstones that surround me, trying to find a spot to lay my blanket down to sit. I find myself coming to the cemetery a lot more lately. There is something about being surrounded by those who have lived and died before me that makes me feel less alone.

Most people view cemeteries as morbid and absent of life. While that's true, I've always found solace in the peace and quiet that comes from being surrounded by the not-so-subtle reminder of just how fragile life is. To live is to know that one day, death's grim grasp will seal your fate, forcing us all to succumb to our end. In a world of endless differences, it is the one common truth we all share.

The stillness that fills these grounds is a sobering prompt to stop and live life before it's too late, because death does not discriminate. Death is not easily impressed by how much money or power one possesses. There is no bargaining your way out of death's inevitable grip. It's a bleak fate that we must all face, one way or another.

As I continue to walk farther, I am grateful for the full moon that lights up the pitch-black sky. The way it shines down on the slate gravestones not only illuminates their still beauty but, since I forgot my flashlight at home, it is the only light I have guiding me through the otherwise dark cemetery.

I spot a section of gravel underneath a tall tree that the moon has practically hand-selected for me, with its gleam making a visible path to follow. I pick up my pace, heading toward the section of rock and stone not yet covered by sod, when I feel my left boot snag on something, pulling me back slightly. Irritated, I try wiggling my foot free from whatever it's caught on when I hear a crunching sound. I bend down to try to feel with my hand what I have stepped on, when my fingers are met with more crunching.

I sigh when I realize the noise is from a wrapper to a bouquet of flowers left by whoever's grave I am standing by. Carefully, trying not to destroy the bouquet more than my foot already has, I remove the cellophane stuck to the buckle of my shoe and place it back by the headstone.

A rush of guilt hits me as I head toward where I am going to set up tonight's spot. No matter how many times I have come to this very cemetery, where I watched my parents' caskets descend beneath the ground, I can never bring myself to revisit the harsh reality of their passing. I've never left flowers or visited them just because. Even with tomorrow being Halloween night, the two-year anniversary of their death, I still can't bring myself to do it.

Well, their murder, to be exact. Death implies it was due to natural causes, a tragic accident, or an illness. But it was none of those things. It was the cold, calculated attack on one of New York's most prominent "businessmen," my father, Matteo Ricci, and his beautiful wife, my mama, Isabel Diaz-Ricci.

I don't know if I would call myself superstitious. However, I can't ignore the fact that this night, Devil's Night, marks the eve of when the sand in the hourglass of my parents' lives ran out. I know most people expect to outlive their parents but losing them at sixteen just seems unnecessarily cruel.

I swear I can hear Mama's voice now as I roll the blanket out onto the cold ground: *"Be careful, mi hija. Devil's Night is not just mischievous kids throwing toilet paper on houses. The Devil walks among us, and if you aren't careful, he will steal what he thinks is his,"* she'd warn every year. It was all superstitious nonsense passed down from generation to superstitious generation in Mama's family. Halloween would come and go, yet all remained the same. That is, until two years ago, when it became the last night, I had with my parents here on Earth.

It still sends chills down my spine when I think that it could have been three that were shot dead that night. I was supposed to be there. *I should have been there.* It was important to Papa to always have Mama and me by his side at formal functions. It was the old-school Italian in him, thinking that the presence of a seemingly tight-knit family absolved him of his daily sins.

Smoke and mirrors, that's all my childhood was. Keeping up appearances to evade the truth. I guess that's why Papa was so good at what he did, until he wasn't. It's hard to stay on top of your game when what got you there was lies.

That's how he became a target, or at least, that's what their deaths have led me to believe. I shouldn't be surprised; that is the risk of the life my father chose to live, but it doesn't make it hurt any less.

Maybe that's why I always found such comfort in Halloween before their deaths. My whole life has been about wearing masks and pretending. Halloween is the one night of the year when pretending to be something that you are not is encouraged. Now, the only comfort that remains on Halloween night is being with my boyfriend, Leo.

Aside from tomorrow's painful reminder of my parents' cruel departure from this Earth, it is also Leo's birthday. I was with him the night my parents were murdered, being the "rebellious" teenager Mama always accused me of being. She called it rebellious, but I call it being independent-minded. I have always been fiercely independent, determined to go after what I want. And she hated that what I wanted involved Leo.

Mama didn't like the idea of Leo and me being together, which never made any sense given that he was the nephew of Rose, her best friend. Rose not only took Leo in as her own when his mother died but they lived right next door to us. I've known Leo almost my entire life, and Mama always seemed to like him when she thought we were just friends. As soon as our friendship grew into something more, out went her approval of him.

Not understanding our desire to always be together, she would make snide remarks like, *"Hija, you don't know what you want, you are too young,"* or *"It won't last past the summer."* Except, it did. We lasted each summer she swore we wouldn't, and here we are today, still together, despite her judgements and supposed predictions of our parting.

It's difficult to put into words the bond Leo and I have. We have felt such a pull to each other from the start. It's like our souls were destined for one another, and our bodies had no choice but to obey.

Despite the deep connection Leo and I have, lately I can't help but hold back from him, particularly about my writing. It wouldn't be such a big deal hiding my writing from him if it wasn't how I cope. Words written and words read are how I deal with just about anything going on in my life. Escapism through words is my ideal form of therapy.

I escape to books and writing sometimes more than I flee to him. I hate to admit that sometimes it is easier to open my legs to Leo than to open the can of worms that are my emotions and past traumas. I guess that is the baggage that comes with being a dead gangster's daughter. The smoke and mirrors dissipate, but the brick wall remains stronger than ever around my heart.

Tonight, being Devil's Night, I expected Leo and I would be going to a party or something Halloween-related. Instead, I am sitting here, surrounded by death, with my notebook in hand, waiting for him to join me. I stare down at the brown, worn leather of my notebook, admiring its well-loved beauty. To me, these pages represent years' worth of therapeutic release. But to Leo, the cracked spine that holds together this notebook is a gift, one that he has been waiting patiently for.

I roll my eyes, chuckling to myself at the fact that this is the only thing he wanted for his birthday. Why couldn't he be a normal, almost-eighteen-year-old guy, who is content with a new bottle of cologne and a blow job for his birthday? But no, that's not my Leo. Only he would want to sit on the dirt-filled grounds of a cemetery, reading his girlfriend's glorified diary as his birthday gift. He is so strange, and I fucking love it.

I sit in silence a few moments more, wondering what is taking him so long. Finally, as if he could read my mind, I hear his car door slam in the distance. At the same time, a breeze picks up, rustling the fallen leaves against the headstone closest to me, instantly making me wish I packed an extra blanket other than the one I brought to sit on.

I cross my now goosebump-covered arms as I see Leo scurry his way over to me. I can't help but stare at him as he comes closer. His deep-side-parted, black hair covers one eye but does not distract from his sharp facial features. He is devastatingly handsome, with a tall, athletic build that always makes me feel lost when I am wrapped in his strong arms. Which would be nice right about now, being that I am freezing.

He meets me on the ground, showing off his iPod in hand. He brings that thing everywhere. Music to him is what books are to me—therapy through art.

"Figure I'd set the mood with our playlist," he says as he goes to sit behind me, wrapping his flannel-covered arms around mine. The warmth of his body mixed with the scent of his woodsy cologne make my heart feel like it is going to burst out of my chest. I love when he holds me close, because it's one of the only times I feel like the world slows down, even for just a moment.

"You're shivering," he says, squeezing me tighter.

"I know. I didn't think it was going to be this cold tonight."

"Sienna, it's late October in New York. What, is this your first rodeo?" he teases.

"Yea, yea, you're hilarious." I brush his comment off playfully as I tilt my neck back slightly to face him. I break free from the bear hug he has me in, as he gently moves the stray piece of my long, chestnut hair covering my face.

"I love you, Sienna Ricci," he proclaims dramatically, as he slowly moves the hair behind my ear.

"And I love you, Leo Cruz."

Noticing how much I am shivering; Leo begins to take off his flannel. My teeth chatter from the cold as he kneels behind me, motioning for me to raise my arms.

"Here, baby. This will warm you up," he says as I begin to lift my arms upwards.

He slides the first sleeve on my arm and then the next. Once his flannel is on me, he gathers my hair in his hands and tosses it over my shoulder, so it all lays on one side, exposing my neck to him, which he begins to kiss. The heat from his lips meeting my skin makes me swoon with desire for him. I feel a warm flush on my cheeks as he plants another kiss on my skin, slowly working his way up to my ear. He gently nibbles my earlobe with his teeth, and just as a moan escapes my mouth from the pleasure it creates in my center, he releases me from his lips. Leaving me aching for more of what he has started.

Even when his touch is absent from my body, the love I feel for him is a constant reminder of the grip he has on my heart. I sometimes wonder, since we are still relatively young, if it's just lust that I feel and not true love. Whatever it is, I can't deny how good he makes me feel. So, if it's love, I'm going to allow my heart that satisfaction. And if it's lust, I'll allow my body that satisfaction, too.

He shifts in front of me as we lock eyes. A playful grin forms on his lips as he glances down at the worn leather that is now half-covered by my leg. Damn it, I was hoping he had forgotten his gift. *My stupid notebook.* The thought of strangers reading my intimate thoughts is more comforting than Leo reading them, because most of it is inspired by him.

"You better not laugh!" I shout at him as he reaches to get the leather-bound notebook from underneath my leg. Extending one hand toward the notebook, he slightly digs his other palm into my thigh, causing the arousal already forming in my center to throb.

"I would never laugh at you. I know this is a big step for you, sharing your art," he says with a look of gratitude that can't go unnoticed.

The vulnerability I feel in this moment begins to increase as I look away from him, trying to deflect the embarrassment I feel.

This is a perfect example of when I would rather toss the notebook aside and lay naked with him on the ground than have him read any of those pages.

"Okay, whatever you say, Leo," I scoff. "I would hardly call my written rants art."

"Why do you always do that, Sen?" I sense immediate agitation in his tone. His usual playful demeanor dissipates as his jaw tenses. Notebook in hand, he inches closer. Even on bent knees, his six-foot frame towers over me.

The wind picks up, intensifying his woodsy scent, sending it past my nostrils and what feels like right through me. The way the moonlight reflects on his face, even with his hair half covering it, makes his usually brown eyes look black as the sky that we are sitting under. I know he doesn't mean to come off so rough, but that's the thing with Leo, he leads with his emotions. He is a gentle giant who sometimes doesn't realize how fucking intense he can be. It's something I love about him, but in this moment, I can't help but to feel intimidation overcome me.

Before I get a chance to respond, he sets the notebook down, taking my hand in his.

"Do what?" I ask, trying to pull away from his tight grip. He doesn't let go. Instead, he increases his grip ever-so-slightly as he pulls me in even closer to him.

"Sell yourself short. You are a fucking goddess. You are perfect to me," he praises as he takes his other hand to my hair, tugging my head back, exposing my neck once again to him. He leans into my ear, whispering, "You hear me, Sen? A fucking goddess," he reminds me before releasing me from his grasp.

We remain in an awkward, intense silence a few moments more. Unsure of what I should say to shift the mood, I remember the iPod he brought over from his car. I scan the blanket, searching for where he placed it. I spot it on the edge of the dark wool fabric, where its blackened screen makes it blend in with the darkness that surrounds us. I reach for it, hoping to put our evening back on track.

"How about some music?" I ask, trying to lighten the mood. Hoping if we put our playlist on, the tense vibe between us will dissipate.

He takes a deep breath in and, as he exhales, the tension that built in his jaw slowly begins to melt.

"That would be nice," he replies, finally softening his tone. He extends his hand so I can give him the iPod. He turns it on, swiping the control wheel, looking for a song.

As soon as he presses the play button, I recognize the somber instrumental immediately. "I Miss You" by Blink 182 begins to play on the scratchy speaker he has the iPod plugged into. *Our song.*

"To set the mood, of course," he says, cracking his usual pearly white smile, bringing me right back to melting for him.

He picks up the notebook once more and begins skimming the pages. I told him he could pick whatever he wanted to read. He shuffles through before landing on a random page.

"Found it," he exclaims, all giddy. It's so cute how excited he is to read my writing, even though I am dying inside.

Dread begins to fill me, as I lick my lips to speak. "Great, just let me know when you're done reading," I say, as I settle back in my spot, trying to focus on the music.

Then, just as I am about to close my eyes, I hear him clear his throat. A pit forms in my stomach as he begins to read ... out loud.

Seriously, dude?

"Fractured we remain, scarred by our past and wary of the future. Together we sit waiting to be mended from a pain that feels like it's beyond repair. Will the God who plagued us with such despair, fix what he started? Or will it be us? The heathens, the heretics, the lost souls, who pick up the pieces he so conveniently has forgotten. Our hearts, both

broken into pieces, can be joined together like a locket. To make what is broken, whole. To make what is full of doubt, full of peace. One side mine, one side yours. Together we will stitch what needs to be repaired. I hold the needle; you hold the thread. Together we weave a wicked love story from the dead."

As soon as the word "dead" falls from his lips, he slams the notebook closed, startling me. I look up at him and can't help but feel the intensity radiating from his stare. He remains silent, though his body language is screaming something primal. Without a word, he lowers himself to where I sit, taking my chin in his hand.

"You're going to be famous one day, Sen. I only hope I will be there to see it." His sultry baritone distracts my body, while my mind is trying to decode what feels like an ominous statement.

He brings his mouth to mine, gently biting my lip before crashing his tongue against mine. Shifting his attention to my neck, his lips travel down to my collarbone making my legs feel weak. Every kiss is full of passion and feels more electrifying than the last.

He continues to kiss me, moving his hands down toward the waistband of my leggings. My mind is fighting my body. I want him, but I can't help but get stuck on what he just said.

He hopes he will be there to see it?

"Be there to see it?" I blurt, unintentionally killing the mood.

"You don't have to overthink me. Just let me in," he whispers as he moves past the waistband his hand has been stationed at. Gliding his palm in between my legs, he moves the lace of my thong to the side as he begins to work his fingers on my clit, making me quiver.

"That's it, pretty girl," he praises. "I like when you come undone for me." The whole time he is pleasing me, I can't take my eyes off him. There is a hunger in his stare, a desperation that is calling me to him. Usually, I close my eyes and let our bodies lead, but this feels different, more intense. I can't help but feel there is something he wants to say, and it has nothing to do with my shitty poem he just read aloud.

I begin to unbutton his pants as he lays me down on the blanket, removing my leggings and thong, so that I am bare from the waist down on the now gravel-covered blanket.

As soon as I finish unbuttoning his pants to release the bulge that has fully formed beneath the denim, he wastes no time entering me. In one swift, abrupt motion, he guides his hard length inside of me, startling me with the intensity of his thrusts. I become lost in the passionate need in his eyes as he drinks me in right here in the middle of the cemetery, probably by someone's poor grandmother's grave. I feel like this kind of late-night tryst would be a one-way ticket to Hell, if I believed in such a thing.

Heaven and Hell, it's all subjective. For Heaven is in this moment with him, ravishing me here for all the spirits to see, and Hell is any moment he is unable to consume me with his presence.

His silent, intense thrusts devour me as our panting echoes into the crisp autumn air. I begin to feel myself working up to a release, as he grinds his hips slightly while plunging his length deep inside of me.

He brings his thumb to the tip of his tongue, wetting it slightly, before lowering it to my already aching pussy. He matches the rhythm of his thrusts with small circular motions of his thumb working my clit.

"That's it," he mutters. "Let go, Sen," he encourages me as he picks up the pace, still focusing his thumb on my now throbbing and ready center. I'm so lost in the moment, I don't have time to reply before he crashes his release into me just as I feel my walls beginning to pulse, meeting his finish with my own. He stays inside of me as I feel him still pulsing against my wet walls. Finally, he releases me from his intoxicating grip as he rolls over, joining me on the blanket.

We both lay there for a moment, entangled in each other taking in the stillness of the night. There is not a star in sight, only the beaming full moon shining down on us like a vibrant lantern in the sky. I nestle my head in his chest as he wraps his strong arms around me, kissing the top of my head.

He speaks, breaking the silence: "Hey, what do you say we go get those locket tattoos tomorrow? Figure it would be a nice birthday outing."

"What locket tattoo?" I ask, confused.

"The one from your poem. Let's get a Jack and Sally locket. My side will be Sally and your side will be Jack. It'll be perfect, our favorite movie. Two broken souls who found love together. That'd make a sick tattoo."

A flutter forms in my chest as I hear his idea. I love that my poem made him think of our favorite Tim Burton movie and, honestly, probably one of our favorite movies of all time. We watch it for Halloween, for Christmas, pretty much year-round. There is such nostalgia intertwined in the animation that has always intrigued both of us. The Pumpkin King and his stitched-together, beautifully broken Queen, destined to be one. There is a somber, yet playful, vibe to it that's so ... *us*.

"You're serious? Won't that like ... hurt?" I ask, unintentionally sounding like a valley girl.

The thought of inflicting such deliberate pain on myself has never dawned on me. I have dealt with enough agony in my life, so paying to be poked by needles hasn't really been on my radar.

However, the more I think about it, that intentional pain might feel therapeutic in a weird way. Momentary pain to remind yourself, "Hey that hurt like a bitch, but I survived with a souvenir I can wear forever." I could get on board with that. As cliche as matching tattoos can be, I kind of like the idea of branding my skin with a permanent reminder of him. I like it even better that he, too, will be marked with a constant reminder of me.

He nudges me slightly with his elbow. "C'mon. It'll be my treat. It'll be our first tattoo. We've been each other's first everything else, so ..." He can't even finish his sentence without flashing a cocky grin.

Blushing from his statement, I move the conversation back to the tattoos. "Shouldn't we have a sketch or something to give the artist for reference, right?"

"Don't need one. Your poem painted such a beautiful picture. My cousin knows a guy in the city who works part-time at the shop in town. He is super artsy. I'll just have him read the poem over, and I'm telling you, he will crush it."

My face becomes flushed. It took me years to finally allow Leo to read my writing, and now he wants some tattoo artist I don't know to read it. *Jesus Christ.* Well, I guess it's better that I don't know the guy and I'll only have to face him tomorrow, as he stabs my skin with a needle. Could be worse, I guess.

"Can I borrow the page with the poem on it? I'll give it back; I just want him to read it so he can visualize it better," he asks, pouting his full lips.

I roll my eyes, of course, I'm going to say yes. He knows this already, but I appreciate him playing along and asking. "Sure, just be sure to give it back so I can crumple it up and sulk in embarrassment as he tattoos us tomorrow," I say sarcastically.

"You sound so emo, Sen."

"Because I am, duh," I tease.

Bringing my hand to his lips for his kiss, he presses his lips on my skin. "I know and I fucking love it," he whispers.

Chapter 2

Sienna

12 YEARS AGO

October 31st Halloween

Hand-in-hand, Leo and I walk toward the tattoo shop. As we step onto the sidewalk, I notice the flashing marquee with the name "Oogie's Ink" hanging from the large window next to the double wood doors. From the outside, Oogie's has a very Vegas-inspired look, with flashing neon lights going off around the window. As we approach the entrance, I notice a large painting of a roulette wheel in the middle of the two joint doors.

Leo goes to grab one of the handles of the door, when I notice it is adorned with a vibrant, multi-colored snake slithering down the curved iron of the handle. As Leo opens the door, I continue studying the ornate design of the painted wheel, noticing the distinct wrought-iron bugs in the snake design. This place is unlike any of the tattoo shops in our town, not that I have been to any yet, but I have lived in this town long enough to notice that most businesses around here have a lackluster appearance, at best.

Still holding his hand, I follow Leo's lead into Oogie's when I suddenly notice how cold and clammy his palm feels. He squeezes my hand as we walk through the doorway, and we are immediately greeted by the scent of burning incense mixed with the distinctly pungent aroma of weed.

The aroma's intent is to create a calming atmosphere, I'm sure, given the amount of piercing and stabbing that takes place here. Though, for some reason, as we make our way through the small vestibule before the front desk, I can't help but get an ominous vibe. I don't know why exactly. There is just something that feels off with Leo suddenly.

He has barely said a word to me since he picked me up from my house, which isn't exactly groundbreaking given that I am more of the talker between the two of us. However, the lack of conversation, coupled with Leo incessantly checking the rearview mirror while he was driving here, has made me begin to feel uneasy. Even now, as our hands are still intertwined, I have caught him twice checking over his shoulder toward the front window of the shop. I even look over my shoulder, squinting, trying to see something, but I see nothing other than onlookers and a car or two pass us by.

Just as I am about to ask Leo what is wrong, I'm met with an even stronger scent of weed as an older man just as tall as Leo emerges from behind the tall oak desk. Leo lets go of my hand as he goes to greet the man. I'm immediately struck by the number of tattoos covering most of the man's body. Despite the sea of ink splashed about his skin, I am drawn to a small tattoo on the side of his face. It's a small frog perched on a branch with some sort of flower to its side, done in a traditional style, with black and grey shading.

He goes to shake Leo's hand before introducing himself. "You must be, Leo. I'm Eddie."

Snapping out of whatever mood has taken over Leo today, he finally opens his mouth to speak. "Nice to meet you, Eddie. Thank you for fitting us in on such short notice."

"Of course, glad I was able to fit you in while I am in town. I'm heading to another shop in Jersey tomorrow, so you caught me at a good time," Eddie says, smiling. His demeanor is the opposite of how he looks. On the outside, he looks rugged, but upon meeting him, he seems poised and sweet.

Leo nudges me forward, as if Eddie couldn't see me standing right in front of him. "This is my girlfriend, Sienna," he introduces me to Eddie, who has his hand out eager for a shake.

"Hi," I say awkwardly.

Eddie shakes my hand quickly, unfazed by my awkwardness. He grabs his sketchpad and pencil, directing his attention to both Leo and I, clearly ready to start what we came here for.

"Alright, so, you mentioned something about a locket tattoo?" Eddie starts. Leo reaches for the page he tore out of my notebook last night to give to Eddie for a reference. I still can't believe we are getting matching tattoos, let alone ones inspired by something I wrote. I don't know whether I want to cringe or jump for joy. In a weird way, I want to do both.

Eddie takes the now crumpled page and gives it a quick read.

"Alright, cool, man. Let me see what I can come up with. Make yourselves comfortable. You can start filling out the paperwork while I draw something up, and then we will get started," Eddie says enthusiastically, pointing us in the direction of a crimson velvet couch in the corner by the door.

"Thanks, will do," Leo says as he grabs two clipboards from the front desk, where Eddie was sitting before. Leo hands me one of the clipboards, and as I go to grab it from him, he lets out a loud sigh. I know that sigh, it's his "I'm fucking pissed off" sigh.

Irritated by the shift in his demeanor today, I go to kiss his cheek in the hopes that it will soften his mood a bit.

As I bring my lips closer to his face, I notice him grinding his teeth. He sighs once more, this time louder than the last one. "Just fill out the paperwork, Sienna," he snaps without even making eye contact with me.

"Whatever," I mumble under my breath, slipping back into my seat.

What the fuck? This was his idea.

We both sit on the cramped couch, which squeaks every time we make even the slightest movement. Judging by the weathered condition of the velvet, this couch has most definitely seen better days. Between the annoying sounds the couch springs are making, and the vast array of flash designs scattered about the walls, not to mention Leo's stoic behavior, I feel too distracted to fill out the paperwork. I just start checking "*no*" for each of the questions about health history and such, most of which do not apply to me, anyway. I just want to get this over with already.

I rush to finish checking the boxes, and just as I am about to sign the waiver, my eyes catch a section of flash art with different variations of the grim reaper. All of them contain the classic image of the reaper in his black, hooded cloak, holding his scythe, though each design is done in a different style. All so unique, all so beautiful in their own way. Though, out of all the reapers displayed, the one with "MEMENTO MORI" etched on the scythe catches my attention. *Remember, you must die.* Somehow, the inevitability of death seems less ominous when it is portrayed in such an artistic way.

I look over to Leo when I hear his pen tap against the clipboard. He begins tapping his leg, shaking the already questionably stable couch, making me shift back a bit. I grab his arm and rub it, trying to put him at ease from what I assume are first tattoo nerves.

"You ok, babe?" I ask, continuing to rub his forearm.

"Yea, I'm fine, I just want to get this going," he says, not sounding too convincing.

My gaze falls to his leg that is still tapping. Just as I tilt my head down, he grabs my chin, lifting my head up to face him. A half smile escapes his mouth as he leans in to give me a kiss. I close my eyes, taking comfort in the small gesture that is much appreciated given how off he has been acting today.

"Alright, we are all set," Eddie interrupts as he motions for us to follow him.

We rise from the couch and follow him to the back corner of the shop where his station is set up. There is so much artwork on the walls surrounding Eddie's back corner of the shop that I don't know where to look first. Then, through a host of morbid images, my eyes are drawn to a canvas painting of a hummingbird kissing a vibrant red flower with its bill.

The bright, yet hauntingly beautiful piece is striking

against the otherwise dark aesthetic of artwork surrounding it.

I inch closer to the painting, feeling a magnetic pull to it. I can't look away. The way the colors drench the canvas captivate me. I continue to admire the painting, trying to memorize every detail of its beautiful simplicity, when I notice in small cursive the word "siempre" beneath the hummingbird. *Always.*

"Beautiful, isn't it?" Eddie asks after noticing me admiring the painting, as he pours ink into the small cups that are on the tray near his seat.

"Yes, very. Did you paint this?" I ask as he now begins sanitizing his station.

"Nope, that would be my wife, Maria. She is from Puerto Rico and always had a fascination with the myth of Alida and Taroo."

My heart begins to flutter as soon as Eddie mentions Puerto Rico. *Mama's homeland.* Despite having her culture intertwined with Papa's Italian heritage growing up, I don't ever remember hearing anything about this myth.

"Alida and Taroo?" I ask, instantly intrigued.

"Yes, according to island folklore, Alida was already promised to a man from her village. But Alida did not want this and instead began a relationship with Taroo, who was from a different village. When her father discovered Alida and Taroo's relationship, he became furious and forbade her from seeing him. Alida was so grief-stricken that she prayed to the gods to escape her fate of marrying a man she did not love. The gods answered her prayers and turned her into a beautiful red flower. Taroo did not know where Alida disappeared to, so he prayed to the gods to find her and to reunite them. The gods listened and turned him into a humming-bird. So, in their next life, they would be together, since the hummingbird would be drawn to the beautiful red flower."

I bring my gaze back to the painting. "That's so tragic and beautiful".

"Talk about fate, right?" Eddie says as he finishes setting up his station.

"Seriously," I reply as I look back at Leo, who is standing with his hands in his pockets, staring out the damn front window again, as if he is expecting someone. I leave my eyes on Leo a few seconds more. He must have felt the heat from my glare because he turns around and tries to shake off the notably concerned look on his face.

Oblivious to the tension forming between Leo and I, Eddie stands from his chair and claps his hands.

"Alright, I'm ready to start. Where are these pieces going, and who is my first victim?" Eddie laughs.

Leo and I briefly discussed the placement of our tattoos last night on our way home from the cemetery. I was surprised that Leo suggested our rib cages. Even I, being a tattoo virgin, know that the ribs are a notoriously painful spot for a tattoo. I was equally caught off guard because Leo has a decent-sized scar on the right side of his rib cage, where he told me he wanted his tattoo. I suggested getting it done on the other side, but he was adamant it needed to go on the right.

He never disclosed exactly what happened to him, I just know it was his father's doing. From the little I know about Leo's father; he was a cruel man who often lashed out at Leo.

Ever since Leo's mother left his father, he doesn't have anything to do with him. So, thankfully I never had to meet him. I don't think I could ever break bread with a man who treated his son the way he treated Leo.

Since Leo doesn't answer Eddie's question, I speak up.

"Leo wants his on the right side of his rib cage, and I want mine on my left."

Eddie chuckles, just as surprised as I was when Leo mentioned the rib cage placement in the first place.

"Alright, starting out the first tattoo with a bang. I like it," he exclaims. "Ok, so, let me know what you think about the design, and then we can get started." Eddie hands both of us a copy of the design he drew up. Just like in my poem, there are two pieces of a broken heart shaped as a locket. Instead of a key going through the keyhole, there is a skeleton hand holding a needle and thread to go through the locket. I love the subtle nod to Jack and Sally in the design.

"Wow, it looks great. You took my girl's art and turned it into a masterpiece," Leo finally says to Eddie.

"Thanks, man," Eddie says with pride. "Alright, sick. Who's going first?" He asks, bouncing his eyes between the two of us.

I say nothing, because I would rather not go first, but naturally, Leo decides to act like a gentleman and suggests that I go first. I oblige simply because whatever mood Leo is in, it's not worth arguing with him about who goes first. Part of me hopes that once Leo sees my tattoo begin to take shape, he will lighten up a bit.

I head toward the coffin-shaped, black leather chair. Eddie instructs me to lift the left side of my shirt up and thread my arm through the armhole, exposing my rib cage. I lay back on the leather chair, which is, thankfully, much sturdier than the old, crimson couch we sat on in the lobby. He begins to prep my skin and I startle as he dabs a cold paper soaked in rubbing alcohol on my ribs.

But the paper isn't the only thing that makes me jump. Just as Eddie goes to sterilize my skin, I hear a loud *ping* come from Leo's phone. The tattoo shop has decently high ceilings, so it makes every sound appear louder than it is, due to the echo.

Leo steps back a few inches from where he is standing near my head to grab his phone from his pocket. The tension in his jaw returns as he reads the incoming text. Without responding to whoever texted him, he just slips his phone back into his pocket and returns to his stoic, silent state.

Me being me, unable to let anything go, I decide to break the silence. "Who was that?" I blurt.

"No one, just Titi Rose," he mumbles.

"Everything ok?"

"It's fine," he mumbles, this time sounding more monotone.

I drop it ... for now and smile at him as I hear the buzzing of the tattoo gun rev up.

Eddie dips the needle into the black ink. "Let's get this show on the road," he says.

"Let's do this," I respond as I stare at Leo. When he smiles back at me, I can't help but look once more at the painting behind him zoning in on the small cursive words below the hummingbird.

Siempre.

The buzzing sensation from the tattoo gun isn't anything as I expected. It hurts, sure, but it's the kind of pain that lessens the more the adrenaline kicks in. With each stroke of the ink penetrating my skin, I become more focused on working through the pain. I can see why people become addicted to this. It's an artsy way of embracing pain you endured while reminding yourself that you survived it. Left with a lifelong, beautiful reminder of that ability to push through, *to survive.*

The rest of the tattoo appointment is spent mostly in silence, aside from some small talk from Eddie. Leo contributed a little bit to the conversation, but not much. Even though the appointment didn't go as I expected, the stabbing pain was worth every second to have such a sentimental first tattoo together. The black and grey design brings my poem to life in a way I never imagined.

About five hours pass when Eddie wraps up the last of Leo's tattoo. After Eddie puts a plastic cover on Leo's fresh ink, we walk up to the desk in the front of the shop to pay. Leo reaches for his wallet and brings me in close, kissing me softly on the cheek.

"It's on me, babe," he says, handing Eddie cash from his wallet.

As Eddie takes the cash from Leo, something, or rather someone, catches my eye from across the street. It's now dusk, so it is difficult to make out exactly who is standing outside, but it appears to be a man. He is wearing some sort of long coat, with an old-school top hat. The man is smoking, leaning against the lamppost that is flickering, like a cliché thriller movie. I squint to try to get a better look at him as he is just staring directly into the tattoo shop, when the register slams shut, making a *ding* sound and startling me out of my investigative trance.

I turn back to face Eddie and thank him for the amazing work he did.

"Take care, now. Thanks again for coming in," he says to us.

When we turn around toward the window of the shop, I am expecting to see the man still smoking and staring. But to my surprise, no one is there.

We walk back out onto the sidewalk, and now I feel like I have traded places with Leo, as I start scanning the area looking over my shoulder.

That's impossible, he was just there.

Leo grabs my hand as we head to his car. He seems less tense, but still not overly talkative.

"That was fun," I say as we stand outside Leo's Cavalier.

He releases my hand and begins fumbling in the pocket of his jeans searching for his car keys. "Yep."

Taking in a deep breath I decide that I have held my tongue long enough. I'm over having to tiptoe around Leo today, and now I'm at a breaking point with the half-assed silent treatment.

"That's it?" I begin to move my hands up animatedly. I tend to talk with my hands often, especially when I am worked up about something. "I thought this was supposed to be a fun date. You look like you just went to a fucking funeral. What's wrong?" I press as he retrieves his keys from his pocket.

He doesn't respond to me right away. Instead, he unlocks the car and opens the driver side door to get in.

I roll my eyes as I get in the passenger side, slamming the door shut.

Turning the key in the ignition, Leo grabs for the stick shift as he begins to drive. "Sienna, it's fine, I just have a lot on my mind. Quit it."

"You know you can talk to me," I remind him.

"It's fine, alright? Just drop it." He shifts gears before accelerating beyond the speed limit, making me grasp onto the passenger door handle to brace myself against the dramatic increase in speed.

Holding tight to the handlebar, I turn to look at him, but his eyes are glued to the road, as he continues to pick up speed. I'm about to tell him to slow down when he finally lets up off the gas, just as he turns onto one of the local cut-throughs that is not too far from our street. His gaze remains intense, focused on the dusk-covered road ahead of us.

He peers at the rearview mirror, then once through the side-view mirror, before shifting in his seat as he reaches for the stereo system in the center console. He turns the knob to raise the volume as "Someday" by Nickelback begins to play. He shifts gears once more as the music begins to fill the car, easing my nerves from his erratic driving. I want to say something to him, but instead, I decide to lean back in my seat and enjoy the song, since we are almost home.

I leave my hand near the gear stick, hoping that he will reach for it. I glance at him as he glides his open palm on the steering wheel, turning into the beginning of our neighborhood. His right hand moves to the gear, shifting it once before he redirects his hand to mine. In a low mumble, he then begins to sing along with the song playing through the speakers.

"Someday, somehow. Gonna make it, alright, but not right now. I know you're wondering when ..."

A smile escapes my lips. Hearing Leo sing one of my favorite Nickelback songs is the much-needed cure for the tension that has been building today. I see the stress melt off him as he finally directs his eyes to me as he slows down, parking in his Titi Rose's driveway.

I go to grab the handle to open the door when, when Leo's arm reaches for my hand, stopping me. I look at him, confused by the intense motion. Before I can say anything, he leans in for a deep, passionate, tongue-swirling, kiss. This is the most like us that we have felt like all day. I revel in it and try to release my anxious thoughts.

"Thank you for today," he says.

"Of course. Never thought I was much of a tattoo girl, but I think today might have changed that."

He ignores my tattoo comment, instead moving his hand to my chin. "I love you, Sen, so fucking much."

"I love you, too, Leo."

I look through the driver window and see my Titi Lana on the front porch, talking across the driveway to who I can only assume is Leo's Titi Rose. I turn to my right and look out the passenger window when I see Rose standing right outside the car.

She begins to knock on the window, as if I could miss her pissed-off expression, standing outside the car.

Leo rolls his eyes, removing his hand from my chin as I go to roll the passenger side window down to greet his Titi. "Hi, Rose."

"Sienna," she nods her head, as if she is obligated to acknowledge me, when it's clear she'd rather talk to Leo.

"I'll be inside in a few minutes, Titi," Leo says, shifting positions in his seat, clearly embarrassed at the way Rose is acting.

"Ay, Leo, I have been texting you. I talked to you about

this, you need to come inside. This isn't the time to play games," she warns.

"I said I'll be right there," he repeats, this time less kind.

She remains standing there with a scowl on her otherwise wrinkle-free face. Rose is much older than my Titi Lana, but you wouldn't guess with how smooth her olive skin is. Even pissed off at Leo, for whatever reason, she looks so elegant. After another few seconds of silently scolding Leo with her tense stare, she throws her hands up in the air and walks away toward her house, muttering something in Spanish.

I roll the window back up and look to Leo. "I guess we aren't trick-or-treating tonight," I joke, reminding myself of what night it is. I was so preoccupied with the tattoos and decoding whatever mood Leo has been in that I almost forgot it was Halloween and Leo's birthday.

"Yea, guess not," Leo says, faking a smile.

We both look through my window and see Rose on her porch, waiting for Leo to go inside.

"Okay, looks like you might turn into a pumpkin if you don't head inside. Fitting for a Halloween birthday boy," I say, trying to make light of Rose demeanor.

The deafening silence returns, as he does not respond to my attempt at humor. Instead, we both get out of his car, and Leo walks around the front of the car, meeting me on my side.

"I'll see you tomorrow. Maybe we can go grab breakfast at the diner?" I ask as we begin to walk in front of his car.

Leo hesitates and smiles but does not answer as he leans in for a kiss instead.

"So, tomorrow is a yes, then?" I remind him since he

glossed over my diner suggestion. He still doesn't answer my question, so I decide to just drop it, knowing I will more than likely see him tomorrow at some point.

"Don't forget to put the aftercare on your ribs," I remind him playfully.

"How can I forget? I'll have you forever on my skin," he says as he walks toward me and grabs my face with both hands before kissing me goodnight. I fall right into his kiss and blush, feeling Rose's eyes still on us.

"Ay, Leo, *ahora!*" Rose shouts from her porch.

Leo ignores her, still kissing me. His tongue dancing with mine, making me come undone.

"Goodnight, Sen," he says, releasing my lips from his.

"Goodnight, Leo."

He locks his car and heads toward his Titi Rose on her porch and I head toward my house. I look back to the porch and see Rose begin to scold him as she guides him with both hands on his shoulders into the house. Just as they pass over the threshold, she looks over her shoulder just like Leo did at the tattoo shop. She quickly scans the street and looks back at me once before slamming the door shut.

I walk slowly over to my front porch while keeping my eyes on Rose's porch. She turns off the light that was just shining down on the wood door, as well as the light she usually keeps on in her entryway.

Rose's house fades to dark as I finally make my way into my house. I hear Titi Lana in the kitchen putting away dishes. I debate going to talk to her, but exhaustion begins to creep in, so I instead head upstairs to my room.

Just as I am about to crawl into bed to unwind with a book, I hear my phone vibrate from inside my purse. I sit up on my bed, reaching over to grab my phone seeing that it is a text message from Leo.

Leo: I love you, just know that I am sorry.

Me: I love you, too. What's wrong?

Leo: I know today is a difficult day for you. I'm sorry I wasn't more present.

Me: It's ok. I think our new matching ink makes up for it.

Leo: Do you ever think about that night your parents … you know?

Me: Um I try not to but it's kind of difficult to forget. Why are you asking?

Leo: Do you ever worry whoever did it will eventually come after you?

Me: Why are you asking me this?

Leo: I would never let anything bad happen to you.

Me: Ok? You're acting weird, what is wrong?

Leo: I love you.

Me: Ok…I love you too. Leo…stop it, you are acting so weird.

My heart begins to pound in my chest as soon as I send the text. I turn my head toward the window that overlooks Rose's house though it remains pitch-black and seemingly motionless. I look back down at my phone, expecting there to be another text from Leo. He has been responding almost immediately since this bizarre conversation he started out of nowhere, but suddenly, his replies stop. Confused, uncertain what to think, I text him again.

Me: Hello??

Still, no reply.

Between the adrenaline crash from the tattoo and the emotional rollercoaster that was today, I don't wait up for a response from Leo. I don't bother getting changed into my pajamas. Instead, I pull the covers over me and drift off to sleep.

Tomorrow will be better. It must be, right?

I wake the next morning to the sound of rain crashing against the roof above my bedroom, as the wind whistles through the windows.

I get out of bed and immediately go to the nightstand my phone is placed on. I touch the side button of my phone and see one new message from Leo.

Instead of feeling relief, there is something inside of me that feels a sense of dread. I can't explain it, but the air has shifted. I feel as though something tragic has happened and I am too late. I take a deep breath, bracing myself, for what exactly, I don't know.

I open the message and my hands turn cold. My ears start to ring. I feel sick.

Leo: Siempre.

Always?

I read the message over and over, not comprehending what he means. My breath stalls, my heart feels like it is suddenly shattering into a million pieces.

Chapter 3

Sienna

PRESENT DAY

A buzzing noise startles me awake as I roll my sore, hungover eyes. Last night, in my drunken stupor, I must have forgotten to close the curtains as sunlight spills into my bedroom. I can feel the warmth radiating from the window, with its strong gleam burning against my closed eyelids.

Buzz, buzz.

Ah, that noise, make it stop.

I begin to slowly open my eyes, wondering if the obnoxious buzzing sound is coming from the vibrator that I keep in the drawer of my nightstand. I had one too many vodka tonics last night, so it is well within the realm of possibility that I could have left it running after using it. If I was coherent enough to pleasure myself, that is.

Just as I go to turn my head to check my nightstand drawers, I hear a faint grunt followed by a shift in the bed. A large vein-covered hand with a tattoo of Beetlejuice's face on it emerges from under the covers. A sigh of relief floods me as

I take in the green and purple ink, remembering I had a guest last night, Eric.

Well, there goes the vibrator theory.

My phone keeps buzzing as I am trying to get enough wits about me to look for where the fuck it may be. The phone finally stops, since it's taken me entirely too long to find it, sending whoever is calling to voicemail. *Shucks.*

Despite not having a clock in my room I can tell from the way the sun is hitting the front of the house that it's early. Too damn early to be getting a phone call from anyone if it isn't an emergency. It's 2022, phone calls should be illegal at this point. If you can't say it through a text, email, or to my face, chances are it can go unsaid. At least, that's how I am feeling now with the hangover from Hell.

Still asleep, Eric shifts in the bed exposing his thick, ash-blonde beard. He is scruffy but not so much that it hides his traditionally handsome features. On paper, he is my type; covered in tattoos, good in bed, tall. But there is one problem: I don't feel anything other than physically satisfied when I am with him. He can turn me on and fuck me, no problem, but he does nothing to make my heart skip a beat or bring my soul alive.

I often wonder if love will ever be in the cards for me again. Leo fucking ruined me in the best and worst ways possible. The internal scars of love lost that I carry with me daily make the prospect of finding a love as deep as what I felt for Leo feel increasingly out of reach. Even though we were young, he left such a mark on my heart that it makes me feel like truly moving on may never happen.

Despite all the time that has passed since he left, I still feel guilty every time I have a new visitor in my bed. I call those that frequent my bedroom, visitors, because that's what they are. Visitors who can please me temporarily, but that's it. I'll give a man a night, but I won't promise any man my tomorrow. Those are now promised to me.

I finally spot my phone on the floor beside my night-stand. I inch out of bed to grab it, trying not to wake Eric, who is now snoring. I take the flat sheet with me to use as a cover, wrapping it around my naked body.

Reaching for my phone, I illuminate the touch screen and see that the missed call is from Nessa, my best friend and total opposite. She recently got promoted to detective in the city and I am the daughter of a professional criminal whose very playground used to be where she now patrols daily.

Sometimes, I wonder if it weren't for the fact that we were roommates in college, if we ever would have become friends. However, opposites attract, both in love and friend-ships. So, early phone calls after a night out of drinking is part of the package deal that comes with being Nessa's friend.

I go to call her back, but she beats me to it, as the phone vibrates once more. This time, I answer it immediately.

"Hey, Nes, what's up?" I ask groggily as I walk toward the large bay window in my room that overlooks the house next door.

"How are you feeling, girl?" she asks, sounding way too chipper for it being morning.

"Eh, I'm hurting," I respond as I rub my hands on my throbbing temples, wishing I had some Tylenol for this headache from Hell.

A breathy chuckle echoes in the earpiece of the phone

as, I'm sure, Nes is about to say something snarky. "From what, the new ink or from Eric laying down pipe last night?"

Yep, there it is.

I feel my cheeks turn red. "Gross, Vanessa, he is your fucking cousin."

I internally cringe at the reminder that Eric is Nessa's cousin. Not that there is anything necessarily wrong with that, but it just makes everything feel more complicated. Especially because I view our arrangement as purely physical, while I know he wants it to be more. He has had a crush on me since he visited the dorms when Vanessa and I were freshmen in college. We have hooked up on and off over the years, but it has never meant more to me than that. A fact I try to remind Vanessa of almost daily, since she is somehow convinced, I'm going to marry him.

"He has had a hard-on for you forever. It's me, Sienna. Cousin or not, you can tell me these things."

"I know, but still. I just don't want to lead him on any more than I probably already have."

"Well, I think it's a little late for that, considering he has landed in your bed almost every night he has been in town," she sarcastically reminds me.

Eric lives in the city not too far from Nessa's apartment, but his new job has had him in town recently. Last time I checked, he is an intern for some bigwig in the city, so what he needs to be doing here, an hour and a half north of the city, I'm not exactly sure. I never asked him, not like there has been many discussions between the two of us since he has been in town. We usually drink, fuck, repeat... and in that order.

"I know, I just hope he doesn't expect an invite tonight when we go out. I was kind of hoping for a girls' night, since it's your last night in town," I say to Nessa.

"Yes! Let's try that new bar on Main Street tonight," Nessa responds. Thankfully, she didn't insist on inviting Eric.

I let out a sigh of relief. "Great, a girls' night is just what the doctor ordered," I say softly in the phone, on the off-chance Eric isn't in as deep of a sleep as he appears to be.

Vanessa's bubbly tone shifts, hearing the amount of relief in my voice. "Sienna, I know this month has always been difficult for you, but it's been twelve years already. Don't you think you owe it to yourself to move on?"

I pause. Twelve fucking years, I can't believe it.

Somehow, losing Leo has stung just as much, if not more, as losing my parents. I know Nessa wants me to move on and stop closing doors in my love life before they are even able to open, but I hate talking about it.

"Alright, Nes, let me get going. I need some coffee before I finish these last few paragraphs that I owe Luke before tomorrow's paper is printed," I lie. Work can wait. As a free-lance writer, I occasionally get some article opportunities for physical papers, but it's nothing that has crazy deadlines. Truthfully, I'm already caught up with the work I had to do. I just don't feel like talking anymore, especially about Leo, Eric, none of it.

"Ok, see you tonight. Say hi to my cousin for me," she teases. "Oh, and don't forget, with you moving to the city, you aren't going to be able to escape seeing Eric," she reminds me.

"I know that Nes."

"I just wanted to make sure," she says with a slight edge to her voice.

I hang up the phone and look up at the brick house of nightmares next door. I need to move out of this place for good. I try so hard to move on, but sometimes, this house suffocates me, bringing me back to a state of grief I just can't handle anymore. The memories are too vivid, and lately, they haunt me more than comfort me.

I ignore Eric snoring as I take in Leo's old house, which looks nothing like how his Titi Rose used to maintain it. The shutters are all faded from the sun. The landscaping isn't maintained, with its overgrown bushes crowding the once pristine walkway. The porch that was once adorned with rocking chairs now remains bare, with chipped paint and weathered wood.

As if Leo leaving the way he did wasn't confusing enough, what happened to his Titi Rose and the house, afterwards made even less sense. There was no for sale sign, no moving trucks, nothing. The house remained vacant, until one day, a woman named Miranda, around the same age as Rose, moved in.

I continue staring out the window a moment more when I hear the mattress squeak as Eric makes his way out of the bed. I turn to look at him. He is in nothing but his checkered boxers that hang low, exposing defined abs with a V trailing down to his groin. His long, golden hair is messier than mine from however many rounds we went at each other last night.

"Good morning," he says in his usual flirtatious tone.

I turn my attention to the window, keeping my back to him. "Hey, Eric."

"You know she doesn't bite," he says jokingly, as I hear him searching the floor for his clothes.

Confused, I redirect my attention to him. "Who?"

He grabs his shirt, pulling it overhead as he answers me in a tone muffled by the fabric hitting his lips, "The woman next door."

"Oh," I respond, embarrassed that he caught me peering out the window. "Yea, I guess so. It's just so strange she never leaves the house, and rarely does she have any visitors," I continue. "I've caught her multiple times, too, just staring out the window."

"What, like you were just doing? You know, it's not illegal to look out your own window, Sienna," he teases, pointing out the hypocrisy of my own statement.

"You know what I mean. It's just creepy, is all," I say, as I turn to face Eric, still holding onto the sheet I have draped around me like a dress.

He flashes me a wide grin, accentuating his dimples that are almost completely hidden by his thick beard. "Will I see you tonight?" he optimistically asks, with puppy dog eyes.

"I think Nessa and I are going to have a girls' night tonight before she heads back to the city."

He rolls his eyes, and the smirk that was just on his mouth disappears. "Alright, I can take a hint."

I know I am letting him down; I just don't feel that way for him. Plenty of people have casual sex. I shouldn't feel guilty for hooking up with Eric, especially when I have made my intentions explicit.

"Eric, why do you do this? I told you we are just friends, nothing more," I remind him in a weak attempt to rebuild some boundaries or sense of normalcy in our friendship.

He shakes his head in frustration at my words. I know I'm coming off harsh, I just don't know how many times I can tell him that it's just physical between us and nothing more.

I go to open my mouth to lessen the blow my words had on his ego when a defeated smirk unfolds from his lips.

"I get it, Sienna. I'm your friend when you want me to be and your fuck buddy when you want me for a good time." The bitterness in his voice is loud and clear. He lowers his hand as my eyes follow his movements. The Beetlejuice tattoo on his right hand is now clenched in a tight fist as he stares at me with harsh eyes.

His anger doesn't scare me. I'm used to this with Eric, he has always been a bit of a hothead.

I meet his intense gaze with my own agitated stare. "That's not fair, Eric!" I say as I roll my eyes.

"Yea, whatever, life is not fucking fair, Sienna," he hisses as he slides on his jeans.

"I told you where I stood before we started hooking up and you agreed. Then, each time after, you make me feel guilty."

"No, I just let you know how I feel. If you feel guilty, there is probably a good fucking reason, Sienna."

"Shut up, Eric," I seethe.

"You know, you can live your life all you want, staring out that Goddamn window, but he isn't fucking coming back. He left you!" he shouts. His words sting, even though it's the truth.

His anger is just masking his pain. I wear the same mask day in and day out. He is staring at the one he wants, while I am staring back at him, wishing he was someone else.

"Well, you are the one who is bringing him up. I was just mentioning the creepy woman who lives next door, but you decided to take it there," I say, getting increasingly frustrated that he isn't even making eye contact with me.

Instead, he continues to scan the floor, looking for his damn belt. Granted, my room could use a tidy-up, but Jesus Christ, my floors aren't that clutter-filled. I immediately spot his black leather belt across the room. I stomp over to it, seething from the way he is jealously starting an argument with me.

"I think it's time for you to go," I demand.

As I begin to toss his belt to him, I forget to hold on to the sheet I have draped over me. Just as the belt leaves my hands, down goes the sheet onto the ground, exposing my naked body.

Eric's eyes instinctively trail down my silhouette as I rush over to grab my robe.

"Don't even think about it," I mumble under my breath as I leave my room, heading toward the bathroom so I can wash my face. But more importantly, get away from him.

I'm not even halfway down the hallway when I hear his footsteps trail behind me. He follows me into the bathroom, and I pretend I don't see him, despite my bathroom being narrow and him being well over six feet tall. It's a tight squeeze, but I shimmy my way around him to grab a washcloth, still ignoring his presence.

I go to lean over the sink to put water on my face, when I feel his hands grip my hips just as I splash the warm water on my face.

"Sienna, I'm sorry. I just like hanging out with you. I

have been busy in the city the last few times Vanessa came to visit, so it was just nice being out with you last night and after." I can hear the sincerity in his voice again now that his anger toward me has dissipated.

I turn to face him. "I know, L– Eric," I catch myself. *Fuck.*

Anger begins to seep back into his jawline as he pulls his hands away from my hips. "Holy shit!" he exclaims. He runs his hands through his hair briefly before slamming his fist on the countertop, causing the water that fell onto the granite to splatter. "You are never going to get over him, are you?"

"I'm sorry, Eric," I say, aware of how bad that must have made him feel that I almost called him Leo.

Fucking Christ, why did I almost call him that? Nothing about him resembles Leo. But in typical Leo fashion, even when he is not around, he finds a way to seep into my mind.

"Yea, me too," he mutters under his breath, heading toward the hallway to leave.

"Let me walk you out at least," I say as I follow him.

"No thanks. I'll pass," he says, increasing his pace.

I ignore him and continue to follow, matching my pace to his as he hurries down the staircase.

He grabs his boots from the landing at the bottom of the steps as I stand there watching him tie the long straps. He loops the last lace, refusing to acknowledge my presence. As he heads to the front door to unlock it, I stop him, placing my hand over his.

He lets out a sigh. "I have to go," he says as he tries to pry my hand from his.

"I know, I just wanted to walk you out, like I said. It's the right thing to do."

He shakes his head. "Really?" he asks. Though judging from his attitude, the question feels more rhetorical than anything.

"Since when have you ever cared about doing the right fucking thing? Now get your hand off the fucking doorknob," he roars. His words cut like a knife, as do his cold eyes.

"What fucking ever, Eric," I say, giving up on trying to be nice to him.

Just as he goes to swing open the door, I notice a black envelope falling down from where it appears to have been wedged under the glass storm door.

Noticing the envelope as well, he bends down to grab it. As he hands it to me, he notices the emblem on the back.

"Oh, I didn't know you applied to Marked Inc.," he says, staring at the gothic-style *M* centered on the back of the envelope.

Marked Inc.? What the hell is that?

"Umm, I didn't. I don't even know what that is," I say, confused. "Should I?"

"Guess you weren't paying attention to me last night at the bar, that's cool." He tries playing off his hurt, but it is evident by the edge in his tone that I've hurt him ... yet again.

"I'm sorry, refresh my memory. I was running on little sleep, a long tattoo session, and way too many drinks," I remind him, meeting his irritation with my own.

"Yea, well, like I was saying last night, that's the public relations firm I have been interning at. I'm mostly just the boss' errand boy, but he pays well, and I'm broke so—"

I cut him off. "I have never heard of Marked Inc. before. I wonder why I was sent something," I say, dying to know what is inside the envelope.

Eric grabs the handle of the storm door, opening it to leave. "Well, looks like you're about to get a crash course in all things Marked Inc. then," he says ominously as he walks out and slams the glass storm door behind him, making his way down the porch steps.

I can barely formulate a goodbye to Eric as curiosity begins to take over. I shut the door and hurry to grab my letter opener from the kitchen, anxious to see what the fuck is inside. I take the blade of the letter opener, tearing the top of the seal revealing a handwritten letter.

I have applied to some papers in the city just for shits and giggles, but no one ever responded. I have never even considered a public relations firm, let alone thought one would follow my practically non-existent writing career to seek me out via personally delivered letter.

I'm immediately struck by the elegant cursive writing that adorns the paper. These days writing in longhand feels like an ancient art. I focus my eyes to the top of the page, as I begin to read the letter out loud.

Ms. Sienna Ricci,

I hope this letter finds you well. My name is Carmine Moretti, and I am the CEO of Marked Inc., a public relations firm with a vested interest in providing our clientele with the best representation possible. This entails having a host of lawyers, media consultants, and writers on our team.

Your vast work as a freelance writer has come

to my attention, and I believe your well-rounded writing abilities would be a true asset to our company.

I am willing to offer you a full-time position, including benefits and paid time off, if you so choose to join Marked Inc. I trust this is an opportunity you will not want to miss out on. I look forward to hearing back from you.

Yours,
Carmine Moretti

I read the letter again, just to make sure I didn't skip over anything. In the top left corner of the letter there is a staple, and beneath it is a matte-textured business card attached to the back of the paper. I carefully tear the card from behind, releasing it from the staple to get a better look at it.

With the business card in hand, I head back upstairs to grab my cell phone so I can find out more about what this Carmine Moretti has to offer.

As I make my way up the stairs and down the hallway to my bedroom, I stop and stare at the threshold to my room. I was already planning on moving to the city, ironically, within the next few weeks, but this feels like a sign. Call it fate or coincidence or whatever, but this feels like the confirmation I needed. The signal from the universe that leaving this place is what I need to move on with my life, to finally feel like I'm living again for me and not for memories that haunt me.

I grab my phone, and just as I am about to start dialing the number, I take a deep breath in to calm the unexpected excitement beginning to stir inside of me.

Here goes nothing.

Chapter 4

Carmine

I swirl the pen in my hand, watching the mouth of my financial advisor, Felipe, move without focusing on his number jargon. Usually, I would be asking questions, crunching numbers, getting involved, but not today. Instead, I am distracted, tense, and feeling increasingly thrown off my game. Though, I can't let any of that show.

Appearances are everything in my line of work, and it is imperative that I do not allow my emotions to ever come to the surface. It's a disguise I have been forced to wear.

As Felipe blabbers on about things I should care about, I pretend to take notes by periodically looking up at him while I sketch out the next part of my back piece I want to get done.

I'm a horrible artist but I have the basic concept down of what I want. I have an appointment next month with the city's most sought-after tattoo artist. People usually wait months for an appointment, but when you're as known in the kind of social circles that I am, all it takes is a quick phone call and your requests become reality. Better yet, I got him to agree to make a house call. That way, wherever I may be, by the time the appointment rolls around, I can still get tatted.

Tattoos have become one of the many addictions I have acquired over the years. I have debated dabbling in the shit I push on the streets, but I know myself. The depressive hole I have sunken into would collapse if I opened that Pandora's Box. So, instead, it's tattoos and booze—whiskey, to be exact —that attempt to fill the endless void in my life.

Felipe continues to ramble about the numbers from this financial quarter as I lean back in my chair, spinning it halfway, so I have the reception area in my view. I side-eye my receptionist, Lizzie, sitting there, flirting with the UPS guy.

Ah, Lizzie. Her father, Enzo, is a longtime friend of my father's, not to mention the previous co-owner of Marked Inc. That is, until I bought him and Father out of their stake in the company. My father feels a sense of responsibility to Enzo and his family because of his loyalty to the Moretti family.

Providing Lizzie with a job as my receptionist is part of that responsibility. The extra work she has put in over the years taking care of my more personal needs is a blurred line that we crossed a long time ago. I should feel more guilt about the professional boundaries we have ignored but I don't. Lizzie has been more than willing, just as I have been. We are just two people fulfilling our physical needs; it doesn't need to be anything more than that.

My eyes focus back on Felipe, who is now gathering the stack of papers back into the folder he came into my office with. Thank fucking God, he is wrapping up this snooze fest.

"Alright, Mr. Moretti, I will finalize those quarter three reports and have them submitted to you for final review by the end of the week," Felipe says as he outstretches his hand to mine, oblivious to my lack of interest I have had for our conversation.

"Thank you, Felipe. That is all for today." I shake his hand, while still side-eyeing the reception desk.

I have waited so fucking long for this moment, to be able to approach our new hire, that the anticipation is beginning to feel torturous. The proposal should have arrived already. I made sure it was hand-delivered, to ensure its safe and timely arrival. The phone should be ringing at any fucking moment now.

Felipe makes his way out of my office when I spot Lizzie's tousled, auburn hair as she swoops in, grabbing the door behind him. She is a vision to be sure, with her enticing blue eyes and manufactured curves, but she is not who my heart or my cock truly desires. She is simply a placeholder. Just a way to pass the time until I claim the one who is rightfully mine.

Both Lizzie and Felipe, as well as the paperwork that lines my desk, have been utter distractions from the task I have at hand. Today marks the first day where my plan to take over all aspects of the family business will be set in motion.

When my father finds out who I have in mind to stand by my side when I do so, he will no doubt burst out in anger, making it even more sinfully sweet.

Lizzie takes her time walking over to where I stand at my desk. Her hips sway with each step of her heels, accentuating her curves in the form-fitting, emerald dress she has practically painted on her body. I sit back down in my desk chair, waiting for her to finish making her exaggerated entrance toward me.

She props her plump ass on the edge of my desk, as she flirtatiously reaches for the knot of my tie. Her eyes glisten as she tries to lure me closer to her. Inappropriate, for sure, but Marked Inc., has never been a straight-edge company. We march to the beat of our own drum here, setting a different standard for our own morality, or lack thereof.

I can already tell Lizzie is more interested in finishing what we started before Felipe barged into my office. This woman is designed to please. Too bad every time she pleases me, I only use her mouth or her sweet, wet slit as a vessel for my imagination. Wishing every touch, lick, and fuck were my queen-in-waiting and not Lizzie.

Normally, I would oblige her physical requests, but the unease that I feel today is mounting. I have a timeline to adhere to, and Lizzie isn't part of that right now.

She goes to place her red-stained lips on my neck when I pull back, looking at the note in her hand. Anticipation takes hold of me, hoping it is the call back I have been waiting for.

Impatience increasing by the second, I bring my hand to her hand that holds the Post-it note. "What's that?"

She moves her hand back slightly from mine, as if she is purposely toying with me.

"Oh, some girl called. Umm, let me see what I chicken-scratched here. Ah, yes, Sienna," she says, smacking her lips obnoxiously with a wad of bubble gum. "She called an hour ago, I—"

"You, what?" I interrupt her. "Just forgot to do your job and tell me? I have told you this, Lizzie, you are not here just to get me off. You are here to work," I roar, snatching the Post-it from her hand.

Shocked by my abruptness, she takes a deep breath. "That's not how you were acting earlier today, Car."

"Yea well, get used to it," I seethe.

She goes back to chomping on the wad of gum in her mouth, as if she is suddenly oblivious to the anger coursing through my veins. "Carmine, calm down." Lizzie has been around long enough to know that, while I try to stay as composed as possible, my anger creeps out more often than it should. She is unfazed by my antics and goes back to trying to undo my tie.

"Not now, Lizzie, I have work to do." I pull away from her, readjusting my tie. I walk toward the large window that overlooks the crowded, smog-infested Manhattan streets below me.

Her heels click behind me as she follows me to the window, pressing her body against my back. "You sure you don't need anything else, Car?" she asks flirtatiously.

"No, that is all. Take the rest of the day off," I command. I have too much I need to get done today and her ravenous appetite will undoubtedly be a distraction I do not need.

"Really? Thanks, Car ..." She keeps talking, but I tune her out.

Not paying attention to what she is still going on about, I begin to walk, gently nudging her in the direction of the door. "Ok, see you tomorrow," I say as she walks through the threshold of the doorway. I don't wait for a response from her as I slam the door shut.

I am so damn close to finally having the last surviving Ricci in my midst. Just the thought of Sienna Ricci in my office in place of where Lizzie just stood brings the blood rushing to my dick.

I go to pick up the phone at my desk when Lizzie knocks, letting herself back in.

Jesus Christ, this woman can't take a fucking hint.

"Yes, Lizzie? What is it now? I thought I told you to take the rest of the day off?"

"Sorry, I was just about to gather my stuff when your dad called. He said that he is on his way up."

"On his way up?" I growl.

This man's timing is impeccable. My father's favorite pastime is to continually get in my fucking way. He is under the delusion that his way is the best way. If that were true, then he wouldn't need me here, taking over all that he couldn't finish on his own.

"Yes, he called from the lobby. The doorman let him up."

Unbelievable. I am surrounded by incompetence. I thought I made it crystal clear to my staff that despite my father's previous ownership in the company, he can't just barge in. The man is a lunatic, and untrustworthy. A sad thing to say about one's father, sure; however, I can say much worse, all of which he has given me ample reasons for.

I rise from my desk, adjusting my suit jacket as I try to wrap my mind around what the fuck is so important that my father needs to barge in today, of all days. "Ok, that's fine," I say, dismissing Lizzie once more.

"Thanks, Car. You know, you can always call me if you need me for anything," she says with desperately enticing eyes as she leaves the door open, heading back to her desk.

Tempting, but no. I have had my eyes set on a different

prize. One that will change the course of Marked Inc. and my life *forever*.

However, I will now have to delay calling back our prospective hire until I can get my father out of here. He'd better make whatever he needs to tell me quick, because there's no telling the anger I will unleash if he sets back my plans any more than he already has.

I hear the elevator ding from the hallway, followed by what sounds like a herd of livestock filtering in, as the distinct thud of heavy footsteps quickly approaches my office.

Disgust rattles me to my core as my father, Armando Moretti, comes strolling in with his two henchmen, who stay by the doorway as he stomps on past them.

My father is your typical, old-school Italian, from the slicked-back hair down to the pinky ring on his pudgy fucking finger. He runs things old-school, I run things new-school. My way has proven to be more effective, a fact he still cannot accept. Every time he enters a room, he acts like he owns it. Pathetic, really. Power is best executed in a swagger-filled silence. When you force it like my father does, it only highlights weakness, and in my father's case, incompetence.

He takes a seat across from me in one of the chairs I have angled in front of my desk as he clears his throat. He reeks of cigar smoke and cheap perfume, there is no question where he was prior to this impromptu meeting. No wonder my mother ran away from him; he is a fucking sleazebag, among much more depraved things.

"And to what do I owe the pleasure of your presence, Father?" I say, trying not to vomit at the sound of that word: *father*. Armando is a sorry excuse of a father. He could give a fuck about me or my happiness. The fact that I must swallow my pride and break bread with this man sickens me.

"Can't a father see his dear son when he is in the neighborhood?" he asks as he signals to one of his henchmen to pour him a whiskey.

I watch as the nameless idiot begins to fumble with the decanted selections that I have on the bar cart I keep in my office. Distracted by this fool's utter incompetence at detecting which of the amber liquids are, in fact, whiskey, I get up from my desk, dismissing him from his failed attempt at being my father's bartender.

I grab the crystal decanter as I pour whiskey into two glasses. "I'm the only son you have left, remember? Cut the bullshit, what do you want?"

I know how much he hates that I am the son he is stuck with. My older brother was his pride and joy. When he died, it sent my father into a tailspin, which forced me here, into the city I swore I'd never come to. He loathes me just as much as I loathe him. It's a fucking miracle we both haven't killed each other ... *yet*.

A vindictive grin forms on his fat fucking mug as I hand him his whiskey. "Always so hostile, just like your mother," he scoffs, lifting his glass, as if that is his idea of a cheers.

I grab his wrist, still extended with the glass in hand as I tower over him, reminding him that he doesn't scare me. My demons are far darker than his could ever be.

"Don't you dare talk about my mother, you piece of shit." I release him from my grip with such force that some of the whiskey rises to the top of the glass, spilling onto his hand. I spit at his feet before retreating to my chair.

I can see the anger I have summoned in him, but he is a

coward; he won't act on it. If he knows what is good for him, he will let my outburst go and cut to the fucking chase, if he wants to get out of here as he came in—in one piece.

He reaches for the folded handkerchief in his suit pocket, bringing it to his freshly spit-shined shoe. "Touchy subject, I see."

I scoff at his comment. The moment he killed my mother, he stole my life from me, making it more than a touchy subject. It became fucking war.

He returns the handkerchief to his pocket as he continues, "Anyway, I stopped by because I wanted to see how the arrangements are going for the firm's Halloween Gala." He takes a sip of his whiskey, letting out a satisfied sigh, only adding to his already obnoxious demeanor.

Marked Inc. has always hosted an over-the-top gala on Halloween night. It's a way to schmooze with prospective clients and keep up appearances. It's also our biggest night to move product. While the city is busy trick-or-treating and distracting the cops with acts of mischief or drunken bar fights, we make our moves. Running some of the finest drugs this side of the Hudson.

Gala night is a distraction. In this line of work, almost everything is a ruse. It's easy to get away with murder when you don't know who you are looking for or at. The Devil is quite literally in the details here at Marked Inc., and the annual Halloween Gala is a huge part of our success in being elusive.

"Yes, the gala is taken care of. Afraid I can't handle a little carnage?" I purposely let the word *carnage* roll slowly off my tongue, hoping that it will jog his memory a bit.

"I know you can take care of it, Carmine. I just wanted

to check in, that's all. Also, if you are referring to the tragedy that happened, that was forever ago. It's time we move on and not let our name be dragged in the mud more than it has been already," my father says, trying to clear his throat. I clearly struck a nerve. *Bingo.*

"The arrangements for the gala are going the same as they always are. I'm in the middle of hiring some new talent that will aid in what we can provide our clients and future clientele," I say with a sarcastic grin.

"Wonderful. I trust that the new hire will be safe in your hands," he says, sipping a fresh whiskey he poured himself this time.

Oh, will she ever be safe in my hands.

Wait until my father finds out I will be having a Ricci in this office. He may croak on the spot. Ha, if only I could be so lucky, that would make the rest of my to-do list a hell of a lot shorter.

Well, one can wish.

"If that's all, Armando, I have some loose ends I would like to tie up before I close up for the day," I say, trying to hurry him out of my office.

"Armando? Really, Son? Ah, cold as your mother, too."

This fucking bastard, he just can't help himself.

I ignore his arrogant remark, I'll have my time to get back at him, but today is not the day. When that time comes, it will be fucking glorious.

"Bye, Father," I say with enough sarcasm that I practically sound like a giddy schoolgirl.

"Bye, Son. Men, let's go!" Barks my father, as his two pathetic pets follow.

Finally, I sit down and grab the paper I took from Lizzie.

Usually, I have my staff reach out to the new hires and deal with all that bullshit, but it is vital that I take care of this one myself.

I stare at the name and number that Lizzie jotted down on the Post-it. Reveling in the name that graces the paper.

Here at Marked Inc., we specialize in making the outside of a problem look like one thing while the real things can fly under the radar. It's why we need her here. Though more importantly, it's one of the many reasons that *I* need her here.

I know she has tried sending her resume to many of the big newspapers and publishing houses in the city, looking for employment. Unfortunately for her, I know all of them, and they all owe me for one thing or another. I sent out a mass email that if Sienna Ricci were ever to put in an application to any of them, they were to immediately report to me. I have not been shy in making my eagerness to get closer to her known.

Alright, Carmine, this is it. Enough distraction. Seal the deal, like you know you can.

I dial the number without even looking at the paper. I have memorized every detail I can get my hands on pertaining to Ms. Ricci. Where she lives, what she drinks, her social media presence, *everything*.

There is nothing she can hide from me. There is nowhere she can run from me.

Anticipation and lust begin to take hold as I hear the other line begin to ring. Oh, how I crave to hear the voice of the woman that has taken hold of my damned mind, making me arguably lose it.

I clear my throat as I wait for an answer, trying to tame the mixture of emotions I am feeling inside.

Please, don't go to voicemail.

The phone rings three times when a clicking sound suddenly breaks the robotic ringing. A mischievous grin breaks through as my nerves melt away when a subtly raspy, feminine voice echoes in my ear.

A voice that was never meant for Carmine Moretti to hear. A voice that I was told would lead to destruction. Yet all I hear is the sound of redemption. There is a debt to be paid and the golden ticket to glory has her fucking name on it.

"Hello?" she says in a deliciously nervous yet breathy tone.

"Hello, Ms. Ricci. It's Carmine Moretti."

Chapter 5

Sienna

It's going on an hour since I left a message with Mr. Moretti's receptionist. I grow impatient just standing and watching the minutes tick by on the clock. So, I decide to kill some time by brewing coffee and straightening up a bit to distract myself as I wait for a call back.

I sigh as I scan the mess throughout my kitchen. My eyes are immediately drawn to the now overflowing pile of dirty dishes in the sink that I neglected yesterday before going out.

Before I head to the sink to start on the mess, I feel for the hair tie on my wrist and begin to gather my hair in a ponytail to get it out of my way. Just as the last of my hair is pulled through the loop of the elastic, the matte card stock comes back into my view. Moving past the messy sink, I walk toward the countertop; my hands graze the business card, focusing on the name centered in bold font.

"Carmine Moretti." I say his name aloud, letting it roll off my tongue in a whisper. *Carmine Moretti.* His name has a familiar ring to it. It reminds me of the kind of cliché, strong

Italian names you hear often in the New York "business" circles my father ran in.

I pick up the card and flip it over, curious to see if there is anything on the opposite side. Sure enough, there is. As I process the image on the back side, a rush of déjà vu begins to fill my head when I see what looks like a hand-drawn sketch of a bat with elongated wings stretched out. The face of the bat has two large black eyes with a stitched smile. The more I study the drawing, I realize just how eerily similar it is to the fresh sternum piece I just got done, minus the menacing face, that is.

Feeling flustered, I place the card back down on the countertop. The image reminds me of Leo and our shared love for all things creepy. I shake my head, as if the gesture alone can prevent my mind from going down that long, painful road. I don't need to start rehashing the past; I need to move on. I just need to forget him, *for good.*

As I grab a paper towel by the sink to wipe down the countertop, I start replaying the brief conversation I had with Mr. Moretti's receptionist in my mind. I couldn't help but detect a venomous undertone laced within her forced pleasantries. She sounded as though she was anticipating my call and judging from the way she rushed me off the phone, she was disappointed by my follow-through.

I was barely able to get a word in when she interrupted me abruptly, saying that Mr. Moretti will call me back "when it suits him." That was it, and she hung up the phone before I could say anything else.

This whole thing feels strange, even down to when exactly this envelope was delivered. I don't understand how the motion sensor by the front door didn't pick up any movement whatsoever. Usually even the slightest breeze sets off the sensor. Yet, an entire envelope was slipped between the storm and front door completely undetected.

I pulled up the activity log on the doorbell shortly after getting off the phone with Mr. Moretti's receptionist to see if maybe I missed a motion notification, but there was nothing. The last motion detected was Eric leaving, and before that, Eric and me coming back to the house last night. I know for a fact the letter wasn't there when we got back home. I doubt Eric slipped it in the door when we got back, because he looked genuinely surprised someone from Marked Inc. reached out to me.

I have applied to almost every major publishing house and paper in the city without so much as one response. So, I guess whatever Mr. Moretti wants me to do is better than waiting on the countless ignored applications. Especially since I am planning on moving to the city, anyway. At least this way, if it all works out with this interview, I will hopefully have some steady work to help pay the bills, instead of running my savings dry.

The majority of what is in my savings is left over from the inheritance I received when Mama and Papa died. Along with this house, they left me a decent chunk of money that I have been slowly taking from to supplement my sporadic pay. It always amazed me how lucrative Papa's business was.

My father would always attempt to leave his business dealings at the office, but the late-night guests and shady demeanor that followed him home never fooled me. I fed into the illusion of a perfect family, not for his sake, but for Mama's. She wore her emotions on her sleeve, despite trying her best to disguise them. Sadly, there is no shade of foundation or hue of lipstick that can cover the scars we wear internally; they eventually come to the surface.

We all played our roles well. Papa provided a privileged existence for us. Lavish vacations, this huge house that I am standing in now, private school, the works. Mama played the role of the doting housewife, PTA mom, and philanthropist. While I pretended to be the blissfully ignorant daughter, who was fully aware of the smoke and mirrors, but never asked any questions, or even cared to. We appeared happy, despite the cracks in our foundation and to us that was somehow enough, deceptive as it was.

I finish straightening up the kitchen just as the coffee machine beeps to signal it's done brewing. I pour my coffee from the pot and don't wait for it to cool down before taking a long gulp, hoping the caffeine will help my hangover and my nerves. I walk over to the dining room off the kitchen and see the silhouette of that damn woman, Miranda, peering out the window again. I don't get what her deal is. She just stands there, as if she is on a watch shift. I swear it doesn't look like she even blinks.

I inch closer to the window to try to get a better look at her. Taking a sip of my coffee, I peer back at her, when suddenly, she raises her hand to her ear, revealing a phone in hand. She moves her lips, speaking into the mouthpiece before stepping back to draw the curtains closed. What is this woman's freaking deal?

While I wait for a callback, I retreat to the living room and settle into my favorite armchair by the fireplace. I should be catching up on emails and writing, but the thought of sipping coffee and milking my hangover by reading some good smut sounds a hell of a lot better. Even though my shelves in the living room are packed with unread books, I settle on my Kindle instead.

Just as I am about to dive into a new read, I startle from the loud ring of my phone, forgetting I turned off the silent button so I wouldn't miss the call. I grab my phone from the pocket of my robe.

I recognize the number as being the same one I called to leave a message for Mr. Moretti. I swipe the green answer button, feeling a sudden surge of unease swarm over me.

"Hello?" I try to sit up, as if moving will somehow help me feel less nervous than I already am.

Then, a deep baritone transcends through the phone, capturing my attention, rendering me momentarily speechless.

"Hello, Ms. Ricci. It's Carmine Moretti," he says. I freeze, trying to sift through my memory. I know I have heard that voice before, or one like it. I just can't place where I have heard it. He speaks into the phone again, snapping me out of my momentary trance.

"Ms. Ricci, are you there?"

"Yes, hello, Mr. Moretti. Sorry about that," I say, trying to compose myself. I'm thankful this first interaction is on the phone, because the nerves that just his voice gives me without even matching it to a face is absurd.

"That's quite alright," he says, his words lingering in an oddly seductive way. "I have been awaiting your call. I trust my proposal arrived to you in one piece?" I swear I can hear his grin through the damn phone.

"Yes, it did, thank you."

"Excellent. Have you had time to consider?" There is an eagerness in his voice.

"Forgive me, but before I get into any discussion of the proposal you had delivered to my house, I am curious how you found me?"

"Oh, I have my ways." His tone is equal parts flirtatious and sinister. I should just hang up, but for some reason, I can't. I'm not satisfied with his answer—it's as vague as his job proposal—but he is intriguing me, nonetheless. So, I continue the conversation.

"I am a freelance writer, Mr. Moretti. I mainly write interest articles while I work on some of my own publications. I have never considered a public relations firm. So, I am uncertain of what my role would be."

"Vital."

"Excuse me?"

"Your role. It will be vital to the company, not to mention to myself."

I can't help but notice the emphasis he is putting on what my presence at Marked Inc. means to him personally.

"You own a public relations firm, and I am a writer. How exactly is that vital?" I blurt, without taking a moment to polish my response.

I feel a rush of heat on my cheeks when he does not answer right away. I know I have a tendency of being overly direct, but maybe I am being too forward? I mean, it is a job interview, I probably should dial back my intensity a bit.

Clearing his throat, he responds after a brief pause. "Inquisitive, aren't we?" he says with a sadistic chuckle. "Who and what I deem vital is as I say. I am in the business of representing my clients the best way I can, and to do so, I need employees who can help me control the narrative. What better way to do that than with someone who has an uncanny gift to manipulate words artistically? Someone who can write the narrative. Someone like yourself, Ms. Ricci."

The way my name rolls off his tongue makes my stomach turn into knots. There is a commanding presence he exudes. It's not just something I can hear through the phone, it's something that I can feel.

Unsure of how I want to respond, I settle for, "Okay."

"Oh, c'mon. I know you can do better than that," he says, trying to provoke me.

He continues. "Don't bite your tongue. What is on your mind?"

"What is it exactly that you need from me, Mr. Moretti?"

"Many things." He pauses, clearing his throat before continuing to speak. "As of now, I need you to work on written statements for our clients for press conferences, things like that. Also, there will be some public functions where your attendance will be required. Just good to have a writer with a face like yours in our company."

A face like mine? What the fuck? How does he know what my face even looks like? The allure I felt upon first hearing him has now dissipated and replaced by utter annoyance. *Fucking asshole.* I do not like that he is basically insinuating I will be some trophy. I want to work, not be his arm candy.

I take a deep breath in, trying to give myself a second to calm my boiling blood. This man is seriously testing me. He must be. Who conducts a Goddamn interview like this? He is ballsy, I will give him that, but his rich, CEO ass doesn't intimidate me. I'm the daughter of a professional conman, his tactics don't phase me so much as they ignite my desire to beat him at his own game.

"I'm sorry, Mr. Moretti, but have we met before? Your last name sounds familiar to me. I just can't place the full name," I ask, wanting to pry more information out of him.

"Sadly, no, we have not. I would like to change that, though. And please, call me Carmine," he says persistently.

"Okay, well, before we proceed any further with this interview, I want it to be known that I want to work and be useful. I do not want to be considered for the position if it requires me standing still and looking pretty," I say, sticking up for myself.

He pauses.

Good, I got to him. Serves him right.

"Let me make something clear to you, Ms. Ricci," he starts in that flirty, sinister tone again. "This is not an interview, and you are not being considered for the position, because my mind has already been made up. The job is yours. It was designed to be yours."

Designed to be mine? Who does this guy think he is?

"Excuse me?"

"You heard me. Now, if you accept my proposal, I want you to start next Thursday," he demands.

I move the phone from my ear and open my calendar app to see what date next Thursday is. Of course, the 31st ... *Halloween.* I was planning on heading down to the city to move the rest of my stuff into Vanessa's apartment next week, anyway, but it still feels rushed starting so soon, despite the prospect of a steady paycheck.

"So, on Halloween, then?" I answer, not trying to mask the bitter memories of that day.

He lets out an unexpectedly delicious chuckle. "Yes, on

Halloween. What, are you not a fan?" he asks, picking up on the apprehension in my voice.

"No, it's not that," I lie. "It's just sooner than I anticipated."

"All the more reason for you to start to get your things in order, then."

I'm about to reply when I realize we never discussed a salary. "Before I start, I think it is important to discuss salary and benefits," I point out. Truthfully, we have barely discussed anything that should be in an interview if you can even call this conversation an interview.

"All of that boring new employee business is in the packet. When you fill it out, just name your price," he says, so nonchalantly that it makes my blood boil ... again.

What packet is he talking about? I grab the envelope the letter was in to see if there was anything that I missed and as I expected, nothing.

"I never received a packet. When should I be expecting that?" I ask, even though I am still internally harping on the *name your price* nonsense. I will circle back to that after.

"Now, if you head outside to where you received the letter, there should be a large manilla envelope with the packet inside. You will need to fill out all the usual boring information such as address, social security number, all that kind of stuff ..." He continues talking as I unintentionally tune him out, heading to the door to see what he is talking about.

I swing the door open, and just as the interior door moves toward me, a large envelope falls to my entryway floor. I bend down to pick it up, staring out the glass of the storm door. Someone must have just dropped this off. I received the first envelope a little over an hour ago. There was nothing else with it, and I didn't hear my doorbell sensor go off. Then again, for some reason, the sensor didn't go off for the first delivery either.

I remove the phone from my ear and open my doorbell app to see if it picked up any motion that I have missed. I look, and just as I suspected, there is nothing.

I bring the phone back to my ear, hearing Carmine still talking. "I trust you received the packet?" he asks.

There is no point in continuing this back-and-forth. He had to have known that it was just placed in between my two entry doors. It's like he wants a reaction out of me.

"You said to name my price before?" I ask, ignoring his question.

"Yes. We all have a price. A threshold of value we place on ourselves. I want to know what you believe yours is to me."

I roll my eyes so hard at his response that it makes my headache from my hangover worse. I can't stand that everything out of this man's mouth is a riddle. An aggravating, confusing, deliciously seductive sounding-riddle.

"Well, to quote you, you deem what is vital. And you have deemed my presence in your company to be, which means my value is priceless. According to your own logic, that is," I say, with a level of confidence that even surprises myself.

"Luckily for you, I am a man with lots of disposable income, and you are correct, you are priceless. I trust an assertive and intelligent woman like yourself can come up with something that feels fair."

I don't even know what to say. I'm teetering between a

thank you and *go fuck yourself*, but my bank account has been dwindling. So, I'll play his little game for now and make it worth my while.

"I assume you will be staying in the city. The commute up north is a bit of a hike," he says, taking my lack of response as a signal to solidify my acceptance, since he clearly is not going to accept no as an answer.

"I am currently in the middle of a move to the city. This makes my move timeline shorter, but thankfully, I'll be rooming with my best friend. So, I can make it work."

"Excellent. I take that as a 'yes,'" he says with an intense baritone.

"It's a yes. I will just look over the packet you sent today and let you know if I have any questions."

"Perfect," he purrs. "Oh, and Sienna? Please, don't hesitate to call my personal cell should you have any questions. It's on the card I attached to the packet."

I flip back to the beginning of the packet, and sure enough, there is a card with the same sketch of the bat, but this time, the rest of the card is blank, except for what I assume to be his cell phone number, handwritten.

"Got it. I'll be in touch soon, should I have any questions," I say, freeing the card from the paper clip it was under.

"Excellent, I look forward to having you join Marked Inc. I'll make sure not to overwork you too much, so that you still have time to write and publish your own works," he says with a sense of encouragement.

"No need to worry. My own writing can wait, I'll be focused," I reassure him.

"Well, don't put it off too much. I do look forward to

reading your inner thoughts someday," he says cryptically.

A blush begins to form once more on my cheeks, as I feel the heat begin to rise on my face. "I won't," I answer.

"I look forward to meeting you, Sen." He ends our phone call before I can even respond or say goodbye.

I remove the phone from my ear and stare at the blank screen, trying to process the conversation we just had. Much like this entire morning, I am having a difficult time processing any of this, and then it hits me. He called me Sen.

No one other than Leo ever called me Sen. He always said it was the perfect nickname for me because he said Sen sounded like "sin," and to him, I was as sweet as sin. It's strange hearing anyone else call me that, let alone my soon-to-be boss, who doesn't know me from a hole in the wall.

My stomach turns, and I feel like I'm signing a contract with a sultry-voiced Devil.

I put my phone, along with the mysteriously delivered packet, down and head back to the dining room to open the large bay window to get some much-needed fresh air in the house. As I unlatch the lock on the window, I look up and see the woman across the street staring at me again.

What is her deal?

I stand there, letting her know that I see her staring at me. There we stay, for what feels like minutes but is just seconds. It's then that I am finally able to take in more of her features. Even with the distance in-between the two houses I notice the long streak of white she has distinctly down the middle of her hair.

We continue to have a stare-off, neither of us flinching; that is, until she lifts her phone to ear and begins to talk to whoever is on the other line. A few seconds pass with both of us staring at each other, until she walks closer to her window, so her face is almost pressed against the glass. She peers at me creepily and winks before drawing the curtain closed.

Shaking my head, I continue staring at her now curtain-covered window, unable to understand her odd behavior, coupled with letters just appearing at my front door as if out of thin air. Suspicion begins to arise, and part of me wonders if somehow this has something to do with Papa.

Revenge runs deep with criminals. Even though he and Mama were killed years ago, I know that the vendettas against made men don't die when they do. They end when all they ever loved ends, even if they aren't on Earth to see it. And with me being the last living Ricci, the chances of an unfinished bounty being carried out on my life is always a possibility.

I head back to my room and grab the largest suitcase I can find and begin throwing my stuff into it. I don't know what awaits me next week in the city, but if it's war on the horizon, I am fucking ready for it.

Chapter 6

Sienna

12 YEARS AGO

The day after Halloween...

I wake up feeling unsettled. I can't stop thinking about the cryptic text messages from Leo last night. I roll over in my bed, immediately searching for my phone. I start moving my hands, patting the bed in desperation, trying to find it to see if Leo tried contacting me again.

After frantically searching all throughout the sheets and under my pillow to see if it might have ended up there, I see it on the floor next to my bed. I pick it up, anxiously anticipating a message from Leo. I flip open my phone and ... nothing. No new messages, no phone calls, absolutely nothing.

I grab a sweatshirt and throw on my UGG boots so I can head next door to check on Leo. I glance at the clock on my phone: 8:28 a.m. I know it's early, but I need to make sure Leo is alright.

I look back to the window in my room with a view of Leo and Rose's house, hoping I can see a light on or a sign that anyone is awake inside. I scan the windows a few times over, not seeing any lights or movement, but I decide to head over, anyway.

I slowly walk past Titi Lana's room, trying not to wake her, because she would stop me if she knew I was going to anyone's house before 10 a.m. on a weekend. I head downstairs to the front door, veering left toward Rose's house. I walk through the meticulously manicured path of chrysanthemum bushes that line the walkway to her porch steps. As I approach the first step, the wood planks begin to creak beneath my feet.

The sound is intensified by the early morning stillness. I walk up the rest of the steps until I am at the front door. Shifting my weight onto my tiptoes, I try to first peer into the window on the upper portion of the front door to check if I can see Leo or Rose awake. Even on the very tips of my toes, I am unable to see into the house beyond spotting the top of the grandfather clock in the entryway.

My hand hovers over the doorbell, but I decide that knocking will be less rude at this time in the morning. I knock once and step back on to the welcome mat in front of the door. I wait a few seconds before stepping closer to knock again.

I end up knocking three times, though no one answers.

I take a few more steps back, until I am at the edge of the porch, for a better look at the house and to see if any lights have been turned on. I know it's a weekend, but for as long as I have known Leo, he's always made mention of Rose being an early riser.

I turn to look at the driveway and see Leo's Cavalier, along with Rose's CRV. So, I know they should be home.

I stand there, scanning every window, until I finally see

slight movement in the window that I know is Rose's room. While the outside of Rose's house is brick, compared to the white siding Mama chose when her and Papa built the house, both the interior layouts are identical.

I head back to the front door to knock again, this time with more exertion. Growing more impatient, I don't wait between knocks. At this point, my knocking has arguably morphed into pounding.

In my peripheral, I see the striped fabric of the curtain move in Rose's room. What the hell is going on? Why is she avoiding me? I know she must have seen me, let alone hear me pounding at the door.

"Hello?" I speak into the door, unclenching my fist from knocking to a flat palm I lay across the wood.

Still, no one answers. I can still see movement by the bedroom curtain. So, I decide to walk down the porch steps and around to the side of the house. There is an all-glass sunroom just off the kitchen that if nothing else will get Rose's attention when she enters the kitchen. At least then she will have no choice but to answer me, instead of continuing to ignore me as she is clearly doing.

Suddenly, I see Rose's purple robe as she walks down the stairs into the kitchen. Her back is turned to me as she turns on the small light above the kitchen sink. She reaches for a coffee mug in the holder next to the sink, and as she walks to the other countertop, where she keeps her coffee machine, she makes eye contact with me.

Flailing my hands, jumping slightly outside the glass sunroom, I shout, "Rose!"

Flustered, she puts her coffee mug down and walks through the kitchen in the direction of the front door.

I pick up my pace and head to meet her back at the porch. I hear the front door swing open. As I scurry up the porch steps, which creak even more this time with my fast pace, I am met with Rose's arms crossed with the distinct look of disapproval on her face.

I try to catch my breath, not realizing how much I exerted myself running to the porch to meet her.

"Rose, I'm sorry to bother you. It's just that I have been knocking and—"

She cuts me off, abruptly, "You need to go," she says in a robotic tone.

I ignore her request and continue. "I'm sorry," I apologize, again. "I know it's early, it's just that I have been trying to get ahold of Leo and I haven't heard from him." I can see she is about to cut me off again, so I talk louder and at a faster pace, forcing her to listen to me. "He left me some weird messages last night after we hung out, and I just want to make sure he is ok."

Unlocking her crossed arms, Rose takes two steps out of the door, meeting me closer on the porch. She looks around, as if she is afraid someone might be watching us. It's a lot like the look she had on her face last night, when she was urging Leo to come inside the house when we got home from Oogie's.

She scans the empty road of our neighborhood once more before clearing her throat to speak. "I wish I knew the right words to say, but I don't," she says, with a slight tremble in her voice. She takes a deep breath, trying to steady her voice, before she continues to speak. "Leo loves you. He has since the day he met you."

I feel my brows lower, pulling closer together as confusion once again begins to settle in. "I know Leo loves me. I just want to make sure he is ok. Can I come in?"

Her demeanor is confirming my worst fears. That something has happened to Leo.

Instinctively, I try to walk past her. As rude as it is, I feel desperation take hold and I just need to see Leo. Even if he is sleeping, I don't care, he'll get over me waking him up. I just want to make sure he is ok, that he is still here.

She steps back onto the threshold of the door, raising both arms as she grips each of her hands on the frame of the doorway, preventing me from getting through. I feel tears begin to form in my eyes.

"I'm sorry, Sienna, you need to go home," she orders. "Leo is not here," she says, keeping her body barricading the doorway.

I try to push past her, but she won't let up. The tears I felt forming just moments ago have now escaped my eyes. Wet droplets begin to fall, turning into a steady stream of tears moving down my face.

Releasing myself from my attempts to get past her, I raise my hands to wipe away my tears, when a revelation strikes me.

If Leo is not here, then something bad must have happened to him. I immediately think of the man I saw standing across the street from Oogie's yesterday. I'm not even sure who that man was, or if he has anything to do with this, but I figure it is worth a shot mentioning, to maybe find out what the fuck is going on.

"Wait!" I blurt, startling Rose. Her thick, black hair piled on top of her head bounces as she reacts to my dramatic outburst. "There was a man watching us when we were in the tattoo shop."

Her eyes widen. "A man?"

"Yes. He was watching Leo and me from across the street. But before I could get a better look at him, he was gone."

She releases her arms from the doorway and inches toward me. Crossing her arms again, she squints her eyes as she tries to piece together what I am telling her. "What do you mean, gone?" she presses.

"I saw a man I did not recognize just watching Leo and me from outside the tattoo shop. It was the strangest thing. He was just standing there, smoking, as if he were waiting for us to leave. Then, he was gone. It's like he just disappeared," I reply, feeling defeated at how pointless even mentioning this now feels.

Rose pauses a minute. Her bun bobs again as she tilts her head, as if she is working through a difficult equation in her mind. "What tattoo parlor did you two go to?" she asks with an intensity that makes me feel as though I am being interrogated, instead of trying to figure out what happened.

"Umm, Oogie's over on Market Street. Why?"

She mumbles something under her breath in Spanish. I wish I could make out what she was saying. Despite Spanish being Mama's first language, she never taught me. The only Spanish I know is what I learned in school, which I had trouble absorbing.

Rose remains quiet, her eyes beginning to well with tears. She is around the age Mama would be now if she were alive and always looked so youthful for her age. Yet, now, with the sadness seeping all over her face, her smooth forty-something-year-old olive skin looks instantly haggard.

"I was hoping that we'd beat him to it, or that he would forget," she says, with a small tear streaming down her face.

"Forget what?" I press, waiting for her to answer me. Again, Rose is deep in thought now with tears streaming down her face. She takes a deep breath as I stand there, waiting in vomit-inducing anticipation, for whatever she needs to tell me. She finally wipes away the tears dripping down her cheek and looks at me with puffy, grief-stricken eyes.

"Did your Mama ever tell you the legend of Alida and Taroo? It was a popular myth our *abuelas* used to tell us as children in Puerto Rico."

How ironic. This is the second time in less than twenty-four hours someone mentions the same legend to me. First Eddie, and now Rose.

"No, she didn't, but Eddie, the tattoo artist mentioned it yesterday. His wife is from the island, and she painted a beautiful piece inspired by the legend. He had it hanging in the shop." I shake my head, trying to figure out how this story has anything to do with where Leo is. "I'm sorry, but what does this have to do with Leo?"

"Do you believe in soulmates?" Rose asks, going over my question.

"I guess?"

"You know, your Mama and I were raised hearing that the concept of soulmates was for fools. We were raised to believe that who we end up with is determined by God. But the story of Alida and Taroo, the hummingbird meeting its vibrant flower, that is a story that gives even the most pessimistic or questioning souls hope. Whether you believe in God or our island's myths, it is important to ground yourself in what feels right to you, Sienna. Do you understand?"

"I guess so," I lie. I'm still trying to understand what is happening. So, the philosophical lesson in soulmates and faith is quite literally soaring above my comprehension.

"Good," Rose says as she reaches into the front pocket of her robe. She takes out a crumpled piece of paper. Before she hands it to me, I catch a glimpse of the sepia card stock and my heart sinks. It's the poem Leo read at the cemetery—my poem that inspired our tattoos.

Suddenly, I feel grief wash over me. An unsettling feeling, considering I still don't know what has happened, but I know whatever it is, it's beyond my comprehension right now.

She outstretches her hand with the crumpled paper. "Here, Sienna. He would have wanted you to have this."

"He gave this to you?" I ask, taking it from her hand.

"No, it was left in his room," she replies.

I look at the poem, wanting to burst out in tears once more. This makes no sense. I don't even know how I should feel. Should I be angry or sad? Worried? Did he leave me? Did something happen to him? Rose clearly knows a lot more than she is telling me. I want to shake her, yell at her, but I don't. Whatever she knows, she isn't telling me for a reason.

"You must promise me that you won't go looking for him," she warns.

"Where is he?"

"Just remember, the soul lives on. It may take different

forms or avenues than you expect, but what the heart wants, you must allow the heart to get."

"Where is he?" I ask again, ignoring her poetic spiel. Ordinarily, such poignant words would soothe me, but at this moment, they are only digging a knife into my heart, making me feel a pain I didn't think I was capable of. Not even Mama and Papa's death left such a hole in my heart as the possibility of losing Leo forever is doing to me right now.

"You need to trust me. Go, now," she says again, looking around nervously.

"But Rose—"

"Go, now!" she repeats.

"What happened to him? Where is Leo?" I burst into tears.

"You know more than anyone, given the circles that your father conducted business in, that when a debt is owed, collection is inevitable."

My brows lower once more, trying to piece together what the fuck she is talking about.

"A debt? What kind of debt" I ask her, hoping that this time she answers me with something I can actually go off of.

"Life," she says.

"Life, really? You can't tell me anything that isn't a Goddamn riddle?!" I shout.

"The price we pay to have life, is death. Death comes in many forms, Sienna. When death closes one door, the universe finds a way to transfer that life to open another door."

"Gone? Rose, what happened to him, please?" I ask, this time begging. I feel a stabbing pain in my heart, I can't handle losing him.

"Sienna, please, go. I've said too much. If I say any more, he will come after all of us, too."

"Who will come after us?"

My mind begins racing. Who is this 'he' she fears so much? Is it the man I saw across the street from the tattoo shop? What are the chances that I see this creepy guy watching us, and then, Leo, my Leo, is gone.

"Who, Rose?" I plead once more.

"Muerte."

Death.

Chapter 7

Carmine

October 30th, Devil's Night

It's going on one week since I spoke to Sienna on the phone and her silky voice still echoes in my ear. Just one more day, *mi reina*. Just one more fucking day.

I have gawked at the calendar like a predator hungry for its prey, counting down the days until I can give into these primal urges that flood the depths of my depraved soul. I feel like I have been locked in a prison of predetermination, stuck waiting, but all that is about to change.

Tomorrow, I will finally have the daughter of my father's deceased enemy shimmying her voluptuous hips and naturally sun-kissed skin into Marked Inc. I become giddy just thinking about the look on my father's face when he sees her, a Ricci, in the building. And not just any Ricci, but Sienna Ricci. The one my father deemed off-limits for a man like me, which only makes my craving for her more intense.

Telling me that I can't have something only makes me

want it more. And when it comes to her, I will stop at nothing until I mark every inch of her as mine.

I have a to-do list a mile long, preparing for her arrival as well as the gala tomorrow evening. I already resent that my first order of business for today is carving out time for an impromptu meeting with Christian, but it's of the utmost importance that this ship run smoothly, and I trust no one other than myself to make sure it does.

Oh, Christian. Our in-house mad scientist. Well, he is not actually a scientist, but he is mad. He was once renowned in his field but now he is a necessary evil in my field, which is all about nipping and tucking the truth.

I am getting tired of having to constantly reprimand him for his incompetence. He was Father and Enzo's hire before I took over Marked Inc., and despite my better judgment, I kept him around a lot longer than I wanted to. Although his role in the company has become crucial, he forgets that the margin for error is practically non-existent. Or it should be, at least. What Christian brings to table is only valuable if done properly, and since he seems to not be getting the message, I have decided to pay him a little in-person visit today in his office

I stand outside the elevator doors awaiting its arrival. Peering over my shoulder, I look back at Lizzie's desk, relieved it is empty. There is something off with how she has been acting lately. The rational part of my psyche wants to chalk it up to her being pissed off about Sienna's arrival tomorrow. However, the irrational part of me, the part that often takes over my mind, indulging my impulsivity, suspects she is up to something more devious.

My attention is brought back to the steel doors as the bell

chimes, just as the elevator doors glide open. Relief once again washes over me when I see no one other than my reflection from the mirrored walls of the elevator as I walk inside.

I lift my hand to the control panel, tapping the cold brass button to bring me to Christian's floor. As I walk to the back wall of the elevator, I am forced to stare at the image of myself that glares back at me in the reflective wall. The little bit of skin exposed from my pinstriped jacket and black button-up shirt is covered in a mural of ink, making it difficult to see where my skin begins and ends.

As I approach the wall of mirrors, I notice the patch of hair I keep longer in the middle is beginning to fall in front of my face. I keep the sides buzzed but the longer section centered on my head always has a way of escaping. I was in a rush this morning and didn't have enough time to tame it properly. I expel saliva into the palm of my hand, to keep my hair in place.

The man that stares back at me is someone I hardly recognize. I swore I would never become what my father is, yet here I am, arguably worse. I look nothing like him, but whenever I glance at my dark—almost black—irises it's clear to see that the darkness I have succumbed to has always been my home.

At least the sins my father commits are because he doesn't know any better. He is too foolish to know what the right thing is and how to do it. But me? Well, I have been choosing to do what I know is destructive simply because doing right never gave me anything but heartache and grief. Every day I choose to veer off the right path. I consciously choose to engage in wrongdoings because it distracts me from the wrongs that have been committed against me.

Once I reach Christian's office floor, I am met with the distinct smell of rubbing alcohol as the doors open. Given the alterations Christian performs for our clients, it is imperative that his working environment be as sterile as possible. Though, the harsh smell of cleanliness is abrasive when it greets my nostrils.

I already had a look at Christian's agenda for the day and there were no clients that needed any procedures or consultations this morning. So, I expect him to be prepping for the few afternoon clients I know he does have.

I hear clinking in the back supply room, so I follow the sound to find Christian sanitizing his scalpel and other surgical instruments. The door is open to the supply room, and with my Vans on, I walk in undetected. I stand a few inches from Christian, still busy polishing his tools, and clear my throat to get his attention.

Christian startles, dropping the scalpel in his hand on the metal tray.

"Shit, Carmine, you scared me," he exclaims.

"Good," I answer, not in the mood for whatever small talk he will no doubt attempt.

Oblivious to my irritated tone, Christian extends his hand out for me to shake, with a friendly smile on his face.

I let him squirm a bit with his hand still extended until he finally gets the hint that I have no interest in pretending I like him. Not today. There is simply no time for it. He spreads his fingers out before wiping his hand on the side of his white lab coat.

I know deep down that Christian wants to tell me to piss

off, but he won't. He has put himself in a situation that places him at my disposal.

Not the wisest decision for one of the city's most prominent figures in his field to owe a gang of criminals an excessive amount of money due to an incessant gambling problem. Now, he pays the debts off, not with money, but with his life. He took an oath to die unto himself and surrender his free will to the Moretti family in exchange for his debts.

I guess he and I both have that in common, at least. Like myself, Christian is indebted to the Morettis, and by default, Marked Inc.

He isn't who he once was, but neither am I. *None of us are.* Long gone are the days we walked these decaying streets as free men. We all have surrendered ourselves to the inevitable evil that ensures our survival in *our* world. A world where truths are kept safe by lies and lies are truths in disguise.

Cleary trying to avoid the tension in my voice, Christian walks back over to his tray and casually begins sanitizing his tools again.

"So, how are you today, Carmine?" he asks, apprehensively with his back turned to me.

Ignoring his attempt to lighten the mood, I go over his question, getting right down to business. "Christian, I already told you, whatever is or isn't going on in your personal life is of no importance to me. You're getting fucking sloppy. Get it together, and do the job I pay you to do, or you're going to leave me no choice but to step in," I huff.

Sloppy is being generous. The piss-poor job he has been doing on his assignments is straight up reckless. His job is to conceal who and what we ask him. Concealing the truth requires attention to detail and leaving any detail up for grabs can lead the cops right to us.

I realize that Christian is not paid nearly as much as he would be making if he was able to use his skills in a more traditional setting. However, that is a privilege he lost a long time ago. So, what he does not earn monetarily, he earns in the ability to live another day ... above the ground he would otherwise be buried in.

"But Carmine ..." he begins to plead.

"*But Carmine, nothing.* This is your last warning," I threaten, my voice echoing in the mostly empty room. I crash my fist down on the tray he has been cleaning his tools on, making the metal of each instrument bounce upwards. The contents of the tray go crashing to the floor as he just stares at me, open-mouthed, as if he is looking at a damn ghost.

He should know better than anyone that the Carmine he met years ago is nothing like the Carmine that stands before him today. I don't want to hear whatever excuses he was about to spew out of his lying, sack-of-shit mouth to defend his incompetence. What I used to put up with, I no longer tolerate.

"It won't happen again," he stammers, wiping away the sweat beginning to form along his brow as he begins searching for the tools that are now scattered on the floor.

"You're right, it won't," I remind him as I adjust my tie, loosening it slightly. I leave him to collect the tools as I begin to walk around the rest of his office. I head over to his desk, which looks to be as disheveled as he has been lately. Papers strewn about, empty soda cans, and cigarette butts fill the ashtray. It's like the sins of the job have caught up to him.

At one time, his work was impeccable, unmatched, even. However, now is a different story. Any assignment he is given, the results are lackluster, at best. I don't pay him for lackluster; I pay him for perfection. Perfection is what helps us evade the cops and run our other operations beneath the line of the law. And when he can't conceal the prints of who I ask him to, that's a fucking problem.

The nice little visit we had earlier this week from a sergeant at the local police precinct asking if we heard from a former employee of ours who, to the police's knowledge, had died months before, is proof enough of how reckless Christian has become. It was a fucking doozy trying to turn my charm on to evade the sergeant's questions when he said he had someone held at the station for petty larceny with fingerprints that match our ex-employee's.

The cops have been suspecting shady dealings at Marked Inc., but with us being a seemingly normal public relations firm—not to mention my cousin, Alex, being a long-time veteran of the department—they'd be hard-pressed to confirm any of their suspicions. If the cops only knew the fucking half of it, *I* would be the least of their worries.

Nonetheless, it will be amusing watching them snoop around. One of the few valuable things my father instilled in me, arguably the only decent attribute that came from him, is the ability to conceal the truth.

I hear Christian futzing with the steel tray once more before the squeaky scuffle of his walk pains my ears, which is arguably worse than the damn metal clacking.

"I can't tell you how sorry I am," he says with pleading eyes.

"You know what tomorrow is, correct?" I ask.

"Gala night. How could I forget?" he asks skittishly, still dealing with the mess on his desk.

I walk in front of his desk, placing both my fists on top of the pile he has been messing with to distract himself from my wrath.

"Good, just making sure you remember how important a night like tomorrow is," I remind him, while he still tries to work around me. My fists harden as I squeeze them in anger.

"For Christ's sake, put the papers down. You can clean that shit later. Look at me when I talk to you, so I know you understand what I am telling you," I demand.

He jumps, dropping the pile of garbage he is collecting from his desk. He is about to retrieve it when I bend down, meeting him at eye level.

"Leave it," I stop him, placing my rough, calloused hand over his clammy trembling one.

"S–s–sorry, Carmine," he stammers.

Now that I have his attention, and more importantly, his fear, I hold his arm down so he can't get back up.

"So," I continue. "Since tomorrow is gala night, I shouldn't have to remind you what happens behind the scenes while everyone is dressed up and schmoozing one another. You know how important it is to be on top of your game, correct?"

"Yes, sir."

"I expect that whoever I send to you the next day, you will be able to properly take care of them, so they are not only unrecognizable but untraceable this time," I remind him, gripping his arm tighter with my one hand and raising my other, drawing attention to my fingers.

"See these fingerprints?" I ask him as I direct his attention to my hands.

"Yes, Carmine."

"What's so special about them, huh?" I ask sarcastically.

"Um," Christian thinks. "Umm," he continues to just stare at my hands, without forming a coherent response.

I remove my hand from his arm and bring both my fists to the collar of his lab coat, lifting him slightly. My jaw tenses as I lean in, as I am but inches away from his now profusely sweating face.

"I'll ask you one more time. What makes these hands that I can easily strangle the life out of you with in mere seconds so special?"

His lips begin to quiver as panic sets in. *Absolutely pathetic.*

I release him from my grip, making him lose his balance, which forces him to fall to the cold tile floor.

"I will remind you, since your memory seems to be a bit hazy," I say, lifting both palms up and toward me. The callouses that run all through them are a product of the hours of work I have put into the gym, chiseling my once slender, lanky physique. "These hands—these fingers—are untraceable. You can run my fingers in any police database, and you will come up with nothing."

"Yes, I know," he says in a defeated tone.

"Good, so then you also remember part of your job is not only to alter but to erase," I remind him. "Don't forget that second part."

Christian used to be able to nip and tuck the flesh like no one else in the business. His role in the underground aspects of Marked Inc. need to be executed with precision. There is no room for mistakes, not at this point in the game. But if push comes to shove, I have no issue reminding him that his altering of flesh doesn't come close to my ability to *sever* the life out of it.

I adjust my suit jacket and crack my neck to the side, giving him one last look before leaving. "I trust that this will be the last time I have to remind you why you are here, yes?"

"Yes, Carmine."

"Excellent. Do carry on," I say as I exit, leaving him trembling, just as I intended.

My head pounds as I exit Christian's floor and head back into the elevator. I try to take a deep breath, to center myself as I run a mental checklist of what needs to be taken care of before tomorrow.

I got a new hybrid blend in that is supposed to offer a super clean high. Even better, it is practically untraceable by drug dogs, sensors, pretty much anything that should pick it up. That's why I coined it *fantasma*. "Ghost," in my mother's native language, which is the only thing I have left of her, thanks to my fucking father.

It's imperative that I set up the proper distribution chan-nels so I can start collecting remittance before I fuel any of these detectives' suspicions more than I already have. I need to make sure every chess piece is in place, every soldier who has sworn their loyalty to me is ready for the war ahead. And now that I hopefully set Christian straight, that will be one less thing I have to worry about, because his lack of craftsmanship isn't helping the matter. He is practically leading the damn cops right to us.

Even with the annual Halloween Gala right around the corner, my father remains a thorn in my side. Knowing the money that we will make because of my hard work, both in the company and in pushing our new product, he still insists on giving me a hard time.

How I wish I felt for him the way most sons feel for their fathers. Full of admiration, love, respect. None of that exists in my heart for my father. The only love I have pertaining to my father comes from the desire to make him pay for the crimes he has committed. Not against society, I could give a fuck about that. He has a long rap sheet of heinous crimes, but his worst crimes committed are not against others but against his own flesh and blood.

My father prides himself in thinking he is the King of Midtown. He has always been a delusional man, assuming the long lineage of made men he derives from automatically makes him a god. Unlike my grandfather and his father before him, who were true mafiosos, he is weak and impulsive. To thrive in our line of work, you must play all parts, while still being ten steps ahead. I have been fifteen steps ahead of my father, just waiting for the opportune moment to take what is rightfully mine, and this time, he will have no fucking say in the matter.

I twist my wrist up to check the time to make sure I stay on schedule today. I have plans to meet Alex later at the bar, but I still need to tie up a few loose ends here at the office.

The elevator comes to an abrupt stop, jolting me forward just a bit. As the doors slide open, I am immediately met with Lizzie's seductive glare as she spots me before I even step foot outside of the elevator. Luckily, she is on the phone, so I have a greater chance of sneaking by her without having to delay my day any more than it has been. I adjust my suit once more before I begin to walk steadily past where she sits. As I approach her desk, she tells whoever she is talking to hold on one minute as she flips her wavy, auburn hair back, revealing her cleavage spilling out of her top.

"One second," she says to whoever is on the other line as she smacks the gum between her lips.

"Car, hey, you got a minute?" she asks, obnoxiously chewing her gum and waving her hand for me to stop by her desk.

I sigh, trying to compose myself from the frustration I feel boiling.

"I'm very busy today. If it can wait until this later, that would be great," I say, trying to continue to move past her desk.

"It's quick, I promise," she starts, still holding the phone in her hand. "I was thinking about how you wanted to send a driver to pick up that girl tomorrow," she says, with the distinct look of jealousy splashed on her pretty face. "Well, that new guy, Eric, I heard he knows her. It would probably make her feel more at ease if you had him drive her."

I clench my fist. "Is that so?"

She continues to chew her gum distractingly loud. "Yea, I think they used to date, or you know," she says as she suggestively winks at me.

I know I shouldn't be jealous. Who am I to get upset over who Sienna has or hasn't fucked? She doesn't even know me.

Either way, I don't like sharing. So, whatever is or isn't going on between them, I need to judge for myself.

"Sounds good," I lie, but I want to see for myself if there is anything going on. More importantly, I need to go check the file on this Eric person. We recently hired a slew of new interns, and I haven't committed them all to memory yet. But if he drives her, and I see for myself there is something there, well, then it will give me reasonable cause to end it.

Lizzie mumbles something into the phone that I am unable to understand, even standing just a few inches from her. I try stepping closer to her desk to hear what she is saying, but she covers the mouthpiece of the phone and finishes whispering.

She lifts her mouth, finally, from whomever she clearly doesn't want me to know she is talking to and licks her lipstick-covered lips before redirecting her attention back to me. Already letting my mind wander into places that make me seethe with rage at the thought of Ms. Ricci with this Eric guy, I begin to walk away from Lizzie's desk, heading toward my office door.

Lizzie's heels click on the floor as she rises from her seat and away from her desk. She is still holding the phone, now stretching the cord. "Okay, Car, I'll go ahead and arrange that for you. Just let me know what time you want him to pick her up!" she shouts down the hallway.

I stand in the doorway of my office and feel the blood coursing through my veins. I loosen my tie and roll my neck in a half circle, until my head is titled, looking up at the industrial-style ceiling. "I'll get back to you," I respond back to Lizzie.

First, I need to figure out who is potentially trying to steal who is rightfully fucking mine.

Chapter 8

Carmine

Shadows begin to creep their way into my office as dusk settles in. As the natural light fades away, I lift my head up from the pile of work I have been engrossed in. My brain hurts from trying to coordinate every little detail pertaining to tomorrow night's gala. I know I have plenty of people working for me who can handle these things, but with the latest round of Christian's slip-ups in combination with the amount of *fantasma* I need to distribute, I would rather handle things myself. At least then I know it will be done properly.

I shuffle the papers on my desk into a pile and toss them into a drawer to get them out of my way. I told my cousin, Alex, to meet me at The Sandy Claws for a drink when his shift is over to discuss things, so I need to get going, anyway.

Just as I finish making my desk somewhat presentable, I notice the folder I requested from human resources behind my computer. I asked to see all the recent interns' files earlier, so I can find out more about this Eric guy that Lizzie mentioned. It did strike me as odd that she barely remembered Sienna's name when she called the other day, yet she knew enough about her to know who she may or may not be screwing.

Just the thought of Sienna being unavailable sends a stabbing pain to my gut. I know it's hypocritical of me. I may have been watching her from a distance, waiting on my chance to snatch her into my existence, but it's not like I have been celibate. Shit, forget hypocritical, it makes me sound fucking crazy, seeing how she doesn't even know who the fuck I am, other than her soon-to-be-boss.

Though in time, she will realize that I am the better option for her. The *only* option for her.

I rise from my chair to grab the folder from behind my computer. As I open Eric's file, I'm not exactly sure what I am expecting to find. It's not like his paperwork will disclose who he is fucking or what football team he roots for or any information other than the usual employee bullshit. But I just need to know something, anything, that gives me even the vaguest inkling as to who he is to her.

I open the folder and thumb through his file. Not that there is much other than his full name: Eric Robert Mendez. In fact, his resume is rather short, with not much on it other than some retail experience through high school, and a short stint working construction afterwards. I flip back to the section on schooling and notice he did not complete college; it looks like he dropped out. I put the file down to reach for my pack of Parliaments I keep in my bottom desk drawer.

Without breaking eye contact with the paperwork in

front of me, I lean down slightly and feel for the pack, opening it and grabbing for the first smoke I can feel. I raise the cigarette to my lips and grab the lighter tucked in the front pocket of my pinstriped jacket.

I flick the lighter to the tip and inhale as I sift back through Mr. Mendez's folder. Aside from the lack of college degree, which isn't exactly a dealbreaker for me. It's not like having a college degree is a prerequisite for working at Marked Inc., given that I, myself, did not even step foot in college to get to where I am today. But what strikes me as odd is that most of our interns who apply are fresh out of high school or about to graduate college, while Mr. Mendez is nearing forty, much older than most interns we usually have working for us.

Holding my Parliament in my mouth, I let it dangle as I take short puffs from it. I take another moment to see if there is anything at all that stands out to me, other than the realization that I should probably make a better effort in knowing everyone that works for me, intern or not.

I close the file and swivel my chair to face the floor-to-ceiling windows behind my desk. As the smoke billows from my mouth, a gut feeling begins to form. Even though his folder was bland at best, I can't shake the mischievous look on Lizzie's eyes earlier when she mentioned him and Ms. Ricci. It's like she was dangling something in front of me. What that is, I don't exactly know, but rest assured, I will find out. I always do.

I rotate my chair back to face my desk, taking one last drag of smoke before tapping the butt into the ashtray. I'm about to text Alex and let him know I am on my way to The

Sandy Claws, when I hear heels clacking their way to my office door. The clacking continues, echoing down the hallway, until suddenly it stops. I wait a moment before walking toward the door.

I decide to get up, since I have to be heading out, anyway. I go to grab my hat and another smoke for the walk to The Sandy Claws, when I see the gold knob of my door turn.

"Car, you in there?" I hear Lizzie's muffled voice speak into the wood of the door.

She proceeds to open the door, but instead of walking in, she stands there, hand on the doorframe, poking her head in. Her wavy hair drapes over her shoulder as she leans there waiting, as if I asked her to just barge in my office.

"What, we don't knock anymore?" I ask.

"Sorry, I just thought—" she begins.

"What do you need, Lizzie? I'm running late," I interrupt her.

"Should I contact that guy about driving Sienna tomorrow?"

I squeeze past her, still waiting there in the doorway. As I walk away, I see her turn her heels to face my back as I head toward the elevator. I press the down arrow and turn to her while I wait for the doors to open.

"Yes, you can contact Mr. Mendez about driving Ms. Ricci tomorrow morning."

"You got it, Car. Have a good night."

"Yes ... you too, Lizzie." I nod goodbye to her as I back into the elevator.

She nods back at me with a surprised grin, as if she

wasn't expecting me to agree to her proposal. I've known Lizzie long enough to know that she is playing some sort of game with me. Too bad for her that games are my specialty, I rarely lose.

Chapter 9

Sienna

Since my phone conversation with Mr. Moretti, I have spent the past few days packing up my belongings so I can begin working for this elusive man. I have tried searching for any information I could find him and Marked Inc., without much luck. Aside from a carefully curated website, I can't find any pictures of him, no links to personal social media, nothing. It's like he is a ghost. That, or maybe he is just that good at this whole public relations gig, because everything appears to be meticulously concealed.

Being the daughter of Matteo Ricci, I have encountered my fair share of sketchy characters, and everything about Carmine Moretti feels sketchy. His presumptuous attitude both insulted and ignited something deep inside of me. I would be lying if I said that his mysterious approach wasn't intriguing, instead of raising the red flags that it should be waving in my face.

I think that's what years of complacency have done to me. Years of staying in this house, waiting for a sign to move on with my life. My idleness has now brought on cravings for thrills that make me think I am more like my father than I probably care to admit.

Now, as I pack the last few boxes, I am indulging the part of me that is sick of being stuck in this house, this town, this life. Maybe getting lost in the unknown is exactly what I need.

As I go to move the tape dispenser across the top of the large moving box, I realize that this was probably a bad sizing choice, considering the number of books I packed inside. This shit is going to be heavy to move, that is, if it doesn't collapse before making it into Nessa's car.

Before I bring the tape down to seal the side of the box, I debate taking some books out to leave here for when I visit. But the thought of not having all my books where I am gives me more anxiety than the possibility of the box breaking in the moving process. So, instead, I do what any introverted bookworm would do when faced with such a first world dilemma: I drag that tape down and lock all those book babies in. They have no choice; they are all coming with me.

Now that the book dilemma is settled, I take one last look at the room I have spent my entire life sleeping in. Not much has changed over the years. The walls are still painted pink with a hideous floral wallpaper border lining all four walls, along with posters of Blink 182, Selena, and Eminem, and a bulletin board full of memories too good not to save. I walk toward the bulletin board that has been pinned with old movie stubs, random postcards from years of traveling with Mama and Papa, and my college graduation picture with Titi Lana and Nessa standing by my side. I smile as I take in the collage of pictures and collected memories that have made up my life.

Taking in the board once more, my heart sinks as I look at the two pictures toward the top that I purposely tried to put high enough that they don't catch my direct line of vision. Not that I don't want them there, it's just that seeing both pictures instantly bring me back a place that saddens me. But today is as good a day as any to look up and see what I have lost before I gain whatever adventure awaits me when I step foot in the city.

I raise my hand to trace the picture of Mama and Papa holding me the day I was born. Even after an excruciating twenty-six-hour labor, Mama looks so elegant. Without a stitch of makeup on, the pure happiness that radiates from her face only complements her natural beauty. Her wavy, black hair frames her face, complimenting her sun-kissed skin.

I run a hand through my now onyx hair. I dyed it a couple years ago, and although I keep mine straight, I see more of a resemblance to Mama in me than ever before now that my hair is the same hue as hers was. I look back to the picture, admiring the way Papa is sitting next to her. He has one hand draped over her shoulder and the other caressing my cheek as he smiles down at me. Judging from the grin on his face, you can see the love he felt in the moment. It's a love that even with them gone I still can feel to this day.

A lump begins to form in my throat as my eyes scan over to the next picture of Leo and me. It's a grainy polaroid selfie, which is ironic, because it's from a time when selfies weren't even coined as such. My hand is outstretched to take the picture, which looking back, seems so much more difficult than it is now, since there was no preview screen staring back at us to make sure we were in frame.

I cringe at the amount of hot pink eye shadow I have on, along with heavy onyx liner. But even with my poor choice in makeup on full display, it doesn't take away from the expression on Leo's face. His lips are half-puckered, kissing my cheek as he lets this adorable smile poke through the corner of his mouth. The look on his face is like the way that Papa looked at Mama in the picture just next to it. The look of true love.

The lump in my throat has now erupted into a stream of tears that escape my grieving eyes. Shit, I don't have time for this. I go to wipe my tears away and then bring my now tear-slicked fingers to my lips as I kiss them, bringing them back to both pictures to say goodbye.

Sadness and hope mix in my gut as I accept the closing of this chapter of my life that I have left open for longer than it needs to be. I can still grieve my losses without losing anymore of myself in the process. Today, I am finally giving myself permission to move on.

I pile the few remaining boxes by the door so I can start bringing them downstairs, and just as I turn to grab my duffel bag off my bed, I hear a car door slam. Confused, because Nessa shouldn't be here yet to pick me up, I head to the window looking over the front of the house from my room. I move the curtain over and look down toward the driveway and see Titi Lana's black Escalade, but I don't see her.

I scan the outside once more until I hear muffled voices coming from the window closest to my bed. I forgot I left it open to let in the cool, late-October breeze that just warms my soul this time of year. Luckily, I'm not leaving the state, so I can hold on to those beloved New York autumns that are so dear to my heart.

I move toward the side window that is open, now hearing the muffled voices more clearly.

I can see Titi Lana's chocolate hair pinned back in a bun as her back is turned in what looks to be a deep conversation with that creepy-ass woman next door, Miranda.

Just as I am about to close the window, Miranda's gaze shifts from whatever she and Lana are talking about directly up at me. *Shit.* Feeling like I just got caught doing something I shouldn't be doing; I panic and slam the door. Granted, I was eavesdropping, and while that's rude, sure, it's not against the law.

Eager to find out what Titi Lana is doing so engrossed in conversation with Miranda, I hurry and gather my duffel bag and the rest of the boxes, minus the heavy one filled with books. That will no doubt have to be a two-woman job.

I trek down the stairs and head toward the front door. Placing the boxes down, I prop the storm door, so it remains open, making moving everything out much easier. I step out onto the porch, trying to discreetly inch closer to the side of the porch that overlooks Miranda's driveway. There is a tall bush that gives minimal privacy, but it is enough that I can eavesdrop hopefully undetected.

As I approach where they stand, I overhear what sounds like Miranda whispering.

"I'm telling you; I haven't seen him smile in ages," she says tearfully.

I try to perch myself toward the bush to get a better look as I see Titi Lana go to embrace Miranda. Lana holds Miranda for a few seconds before releasing her. "Miranda, it will be okay. It's all going to work out, just as we all discussed."

I go to shift my stance, forgetting that my heavy duffel bag is still slung around my shoulder, when I so gracefully lose my footing and trip. I scratch my cheek on the bush that I was attempting to use as a cover. My duffel bag drops, and even with the small cover I still have despite my fall, I feel both of their eyes on me.

"Sienna?" I hear Titi Lana call out.

I collect myself before I wave over to their direction.

"Hey, Titi, I was just packing and heard your car door slam. I wanted to see if you could help me move a few heavier boxes downstairs before Nessa gets here." I say, trying to make my presence on the porch seem more legitimate than nosy.

"Ok, no problem, Sienna. I'll be right there," Lana says, unaware of the frigid stare Miranda has on me. This is the closest I have been to her, other than our daily window staring contests. The white streak I knew Miranda had looks even more pronounced as we stand but a few feet from each other. Even more distinct than her hair is the eerie way her eyes match the ebony of her hair. Black as night and fixed on me with an intense look of disgust mixed with what I can only assume to be pity. She holds her gaze on me a few moments more before redirecting her attention back to Lana.

I'm about to head back inside when the sun pokes out from the clouds, shining down on the patch of grass between both houses. It's as if the sun is a spotlight trying to highlight Miranda, because as she and Lana go back to whatever they are talking about, I suddenly notice the gold chain around her neck. I notice that the chain that graces her décolletage has a charm of a *coqui* dangling from it.

My heart flutters with the unexpected reminder of Mama. I remember the first time we visited Mama and Titi Lana's hometown of Caguas, Puerto Rico. At night, my Grandma Isa would leave the windows open, and the sound of the *coquis* chirping filled the air. The singing frog of Puerto Rico, a symbol of the island that I wish I was able to visit more.

My Grandma Isa never approved of Mama and Papa. She felt that Mama was betraying the Diaz name by marrying a Ricci. My Grandfather Rico died when Mama and Titi Lana were both young, so he never was able to choose who Mama could marry. When Mama went to New York for college and came back to the island with an Italian man, Grandma Isa saw that as a betrayal to the family. As the years passed, Mama gave up seeking her mother's approval, so the trips to the magical island dwindled, until we just stopped going all together.

Maybe Miranda is someone Mama and Titi Lana knew from Puerto Rico?

I hear Nessa's car pull up to my house, stealing my attention from Lana and Miranda. I walk across the porch and down the steps to meet her.

"Hey, girl, you ready?" Nessa asks as she slams the door of her Civic.

She recently got promoted to detective, so she doesn't have to wear those God-awful, navy blue, rigid police uniforms. Instead, she has on a pair of black, flared pants with a black bodysuit underneath a gingham blazer. If it weren't for her badge and Glock attached to her work belt, you'd think she just left a corporate job or a swanky dinner spot.

"Yea, I just need your help putting these boxes in your car, and I have one more upstairs that's pretty heavy," I say, pointing to the stack I made before I tried listening in on Lana and Miranda's chat.

"You got it." Nessa takes off her blazer, resting it on the rail of the porch before she bends down to collect the first few boxes she sees.

I grab my duffel bag and the remaining boxes and follow Nessa to her car. She's been driving the same Civic hatchback since our freshman year of college.

I wait with her as she fumbles with the key fob, trying to get the button to connect to the trunk so it can open. Flustered, she decides to flip the fob side over to the key side and manually open the trunk.

We pile the boxes into her trunk as I look over to see Lana seeming to hug Miranda goodbye and head over to me and Nessa.

"This car is such a piece of shit. I only use it when I come up to visit you, and now that you will finally be in the city, it's about time I say peace out," she says, slamming her trunk shut with visible excitement.

"Oh, shit, Nes. We still have that heavy box I was telling you about, upstairs in my room that I need your help with," I remind her.

"No worries," I hear Titi Lana say to Miranda as she comes over with puffy eyes. It looks like she has been crying.

"Titi, are you ok?" I ask as I see creepy Miranda still standing in her driveway, staring. *Fucking shocker.*

"Yes, I'm fine. I'm just sad that you are leaving," she says, bringing me in for an embrace.

"I told you, I'll come back home in a couple weeks, and you are always welcome to visit. The city isn't that far," I remind her.

"Yea, Lana, seriously, you are always welcome," Nessa says, backing me up.

Lana takes a deep breath and shifts her attention to Nessa. "Thank you, Vanessa, I appreciate that. Ok, you girls all set?"

I'm about to say yes when Nessa reminds me of the box of books upstairs that I just told her moments before that we still needed to get. Before I could say anything, Nessa and Lana head back inside the house to grab the box of books together, leaving me to get one good look at the house before we head down to the city.

Mama always took such pride in housekeeping, and she kept the exterior just as pristine as she did the inside of the house. I definitely do not uphold the same standards, but I think I've done a pretty good job at honoring the home that I have spent my entire life in, up until this moment.

I glance over at what once was Leo's house and I can't say the same. With the chipped porch paint and weathered shutters, it stands out like a sore thumb amongst the rest of the pristine homes on the block.

A moment later, I hear Lana and Nessa laughing, struggling to get my box of books through the front door.

"Jesus Christ, Sienna!" Nessa shouts. "Are you planning on leaving the apartment anytime with all these books you have?" she teases.

I run over to Nessa's car to open the passenger door and slide the seat forward to fit the box in the back.

"Here you go, bookworm," Nessa says as she and Lana lug the box in the back seat.

"Very funny," I say back to her, laughing at how ridiculous of a sight it was to see them struggling with the number of books I have packed.

"All I'm saying is, tonight, you better be ready to let loose a little bit. We have a move and a new job to celebrate." Nessa claps in excitement.

She turns to Titi Lana and gives her a hug goodbye before reaching for her ringing cell phone clipped to her work belt. She answers quickly and heads to the car, waiting for me to say goodbye to Lana.

"Well, this is it," I say, feeling those damn tears I had streaming down my face from earlier in my room start to surface again.

Lana smiles warmly at me and lifts her smooth, manicured hand to my cheek.

"Your parents would be so proud of you, for following your dreams and going for it in the Big Apple," she says as I raise my hand to meet hers that still rests on my cheek.

"I hope so," I say, unsure if they would really love the idea of me heading to the city that they sadly died in, let alone on the eve of the anniversary of their passing.

"I know so," she declares with confidence. "Just do me a favor, please be careful."

"I will, Titi. I'll call you when we get to the city," I promise her as we go in for one more hug before I meet Nessa in her car.

Lana remains in the driveway for a moment more and

waves goodbye as I buckle up. Nessa hangs up the phone as she throws the car in reverse. She begins to back out of the driveway as she excitedly goes on about what she has planned for us tonight once we get to the city. I am half-listening as we pass Leo's old house, where Miranda stands, still staring. Except this time as we pass by, she is making a peculiar motion with her hands. I turn my head to look back at her to and it is then I notice she is doing the sign of the cross with a sinister grin smeared all over her face.

What the actual fuck?

Chapter 10

Carmine

As much as becoming involved in Marked Inc. was something I never wanted, I am appreciative of the perks that come with now being its CEO. The main one being how lucrative the underground drug trade is. It's what gave me the funds to purchase the business venture I am the most passionate about: The Sandy Claws. My home away from home.

The Sandy Claws is a misfit's Heaven or Hell, depending how you look at it, with its gothic appeal and its dark opulence. I've worked hard to create an atmosphere where people can feel like they can let loose—inhibitions and morals alike.

At one time, it stood as a Catholic church; though, when the congregation didn't donate enough to run it or fill the priests' pockets, they abandoned ship. *Shocking.* Churches are no different than the businesses I run. While they may pretend to be holy, their end goal is monetary, manipulating the truth however they can so that seats are full, and pockets are fuller. Only difference between them and me is that I have no interest in pretending to be holy. Being unholy is far more fun.

I light another cigarette as I continue to saunter my way over to The Sandy Claws. Alex hates meeting me there. He says that it's risky, as he may run into repeat offenders, since our patrons aren't always society's finest. Not to say that those who break the law are scum, because that would make me the world's biggest hypocrite. It's just that The Sandy Claws has always been a refuge for those who feel like victims of the world's righteous standards.

I like to remind Alex that when he is in my company, he is safer than with the gun he keeps holstered to his side. That is the perk of being the owner. No one dares try me on my turf. As much as Alex likes to pretend that he is above the discretions I commit daily, he is right there with me, co-signing all my devious moves. Cop or not, his loyalty is to me. And it runs much deeper than his allegiance to the badge he wears around his neck.

As I continue to walk, I see an unusual amount of people flooding the streets. Granted, this is New York City, a notoriously crowded, bustling metropolis. Still, most of the people that roam these streets are in a rush, uninterested in hanging around or fraternizing.

I twist my wrist in an upward motion, illuminating my watch. The screen lights up with its obnoxious reminders of how little I moved today. Aside from the unmoved rings, I stare at the date: October 30th. Ah, Mischief Night. The evening before Halloween, which your average folk use as an excuse to be up to no good. I pity them, really. Mischief Night is my every night.

Just a block away from the entrance of The Sandy Claws, I toss the butt of my cigarette into an overflowing trash can. I decide to hang back and have another smoke while I wait for Alex. I grab another Parliament from my jacket pocket and settle it between my lips as I flick the lighter. The second the tip lights, I inhale the calming, toxic bliss, letting the nicotine fill my lungs.

An elderly woman scowls in my direction as she walks past me. She's swiping her hand in front of her face to waft away the smoke that billows her way. The woman quickens her pace past me, making sure to roll her eyes exaggeratingly as to solidify her disapproval of my smoking.

A condescending grin forms on my lips as I lift my hand to wave to her. She rolls her eyes once more, muttering something as she gets lost in the crowd filled streets.

Even as the woman leaves my view, the grin I gave her does not leave my lips. Instead, I am hit with a pang of nostalgia as the stranger's disgust at my inhaling tobacco reminds me of the disdain my mother had for it.

If my mother were still alive, she would be having a conniption over seeing me light up a cigarette. *As if that were my only sinful vice.*

I remember when I was young, she scolded my Uncle Victor for smoking one night when he lit up at the dinner table. She went on about how distasteful of a habit it is. My choice to inhale the toxic fumes of cigarettes is practically candy on the scale of where my morality now lies. Hell, Mother would resurrect herself if she even knew the half of the heinous transgressions that have defined the last few years of my life.

Taking another drag, I exhale the smoke with closed eyes

as I tilt my head up toward the dark blanket of autumn sky above me. October nights like this, where the scent of foliage strewn about is potent and the air is sharp against my face feel like a refuge from the chaos that consumes my life. Head still tilted upwards, probably looking like a madman amongst the influx of people zooming past me, I remain on the sidewalk basking in the moonlight, I feel something take hold of my forearm.

I lower my head, opening my eyes to see Alex now standing next to me. He lets go of my forearms and brings his hand to mine, bringing me in for a handshake.

"Sorry, didn't mean to disrupt your star gazing," he jests.

The sheen of his badge still slung around his neck beams from the full moon overhead. I reach for his badge, in a half-joking way of bringing to his attention he is still wearing it. Which, knowing Alex, is by mistake. He never wears his badge outside his clothing or his uniform when he comes out with me.

"I thought you coppers were supposed to be smart. Can't gaze at the stars with closed eyes," I say as I tug on his badge before he looks down, frantically tucking it into his shirt.

"Yea, well, forget your eyes being closed. Even if they weren't, I don't know how you would be able to see shit with all that smoke always blowing around your face." He zips his black hoodie up toward his neck, before slipping his hand into his jean pocket.

Lighting up a cigarette of his own, he laughs. "Didn't anyone tell you those are cancer sticks, bro?" *Smart-ass.*

"Didn't anyone tell you that you can't pull off saying *bro*? It makes you sound like an asshole," I taunt.

"Very funny, *dude,* is that better?" he snaps back as he goes to take his first drag of his freshly light cigarette.

"Honestly, no." I chuckle.

Alex returns a quick chuckle in between drags, and even through his attempts at humor, I know my cousin well enough to spot the tension spreading along his jawline.

"Long day, huh?"

Alex nods.

"Yea, I can relate," I say as I step on my smoke, putting out the light.

"I know, Boss," Alex says. "Fuck, I still can't get used to saying that."

"Well, it's been how long? Get used to it, at least for the time being." I sneer.

"Yea, man, I got it. Calm the fuck down," he says, stomping on what little is left of his cigarette.

"Let's go to the kitchen entrance tonight," I suggest, as we start heading to the back of The Sandy Claws.

He draws in a long breath as we begin walking. "Yea, good idea. I need a fucking drink. Shit is starting to stress me out at the department. I can only deflect so much until they start looking at me, too, especially given what tomorrow is."

"Oh, what, Halloween?" I say with a sarcastic grin trying to ease his stress. I try to remind Alex that since we do not share the same last name or similar facial features, for that matter, most people would never put our familial connection together. Our mothers are sisters, and where I look more like my mother, Alex resembles his father, Victor, especially with his rounded face and now salt and pepper scruff.

"Yes, Halloween, smart-ass. But you know what I am getting at here, Carmine. Gala night. The chief is requesting that some of the guys, and that girl they promoted to detective, stay within a couple blocks of the gala."

Fuck, this is the last thing I need right now.

I can see the stress oozing from Alex's expression, and I feel a tinge of that stress rubbing off on me. But the both of us getting all worked up isn't going to do either of us any good. "Fuck, sounds like we need a drink, then," I say as I grip his shoulder to try to get him to loosen up a bit.

"Yea, we fucking do," he jokes, slowly starting to loosen up a bit.

Once around back, Alex and I step down into the lowered entrance door to the kitchen. I tap the camera doorbell once and wait for José, my head bartender, to let me in.

The double bolt lock slides, making a loud sound as José swings the door open. He has a dingy bar mop towel draped over his shoulder, as I hear him yell something in Spanish to his wife, Wanda, who also bartends for me a couple nights a week. I could only make out bits and pieces of what he is saying to her. Despite Spanish being my mother's native language, she wasn't around long enough to teach me the language fully.

José is around my father's age, in his upper sixties, though, you would never guess it with how physically fit he keeps himself. The only thing that gives away his age is the not-so-subtle limp he has acquired after an accident on a construction site he was working at over a decade ago. Most days, it doesn't affect his ability to work the bar, but on the rare nights like this one, where the patrons expand past the usual townies that frequent The Sandy Claws, having the help of his younger wife, Wanda, is much needed.

"How's it going, Boss?" José asks as he turns his back to

the heavy metal door, keeping it open for Alex and me to walk past.

"Pretty good, José. How's business tonight?"

"Crazy, man. It's fucking wild tonight. All these out-of-towners and college students. I hope you don't mind, I had Wanda come in, just to give me an extra hand," he responds as he slides the bolt lock back in place.

Wanda's caramel-highlighted curls bounce as she waltzes over with a pissed off expression on her face. Her eyes widen when she looks past Alex and me toward José. "Sorry, I don't mean to interrupt, but I need his help. It's a madhouse out there."

I nod in agreement. "Of course, I won't keep your husband any longer. Thank you, José."

Wanda smiles at me, then directs a stern expression back toward José as she motions him to keep it moving and leads him back to the bar.

Alex and I make our way through the bustling kitchen to our usual spot at the back corner of the bar. It's my preferred place to sit, since it allows me to look at all who enter the bar while I am there. It is crucial that I never have my back turned. I never know who is going to attempt to stab me in it, so I need to always be on the lookout.

José finishes serving two blonde women sitting at the bar before he shouts over the loud music in our direction.

"Usual, Boss?" he asks.

I nod, holding up two fingers, indicating that tonight's whiskey on the rocks needs to be a double pour.

"You got it!" shouts, directing his attention over to Alex. "You too, Alex?"

Alex nods as he sinks into his chair, as if trying to blend in.

I loosen my jacket and chuckle at Alex's demeanor. "Yes, make his a double, too," I answer for him, since José is still staring at us, confused by Alex's body language.

José turns to grab the bottle of Jack from the glass shelf, when I notice one of the blondes he just served has her eyes locked on mine. She twists around on the tall barstool, revealing a form-fitting bodysuit that has her full tits spilling out and on display. She flashes me a pearly white smile before she seductively bites on her plump lower lip. I smirk back, briefly, then continue to take off my sports coat and turn my attention back to Alex, who I see is practically drooling over said blonde.

"Shit, Carmine, that chick is sexy as hell." He adjusts his hoodie, leaning forward in his chair, glancing at her once more. "She is here almost every week, always eyeing you. I don't know why you waste your time obsessing—"

I raise my hand to cut him off. Alex shifts his gaze from the seductive blonde to my now raised hand, signaling him to think about what he is going to say before he continues.

Before either of us can say anything, José comes over and sets both double whiskeys down on the small round table in front of us. I grab the glass quickly, causing some of the precious amber liquid to splash up and onto the outside of the glass. I take my index finger and run it along the whiskey now dripping down the glass. I bring my whiskey-soaked finger to my mouth as I shoot a devious side-eyed glance over to the blonde, who hasn't taken her sights off Alex, or I since we sat down.

I watch as she shifts in her seat, biting down on her lip

even harder than before as I suck the whiskey off my finger. She is so visibly turned on by my blatant flirting that her friend, with hair so light in comparison it looks white, is even eyeing me in anticipation of what I do next.

Alex clears his throat after witnessing my little flirtatious game and interrupts.

"That's what I mean, Carmine. You can have any woman you want. I just don't understand why you waste so much energy obsessing and creeping after ... you know," he says, raising his bushy brows.

"It's not obsessing," I lie. "You of all fucking people should understand why I am the way I am."

It's not a matter of me being able to have anyone I want. I know that, and it's not even me being cocky. Facts are facts. Most women I run into seem to throw themselves at me, much like Blondie One and Two over there. It's not that I can't get anyone, the problem is I don't want just anyone. I want her, and until I can make her mine, the rest of the world can go fuck right off.

Shaking his head at my response, Alex gulps his whiskey down, letting the last sip drip down his chin. He wipes away the mess from his face and slams the glass down, looking past the two flirtatious blondes and signaling to Wanda for another round.

"So, you said you have updates," I try to bring the conversation back to business as I light another cigarette.

"Dude, you are not supposed to smoke in here," he pesters.

A deep chuckle forms in my throat before I take another puff. "What are you going to do, dear cousin, arrest me?"

Alex rolls his eyes. "Fucking Christ, Carmine, work with

me here a little. It's always something with you. Anyway, let's fucking get down to it, because I don't have all night. I have to head home at a decent time tonight before the Mrs. starts chewing my ass."

"I thought you liked that," I tease.

"Fuck you, man." Alex laughs.

Wanda brings over our next round of whiskeys before a rowdy group a few tables over, closer to the bar, steals her attention.

"Anyway, like I was saying," Alex grabs his glass before continuing. "We got this chick who was recently promoted to detective. She occasionally will work with the drug unit, and I swear, man, she has a sixth fucking sense for that shit," he warns.

I grab my glass of whiskey from the table and give it a swirl before bringing it to my lips. "Oh, is that so?"

"I'm telling you, she is fucking good, which means she is going to be a problem. Not to mention, she started reading over some open case files, and I can tell her wheels are turning," Alex says before he proceeds to slurp down almost his entire whiskey in one pronounced gulp.

"Slow down there, buddy. You're drinking like you're scared," I say as he wipes the whiskey that dripped down his lips.

"I'm serious, she's going to make things even more difficult for me to cover for you."

Alex continues talking, though my ears stop working momentarily. All my brain is focusing on is the word "she." Being in the business of evading law enforcement as long as I have has taught me a few things. One being, while male cops think with their muscles, a female cop, well, they are usually a whole other breed. Smart, quick on their feet, and on a mission to prove any asshole who may underestimate their power wrong. Alex is right, she is going to be trouble.

I snap out of my daze and try to jump back into the conversation.

"Not to mention, he is putting her on surveillance tomorrow night at the Halloween Gala."

This is going to be a problem, because a large part of the success of gala night has always rested on Alex convincing the chief to let him work security that night. Aside from the drug force gig, Alex has always worked per diem security gigs. I have had him on retainer for Marked Inc. function nights, and since the chief, for some reason or another, has taken a liking to my father, I have always been able to have Alex guarding the front, while I have the products run through the back.

But now, if this detective, whoever she is, suspects that we are, in fact, running drugs at the gala and she is out to surveil ... well then, that puts a damper on things. Big fucking time.

"Did you remind the chief that, since you work security for me on gala night, that will be unnecessary?"

"I tried, Carmine, but she is on her game. She heard me talking to the chief, inserted herself in the conversation and got him to stick to the original plan they discussed."

"Fuck," I grunt, taking the last drag of my cigarette.

"Yea, fuck, is right," he echoes. "Oh, there is one more thing," Alex says with a genuine look of concern on his face.

"Yes?" I ask hesitantly.

"She also is looking into the Santiago file."

Ah, Santiago. One of our biggest disappointments at the

company. My father insisted he wouldn't be a flight risk, but it's near impossible having a recovering addict sell drugs. Not to mention, Santiago failed to follow protocol after Christian performed the necessary alterations.

"I was thorough with my disposal. I followed the strict protocol that I instated myself. There should be nothing left to dissect," I say confidently as my blood begins to boil. Santiago was a loose cannon, which is why I went around my father and finished him myself.

"Well, it looks like Christian may have forgotten to complete the job on the prints. This chick is fucking smart, Car, it's only a matter of time before she starts putting the pieces of the puzzle together."

Fuck.

I try to conceal the worry that is beginning to attack my mind. Swirling my glass once more, I try to buy myself time to figure out how to handle this.

"She sounds like she knows what she is doing. Too bad she is so driven to take down the wicked. Otherwise, I would offer a vulture such as herself a job," I joke, trying to conceal the doubt that is momentarily hitting me.

"She a fucking fox. Smart and determined to make a name for herself in the department. Busting the city's biggest drug lord would be the highlight of her career. Shit anyone's, really." Alex has a point, except he left out a keyword.

"Rumored," I reply.

"Huh?" Alex slurs, sounding like the double whiskeys are starting to work their magic.

"I think you meant to say, the city's biggest *rumored* drug lord. There is a difference. No one has been able to prove shit. From the outside, I am just a wealthy businessman running a public relations firm by day and this gothic oasis by night," I remind him as I lift my hands, taking in the smog-filled air of The Sandy Claws.

My tone is more intense than I intended it to be. He is like a brother to me, although, I know he isn't doing this for me; he is doing this to honor my mother. Sometimes, I am jealous that he knew her better than her own son did. Sadly, my father stole her from me before I had the chance to build the memories that I so wished I could have and because of that, Alex and I share a mutual disdain for my father.

"Remember, Carmine, you aren't untouchable. Eventually, this is going to come to the surface. Especially if you have a loose kink in your midst. You can send them up to Christian all you want, he can work magic on the flesh, but unless he can alter flawed souls, you still need to be careful."

Anger begins to settle in as I grow increasingly resentful with the position my father has put me in. Although this life comes with power, it also comes with an immense amount of pressure. This war that my idiotic father started with the Ricci family after they completed their merger with my father's other enemy, the Marinos, has completely changed the trajectory of so many lives.

I digress from my own thoughts and bring the conversation back to Alex. "Christian works their flesh, but I will put the fear of Carmine in them."

"You mean the fear of God?"

"No, because when I hold the cold steel of my Glock to the temple of whoever dares test me, it will be a gentle reminder of who they work for. God won't be there to save them from my wrath," I declare. "No one will."

I am not interested in redeeming the unredeemable.

Very little in this world is redeemable; I should know, considering how far I have fallen. And in the off chance my soul can, indeed, be saved, it won't be God who can redeem it. It will be her. Only she can grant absolution to a man as wicked as I.

Chapter 11

Sienna

"Hurry up, girl, we have twenty minutes until the Uber gets here," Nessa announces as we walk through the doorway into her apartment with the last of my boxes. As soon as we enter, it is immediately evident how much Nes works and is not home. The whole place looks un-lived in, almost. Most of the walls are bare, without any décor or character. There is not a mess in sight, other than a takeout bag I spot on the otherwise untouched kitchen countertops.

"We literally just walked in the door, Nes, you don't want to chill for a little bit before going out?" I ask, pouting my lower lip playfully.

I figured I would ask, but I already know the answer. Nes runs on her time only. It's what she wants when she wants, and everyone usually just follows suit, me included. Some would call her bossy, but I admire how determined of a person she is. This world needs more women like her who are unapologetically themselves.

She heads to the fridge, ignoring my playful plea for

more time. "Nope, those puppy dog eyes, and pouty lip don't do shit for me," she says as she grabs a beer from the fridge for her and me. Handing me a Corona, she glances at the clock on the wall of the kitchen. "Come on, Sienna, that is plenty of time. You already have your clothes hung up in the spare bedroom closet. Just go pick something from there and you'll be good to go." She nudges me in the direction of the spare room.

I take a swig of my beer, swishing the fizz around my mouth before letting it coat my throat. Sighing, I begrudgingly head to get changed. I know Nessa having a night off is rare. She purposely swapped shifts to work earlier so she could pick me up and bring me down to the city. So, the least I can do is suck it up and go out for a drink or two.

I flip the light switch to what is now technically my bedroom and head to the closet. It's a small room, nothing lavish, but it's enough for me. I'm not high maintenance; there isn't much I need other than a place to sleep, hang my clothes, and store my books. If I can do that in a space, I am all set. I look to the large window with a view of the crowded streets and notice a picturesque park across the street. The view is oddly serene, despite being set smack dab in the center of the city.

There are two closets in the room, one smaller than the other, so I moved my clothes into the larger of the two. I head to the large closet that has a mirror attached to the front, which reminds me of the one Nes and I shared in our dorm years ago. Knowing Nes and how frugal she is, it is more than likely the same mirror from our college days.

I halfway open the door and begin to sift through the clothes. I don't even remember what I have in here, because I brought this batch of clothes to Nessa well over a month ago. As I glide the hangers on the metal bar of the closet, I see mostly going out or what would be considered work attire. Nothing like my usual black leggings and concert tees that I prefer wearing.

I look through a few moments more. Not finding anything that I am crazy about, I step back from the clothes and shut the door. I look at myself in the door mirror, debating just leaving on my leggings and Aerosmith tee shirt I have on now and calling it a day.

As if Nes is reading my mind, she knocks on the open door before letting herself into the room.

"No, you're not wearing that out. Don't even think about it." She walks past me and swings the closet door fully open. She hums to herself as she sorts through the clothes until she finds something for me. "Ah, here. This is perfect!" she exclaims, dangling a black off-the-shoulder dress in the air. "This work?" she asks, already handing me the dress.

"Sure. That will work," I say, laughing, as if she is giving me any choice in the matter.

"Excellent," she says, taking the final gulp of her beer. "Now, hurry the fuck up and get dressed. Then, meet me in the kitchen for shots."

She starts heading back out toward the kitchen. In the doorway, with her hand on the doorknob, about to shut it, she turns back to face me. "I'm glad you are here, Sienna. I have a feeling that you will finally be able to start over here." She smiles and closes the door behind her.

Fuck I hope so.

I quickly slip on the dress, throwing my previous outfit on the bed. I debate sprucing up my hair, but after seeing my reflection in the mirror of the closet door in front of me, it doesn't look half bad. Nes did pick an awesome dress for me. I love how this hugs my curves without being too tight. Plus, it has pockets. *Winning*. It also highlights my tattoos nicely, especially my stitch marks I recently added to my collarbone area.

Scanning the small vanity next to the closet for my lipstick, I realize it is in my purse, which I left in the kitchen. Perfect timing, as I hear glasses clanking from the kitchen cabinet.

As my foot hits the kitchen floor, Nessa has already poured shots for us and is handing me one.

"Cheers to best friends taking on the city together. Fucking finally!" she cheers as we clank our shot glasses together before downing what smells like cinnamon whiskey. I make a sour face. Whiskey has never been a go-to for me.

"And hopefully, to getting some dick tonight!" she adds, giggling as she grabs another Corona for each of us.

"Nessa!" I blush.

"Oh, stop! You are just as vulgar as me." She rolls her eyes, handing me another beer.

Ha, she isn't wrong. One of the many reasons Nessa and I became instant friends, despite our differences, is our love for sarcasm and vulgarity. That has always been one of our bonds.

Lifting her beer up toward mine, we clink the glass bottles together in a toast.

"Here is to wherever the night takes us, and whoever it takes us with," I concede.

"That's my girl!"

We both take a long sip of our beers, almost downing

them in a single go as her phone goes off. "Alright, Uber is downstairs. Let's go!" she exclaims, grabbing her purse as I grab mine and follow her lead.

As we head to the lobby of Nessa's apartment, I get an email from Lizzie, Carmine's assistant.

Sienna,

Mr. Moretti has arranged for a driver to pick you up tomorrow at 8 a.m. sharp outside of the address you provided.
Good luck,
Lizzie

"Who was that Ms. Big Shot Journalist?" Nes asks, peering over my shoulder to look at my phone.

I roll my eyes as I close the email. "I would hardly say big shot," I respond to Nessa. "It was just my new boss' assistant. Apparently, he is sending a private car to pick me up tomorrow," I say in a surprised tone. That was totally unexpected, however, I am not complaining, because it buys me some time to learn the ropes of the New York subway system.

"Oh, fancy," Nessa says as she downs the rest of her beer and throws it in the recycling bin outside the apartment building. I follow suit as we both get into our Uber parked out front.

As we make our way through the crowded city streets, I stare out the window of the car, taking in the bright lights and observing the vast array of people spilling out onto the sidewalk. I zone out a bit, taking in the chaos of cars and people that surround us as we drive, losing track of how many blocks we have passed since leaving the apartment.

When the Uber comes to a stop, it snaps me out of my trance. I was so busy in my own head, as usual, I realize that I forgot to ask Nessa where the hell we were even going tonight.

I nod, thanking the driver before shimmying my way out of the back seat. I slam the door and meet Nessa on the sidewalk.

"Hey, Nes, where are we going tonight for drinks?"

"Right over here." Nessa points. "The Sandy Claws."

There is no mistaking which bar is The Sandy Claws. It stands out among the modern store fronts that surround it, with its opulent cathedral-like aesthetic. I've always had a fascination with gothic architecture. There is something so haunting and sensual within the details. The spire on the roof catches my eye immediately. The stunning ogival arches above every stained-glass window remind me of the churches I saw as a young girl when traveling throughout Florence during summer breaks.

We traveled to Italy more frequently than Puerto Rico, since Mama grew tired of the constant digs her mother would get in about how much she hated Papa for her. Regardless of why we went there more than the island, warm memories briefly flood my heart. Those summers in Italy were some of the only times that Papa was present. Granted, even as a young girl, I knew that Papa's work followed him wherever he went. Work always needed to be done, contacts needed to be secured, and business always had to continue. Even on vacations. In Italy, however, Papa was able to relax more being closer to his side of the family, away from the countless enemies he made in New York.

Given the way that The Sandy Claws resembles an old cathedral, it wouldn't surprise me if it once stood as a church. However, I am sure there are now more demons than saints within its walls. Quenching their insatiable thirsts and giving into their carnal desires, which only makes me more eager to see what is lurking within its walls. Which speaks volumes because, despite my fondness of booze, bars have never been my thing.

Most bars I have been to are overpriced and over-crowded. Filled with people who can't handle their booze, or people glued to their phones, instead of interacting with the people they came with. The whole bar scene usually annoys me. Give me a bottle of wine and a good book at home and I'm a happy girl. But if more bars looked like this place, I might become a convert ... and I haven't even ventured inside, yet.

I follow Nessa's lead as we approach the dark walnut doors, equally as ornate as the rest of the building. We completely bypass the long line of impatient patrons waiting to make their way in. I can tell by some of their body language that their impatience is starting to reach a breaking point. I forgot tonight is Mischief Night, so the bar scene is even more packed than usual, especially for a weekday evening.

Nessa seems oblivious to the line of people that have clearly been waiting to get in, because she heads directly toward the two bouncers standing in front of the massive wooden doors.

Unlike me, Nessa loves going out to bars. Whereas I would rather drink at home, she thrives off meeting new people, especially when she drinks. Judging by her overconfident demeanor, and the exaggerated way her hips swing as she walks in the direction of the bouncers, she either already knows them or has fucked at least one of them. Both men are tall, easily over six feet, with arms full of muscle and ink. Their choice of short sleeves is interesting, given how damn cold it is for this October night in New York.

She walks over to the more attractive of the two bouncers. I see her leaning in to kiss him on the cheek. I get a quick glimpse of the bouncer she has her lips on as I catch up to her and he is stunning. He has chiseled cheekbones with a strong jawline that is covered just slightly by a five o'clock shadow.

Nessa releases the bouncer from her grip on him as she motions to me to follow her through the front doors. "Thanks, Miles," she says flirtatiously as we head to the entrance.

"Nes, who was that?" I say, trying to discreetly tilt my head in the bouncer's direction.

"Oh, Miles?" Nessa says coyly. "He is just a friend. I arrested his brother, Trevor, not too long ago. Miles came into the station furious at Trevor, who was starting to become a regular. Petty crimes, mostly. Then, he started getting caught up in using the new drug that's been making its way all over this damn city lately. Miles is tough on Trevor since he basically raised him. I told him I would keep an eye on his brother. So, he just thanked me for looking out for him, that's all."

"That's all?" I nudge her arm, knowing she is leaving out major details here.

She giggles as a faint blush paints her cheeks. "And we may have hooked up once or twice ... or ten times."

"I knew it. Whatever, get it. He is fucking hot," I say as we make our way through the long vestibule that leads to a set of long velvet curtains that separate the main entrance to what I am assuming must be the rest of the bar. The sounds of muffled music and laughter come from the other side of the curtains. Such a dramatic entrance for a bar, not that I am complaining, because it's definitely unique.

The air is thick as we peel back the dark velvet curtains, making our way deeper into the crowded bar, toward the mixture of body heat and cigarette smoke. We find an empty spot at the bar, which is lined with skull-shaped ash trays spaced out every couple of inches, as do the high-top tables. It's odd, since indoor smoking has been a thing of the past for a while now.

The Sandy Claws looks like it has been frozen in an early 2000s millennial time warp. Everything in this place screams emo bliss. From the Seether playing in the background to the dark baroque patterned accent wall against the otherwise all-black painted walls. The antique chandeliers that hang from the high ceilings provide a warm amber light, which adds to the overall ambiance.

The intentional disregard of trying to fit into today's social media-saturated mold is noted, making me like this place already. *I feel like I'm home.*

"José!" Nessa shouts over the loud music.

José, the bartender, is just as tall and muscular as the bouncers. Older, but not any less attractive. He walks with a subtle limp, and as he approaches us, I notice a scar under his left eye, which makes me wonder how he acquired such a mark on his skin. When you grew up surrounded by men who made a living dealing and scheming like I did, you often saw scars like the one José is sporting. Though, if my assumptions are correct, men like José take the scars as a blessing. Better scarred and marked above ground than buried six feet under.

"Vanessa, good to see you," José says, flashing a smile. His accent reminds me of Mama's: New York mixed with a faint Caribbean accent. "What can I get you ladies?" he asks as he quickly wipes down the bar surface in front of us before he places two coasters there.

As Nessa leans over the bar trying to talk to José over the searingly loud music, I look down at the coaster on the bar top. A knot forms in my stomach as I pick up the heart-shaped coaster. There is a stitched design in the middle, with one-half of the heart black and white, the other half teal with accents of red, purple, and yellow. Suddenly, my mind is transported back to love-struck teenage Sienna. To a time when symbolism like this felt nostalgic, not heart-breaking.

I take a deep breath in and brush off the rush of feelings that have just overcome me. How fucking idiotic of me. It's Halloween Eve, of course there would be Jack and Sally coasters. The whole place is decked out in Halloween décor. This is just part of the theme. I shake my head. I hate how, even after all this time, little lingering reminders of what I once had, when I had Leo, haunt me like the fucking succubus he was.

I put the coaster down and interrupt Nessa and José, "Vodka and tonic, with a round of tequila shots, please."

Nessa claps with pride. "You heard my bestie!"

"You got it, ladies. Be right back," José says, heading back to grab the bottle of Tito's.

"I'm so happy you are finally here, Sienna. This is our time to take on the Big Apple, just two best friends," she says as she gives me a side hug, with her arms stretched out around my shoulders.

José comes back with our drinks, and I try not to pay any more attention to the stupid themed coasters he puts the drinks down on. I have waited too long to leave the heartbreak that bound me to my hometown. Here I am, a new Sienna. Here, I will shed the misfortune of my family and life to finally start anew. But all that starts tomorrow. Tonight, I plan on getting fucking hammered.

Cheers.

Chapter 12

Carmine

As I wait for Alex to meet me back at our table after a phone call he had to take, I sit, sipping on whatever number whiskey this is for the evening. I down the last of the watered-down amber liquid, as most of the ice has melted at this point, making it more of a Jack and water than a Jack on the rocks.

I feel a hint of unease as I see more and more patrons beginning to enter through the velvet entry curtains. While I appreciate the business beyond our usual suspects, who have made this their go-to watering hole, I'm not used to crowds like this.

When Alex comes back to our spot, I'm going to wrap things up here and head to the brownstone to try to get in the proper headspace for what and *who* awaits me tomorrow.

Like clockwork, José catches me putting my now empty glass back down on the table. He waltzes over, ready to give me a refill.

"Another one, Boss?"

I hand him the empty glass. "Thank you, José, but I am good. I need to get back home to walk Nada soon, anyway."

Nada, my albino pit bull, surely has been walked plenty of times by now by the private dog walker, Noel. But I miss him and enjoy taking him out myself to spend some extra time with him, since I tend to work double time these days.

José nods and heads back to the bar just as Alex reemerges, looking less on edge than before his phone call. Practically beaming, Alex seats himself where his still-full whiskey is awaiting him.

"Good news?" I ask.

Grabbing hold of his glass, he lifts it just a few inches from his mouth while he raises a cocky brow, tilting his glass up slightly.

"I'd fucking say so." He proceeds to chug his whiskey, releasing an audible "ah" sound as he slams the cup back down on the wood table.

"Do share." I nudge him, now with equally matched anticipation as his.

"It's your lucky day, because the chief called me and said I can still work security at the gala tomorrow night."

Excellent. I like where this is heading already.

"I'll have a burner phone tomorrow for both you and me," Alex begins. "So, you tell me when things start moving round back and when I need to start deflecting guys' attention to the front of the building."

"Will do, Alex," I say, trying to wrap up our conversation, since it appears everything will go according to the original plan, despite this woman that Alex is so afraid of.

Reaching for my sport coat, Alex continues. "I have seniority, and more importantly, the respect of the guys working surveillance with Mendez. Now that I know Chief is letting me work security, deflecting attention should be a breeze. I need to make sure she is distracted, otherwise, I'm telling you, it's going to be fucking game over for us," he warns, oblivious to the chill that just hit my spine as I repeat the name he just said once more in my head.

Mendez. Why does that name sound so familiar?

Continuing to put on my sport coat, I process the name once more, until I remember the file from human resources I went over before heading out for the evening. *Eric Mendez.* Interest peaked, I lean in toward the table so that my elbows meet my knees, hunched toward Alex.

"Mendez, you say?" I ask, "That wouldn't be the woman that has you all hot under the collar, is it?"

Expecting Alex to answer me, I remain hunched over. Instead of answering, I notice him take a deep gulp, forcing his Adam's apple to slowly and visibly protrude as it glides down his throat. A gulp like that is what you would expect from downing a glass of whiskey, but it's then I see that the agitation that briefly escaped his face is back, suddenly, with a vengeance.

He clamps down on his jaw as he bobs his head to the side. "Fucking Christ," he mutters through a visibly tight jaw. "Speak of the fucking Devil."

Curious as to who has Alex so perturbed, I turn around to scan the crowd behind me when I spot a petite beauty with bronze skin heading our way.

"Of course, she would remember I said I liked this place," I hear Alex say as my back is toward him, still taking in the woman a mere few feet from us.

An uncontrollable grin begins to form as I refocus my

attention toward Alex. "Well, that was your first mistake," I begin to lecture him, teasingly. "If you didn't want anyone knowing you frequent such places, probably would have been best to, you know, not mention it." My grin is now turning into a mischievous chuckle.

"Oh, fuck, here she comes," Alex says nervously, sweat visibly forming on his full brows. His eyes still locked on the woman walking up to us, he goes to grab his glass, forgetting he just drained it of its contents moments before.

"Fuck!" he exclaims, realizing just now that he is out of whiskey. Alex turns his head toward the main bar in a last-ditch effort to get José or Wanda's attention, but both are busy tending to other patrons.

"Calm down," I say, trying to reassure him. Just as the words leave my mouth, I am met with the scent of vanilla and the sound of a raspy woman's voice saying his name.

Tugging on his hat, as if that will somehow make him disappear, Alex bows his head with a brief sigh before lifting his gaze to the woman, who is now standing by our table.

"Mendez." He nods in her direction.

"Oh, please, Alex, we are off the clock. You can call me Vanessa," she says as she runs her hand through her wavy, brown hair, tucking it behind her ear and revealing lobes full of dainty gold hoops.

As I sit back, waiting for Alex to introduce me to said Devil, as he likes to refer to her, I try to assess what it is about her that frightens Alex. She can't be more than five feet tall, even with her heels on. She is striking, with her warm, bronzed skin and well-defined facial features. There is a warm glow to her face that is both inviting and intimidating. Though, beneath her pearly smile she has flashed to Alex too many times to count in the mere minutes she has been standing by our table, I detect a fierceness in the way she commands attention.

It's not just her undeniable beauty that intimidates Alex, it's her intellect. That is what terrifies him. A smart female, let alone a smart female detective, is going to be hard-pressed to believe the lies that I instruct Alex to spew to cover not only my ass, but his. So, if my inclination about her is correct, he is right in his fear of her.

Time to work my charm.

I lock eyes with Alex as he is flailing while talking to this Mendez woman. "Alex, don't be rude," I interrupt, immediately seeing the tension in Alex's shoulders go down a few notches in the hopes that I will save him from his discomfort.

"Aren't you going to introduce me to your colleague?" I say as I stand from my chair and turn toward her, extending my hand out to hers.

"This is Vanessa," Alex introduces quickly.

She brings her hand into mine as her gold bracelets fall to her wrist.

"Pleasure to meet you, Vanessa." I kiss the top of her hand, making her blush.

She parts her lips to speak, and just as I release her hand from my grip, my vision suddenly begins to tunnel. Vanessa is moving her mouth, but I hear no sound. The bustling, noise-filled space suddenly feels like a blanket of silence has engulfed it, while everything feels like it is moving in slow motion.

I shake my head in disbelief, which unintentionally releases my not-so-slicked back hair from its position, temporarily blocking the little vision I feel like I have left right now. Quickly, I run my hand through the center of my hair to put it back in place. I blink to make sure my eyes are not failing me, but sure enough, there stands the object of my depraved desires.

The walking, breathing embodiment of perfection. The commencement of my untimely demise if I don't play my cards right. The rag doll in the flesh, standing here in my bar. Ms. Sienna Ricci.

I knew this moment would happen. I mean, *fuck*, I've made sure of it. However, in my planning for this very moment, when I could make myself known to her, I did not anticipate her being at The Sandy Claws. At least, not the night before her first day at the office.

A nervous chill takes over my spine as I try to remain stoic to disguise the unease building inside of me. Thankfully, Alex has snapped out of his mood toward Vanessa as he takes over the conversation I so rudely abandoned.

As she continues to make her way through the crowd, I can't take my eyes off her. My gaze is glued to her, as if she were quicksand and I the helpless fool sinking.

"Sienna, I was looking for you!" Vanessa shouts over the blaring music, snapping me out of my trance.

Fuck, she is exquisite. Even in the dim light, she fucking shines. Equally as petite as her friend, Vanessa, though exceedingly gorgeous, with curves for fucking days. She is a vision of beauty that could summon desire from the dead. I swear just one look from her sultry, dark stare would be enough to make a saint sell his fucking soul to the Devil himself.

With her drink in hand, she gives Alex and I a quick side-eye before redirecting her attention to Vanessa. "Sorry, I went to the bathroom and got turned around. It's kind of dark in here."

Sienna shifts her stance onto her heels as she tosses her jet-black hair back, revealing a sliver of skin exposed from her off-the-shoulder dress. I notice throughout the collage of designs on her skin, there are long, delicate lines wrapping around her clavicle, with smaller horizontal lines going through each of the longer strokes of ink. She tucks a stray piece of hair behind her ear, and the same stitched design runs from her index finger and down through her wrist, as well.

"Yea, it's dark as shit in here," Vanessa agrees. "Not to mention, smoky." She dramatically wafts her hand. "I can't believe they allow people to smoke in here," she complains.

I clear my throat, finding a way to insert myself in the conversation, while still proceeding with caution. It's then, I realize, that I haven't yet introduced myself to Vanessa, and by default, Sienna.

"I believe we are all adults here. So, if a patron decides to come into my establishment to pay for some drinks and decide they want to light up, who am I to judge?" I smirk, trying to mask the nerves I feel brewing.

"Oh, shit, sorry," Vanessa says, straightening her posture, as if I'm going to scold her. "I didn't realize you knew the owner of this place," she huffs, looking at Alex.

"What can I say?" Alex shrugs. "Must have slipped my mind."

"That's because you always have a stick up your ass, Marino," Vanessa says, playfully taunting him.

He darts his eyes at me, trying to signal how to proceed. He knows exactly who Sienna is and doesn't want to make any abrupt moves to blow any covers just yet. Judging by the way Sienna's seductive gaze is on me as she runs her hands through the ends of her thick, straightened hair, I can tell she has no idea who I am.

I make a conscious effort to have no images of myself in the tabloids or my website. I don't want her figuring out who I am until tomorrow. I mean, I could tell her tonight, but where is the fun in that?

"Yes, this is one of my many business ventures. It used to be a church. I always felt a structure as distinctive as this would be best suited as a place people can indulge them-selves after a long day, rather than feel guilty for their perver-sions. I had it converted, and here we are." I raise my hands, emphasizing the unique ambiance that surrounds us.

"Cool," Vanessa says, seemingly unimpressed.

"I had a feeling this was once a church. The architecture reminds me of cathedrals I saw traveling with my parents in Europe," Sienna responds with a delicious smile.

Ah, yes. Of course, Matteo Ricci spent summers in Europe with his family. Say what you want about his reputa-tion on the streets, but the man loved his family. Something my pathetic excuse of a sperm donor is incapable of.

Poor girl, she has no idea what I have in store for her. She may be all smiles now, but I know that the scars she wears go deeper than the ones she has painted on her skin. There is a darkness inside of her that lays dormant, and I intend to extract what she keeps hidden as I undo her seams, stitch by delicious fucking stitch.

I feel Vanessa's icy stare on me as I'm entranced by her friend.

She steps slightly, creating a barrier with her body,

blocking the full view I have of Sienna. Alex is right, she is going to be a problem.

Her suspicious scowl stays on me as she parts her lips to speak, "Well, hopefully, your friend, Alex has let you know that owner or not, smoking indoors is beyond frowned upon these days," she reprimands, as she inches toward me once more, solidifying the barrier she has built between Sienna and me. "It's kind of illegal, but you knew that already, didn't you?"

Keeping her stern eyes on me, she steps back, releasing the imaginary wall she was attempting to build. She should know better, nothing and no one will keep me from Sienna. Not even her cop best friend. Vanessa flashes a smile, as if to soften her not-so-subtle warning, focusing her attention back to Alex, who is wide-eyed and staring at me, as if waiting for a cue on how to proceed with her and Sienna.

"Got it," I snap back as I reach for ... What's that? Ah, yes, another fucking smoke. Vanessa may intimidate Alex, but she is going to have to try a lot harder to do so to me. This is my turf and I make the rules, not her and the arguably-more-corrupt precinct she works at.

Both Vanessa's and Sienna's jaws drop as I light a Parliament in front of them.

Reveling in the rage I see forming on Vanessa's face, I turn my attention back to Sienna, who is noticeably fidgeting with her empty glass, swirling the ice around, as if in the hopes that the booze will reemerge.

I blow smoke out of my mouth and away from them, making sure to be considerate of Mrs. Officer, as I glance back at the bar, waiting to catch Jose's attention.

Ignoring Vanessa's vicious gaze, I shift my attention to the object of my desire. "Sienna, is it?"

Licking her lips, she responds, "Yes."

"What are you and your friend drinking tonight?" I ask.

Before she can answer my question, Vanessa places her forearm in front of Sienna as she clicks her feet forward. Even in heels, I tower over her.

She lifts her head up, trying to level eye contact. "I'm sorry. We were interrupted before, I didn't catch your name," Vanessa says, squinting as if she is trying to decode my evasiveness.

I grin, deciding to play coy. "I didn't realize my name would be required to gift you ladies with drinks on the house."

Vanessa crosses her arms, as Sienna stands there with a flush on her cheeks. Clearly embarrassed by her friend's behavior. She should cut her friend some slack, she is only trying to protect her from a suspected snake in the garden ... for now, at least.

A frustrated huff escapes Sienna's gorgeous mouth as she removes Vanessa's hand from her forearm. "We will both have a vodka tonic," she responds.

"Excellent." I beam in triumph as I grab Jose's attention once more to give him their drink order.

Looking even more angry than just moments before, Vanessa throws a dangerous stare my way before she whispers something in Sienna's ear. I know Sienna is not listening to a fucking thing her friend is probably warning her about, because her attention is fixed on me. Just where I fucking want it to be.

José walks their drinks over, though I can tell from the

way Vanessa's jaw tenses, she still has something to say to me.

"Thank you," Sienna says nodding as she lifts her glass as if to give a subtle cheers.

"Of course, the pleasure is mine."

Vanessa stirs the red straw in her drink, looking down at the ice swirling in the clear liquid. Sienna gives her a nudge with her eyes, as if to remind her friend of her manners.

Begrudgingly, Vanessa looks to me. "Yes, thank you," she says as she takes a long sip. Just as the liquid works its way down her throat, she pauses. "And who, exactly, am I thanking? Is it Mr. Sandy Claws, or do you have an actual name?" she presses once more.

Alex clears his throat, ready to step in and say something. He knows tomorrow was set to be mine and Sienna's official meeting and is fully aware that Vanessa's overly inquisitive demeanor would not help with the vibe I am trying to unearth between Ms. Ricci and me.

Before Alex can swoop in, to help me dodge Vanessa's questions, I hear the faint ring of the phone over the music that is blaring through the speakers. I shift my attention to the bar where José jogs over to the phone. He quickly picks up the phone, sandwiching the earpiece between his ear and shoulder.

He darts his eyes up and over in our direction. With his cheek still pressed to the phone, he motions for me before straightening his neck to shout over the music, "Boss, phone call!"

Relief floods me, even though I know that will fade the instant I speak to whoever awaits me on the other line, due to the tense look on Jose's usually mellow face. Whatever problem lay on the other line is welcome in this moment, as it buys me a little more time to play this thing out with Sienna, *on my terms*. And more importantly, it helps me evade Vanessa's interrogation.

I nod to José and glance at Alex once, which is the signal he needs to head to the back entrance we came in through.

I turn my head back to where Sienna stands. She takes a final swig of her drink and places it down on the table behind us. As she turns and lowers her hand to her side, I feel the primal urge I have been trying to keep at bay since I first saw her this evening begin to rise. Before her hand lowers fully, I reach for it, snatching her delicate skin in my large, calloused palm. Not sure how she would react to my bold gesture, I tighten my grip slightly as I pull her closer to me. The smell of vanilla and a floral note I can't identify tickles my nose as I drink her in, now mere inches away from me.

Her hand now in mine, I bring her soft skin to my lips. "It's been a pleasure," I say as I seal the top of her hand with a kiss before tragically having to let it go.

To my surprise, as I release her hand, she takes another step closer to me as she cocks her head to the side playfully.

"Yes, it has been." She raises her manicured index finger to my wrist as she slowly trails her digit down the front of my hand, sending a fucking rush of pleasure to my cock.

Her index finger meets the knuckle of my middle finger as I grab hold of it, a tantalizing smile draws from her lips. Perhaps, Ms. Ricci is beginning to recognize what it feels like to be in the presence of a wolf in sheep's clothing, or a ghost in a chiseled, inked shell. Her friend should worry less about me and concern herself more with what Sienna hides deep in her subconscious.

There is something there. I know she feels it, too, and I intend on using that to help me seal the deal I was promised long ago.

"Unfortunately, I have to get going. Work calls."

"Yes, maybe another time," she whispers back.

I shift my stare to a seething Vanessa, before returning my gaze to Sienna. "Oh, I'm sure of it." I wink. "It was a pleasure, ladies," I repeat, as I exit toward Alex, who is no doubt reveling at how perturbed I have made Vanessa with my blatant refusal to answer her questions.

Little does she know that I hold many answers. Except, they are for Sienna to figure out, not her.

Just one more day, and the dominos will begin to fall. One by fucking one, until they topple in the direction that leads her to me.

Chapter 13

Sienna

A wet warmth begins to form between my legs as my mind places invisible caution tape all around the path the nameless stranger walks.

I hear Nessa's muffled voice in the background of my thoughts, but I can't bring myself to shift my focus back to my friend. My eyes and my aching center are controlling me, forcing me to follow the black and white pinstripes that mask the thick muscular frame of what feels like the Devil in disguise.

I continue to watch as he makes his way behind the bar. He takes the phone from the bartender's hand and turns his back to the row of thirsty patrons that line it. This should be my cue to stop staring, but instead, I take this as my opportunity to study him some more. If nothing else, he is perfect spank-bank material which, if I don't bring someone home with me, I can utilize later.

As he raises his hand that holds the phone it reveals a sea of ink that I somehow didn't notice before. His knuckles are covered in Old English lettering with what looks like, from a distance, to be a skull with piercing irises. In contrast to the dark center of his hand tattoo, there is an array of colorful flowers that surround it.

Even with his back turned to me, I can't help but admire how wide and strong his shoulders are. They make the perfect tapered V shape down his back. His exceedingly tall frame is well-noted. His body is a work of art, both in the tattoos that adorn it, from what I can see, and the defined muscles that can still be distinguished through his suit. I can tell from the way he is dressed that he is a man with power, and he has a silent but commanding presence. A presence that I have been unable to look away from in the few minutes I have made his acquaintance.

He hangs up the phone, finally, and just as he heads to the exit door, he moves his head back, directing his dark eyes in my direction. The slick warmth that began to form is now slightly dripping past the lace of my thong as I settle my eyes on his. I feel a flutter form deep inside of me. I would say it is coming from my stomach, but somehow, that doesn't feel like an accurate enough origin for how deep of a feeling is being stirred within me.

His friend is already through the back door, yet, he remains standing there, taking me in with a menacing grin on his chiseled face. Keeping his eyes on me, he reaches the inked hand I was just studying to the top hook of what seems to be a coat tree. The design on his hand is suddenly covered as he grabs a hat from the rack.

He shakes his head slightly, shifting the patch of jet-black hair that adorns the middle of his head. I notice how much longer that section of hair is compared to the buzzed length he keeps at the sides of his head as he slips the hat on. He lowers his gaze, bringing the same skull-and-floral-covered hand to the brim of his hat, giving a subtle nod in my direction, before following his friend. As he exits the door, I have this sudden overwhelming urge to chase after him, even though I know I won't.

He's alluring, sure, but I'm not going to chase after a man, let alone one I do not know. I can tell from the little interaction I had with him that he is trouble. I can't trust myself around that kind of man because there is no telling what that will unleash in me. So, I shake the thought out of my head, chalking the encounter up to the result of having one too many drinks and just being horny for the first devastatingly gorgeous guy I have seen so far in the city. That's all. A man like that, with the wicked energy he exudes, would be the end of me. Despite how delicious a descent into Hell being caught in his web may be, I can't risk the burn he would undoubtedly leave on me.

"Well, that was fucking weird," Ness slurs slightly, bringing me back to reality and out of the trenches of my own thoughts.

"Who doesn't answer a simple question, like *what is your name*, when they are asked more than once? Makes sense Alex is friends with him," she scoffs.

I nod and half-listen to Nessa say something about how much of a dick Alex is, before she makes her way over to the bar. The whole time she went on about Alex, all I could picture was his friend.

I need to snap out of it.

Fuck, Sienna, get it together.

I look over at Vanessa, who is now leaning over the bar,

spilling her cleavage out. She's talking to the bouncer from before, who has made his way into the bar area instead of manning the front. By the way she is flirting, I am assuming she will be bringing him home. So, I head over to close our tab.

As I wait for the bartender to bring back our tab, I suddenly feel a familiar presence before it grabs hold of my shoulder from behind. I look over to discover a certain Beetlejuice-tattooed hand.

Eric.

Confused as to why he is here, I glance over my shoulder. "Oh, hey, Eric," I say, instinctively turning toward him, shifting to my tiptoes to give him a hug.

"Hey, sorry, I'm late. Traffic was crazy," he says, sounding out of breath, as if he just ran here.

"I didn't know you were meeting us, otherwise, I wouldn't have closed the tab. Nes didn't tell me," I say, still confused that neither he nor she told me he would be joining us.

"It was a last-minute thing. I just got a sick town car today to start driving around Mr. Moretti and his clients. I was in the area, and I remember Nes mentioning you two would be stopping here tonight. I was hoping I would catch you," Eric says with a flirtatious hope in his eyes.

Judging from the way he moves his thick forearms toward the small of my waist, it's safe to say he is over the little scuffle we got into last week when he left my house. The hope in his eyes is more than likely stemming from his assumption that meeting me here tonight and driving me back to Nessa's will get him laid. Even though the vision of the nameless bar owner is still fresh in my mind, making my thong damper than I would care to admit, I can't keep leading Eric on. No matter how good the sex is. Him being my best friend's cousin just makes things too complicated, and I have had enough unprovoked complications in my life, I can't keep adding to them.

"Miss?" I direct my attention back to the bartender, expecting him to have my bill for me to sign.

"Yes?" I reply, staring down at his empty hands.

"It's on the house, courtesy of the owner."

I can't help but smile. *That Devil.*

Arms still wrapped around my waist, Eric squeezes them beyond the point of feeling playful, or pleasurable, for that matter.

"Ah, well, tell the owner thank you for me." I blush, ignoring Eric's weird aggression. I release myself from his tight grip and turn to him to see what the fuck is his problem.

His chest rises as he looks noticeably irritated. "Typical, Sienna. You are in the city for not even one full day, and you already have an admirer," he grunts.

"Hardly, Eric. He is a friend of one of Nessa's coworkers. He was just being nice."

He rolls his eyes at my comment, taking a second to respond to me. "Yea, whatever you say," he barks back.

Awkward silence begins to form between Eric and me, as I try to get Nessa's attention so we can head out of here. I make eye contact with her, giving her the signal that I am ready. She finishes her conversation with the bouncer and gives him a kiss goodbye.

"Alright, I'll see you when your shift is over," I hear her shout over to Miles as she begins making her way to Eric and me.

Nes walks over, noticeably as surprised as I was to see Eric here.

"What, are you following us, weirdo?" she jokes.

"Very funny. I remember you said you and Sienna would be here tonight, and I was in the neighborhood, so—"

Vanessa stumbles, interrupting him, "Yea, ok. Listen, I need to get home and freshen up. Miles is meeting me back at the apartment in a little over an hour, so chop, chop." She claps her hands, leading the way out of the bar.

"Ok, I'll get an Uber for us," I suggest as I reach for my phone to pull up the app.

But Eric grabs the phone out of my hand. "No need, I'll drive you guys' home," he says, dangling a set of keys in his hand, along with my cell phone.

Vanessa, clearly drunk, laughs. "Ah, there is my cousin, the big, bad chauffeur," she says with her back to Eric and me.

Annoyed, I rise to my tiptoes, trying to get my phone back from Eric, but he laughs, reaching his arm up higher so I can't get it.

"Give it back, Eric," I say, in no mood for whatever shit he is trying to pull.

This is exactly why I am done with him; he just doesn't know how to be chill with me anymore. Sex complicated that for him.

He lowers his arm, handing me back my phone. I take it from him as I quicken my pace, following Nes to the entrance as Eric follows my lead.

The three of us make our way out of The Sandy Claws and I spot the black town car parked across the street. How Eric was able to find on-street parking by the bar is beyond me, but I'll take it, because my feet are killing me from these damn heels.

We cross the street as Eric unlocks the car. I go to sit in the back with Nessa, but of course, she needs to bust my chops. "Ok, you two lovebirds can sit in the front together, I'm going to lay down in the back seat and take a power nap."

Before I can protest, she is already sprawled out in the back seat. *Great.*

I get in the front seat next to Eric, hoping he won't try to get an invite to spend the night with me tonight. Eric starts to drive and I'm relieved that he is quiet. It's been a long day, and I need to sober up so I can prep for tomorrow.

The awkward silence breaks with Nessa's loud snoring, which makes Eric and I both burst out laughing.

"That was quick." Eric laughs, as he begins driving.

"Seriously. We are going to have fun waking her up. That girl can sleep through a hurricane," I joke.

"I know, she has always been like that." He smiles back at me. "So"—Eric clears his throat—"you ready to start tomorrow?" he asks as he runs a hand through his thick beard.

Ah, how can I forget having to work at the same place as Eric? I really hope this place is big enough, and given the fact that he is an intern, we won't cross paths too often. But what's weird is that I haven't talked to Eric at all since last week. So, unless Nessa told him when I was starting, I don't know how else he found out.

Just as I am about to respond to Eric, we startle as both of our phone's buzz with incoming messages at the same time.

"Jinx, you owe me a blow job," Eric jokes.

Smooth, Eric. Real fucking smooth. Absolute disgust

rattles my expression as I roll my eyes at him. I am not one to shy away from a crude joke, but he isn't joking, which makes it even more cringe worthy.

"Ha, good one," I mutter, as I go to open my email.

"I'm joking. That is, unless you want to," he says, flashing his hazel puppy dog eyes.

I ignore him as I pull up my email. It's from Lizzie, Mr. Moretti's secretary.

"Ah, work," Eric says with his phone in hand, as I begin reading the email to myself.

Something came up last minute for Mr. Moretti. He will now send a car for you at 9 a.m. sharp.
-Lizzie

"Yea, me too. It was Mr. Moretti's secretary. Guess I have one more hour to work off this hangover I feel brewing," I joke as I playfully slap Eric's arm again. Except, he doesn't have any jokes to say back to me this time. Instead, he remains silent, pissed off almost, out of nowhere.

"Everything good?" I ask, but still, he continues to drive as we are just about to approach the front of the apartment building.

He aggressively throws the car in park. "Yea, I know, I'll pick you up at nine o'clock sharp," he mumbles.

What? Great, my driver is Eric. Usually I wouldn't care, it's not like I hate the guy, anything but. However, having to deal with him every day is going to make him not getting that the hint that I just want to be friends more evident.

Before I can say anything else to him, he mumbles something else under his breath and gets out of the car. He slams the door shut with the level of rage you would expect from someone punching a hole in a wall.

Alrighty, then. I unbuckle and lean over the passenger seat toward the back to wake up Nessa, who remains sprawled out on the backseat, still snoring.

Eric walks over to the back of the car, opening the back passenger door. He inches into the back seat trying to swoop her into his arms.

"Come on, sleepyhead, we are here," I say as Eric brings Nessa into his arms.

She finally comes to once she is out of the car. The brisk autumn wind hitting her face wakes her up.

"I got it, Eric," she slurs as she groggily walks past Eric and me. She stops by the door and turns to us, with one hand on the handle. "I'll wait in the lobby for you, Sienna. I'll give you two lovebirds a minute." She winks before grasping the long door handle, stumbling on in.

I hear Eric's phone go off again. I watch as his tense hands swipe to read the incoming message. Whatever he is reading is pissing him off, because he lets out a chuckle that reads more like, "I'm trying not to slam my phone into the pavement" than "ha ha funny."

Either way, I take this as my moment to make my exit into the apartment. Solo.

"I think I'm going to head inside. I'll see you tomorrow, 9 a.m. sharp, right?"

Eric, clearly not listening to me, shakes his head. "Fucking prick."

Uncertain of who he is referring to, I can't help but ask, "Who?"

"Ha, you'll find out tomorrow, that's who," he says, cryptically, as he doesn't bother giving me his usual goodbye hug. He steps off the sidewalk and goes back to the driver's side of the town car. I want to go inside the apartment, I'm beginning to feel kind of dizzy, and my feet are killing me, but my curiosity is piqued.

Eric rolls down the passenger side window halfway, enough for me to make eye contact with his growingly angry expression.

"Who?" I say once more.

"Your keeper, that's fucking who," he seethes.

My keeper?

"Excuse me?" I press him once more.

"You heard me," he repeats in a sinister tone. I've seen Eric angry before, but this—the way the words are spewing out of his mouth like daggers—is new.

He is about to roll up the window, when I instinctively run toward it, putting my hand on the edge of the glass, forcing him to stop. "Eric, what are you talking about?"

He stares straight ahead, past the steering wheel that he is gripping aggressively.

"Eric," I repeat.

"The boss, that's who." Seeing my blank expression, he notes my confusion and thankfully, spares me from having to extract answers like I'm pulling teeth. "You seriously didn't think he picked up your tab out of the kindness of his own heart, did you?"

"Wait, the boss? How would he know where Nes and I were going to go out tonight?"

Frustration takes over his face as his grip tightens on the steering wheel. His knuckles begin to turn white from his firm grasp as he directs his angry eyes ahead.

"Jesus Christ, Sienna, I hope you have your shit together tomorrow more than you do right now."

I take my hand off the car window and cross my arms, deep in thought.

"Goodnight," he says as he brings the car window up and drives off into the still lively city streets.

I walk to meet Nessa, who is still waiting for me in the lobby. She's on the phone with from the sounds of it is Miles from The Sandy Claws.

We head into the elevator and once it reaches our floor, I grab the keys out of Nessa's hand and lead the way as she continues to talk on the phone. I unlock the door, leaving it a crack open for Nessa, who is taking her time walking down the hallway to let herself in. I put the apartment keys in a glass bowl on the entry table and head straight for my room. As I shut the door, I lock it behind me.

Anger, confusion, and booze all mix in my system, leaving me drained. But as I slip off my heels and begin to take off my dress, I feel the lingering warmth from earlier in the bar. When I saw him. Whoever he is.

I let my dress drop to the floor as I stand there in front of the mirror by the closet. The bare windows reveal a bright night, lit from the apartment buildings and streetlights that surround where I stand. The outer glow reflects against the mirror, highlighting my now almost naked body.

Arousal takes over as I slowly run both my hands to the lace sides of my thong, bringing the lace down my thighs. The lower I bring the lace, the more I feel my clit begin to throb. I drop the smooth fabric, letting it fall to my ankles, and with one hand, retrieve it swooping it up and tossing it across the room.

Now completely naked, I can't ignore the way the city lights shine against my now glistening center. I lay back on the bed, spreading my thighs apart as I inch my hand closer to my clit. I dip my hand deeper into my wetness as I settle into the pillows, allowing myself to release the arousal that has been building within me.

With each motion I make to please myself, it is not my hand I envision but his. The charming Devil whose ink-drenched hands I wish were here on my swollen warmth, eager to relieve me of the aching desire he has left me with.

I close my eyes, imagining his dark irises consuming my soul as he devours my body in the process. The more I think about him ravishing my every curve, the closer I am to release.

Moving my hand faster and deeper into my needy center, I lift my hips up, trying to brace myself for the euphoria that is about to take over my body. I let out a muffled moan as my whole body begins to quiver. My pulsing release leaves my body tingling.

As I lift the covers over my naked skin, I can't help but indulge my mind as I think back to the way his eyes felt like they were searing into me. His piercing stare felt ominous, like a flare warning of impending danger that lay ahead. Even with my eyes closed as I lay in bed alone, I feel hypno-tized by the mark he has left on my subconscious with his memorable stoicism. His gaze haunts me as much as it has suddenly unearthed something deep inside of me that wants to come out and play.

Chapter 14

Carmine

"Son, we have a bit of a dilemma on our hands," my father says in an irritating, nonchalant tone. The fact that he can display such composure, while briefing me of a supposed dilemma on the eve of our Halloween Gala, is absolutely maddening.

"Care to elaborate, or are we going to keep pussyfooting around the issue?"

My father takes a step toward me, as if that has any ability to intimidate me. He is incapable of striking any emotion in me other than pure disdain. I, too, step forward, meeting his stern eyes with mine. Except, I tower over him, which I know intimidates him as he looks down to his scuffed-up shoes.

He clears his throat before looking up to respond to me. "First of all, don't you fucking forget who brought you into this world, boy, you hear me?"

Ah, don't remind me.

"Again, Father, the fucking point." I gesture with my hands for him to go on with whatever was so important that he had to disrupt my evening. Granted, a part of me is grateful for the escape route. It's not that I didn't want to stay longer at The Sandy Claws in the presence of my ink-stitched goddess. Though, if I stayed any longer, it could have made for a disastrous meeting tomorrow morning at Marked Inc.

Even in the few minutes I was in her presence, I began to feel all semblance of self-control leave my body. And if it wasn't for her friend, Vanessa, pressing me with her questions, I would have swooped her up and taken her to the back office to spread her luscious thighs open and eat her for dessert.

Fuck, I feel the blood rush to my member just fucking thinking about it.

Lost in my hedonistic thoughts, I snap out of it as I hear my father's sadistic cackle echo in my eardrums as he turns to one of his henchmen.

"This kid, always out in fucking la la land," he sneers, snapping his fingers in my face. My jaw tenses, as I swallow my pride so I can get whatever information my father has when, really, all I want to do is bash his head into the brick wall his fucking minions are standing in front of.

"The problem, Armando," I remind him. "Fucking get to it."

He calms down from his obnoxious chuckling, choking on his saliva, causing him to hack.

I stand in front of my father with a satisfied grin on my face, hoping that he coughs up a lung and fucking chokes himself to death. One can dream, right?

That's what years of chain smoking and consuming too many cheeseburgers will do to you. It's a travesty a heart attack hasn't taken out this sack of shit yet. Not that I am one to talk, I arguably smoke more than my father does, but other than an addiction to nicotine, I take care of my body. I work out, eat decently, and can run laps around his sorry ass.

"Jake was mugged when going to transport the remaining product we are pushing tomorrow night." Again, I can't help but notice the eerily calm way my father states what should appear as a catastrophic problem.

Except, I am always ahead of my father, and have had my suspicions that there may be a loose kink in our midst. So, the drop he is referring to only contained a fraction of the drugs that are set to be run tomorrow evening, coming directly from the brownstone. That way, I can see the face of anyone who dares try to steal from me, and they will have to answer to me. While this setback and loss of product is concerning, yes, it only solidifies my growing suspicions that we have a kink loose in our operation. One I intend on eliminating.

I grit my teeth, with a tense jaw, playing along. "When did this happen? Jake was supposed to go into transport hours ago," I say, looking at my watch to confirm the time.

"I don't know?" my father says, stumbling over his words.

"I'm sorry, is that a question or a fucking statement? You either know or you don't," I snap at him. "And why is this the first I am hearing of this? I'm Jake's direct line, not you," I say, reminding him of his place.

"First off, you will fix your tone when you speak to your father. Secondly, you are being careless with arranging these drops. This was bound to happen." His anger is still not convincing me, he clearly rehearsed this. Why, I don't know, but I'm going to fucking find out.

"Thing is, *Father* ..." I let the sarcasm roll off my tongue. I hate that I share DNA with this piece of deplorable scum. "I was the one who suggested switching up locations each time we have a drop or pickup. It's the system that I implemented that has made this operation run smoothly for as long as it has. Don't forget, when you were running this ship, these kinds of mishaps happened all the time before I stepped in," I remind him.

"Yea, well, I never had a mishap happen on the eve of one of our biggest nights." He spits at the ground near my feet. A dangerous move, one I am in absolutely no fucking mood for.

I step to him now, asserting not only my size over him but reminding him of the power I have that he does not. That he never had, because he couldn't gain the respect of a fucking fly, let alone an entire operation, like I have.

I flex my palm at my side, resisting the urge to kill him right here and now. *In due time, fucker.*

Through tense teeth, I lower my brow to him. "Spit at me again and I will tear your fucking tongue out of your mouth so fast you won't know what hit you. Then I will slice you to shreds, providing Nada with enough food to last a fucking lifetime, Father." I spit back at him. Except, where he aimed for my feet, I aim right for his pudgy fucking cheek.

I step back in satisfaction, admiring the way he winces at my words. Fear strikes his face because he knows, deep down, that I will follow through. I'm a man of my word, unlike his sorry ass.

One of his minions grabs a handkerchief from his back pocket, as he goes to wipe the spit that drips down my father's face away. Flustered and clearly embarrassed, he grabs the cloth from his little helper's hand and cleans up my smeared saliva on his face himself.

"If this happens again, Son, you will have a price to pay, you hear me?" He tries to warn me though his tone is already drenched in defeat.

"Name your price, Father, and I will pay it because I have nothing to apologize for. This is an obvious setback, but this isn't on me. Instead of patronizing me, you should be equally as concerned about the obvious rat we have in the operation."

"Yea, well, listen, smart-ass, if you are so all-knowing and wise, fucking fix it."

Oh, I will.

I have my driver, Rufus, drop me off at the brownstone I now call home. It's taken me years to make it exactly as I want, and it is my true oasis from the hellish day-to-day that makes up my present existence.

I light up a cigarette, and as the smoke billows out of my mouth, I notice that the lights are on in the living room. Which is odd, because I wasn't expecting any company this evening, and I know I did not leave any lights on when I locked up this morning. I let my cigarette dangle from my mouth as I reach for the pistol secured in my waistband. I approach the door with caution, my weapon aimed upright.

Taking slow steps toward the concrete steps that lead to the door, I inch up, when I realize the front door has been left ajar.

Gripping my pistol tighter, my mind begins to swarm, wondering if this uninvited guest has anything to do with tonight's failed drop. I use the end of my pistol to open the door wider, continuing to lead the way with it.

I scan the entryway, ready to kill whoever broke in, when I notice music playing faintly in the background. Taking another step forward, I detect that the music sounds like it is coming from the study.

The music grows louder as I approach the outside pocket doors of my study. Technically, it is a den, but I converted it into my library and office area when I had renovations done to the place.

Even standing in the hallway, I can feel the heat from the fireplace that, judging from its vibrant glow, must have just been set. Seriously, what the fuck is going on today? Someone breaks into my house to what, read a book and cozy up by the damn fire?

I can hear "Limits" by Bad Omens playing through the Bluetooth speakers I had installed recently. Ironic song choice, being that I have coined it as my unofficial anthem. Much like the lyrics express, I too have been fed to the lions however death, doesn't scare me so much as it highlights the mission I must embark on.

With one hand, I quickly slide the remaining part of the pocket door open. Entering first with my pistol, I am met with the distinct hues of shiny auburn hair that belong to Lizzie.

Fucking Christ, I forgot she still has a key.

Startled, Lizzie lifts her gaze to mine. She is seated on the loveseat in front of the fire, petting my loyal pit bull, Nada. "Jesus Christ, Car, you scared me," she says, oblivious to the fact that she let herself in without letting me know.

I flinch as the small cigarette butt, that I forgot was still in my mouth, nearly burns my lips, adding to my aggravation. As I lower my weapon back into my waistband holster, I grab the nearest ash tray I have in the study to get rid of the ash-covered butt.

Nada hops off the loveseat as he excitedly wags his tail to greet me. I kneel to pet his smooth, white fur, before addressing Lizzie.

"What are you doing here?" I ask her plainly.

She doesn't pick up on my disinterest and walks over to where I kneel petting Nada. "Well, I figured, since tomorrow is a big day, you would need a little stress relief, that's all," she says as she brings her arm to my shoulder with a flirtatious expression.

Brushing off her advance, I continue to pet Nada. "I'm fine, Lizzie."

"You sure, Car?" She goes to bring her lips to mine. I inch back. I must end this thing I have had with Lizzie. It's going to get too complicated with Sienna here. I don't need Lizzie, I need *her*.

She looks surprised that I don't give in to her advances. Ignoring her reaction, I head to fix myself a drink, as Nada follows me to the bar cart. Before making myself a drink, I grab the jar of treats I keep next to my decanted whiskey. I twist the lid open, grabbing a pumpkin-flavored biscuit for him.

"Here you go, boy," I say, tossing the treat at Nada,

which he retrieves with a wagging tail, bringing it with him to his plush dog bed by the fireplace.

Lizzie walks over to me and wraps her arms around my neck.

"You're tense, Car, let me fix that for you." She begins to run her hands down the sides of my jacket, searching for the center button in the front.

I try to pull away, but she strengthens her dainty grip on me with unexpected force.

"I said, I'm fine," I reassure her, finally pulling away from her grip and return to pouring myself a whiskey.

She lets out a frustrated sigh. "Bull-fucking-shit, Carmine, you are not fine. You haven't been fine or okay or fucking normal since you found her," her voice cracks, and I'm not sure if it's out of anger or sadness. Probably a bit of both.

I keep my back to her, as I take my time sipping my whiskey. "Found who, Lizzie?" I ask, still facing away from her.

Her heels click closer to me, once again bringing her hands to my sides. "Cut the shit, you know exactly who I am talking about."

Of course, I do, how could I not? I have waited what feels like two lifetimes to get this close to Sienna Ricci. A forbidden last name in the Moretti family, which will make having her trapped in my grip that much sweeter.

I turn toward her, forcing her hold on me to loosen. "Lizzie, please, as your boss, I'm telling you I am fine. I'll have my driver come pick you up to take you home." I go to grab my phone to call Rufus to come back to the brownstone when she places her hand over the screen to stop me.

"I'm not here as your secretary, and I'm not here pretending to be the girlfriend you don't want me to be. I'm here to fill the void you have buried deep in that cold heart of yours," she says with gloom filling her irises.

"Lizzie, please stop."

"I'm here, willingly. It's okay," she says as she brings her lips to my neck. In between kisses, she continues to talk. "Use me," she whispers. "Like all those times before."

I shake my head, feeling sorry for her that I have led her on in this way. "Why do you let me do this to you?"

She raises her hand and brings it to my chest, just above my heart. "Because I can't have this," she says as she traces where my heart lay underneath my flesh with her fingers. Continuing to slowly trace above my heart, she says, "I'm not a fucking idiot, Car. I know every time you fucked me, you thought of her. I know every time I was with you, you wished it was her and not me that you were inside of."

She is about to continue, but I cut her off. I remove her hand from my chest, draping it back by her side. "I don't know what you are talking about," I lie, coming off as cold as ever.

She shakes her head. "You may have a lot of people fooled, but you don't have me fooled one fucking bit. I just hope that once you get her, she is worth the trail of blood that will be left behind."

We stand there as if we are two pieces on a chessboard, strategizing and waiting on the other's next move. The sadness in Lizzie's eyes has notably dissipated, and instead, I am standing in front of a woman who has vengeance on her mind.

I flick my wrist up to illuminate my watch, seeing the

time. It's getting late, and since this little meeting seems to be mine and Lizzie's unofficial fuck buddy breakup, I'd rather part ways for the evening and call it a night.

"I think we are done here. I will have Rufus drive you home if you'd like," I offer, but she rolls her eyes, looking completely uninterested in that option.

She heads to the door, dangling the set of keys she used to let herself in. "No, thanks, I'd rather walk!" she shouts, with her back turned, as she drops the keys on the small table by the door.

I wait until I hear the front door slam to ensure she is gone before I walk over to lock it. When I make my way back to the study, I grab the spare set of keys and put them in my pocket, relieved that I won't have any more surprise visits from Lizzie.

I pour myself another whiskey before I head to the bookcase that holds my black box of secrets. It has remained dormant on the shelf for far too long, and tonight of all nights, I need it to provide me with the motivation for the task that lies ahead, beginning tomorrow.

Bringing the box down from the shelf, I carry it over with me as I sit by the fire. I take another sip of my whiskey, swishing the amber liquid around in my mouth, allowing the bittersweet sting of the alcohol to give me the liquid courage I need. I raise the glass to my lips once more and drain it of its contents before I go to open the box.

Taking a deep breath, I grab the key on my chain, inserting it into the locket on the front of the black box. With so much on the line and so much still left to do, I need a reminder of why I am on this wicked mission I have assigned myself. I need to feel justification for my questionable actions. I need to remember why I am here, despite the carnage that follows me. This box is a refresher on who I needed to eliminate to get one step closer to finally having all of her.

Sienna

I wake up to the ever-so-pleasant sound of kitchen cabinets being slammed, repeatedly. Feeling disoriented, I squint my eyes open as I am immediately met with a throbbing headache piercing through both of my temples. Between the hangover I feel, and the incessant slamming of cabinets Nessa is doing, it looks like this headache might be hanging around for a while.

"Sienna! Wake up, you are going to be late!" Vanessa shouts, taking a break from slamming the cabinets, and instead, moving on to what sounds like the utensil drawer.

"Okay, I'll be right out!" I shout back. I finally sit up in bed, trying to get my wits about me as I go to grab my phone to see what time it is.

Fuck. Where is my phone?

I pop out of bed and start feeling around the mattress for what I did with my phone last night when we got back from the bar. Finally, I see it on the floor and realize I was too preoccupied with trying to get myself off that I never charged my phone last night.

I reach for my phone on the floor when the time flashes, illuminating the lock screen.

Shit. I have ten minutes until Eric is supposed to pick me up. I throw my phone on the charger to get at least a few minutes of charge while I run, still ass-naked from last night, to my closet to try to find something to wear.

I grab the first things I see, which so happens to be a black blazer and a pair of black dress pants. As I throw them on the bed, I realize I still need a shirt to go underneath the blazer. Heading back to my closet, I glide the hangers to see what will go with what I already have picked out.

Beginning to get flustered, I pick up the speed that I am sorting through my hanging clothes, and spot a sleeveless, silk blouse. I can't even remember the last time I wore it. There is heavy black stitching through the teal shirt, along with a small purple pocket in the front with black polka dots. I'm not sure what the vibe is at Marked Inc. dress code-wise, but whatever, this will have to do.

Before I get dressed, I tap my phone screen again still on the charger to see how much time I have left. Five whole minutes. Dropping the phone, I throw on the outfit I picked out as quickly as possible before looking in the mirror to assess what to do with the rest of me today. To my surprise, my eyeliner is still intact from last night, which buys me some time.

As I go to put on some brownish-mauve lipstick, I hear Vanessa, yet again, in the kitchen, but this time, she is talking to someone instead of just aimlessly slamming cabinets and drawers.

I finish swiping the lipstick on, rubbing my lips together to spread the pigment throughout, as I open the bedroom door to figure out what the commotion is about.

As soon as I open the door, I see Nes and Eric so deep in their conversation that neither of them notice that I am now standing in the kitchen. I take two steps forward as my heels clack against the hardwood floor, which finally gets both of their attention.

"Good morning. Everything okay?" I ask as subtly as possible.

Before Nessa responds to me, she shakes her head, giving Eric an ice-cold look. "Yes, it's nothing, just some family drama, that's all," Nes says, obviously lying. She forgets that I've known her long enough to know that she is a horrible liar. Thankfully, she has a better ability to detect lies, which helps her at work. But her telling lies? Nope, horrible at it.

I look to Eric, hoping that whatever mood he was in from last night when he dropped Nes and I off has dissipated. But judging from the scowl he is currently wearing on his face; I'm going to venture a guess and say that's a no.

He ignores me and looks back to Vanessa, who is pouring herself a coffee to go. "Nes, I am sorry, I didn't know. I swear," he pleads.

"Eric, we will talk about this later, ok?" she says sternly. Nes grabs her things as she heads for the door. "I'm going to be late tonight, Sienna. I am working overtime tonight, so I'll be home late."

"Alright, no problem," I reply, but she is already out the door. I turn to Eric, awkwardly, just as Nes abruptly reappears through the apartment door with an intense look of concern on her face. She briefly glances at Eric before bringing her full attention to back to me.

I break the tension. "What is it?"

She shakes her head. "Listen, Sienna, just be careful today. Promise?"

Caught off guard by her concerned look, I laugh trying to lighten the mood a bit. "You are so dramatic, I'll be fine. Eric is going to be driving me today to work, stop worrying."

Once again, she gives me a look of concern, although this time, her eyes widen a bit as she shakes her head. "I know, that's what I am worried about," she says without giving me the opportunity to reply, as she heads back out the door.

The car ride to the office is as to be expected: awkward as fuck. Eric and I have barely spoken more than two words to each other since we got into the car. I put my headphones on to distract myself from the deafening silence between Eric and I as we make our way through the crowded New York streets.

As we get closer to Marked Inc., I notice Eric's gaze fixed on me through the rearview mirror, but he remains silent.

Making eye contact with Eric, who is still peering in the rearview mirror back at me, I smile. "Hey."

Keeping a stoic expression, he answers back, "Hey."

"Done being a dick?" I tease.

He lets out an aggravated sigh. "That depends. Are you done pretending like you care?"

Before I am able to unravel that loaded comment of his, we pull up to Marked Inc. I look out the car window and stare at the modern, nondescript building. Unlike The Sandy Claws' gothic charm from last night, this building looks boring and sterile, almost.

Back to our silent gig we have going, Eric opens the car door for me as I follow his lead. We make our way through the lobby, which is minimally decorated. Not much to settle the eye on, other than the shiny, marble flooring and a sleek, black desk located by a set of black elevators. I was expecting the lobby to be bustling, kind of like how I remember the lobby of Runway, when Andy had her first day of work in "The Devil Wears Prada." But there isn't a soul in the lobby, except for Eric and me.

"Your floor is on the 15th, Mr. Moretti's floor," Eric mumbles as he presses the button.

"What was that?" I ask playfully, hoping to warm him up a bit. But to no avail, he isn't impressed, and instead, remains closed off to me.

When the doors slide open, Eric gestures his hand out for me to get in first. "After you."

I nod as I walk in, Eric following behind me. I glance over at him, noting he has his hands clasped together at his front as he rocks onto the balls of his feet.

We make awkward eye contact, which brings his rocking motion to a halt.

"Sorry, still working off the booze from last night," he says with a half-smile.

"You didn't drink at the bar last night, cut the shit," I joke.

But he isn't laughing. In fact, my joke somehow makes him look more upset with me.

"Yea, well, I drank when I got back home by myself." He

rolls his eyes, letting the last part of that sentence linger slowly off his tongue. No doubt, he is trying to make a jab at me for not giving in to his need to hook up.

When we reach the 15th floor, Eric motions for me to step out of the elevator ahead of him. Just like the empty lobby, this floor is quiet. Too quiet. I walk down the hall with its floor-to-ceiling windows on either side making me feel like I'm suspended midair, instead of walking in an office building.

There is a round reception desk across from the elevators, which I assume is Mr. Moretti's assistant's desk. I hear a woman's voice come from the other side of the desk, which is so high that it's difficult to make out who is sitting there.

As my heels click closer to the reception area, the woman hangs up the phone before making her way to the front of the desk. She is stunning with her thick, flowing auburn hair with large doe-like eyes. She is wearing a skin-tight dress that hugs her enviable curves.

Despite her beauty, her face remains stone cold, and more notably, she gives Eric a mischievous nod before fixing her gaze back on to me. I can tell from her body language she is irritated by my presence.

"Eric," she says with another nod, this time more flirtatious than the first. Another moment passes before she acknowledges my presence.

Great, I'm back in high school. Except, this time, the mean girl is a fucking model.

"You must be Sienna." She quickly scans me up and down. "I'm Lizzie."

"Yes, nice to meet you," I say, reaching out my hand for

her to shake. Except, she doesn't. The disdain seeping from her pores is palpable.

"You're late," she hisses. "You should have been here ten minutes ago, but you can take that up with Carmine."

For someone who seems to be such a stickler for the rules, she seems unusually comfortable calling her boss by his first name. Her smirk, while rolling his name off her tongue, suggested that she may be more than just a receptionist.

"Follow me this way." She remains cold as she motions her hand for me to follow her down the hallway to the office door.

Before she heads toward Mr. Moretti's office, she looks back at Eric, who is standing with his hands in his pockets.

"Don't you go anywhere; I'll be there to help you once I take care of her." She winks at Eric, who suddenly refuses to make eye contact with me.

Just outside of Mr. Moretti's office door, she knocks once, not waiting for a response before she takes it upon herself to swing the door open. She sways her hips exaggeratedly into the office, where Mr. Moretti, upon first glance, is nowhere to be found. As we enter the office, I scan the room when I notice a high-back chair, where I assume Mr. Moretti is sitting. It is turned, overlooking the expansive windows that line the entire area behind his desk.

I expect the chair to swivel in our direction, since the collective clacking of our heels, as well as the door swinging open, should make it obvious enough that he is not alone anymore. However, his chair remains facing away from us. Lizzie walks over and leans over whispering something in his ear, not breaking eye contact with me. I remain in the threshold of the doorway, waiting.

"Thank you, Lizzie, that will be all," he dismisses her, still not turning around.

Lizzie suddenly looks more pissed off than she has in the entire three minutes I have known her. She walks right past me, slamming the door behind her.

I stand there, waiting for him to turn his chair around, not sure what the hell he is waiting for. There are two chairs in front of his ornate desk. I debate seating myself in one while I wait for him to acknowledge my presence.

He keeps his back toward me, still facing the fucking window. I wait for another minute. Growing impatient, I decide to make my way closer to his desk to wake him up from this rude trance he appears to be in.

Just as I am about to open my mouth to get his attention, the chair slowly begins to turn. I remain frozen as he makes his way around the desk toward me.

My relief morphs into horror as he approaches, revealing himself to me.

Holy shit, it can't be.

He stops mere inches from me as I am hit with the heady aroma of driftwood cologne mixed with tobacco. An intoxicating scent mixed with the vision of his muscular physique in a tailored black and white pinstripe suit.

He extends his hand out to grasp mine.

It can't be.

Veins course through his strong, ink-covered hands. Ornate, Old English-style letters decorate his knuckles, spelling the word "king," and then, to only solidify my fear, I see the skull with colorful flowers surrounding it.

My stomach drops as my cheeks turn crimson.

"Carmine Moretti, it's a pleasure," he introduces as he extends his hand for me to shake.

I raise the hand I used to make myself come to the hand of the man I fantasized was touching me instead. The mysterious stranger who summoned a deep arousal within my soul now has a name.

Mr. Carmine Moretti.

My new boss.

It's going to be a long fucking day.

Chapter 16

Carmine

Surprise. The shocked look on her face brings with it a ghastly white hue, draining the pigment from her usually glowing skin. Even in a state of confusion, she stands before me just as much of a vision as she was last night.

With her hand interlocked in mine still, I take notice of more crisscrossed stitch lines drawn around her wrists, spilling down her fingers. Much like the stitched ink that adorns her collarbone, these are just as delicious as they are delicate on her supple skin.

Her palm becomes clammy, intertwined with my calloused one. Having her supple skin in my rough palm, I feel a rush of blood flow to my cock. I try to discreetly adjust my aroused length to conceal the animalistic attraction I feel for her. How I wish I could skip these forced pleasantries and bend her over my fucking desk right now and have her squealing my name loudly enough that it could summon the dead. However, I need to let this unfold organically, as it was destined to be.

I allow her a few moments to process that she is peering into the same black irises that she looked at lustfully just last night. There is no denying the attraction we felt the second we locked eyes at The Sandy Claws, because it's the same animal magnetism that is clawing at both of our flesh now as we stand mere inches apart.

I hate that I had to bring her here under the guise of employment, but that was the only way I could think of to get close to her that would seem *legitimate*. Not that I've ever let that dynamic ever stop me from getting my dick wet. But with her, I want much more than her body. I want her soul. I want her to be mine.

She brings her tongue to her lips moistening them before she finally opens her beautiful mouth.

"It's you," she says as she tries to release her hand from mine.

Not yet, you don't.

I squeeze her hand as a mischievous grin escapes my lips. "And it's you," I purr back.

I release her hand and motion for her to take a seat as I approach my desk chair. She does not go to sit. Instead, she remains standing, studying me.

As I sit down, I take her in once more. Her long, onyx hair frames her gorgeous face, which is now regaining its sensuous olive hue.

"I can assure you, Ms. Ricci, I don't bite. Please, do sit down."

I can only imagine what is going through her mind right now. The main thing being how perturbed she is that I didn't introduce myself last night. But where would the fun be in that?

Finally, she retreats to one of the chairs in front of my desk, plopping her plump ass down. "I would hope not," she says, playfully. She sits with her legs crossed as she runs her hand that was just held prisoner by mine through her long, dark hair, tousling it over her shoulder.

I rub my chin, dragging my digits in front of my mouth, partially covering it. "Not unless you want me to," I mumble under my breath.

She bobs her head slightly. "What did you say?"

This is going to be more difficult than I anticipated. I can't seem to behave around her already, and by the looks of it, neither can she.

I let her sweat it out a bit before I respond, for no other reason than I like the way she looks when she is angry. She is incredibly sexy when she is exasperated.

"I'm so glad to have you join us here at Marked Inc., Ms. Ricci," I say as I bring the cuff of my shirt to my mouth, and in one swift motion, loosening the grip of the cuff on my wrists. I take my time rolling up my sleeves. I notice her taking in the ink splashed all over my forearms.

"Yes, thank you for the job offer, Mr. Moretti." She shifts in her chair, crossing her legs. "If I may be bold—"

I interrupt her. "Be as bold as you need to be, Sienna, and please, call me Carmine."

She blushes. *Fuck, she is stunning.*

"Well, thank you. As honored as I am by the more than generous salary and benefits, I am just a little uncertain of what I am doing here ... still." She looks around my office, as if anything in this room could possibly have the power to reveal the true reason why she is here, right now ... with me.

She continues, "You were a bit vague on the phone last week with what you needed me to do here."

Inching forward, I rest my forearms that are now free from the confines of my shirt onto my desk. "I already told you that your role here, with me, is vital. Don't you remember?" I click my tongue at her.

She bites down on her lip, as if she is trying to stop herself from telling me off. Fuck, I wish she would, but since she is trying so hard to keep whatever it is that she really wants to tell me in, I decide to continue.

"Per our phone conversation, as you should remember, we represent some exclusive clientele. People come far and wide to acquire our representation. Think of us as a high-end clean-up crew. When a high-profile client needs to fix a mistake, to lay low, or even hide, we work closely with their attorneys to rewrite the script as we fix the problem."

She shifts in her chair. "So, you want me to write lies for you, is that it, Mr. Moretti?"

"Again, call me Carmine," I remind her.

She tilts her head with a confidence that looks divine on her. "You are my boss, and I am my own person. Mr. Moretti feels more appropriate." The tone in her voice sounds more like she is trying to convince herself of that rather than tell me.

"As you wish," I say in agreement.

She settles back in her chair, motioning for me to continue.

"A large part of what we do here is writing and rehearsing public statements. Our previous writer didn't fit the bill." I leave out the little tidbit about the previous writer also being a lying cokehead who started stealing, and that I had to remind him where he stands with the company. *Demoted and six feet under the fucking ground.*

I lean back in my chair, reaching for a cigarette. "Smoke?" I offer as I run the filter through my lips before flicking the switch on my lighter.

"No, thanks," she says as she lifts her hand to decline.

I continue to light up when I notice she looks like she has something to say. She is biting her lip, as if to keep the words from spilling out of her mouth. I sit back, waiting for her to speak what is on her mind.

"So, it's not just at the bar you allow people to smoke, it's in the office, as well?" she blurts.

There it is.

I knew she was stewing over last night. I'm surprised it took her so long. Just as I am about to say some smart-ass remark, as I am known to do, we are interrupted by a knock at the door.

Assuming it is Lizzie, I keep my eyes on Sienna as I answer the knock. "Come on in, Lizzie."

Slowly, the door opens, revealing a man about as tall as myself, with a blonde, scruffy beard. He enters my office awkwardly, as he gazes at Sienna sitting in front of my desk.

Noticing his eyes falling on what is mine, I interrupt his gawking at her. "Can I help you?"

Finally, his love-struck eyes that have been googling over Sienna shift in my direction with the complete opposite sentiment. Daggers form in his light eyes, as he approaches my desk.

"Uh, Mr. Moretti, it's me, Eric," he introduces himself. I immediately see through this coy persona he is putting on in front of Sienna. He is acting with apprehension, but I know that look shooting from his eyes. It's a visual checkmate, the look of scoping out the competition.

"Yes, I know. What can I do for you?" I ask, expecting him to brief me on whatever was so important that my meeting with Sienna be interrupted.

He ignores my question and, instead, walks over to where she sits in front of my desk. I look down and notice there is a leather bag in his hands. He kneels to the side of Sienna, and she looks up at me uncomfortably before turning her attention to him.

"Here, you left your bag in the car," he says, handing her the black leather bag.

"Thanks, Eric." Her face warms from the simple gesture, making me seethe inside.

Their seemingly simple interaction fuels my suspicions, making me believe that Lizzie may have been correct in thinking there was something between them.

I pucker my lips around my fading cigarette as I watch Eric whisper something in Sienna's ear. A half-smile forms as she looks up to him as he rises.

"Sounds good, I'll see you later," she says to him.

Eric heads back to the door, not even attempting to acknowledge my presence as he slams the door shut.

What a fucking arrogant prick.

Sienna's face flushes at Eric's dramatic exit.

"Well, now that whatever that was is over, let's get back to it, shall we?" I ask, trying to redirect her attention to where it belongs, away from Eric.

Confused at the attitude weaved within my words, she side-eyes me as she rests her purse on the empty chair next to her. She flips her hair back, so it falls behind her shoulders. I admire the stylish outfit she has on, but I'd be lying if I said I didn't wish I could see more of her skin. Even a sliver, something to feed the wicked thoughts brewing in my imagination.

"Sorry, I left my bag in the car that you had Eric drive me here in."

"Ah, yes, how's Eric working out as your driver?" I ask, grabbing another cigarette. I watch her eyes roll as I go to grab one.

"Fine. We have known each other a long time," she says casually, clearly not picking up on the territorial war that has just been cast in my head.

"Interesting," I mumble.

"What is?" She shakes her head.

I let the smoke billow out of my mouth as I take my time answering her. I like seeing her squirm a little bit. "You. I find you very interesting." As the words spill out of my mouth, I take notice of her adjusting her legs once more. If I were a betting man, I'd say all the shifting in her scat has less to do with a nervous habit and more to tame whatever is brewing between those luscious legs of hers.

Tucking her hair behind her ear, she whispers, "Thank you." I watch as she swallows hard. Clearly, I have gotten to her. *Checkmate.*

The smoke still flows from my half-finished butt. I place it down on the ashtray on my desk as I reach for the intercom button on my phone.

It rings twice before clicking, with Lizzie's voice on the other end.

"Yes, Car," she purrs in the speaker.

I take notice of Sienna's eyes as she witnesses the cringe-worthy lust in Lizzie's voice.

"Please send up Natasha, so she can show Ms. Ricci around," I command.

"You got it, Car," Lizzie says once more in her bedroom voice. *Oh boy.* Lizzie is going to be a bigger problem than even I could have anticipated.

I look over to Sienna who is pursing her lips, more than likely at the sensual inflection in Lizzie's voice. Although Ms. Ricci is here to work, *or so she thinks,* I want to reassure her that Lizzie is nothing to worry about.

Just as I wet my lips to speak to Sienna, the door to my office swings open, with Lizzie letting herself in. I notice the way she side-eyes Sienna the moment she barges through the door.

In no mood for her games, I slam my fist down on my desktop, startling both Lizzie and Sienna. "Next time, knock and wait like everyone else, Lizzie. Do not make me remind you of this again," I snap.

Both women look equally shocked at my frank tone.

"Sorry, Car," Lizzie says as she crosses her arms, moving her weight to one hip.

I open my clamped fist and bring it to my tie to adjust it. "Anyway, did you call Natasha like I asked you to do?"

Arms still crossed; she lifts a finger to wind a loose curl around as she obnoxiously smacks her lips on a wad of gum in her mouth. "Yes, Car," she snaps back at me.

"Excellent. Oh, and Lizzie, what did I tell you about the gum chewing in the office?" I remind her as the smacking sound practically pierces my eardrums.

"The same thing you told me the other night. Need me

to jog your memory?" she says as she begins to blow a bubble. Letting it continue to grow until it pops. She takes her time snatching it back into her fresh fucking mouth, which at this point has me seeing red.

"Enough!" I roar as I rise from my desk, seething with anger at Lizzie's remark. "That is enough. You are not needed here, anymore, go," I order.

"Whatever, Carmine," she huffs as she exits my office, slamming the door behind her.

The look of discomfort on Sienna's face makes me shift gears, trying to calm myself. I finally have her here, I can't afford to scare her away.

"Sorry about that," I say, trying to reassure her.

Unconvinced, Sienna nods in silence.

Another knock interrupts us, I sigh in anticipation of what could possibly go wrong next today.

"Yes," I answer.

A muffled voice speaks through the door. "Mr. Moretti, it's Natasha. I'm here for Ms. Ricci."

Relieved it's not Lizzie, I walk to the door and open it myself to let Natasha in.

"This is Sienna," I introduce her to Natasha. They shake hands as Sienna follows Natasha to the door. I notice the look of relief on Sienna's perfect face, as Natasha whisks her away with a clipboard of boring new employee forms for her to fill out. Between Lizzie's antics and Eric interrupting us, this morning has been more of a shitshow than I anticipated.

"I will see Ms. Ricci to her office, once I am done going over things with her," Natasha says as she guides Sienna to follow her to the hallway.

"Very well." I nod, though my focus is on Sienna. I hate

watching her leave, after I've worked so hard for her to be here. "It was a pleasure," I say to Sienna, as I bite down on my lip.

"Yes, it was," she says with an adorable innocence I would like nothing more than to corrupt out of her.

She walks ahead as Natasha follows her, closing the door behind them.

I look at my agenda laid out on my desk. I try to rest my eyes on the first item of business that needs my attention, but I can tell that is going to be nearly impossible today. Instead of pretending to give a shit about the things I should, I allow my mind to marinate over the fresh memory of Ms. Ricci from just moments before.

My mind drifts off in pleasurable bliss as I look out the window behind my desk, when suddenly the phone rings, robbing me of my moment to distract myself from the responsibilities that await me.

Unenthusiastically, I turn to answer the phone.

"Sorry to bother you, Mr. Moretti." My nostrils flare as soon as my ears are met with the sarcasm that oozes from Lizzie's voice.

"Yes?" I respond, not hiding my disinterest in conversing with her.

"Your father has called three times in less than five minutes. I think something is wrong."

Jesus Christ, today. Not this man now.

"Did he leave a message?" I ask, growing bored of this conversation.

She stammers before she responds, "Well, no."

"Then, how do you know something is wrong?" I interrupt her.

"Well ..." she begins again.

"Well, nothing. Whatever he wants can wait, thank you, Lizzie." I'm just about to hang up when I hear a commotion coming from down the hallway.

"I told you, Car, something is wrong. Maybe you should spend less time reprimanding me and pay attention to what is going on around you. She doesn't belong here," she warns.

My fist clenching the phone, I bring the mouthpiece to my lips as I rotate the earpiece away from my range of hearing. I'm not interested in what else Lizzie has to say.

"You're right, she doesn't belong here, that's why I don't plan on keeping her here for long," I say as I slam the phone down.

Chapter 17

Sienna

I must be cursed. That, or I am out of my Goddamn mind. If I'm being honest with myself at this present moment, I think it's safe to say that I am probably both.

The fact that I had such a visceral attraction toward Carmine last night at the bar solidifies the ill-fated feeling I now have as I reflect on the last twenty-four hours. Granted, that was before I knew the fucker was my boss. But still, what are the chances my first night in the city I meet someone who ignites such carnal desire and curiosity in me, only to find out that he is the one who sought me out, and even worse, knew who I was the whole time he played coy?

Ah, I could strangle him for being so deceptive. He knew exactly who I was when I saw him last night, yet he still insisted on playing his games with me.

My head has been spinning as I try to piece together moments from last night and this morning with Carmine that I pay no attention to the button Natasha pressed in the elevator. As the doors open, my ears are met with an abundance of noises. Phones ringing endlessly, people talking amongst themselves, printers and fax machines chirping. All causing my head to begin hurting before we make it out of the elevator.

Assuming we are headed to Natasha's office, I continue to follow her through the sea of curious onlookers who sit in their cramped cubicles as we walk by. Not much taller than myself, Natasha practically disappears amongst the tall half-walls that surround each of the desks we pass, creating a claustrophobic hallway. If it wasn't for the distinct grey of Natasha's tightly wrapped bun she has secured to the top of her head, she would disappear in the crowd of employees we pass by.

Oblivious to the inquisitive eyes that gawk at us, Natasha continues her new employee spiel as I trail slightly behind her.

"Okay, so, I went over all the basic info, if you need me to repeat anything, don't hesitate to ask," she says.

Yes, if you don't mind, I need all of it repeated, because I retained none of it. Thanks.

"Thank you, I will," I lie, following her into what looks more like a dressing room than the bland Human Resources office space I was expecting.

"Excellent," she says as she leads the way into a brightly lit room that reminds me of a boutique that I went to years ago with Mama. A mannequin with a tape measurer wrapped around the bodice stands in front of rows of carefully curated garment racks.

Natasha walks past the racks of clothes as she reaches for a pen on the sewing table that was hidden amongst the garments hanging. She lifts the clip of the board in her hands, placing the pen beneath it. "While you fill this out, I will grab Elaine so she can confirm your measurements."

"Measurements?" I ask.

She raises her softly wrinkled brow. "Yes, your measurements. Didn't Mr. Moretti tell you?"

I squeeze the clipboard in my hands, bringing it closer to my chest, wishing it was Carmine's head. I want to shout at her in my frustration because this man has told me nothing, and even if he did, I feel like everything that comes out of his smug mouth is a lie, anyway.

Reading my exasperated expression, she places her wrinkled hand on my arm. With slight pressure, she brings my arm down so the clipboard is once more in front of me, where I can see it, and not clenched against me.

"I take it he didn't tell you," she says warmly.

I shake my head, unable to speak through the frustration I feel.

"Your presence has been requested this evening at the Halloween Gala, Ms. Ricci."

"The gala?"

She releases her grip on my arm and walks to the sewing desk, where she retrieved the pen from earlier, and toward the intercom that rests on the corner of the table. Her head bobs around, looking for this woman, Elaine, I assume.

"She must be in the back storage room. Hold on a second, let me ring her." She presses the intercom button as a loud beeping noise comes through the speaker.

Before Natasha can say anything, a voice says, "I'll be right up."

Natasha nods and presses the button once more. "Thank you."

Redirecting her attention to me, she purses her lips at me, shifting from the sweet to stern in an instant. "You know, most would be envious of the position you find yourself in. Mr. Moretti doesn't bring just anyone to these events."

She lowers her brow as her eyes scan the room. "Between you and me, he has never brought a guest with him to any event. It's an honor," she whispers.

"I'm sure it would be perceived as an honor to some, but I am not here to play dress up. I'm here to write, which is what I was brought here for."

"If you were brought here to write, then I'm sure you will be able to, in addition to whatever privileges Mr. Moretti deems you worthy of." The condescension in her tone makes my blood boil. I ignore her ridiculous comment as I instead begin filling out the paperwork that she handed me from before. I shake my head at the fact that this man thinks that his presence alone is an honor. It only highlights the delusional privilege he has anointed himself with. Even worse is the fact he has his staff believing such bullshit.

As I finish filling out the paperwork, I feel my phone vibrating in my purse. Trying not to be rude, I shift my gaze to the inside of my purse where my phone lays flat. I move my shoulder, so the lock screen of the phone shakes awake. A message from Titi Lana pops up.

I miss her. I can't wait to vent to her about the happenings of today.

"Hey, Sienna, text me later to let me know about your first day! I'll be ..."

. . .

The message cuts off just as I hear a bell chime.

Looking up, I notice a woman enter the dressing room. She walks past Natasha, outstretching her hand to me. "Hi, I'm Elaine," she introduces herself with a crooked smile. "It's so nice to finally meet you, Sienna." She looks like she could be Natasha's daughter, or at least, some form of relative. There is a similarity in their facial features, despite there being at least a twenty-year age difference between the two women, if I had to guess.

Elaine steps back and squints as she takes me in. Expecting her to take my measurements, like Natasha said she would, I stand there awkwardly waiting.

"I think it's going to fit you like a glove." She beams as she disappears into the rows of garments past her sewing station.

Natasha is busy squinting on her phone and doesn't catch my confusion at Elaine's comment. I continue staring at Natasha, waiting for her to look up at me, to give me any more instruction, but she doesn't.

"Shit," she mumbles under her breath.

"What's wrong?" I ask, taking this as my opportunity to regain her attention.

Lifting her nose from her phone, she yells back to Elaine. At first, it sounds like Spanish, though there are distinct differences from words I have heard Mama or Titi Lana speak. If I had to guess, it's in Italian, and if I were to venture another guess, judging from the infliction in her voice, it isn't good.

Returning her attention to me, she answers, "Nothing, I hope."

Well, that's reassuring.

Elaine reemerges from the back with a garment bag in hand just as the familiar chime of the elevator goes off once more. Simultaneous panic strikes both of their faces as two men emerge.

The first man I see is wearing a crisp white lab coat. However, that is the only thing I could describe as crisp on him. His facial hair, much like the hair that adorns his head, is disheveled. He also looks notably startled to see us standing in his view as he guides the second man out of the elevator.

The other man's face is visibly swollen, even beneath the extensive wrapping that looks like surgical tape fastened around his face. The slow way he drags his feet as the man in the lab coat guides him makes the man appear as if he is drugged.

"Christian, I didn't know you made it down from your tower during the day hours," Natasha sneers.

"Natasha, always a pleasure." He nods, though his words come off more sarcastic than genuine. "I was just helping my friend get familiar with the place. Figured I'd give him a brief tour and get some new clothes. I'm surprised that anyone is on the floor at this time."

I look to the bandaged man, who is swaying as he tries to stand. The man looks like he is in desperate need of a new wardrobe and most certainly a shower. I can't help but notice the dark crimson stains on what once used to be a white shirt beneath the black leather jacket he is wearing.

"Not as surprised as I am," Natasha scoffs. "Maybe if

you read your emails, you would know that the fitting room is occupied today. Plus, this level is usually reserved for current employees during traditional business hours."

Directing the bandaged man to a chair right outside the elevator door, Christian helps him sit before he responds. "Cut the bullshit, Natasha. I am a current employee, and I'm helping a newbie, just like you are." He directs his angry gaze to me now.

Apprehensively, I make my way toward him with an outstretched hand, hoping if I introduce myself, it will cut the tension building between Natasha and him. "Hi, I'm Sienna."

"Yes, Ms. Ricci, right? It's a pleasure to meet you," he says as he takes my hand in a strong hold, bringing it to his lips for an awkward kiss.

I immediately release my hand from his and step back. His attempts at charm come off sleazy compared to Carmine's.

"Yes, it is. Nice to meet you." I don't bother disguising the disgust or hesitancy in my voice. Kind of ironic that, according to Natasha, this man can't pay attention to an email, but he already knows who I am.

"Well, if that will be all, we have work to do," Natasha interrupts.

"I won't keep you anymore. It was nice meeting you, Ms. Ricci, and Natasha, have a good one." Christian leans toward the bandaged man sitting, whispering something to him that makes the man move faster than he has since he got off the elevator.

I debate asking Natasha who those men were, when

Elaine swoops in, grabbing my arm. "Follow me," she directs as we walk back to a small, curtained-off area.

"Here you go, try it on." She hands me the garment bag she has been holding. "I already know it's going to fit, but I need to make sure."

I draw the curtain, making my way into the cramped space.

Elaine shouts from the other side of the curtain, "Don't forget to show us once you have the dress on!"

"I won't forget," I reply as I unzip the garment bag, revealing a stunning, long black gown.

I slip into the gown and admire my reflection in the mirror. The dress has a halter top with a black collar leading to a mesh section right above my cleavage. The bodice of the dress is fitted, hugging my wide hips that I inherited from Mama, and it has an offset slit as the bottom flows. It's a gorgeous dress, and I can't lie, it does fit me like a glove.

I move the curtain with one hand, grabbing the fabric that drapes down with the other as I step out to where both Elaine and Natasha stand, eagerly awaiting me.

"Absolutely stunning, Ms. Ricci," they say in unison. Their eyes linger on each other, as if saying some secret between them before looking at me once more.

"You can have this pressed in time for this evening, right?" Natasha asks Elaine.

"This evening?" I ask Natasha.

"Yes, Ms. Ricci. This evening. As I said to you earlier, tonight is the big company charity gala. It's a huge night on our social calendar. Lots of current and prospective clients will be in attendance. You are now part of the Marked Inc. family, so you will attend as Mr. Moretti's plus one."

I look at her absolutely dumbfounded. *His plus one?* Unbelievable. Was he planning on telling me this today, or just springing this on me, as well?

"Ok, you can get changed and head home for the day. Mr. Moretti just texted me that your only job for today is to relax and get ready for tonight's gala," Natasha says, unaware of the anger reemerging inside of me.

"Once you get changed, just hand the dress to me so I can have it pressed," Elaine chimes in.

Internally seething, I walk back into the curtained area and quickly change.

Natasha says something else to Elaine in, again, what I am assuming is Italian, before Natasha clears her throat.

"It was wonderful meeting you, Sienna. Once you hand Elaine the dress, you are free to go."

Whipping the curtain open as I fasten the solo button on my blazer, I startle them. "What do you mean, free to go? I just got here an hour ago," I press Natasha.

Not expecting my abrupt questioning, she shoots Elaine a confused glance. "But Mr. Moretti said that you can head home," she says, apprehensively.

I hand Elaine the dress, thanking her for her time. As I go to shake Natasha's hand, I say, "Thank you for your help. If I am all done here, I am going to head back to the 15th."

"But that's Mr. Morettis—"

"Yep, I know," I say as I waltz past them, about to give this asshole a piece of my mind.

Carmine

Judging by the monstrous-sounding footsteps that echo down the hallway, I can already decipher who is responsible for the commotion. I recognize the distinct heavy thud of my father's footsteps as the glass top of my bar cart rattles from his exaggerated stomps. Each step vibrates the bar cart more, as he makes his grand, unwanted entrance.

He is angry, just as I expected.

Lizzie excuses herself, looking at me with apologetic eyes as she scurries out of my office. She forgets to shut the damn door, as if my father wouldn't tear it down to get to me if it were closed. But at least, if it were shut, it would be an obstacle for him to have to break through before getting to me.

Before I have time to stand up from my desk to prepare myself for what will undoubtedly be a fight, he storms into my office solo, no henchmen to be seen. A surprising move by my usually cowardly father. Everywhere he goes, he has at least two nameless minions by his side to help do his dirty work for him. Or, at least, that's how it is now.

Once upon a time, Armando Moretti used to hunt and kill his own prey, until the list of enemies became greater than his ability to end them. That is a problem I've never had. I have the blood of many who deserved it on my hands, and yes, some who didn't. Either way, I know how to handle my problems. This man, this despicable prick that I have the misfortune of having to call Father, is better at causing problems than having enough brain cells to solve them.

"I should beat your fucking ass for the shit you just pulled!" he shouts as he digs his pudgy digit into my chest. He is seething to the point of trembling. I knew this was coming, it was only a matter of time before he found out about my new employee.

"I will warn you once, get the fuck off of me."

He grits his teeth, still trembling from "Or what?" he says, unintentionally splashing his disgusting, warm saliva on me.

"Or I will toss you through the fucking windows that line my office and put on a show for the busy city folk outside, that's fucking what."

"You have a lot of fucking nerve, you know that?" He removes his finger from me, heeding my warning.

"Do I, now?" I snicker. "Can't fault me, Father, I learned from the best."

"Stop playing games!" he shouts, flustered. It's so easy to throw him off his game. "I'm talking about the fucking nerve you have for inviting a Ricci into this establishment, and not just any Ricci, Sienna Ricci. Have you lost your Goddamn mind, Son?!" He lifts his finger once more in my direction.

I click my tongue, warning him that I make good on my threats. He lays another finger on me, and he is roadkill. "I made sure to have the windows cleaned for today, it would be a shame for your body to make smudge marks as I crash you into them."

Heeding my final warning, he lowers his hand.

"And don't call me 'son,'" I snap.

"Whether you like it or not, Carmine, that's what you are, my son. You are a Moretti; she is a Ricci. Morettis and Riccis do not mix ... not anymore, anyway."

"Yes, I remember, Armando. Thank you for the adorable family history lesson. Now, would this be before or after the Riccis decided you were an abusive flight risk that they no longer wanted to associate with?"

"Is that why you brought her here? You think she is going to save you, Son?" He laughs. "You're more delusional than I thought. Shit, you need to snap out of it. She is just as evil as her parents and those fucking Marinos."

"Don't you dare talk about the Marinos, you hear me? They were more of a family to me than you have ever been. Fuck, they *are* my family. Do not punish them for trying to take care of the messes you made."

He flinches slightly, and I can tell that I am starting to get to him. All these years, he has convinced himself that he has been wronged, when it was him who has been in the driver's seat of this train wreck.

I wait a moment more, giving him a brief window of opportunity to redeem himself, or at the very least, own up to what he did to get to where we are now. But just as I expected, he says nothing.

"That's what I thought. Thing is, all these vendettas you

have created that paint everyone the villain except yourself, well, they are getting in the way of what I want."

He coughs, clearing his throat before finally speaking, "And what do you want, Son?"

My blood boils once more at the word *son*. Would a father who loved his son treat the mother of his child like a punching bag or go after anyone that tried to protect her from his wrath? Would a good father manipulate and kill anyone or anything that brought his son happiness? The answer to all the above is no. Because Armando Moretti is many things, but a good father is most definitely not one.

I step toward him, my jaw tense. Rage consumes every cell in my body. "What I want, is you gone. From here, from my life, forever."

"Let me remind you of the mess I saved you from, Carmine. The gift I gave you, a second chance. I gave you power, and all I asked was that you dissociate with anyone I perceived to be an enemy. The Riccis and Marinos both being enemy number one," his voice begins to crack, as has the weak foundation he has built his lies on.

"You didn't save me. You ruined me, and now, I will give you one last warning to drop your unjust vendettas, or you will force me to do so myself."

He steps away from me, sitting down at the chair by my desk. Sudden concern washes over his face. "What did I do to deserve this?" An unexpected sadness cracks in his voice.

I don't let the false display of emotion fool me. Even when he appears sad, it's usually just to manipulate whomever he is trying to fool. He has fooled many, but he has never had that ability with me. Not then, and certainly not now. If he feels sadness, it is not for the carnage he has created. Whatever remorse his conscience allows him to feel is for himself, and himself only.

He stares out the window as I go to sit at my desk chair, blocking his view as I bring him back to the harsh reality of the mess he has created.

I snap my fingers in front of his zoned-out face, redirecting his gaze from the window back to me. "The fact that you question what you did to deserve what I have now set in motion is fucking comical. Shall I remind you of what you have stolen from me? What you have forced me to become?"

"Everything I have done is to protect you. To give you the power you deserve," he says trying to defend his inexcusable actions.

"You got me there." I point at him in agreement. "I do deserve power. However, the power that is rightfully mine is on my terms, not yours. I am rewriting the script. I am the master; you are the soon-to-be-forgotten puppet. Now, this is your last chance, if you admit your transgressions against me, your own flesh and blood, maybe, just maybe, I will let you live."

He looks to me with pathetic eyes. "I stand by my decisions. One day, you will see that and thank me."

"Thank you," I say condescendingly.

Confused, as if he should celebrate my words, he raises a brow. "For what?"

"For making my decision so fucking easy."

He doesn't bother asking more questions. The fear that drips from his face lets me know he is already aware of what the fuck I am talking about.

"Oh, and while I have you here, Armando, if you think telling Christian to half-ass his work is going to destroy everything, I have worked so hard for, you are mistaken. Don't forget, if you set me up to go down for his mistakes, we all go down, and that includes you."

He shakes his head, and now, I'm not sure if it's out of genuine confusion or utter stupidity. "The fuck are you talking about?"

I let out a devious chuckle. "Don't play dumb. It makes you look weaker than you already are. Now, get the fuck out of my office."

He rises from his chair with a heavy breath. Just the simple motion of rising from a seated position is too much for his lungs or heart to bear. Luckily for him, this meeting sealed his fate, and his heart soon won't have to work over-time pumping blood to keep him alive. Oh no, what I have planned for him will drain every ounce of blood flowing through his body.

"She is trouble. She will get you killed; I'm warning you."

I laugh at how comical a statement that is. "And how is that?" I ask, humoring his delusions.

"Because she will expose a weakness in you. She will expose the truth, and when she does, I won't be there to help you. I'm telling you, Carmine."

Ah, the truth. What a foreign concept, considering this empire has been built on the blood of its enemies. Until I stepped in, that is.

"The only truth you should be afraid of being exposed is what you did to her and her family. Once she finds out, it's her wrath you should fear more than mine," I warn with glee.

I see the anger start resurfacing in his face. "Listen here,

I still have a say in this company. I am the one who fucking started this—"

I interrupt him. "This corrupt shithole of an enterprise that I will soon demolish, and when I do, you won't know where to find me. That is, if you are still breathing."

"I want her out of here, Carmine, you hear me? She needs to get out of here, she is going to get you killed!" he bellows.

I shake my head at him thinking she can possibly get me, an already lifeless sack of bones, killed.

"Death doesn't scare me. My soul departed long ago from this shell I exist in. Now, leave," I demand as I take the gun out of my waistband holster, pointing it right at him. "Before I have you escorted by a bullet with your name on it."

He raises his hands in surrender, for now. My father pretending to be concerned for me only means that he is up to more than I am currently aware of. Just another thing I need to add to my to-do list today.

Chapter 19

Carmine

Between the adrenaline still coursing through me from this morning's excitement and the anticipation of what is to come next, sitting in this office feels torturous.

I'm about to dial Alex to discuss any updates on the surveillance front, when a fast-paced clicking catches my attention. The tapping becomes louder, feeling as though the noise is penetrating my ear drum. The noise continues, reaching a crescendo, when I am met with the sudden swing of my office door.

Does no one knock anymore?

There, stands a baffled Lizzie trying to block the doorway as an irate Sienna peels Lizzie's arms away, making her presence known. Although I think I have a pretty good idea as to what provoked such an intense reaction from Ms. Ricci, the anticipation mounts, as does the twinge I feel in my slacks while I watch her force her way past Lizzie's weak barrier.

Unable to contain the ear-to-ear grin smeared on my face, I motion for Lizzie to stand down. "It's ok, Lizzie, leave us."

"I tried to stop her," Lizzie pleads.

Eyes fixated on a beautifully perturbed Sienna, I repeat once more, "I said it's ok. Now go." I swipe my hand at Lizzie, welcoming whatever volatile mood Sienna is in. She may be a Ricci, but the Diaz blood she inherited from her mother's side runs deep, causing her to be hot-tempered, especially when provoked. And something tells me the gown that awaited her upstairs most definitely provoked her. *How fun.*

I can't peel my eyes off her, even the way her chest rises and falls in her anger is divine. The door clicks, confirming we are alone. I was so busy studying Sienna that I didn't even pay attention to Lizzie leaving.

She clicks her heels, one in front of the other, each step swaying her hips, until she is mere inches from me. If I wasn't so intrigued by her, so blinded by the incessant need to have her exactly where she is finally standing right now, I would deem her proximity to me in the workplace to be inappropriate. However, the only thing inappropriate about this encounter are the thoughts coursing through my mind that are making their way down to my dick. Thoughts of the depraved things I'd love to do to her in this office, the elevator, and everywhere in between.

"What can I do for you, Ms. Ricci?" I begin.

"Let's skip these forced pleasantries, they don't suit you, anyway." She sneers. "I want to know what your endgame is here."

Oh, sweetheart, this isn't an endgame, it's just the beginning of the games we will play.

"Endgame? I'm sorry, I don't understand what you are referring to?" I play dumb, although, I know such a response only feeds into the anger brewing inside of that perfect frame of hers.

"Please, sit." I motion to her.

"No, thank you." She shrugs. "I'm trying to understand what you want from me?"

Everything.

"You knew I was a writer when you strangely sought me out for employment, yet, here I am, playing dress up, with no talk of how I will be utilized in this company."

"Dress up?"

"Yes, dress up. Natasha made sure to introduce me to Elaine in the dressing room so I could be fitted for dresses for company events. Ring any bells?"

"I don't know what you are insinuating, Ms. Ricci. I hired you to work in the writing department. I thought I made that clear?" I am being a bit cruel, yes, but there is something about her fiery Latin blood getting boiled that turns me on. I push her a little more, indulging myself a bit.

She moves herself one step closer to me, the scent of cinnamon-vanilla mixed with floral accents in her perfume working their way down to my length as I feel it beginning to harden.

"I can spin whatever you need me to, I can convey through words what most can't even drum up in their closed-off minds. I just ask that you see me as an asset here and not see me for my assets."

"Are you implying that I don't know how to run my own

company? That I would hire you just to keep you around as my personal toy?" This back-and-forth bickering is nice, it reminds me of something I once had many moons ago and ignites something in me that has been long forgotten.

"I said what I said. If you are trying to extract something from me, you are going to have to work a lot harder than throwing fancy drivers and even fancier dresses my way. Don't insult my intelligence."

"Never," I say, diverting my attention to the glass bar cart conveniently located near my desk. "Vodka tonic, right?"

She shakes her head, thrown off by my question. "Yes. Wait what, a drink, now?"

"Why not?" I shrug off her judgment as I begin to pour our drinks. Is it too early for a drink? Yes. Is it highly inappropriate to offer my new employee, who is already pissed off with me, a drink during work hours? Also, yes. Will that stop me? No, not a fucking chance.

I hand her the freshly poured vodka tonic, admiring her beautifully stunned face.

"Thanks," she mumbles, still agitated. Her fingers brush up against mine for a fleeting moment as she grabs the glass from my hand, and it is enough to get the blood flowing to where I wish her hand was instead.

"I didn't mean to offend you, Ms. Ricci. I just assumed that a beautiful woman like yourself, with such talent and all, deserved those finer luxuries in life."

"What I deserve and what I want are two very different things. I know what I deserve, but what I want is to work. Don't underestimate me." She lifts the glass to her lips, and in a swift motion, chugs the cocktail down.

"Of course, and work, you will. You just so happen to be

starting on gala night. Every Halloween, we host a charity gala, and I just like our staff to look their best, that's all."

"Is that why everyone here seems to be made of plastic?" she mumbles into her empty glass, as she shakes an ice cube in her mouth.

I sip my whiskey, moving right past her snide remark ... for now. It won't take long before her comments will turn into suspicions that demand answers. It's just a matter of time.

She places her now empty glass on the bar cart and directs her sultry gaze at me once more, trying her best to be professional, but I know she feels it. *She has to*. Her tone is all business, but her body language is craving pleasure. She can try to hide behind the walls her parents tried so hard to force upon her, but those are walls I am more than willing to break down.

As if she can hear my inner monologue, she clears her throat, appearing increasingly flustered. Not that I am surprised, that's what happens when your soul is predetermined to capture the attention of one as wicked as myself.

"I do thank you for your generosity, however, I will determine who can provide me with such luxuries. I'm your employee, not your girlfriend, or whatever else you think I am," she says, tilting her head in the direction of the door, where Lizzie's desk sits.

I can't help but let out a chuckle. If she only knew that the role that she is insinuating Lizzie previously held was a placeholder until I could get my hands on her.

"I'm sorry, but I don't see what is so funny."

"You."

"Excuse me?"

"It's just that I've never had anyone I have had on my payroll speak to me like you have. Much less someone who was in such desperate need of standing exactly where you are, right now."

"You approached me, remember? I never even knew you existed until your sketchy envelope showed up on my doorstep. I'm not the desperate one here."

"If it was so sketchy, why did you pursue the next steps?" I challenge her.

"You seem like a smart man. I'm sure if you found out my address, then you probably already did your research and know who my parents were. Riccis are well-known in this city, and sketchy doesn't scare me so much as intrigues me."

"So, I intrigue you, huh?"

"You confuse me, but like I said, I am here to work, and for whatever reason, you are the only person who wants me so desperately to work for them."

"Well, since I am so desperate for you to be near me, why don't I give you a proper tour?"

"I didn't mean for it to come out like that," she fumbles her words a bit, as if she realizes how intense she is being.

"It's ok, how about you make up for it by wearing that pretty dress Elaine so graciously picked out for you, and join me for dinner tonight? Strictly to discuss business, of course." As soon as the words leave my mouth, regret hits me. Maybe I came on too strong? *Shit.*

I know what I want, it's her. It's always been her, but now, I fear that I have let this persona of the scorned man in charge cloud my ability to talk to her. To find the words to convince her to stay where she belongs.

Scrambling to think of something to say to lessen the

intensity of my words, I am about to open my mouth to say something, anything, but then, I look at her. There is an intoxicating grin on her face.

And to my surprise, she licks her full lips before she speaks. "Sure, what time?"

Chapter 20

Sienna

This man is absolutely infuriating. I have never wanted to strangle someone as badly as I want to wrap my fingers around his sturdy neck right now. Sure, he looks strong, no doubt he would put up a pretty good fight, but muscle mass has nothing on a woman who has walked through fire. And I, Sienna Ricci, have walked through an inferno. The wounds I carry have made me an unstoppable force. I'm stronger than he, or anyone else, gives me credit for.

The only reason I accepted his dinner invitation was so I could get a better idea what his true motives are. If playing along with his antics will provide me with the answers I need, then so fucking be it.

But what makes no sense to me is, if gala night is so important, why he has me meeting him for dinner before? It would make more sense to meet at the gala, as I'm sure he has a lot of last-minute things to do to prepare. However, in the short time I have known him, I have come to realize very little makes sense about Carmine Moretti.

Suddenly, it hits me. He didn't just refer to it as any event; he said it is their annual Halloween Gala. So did Elaine, earlier today in the fitting room. *Halloween Gala.*

My stomach turns with a twinge of grief. I wonder if it's the same Gala that Mama and Papa were at all those years ago, when they were murdered? It has to be a coincidence, what are the chances? In the social scene of New York's elite, Halloween parties and galas are not anything ground-breaking.

Then again, the world of organized criminals is smaller than one would assume, and if it is the same gala, it would explain why I have been called here like I have. I need to play my cards right or I might end up being the next and *final* Ricci dead.

I glance down at his ink-covered hand, trying to distract myself from the unease that I feel building inside. His hand flinches as if he is startled by me taking in his tattoo. The black ink mixed with the veins that run through his large hand is transforming my internal angst into arousal. Suddenly, the thought of his strong hands wrapped around my throat, robbing me of air as he pins me against the wall flashes in my mind. The thought sears itself into my brain, making me want that fantasy to come to life, despite the obvious reasons it shouldn't.

Fuck, it can't. What am I thinking?

I try to steady my breath and focus back on my next move in this never-ending game of chess we have found ourselves in.

Adjusting my gaze to his is an arguably worse move, considering the fantasy I was just conjuring in my mind. As our eyes meet, it feels like we are tearing into each other's souls. There is something about his presence that feels oddly familiar, comforting, even. His dark irises summon me. They call to something deep inside of me.

This is too much. I don't know where to look.

I'm about to open my mouth to say something, anything, to detract from this tension that is building by the second between us. Carmine clears his throat, again, with a shit-eating grin on his face, immediately bringing me back down to reality. Angry Sienna is back, I can work with angry. Lustful Sienna, well, she is unpredictable, and there is no time for unpredictable right now.

"If I may have your attention," he jokes.

Fucking arrogant asshole.

"You have it, go on," I say.

"I will tell your friend, Eric, to pick you up at seven, then."

"You mean, your employee, Eric?" I say, not hiding the annoyance in my voice creeping back in.

"Am I wrong? Is Mr. Mendez not your friend?"

I don't know what this guy's deal is. Eric worked for him before I did, and regardless of the status or level of my relationship with Eric, it is none of his damn business.

"Yes, we are friends, nothing more. That should be obvious." Fuck, why did I say it like that? *Sienna, stop, you don't owe this man any explanations.*

"The only thing that is obvious is your dislike for me. Don't worry, in time, I trust you will understand why I am the way I am. In the meantime, let's holster the metaphorical gun you have aimed at my cock and allow me to give you a proper tour of your office."

He motions to the door, waiting for me to take the lead. I

hesitate, momentarily. Trying to read this man is going to be a feat in and of itself. I really want to storm out the door and tell him to take this made-up position he is appointing me to and shove it. I don't need him, but for some odd reason, he needs me, and that intrigues me enough to stay for now and find out why.

Carmine walks ahead of me, opening the door, startling Lizzie. She likely overheard our bizarre scuffle, judging by the look of jealousy that is smeared all over her face. I walk past her; I don't have time for her petty bullshit. I'm a girls' girl, and I refuse to engage in whatever nonsense she is thinking. If it's Carmine she wants, she can have him.

An awkward silence forms as we make the short walk down the bright, glass-filled hallway. It has become instantly apparent that the only way we are able to speak to each other is through bickering. The fact that I am not already fired only shows me that he knows who I am and needs me here for whatever reason. I don't know what version of Sienna Ricci he thinks he ordered, but it isn't the woman he is getting, that's for sure.

Finally, we reach our destination as Carmine opens the door and reveals my office. I step inside and nearly gasp. A chill instantly works down my spine. Who did he hire to put this office together? Unlike the modern vibe of the building, the feel of my office is reminiscent of the decor at The Sandy Claws. Rich wood built-in bookcases line the side wall behind an antique, baroque-style desk. A Mac computer rests on top of the desk, along with a sugar skull planter filled with deep purple and vibrant yellow florals.

"What do you think?" he asks, almost giddy.

I try to mask my genuine love for how unique the space is. "It's nice," I lie, intentionally holding in my excitement.

"It's more than nice, not even the VPs of the company have an office that look as good as this, but that's beside the point." He sneers.

Clearly, I struck a nerve, because whatever temporary excitement Carmine felt in showing me my office is gone and the jerk is back. He seems disappointed with my answer, and truthfully, I am too. I want to express my gratitude for this beautiful office, but I have to maintain some sort of boundary between him and me. From the moment I have met him, I feel like we have been dancing on this line of no return. So, for now, I will lie to him, acting like I don't give a shit about how nice it is.

"Well, thank you, then."

He glosses over my thank you. "And since you think that I am some creep who hired you as office eye candy—"

I interrupt him. "Your words, not mine, but go on."

His jaw tenses at my quip. "As I was saying, I have your first assignment on your desk. I also had the files transferred onto a flash drive, if you prefer to view everything on the computer versus the printout."

I walk over to the desk and see a decent-sized folder. I open it and see a whole bunch of court documents and other random papers. I scan through the folder a bit more and see a mug shot.

"Ok, so, what am I looking at here?" I ask, still flipping through the documents.

"A high-profile client of ours has found himself in a bit of a jam, you can say, and we need to make it disappear. I first want you to read the details in the file, and then we can discuss with the client's attorney how to put forth proper statements and proceed from there."

"You got it."

"Well, I will leave you to it, so you don't think I have you here solely as eye candy," he scoffs.

I snap my neck to him in disbelief at the weird mixture of emotions he brings out inside of me.

He leaves me with a smile that I swear haunts me. All that fighting him to let me work and now I can't seem to redirect my brain to do so.

I spend the next few hours uninterrupted, sifting through the file Carmine prepared for me. There are a bunch of newspaper articles about a man named Jake Owens, who is wanted for tax evasion and a bunch of other white-collar crimes. The more I sift through the file, the more I am confused as to why I am looking at this. It doesn't feel like something that should be taken care of by a public relations firm. It almost feels like something I should be handing to Nessa.

It's then that I remember what Carmine said when he directed my attention to the file: *We need to make it disappear.*

Does he want me to lie and write something to clear this man of the crimes that he is being accused of?

A knock interrupts my train of thought as I look up from my desk.

"Come in," I say.

Carmine stands in the doorway. He leans against the doorframe, running his hand in the small section of hair that keeps escaping, trying to cover his eyes. There is an unlit cigarette dangling from his mouth. He puckers his lips around it, highlighting his already chiseled cheekbones.

"Eric is waiting downstairs to drive you home. Perhaps you can take the file with you while you drive home? I want to make sure you have plenty of time to prepare yourself for me," he says, somehow grinning even with the cigarette perched between his lips.

"I think I have time still, it's not even five o' clock yet," I say as I check the time on my watch.

"That wasn't a suggestion." His tone sharpens, intended to intimidate me, but it does something inside of me. "Tonight, is a busy evening, with the gala and all. I need to make sure we adhere to the timeline I have predetermined for us."

Why is it every word that comes out of this man's mouth has me teetering between thinking he is delectable and despicable?

"Ok," is all I can muster up, as I try to distract my body from the unintentional lust that is stirring inside of me.

Still in the doorway, he brings a lighter to the cigarette, finally lighting it. "Oh, and Ms. Ricci ..."

"Yes?"

"I know you and Eric have a history together. I want none of that happening in my office, or in my town car he drives you around in. I will only warn you once about this. Next time, I won't be as nice." He exhales the smoke as he closes the door.

The moment the door shuts, my phone is already buzzing with a text from Eric.

I read, "**Boss has me downstairs waiting to bring you home**."

Of course, he does.

"**Got it, be down in five,**" I text back to Eric.

I grab the folder and throw it in my purse as I take another look around at my new office, with the beautiful wood bookcases that look as though they came from a turn of the century Victorian home. I scan the books and decor that line the shelves for the first time since Carmine brought me in here. There are mostly reference books, some grammar guides, and some random decor accents. I plan on filling the shelves with books that bring me inspiration. I may be writing more technical pieces at this job, but I can envision myself in this space, finally writing the novels I have wanted to for years.

As I go to shut off the lights before closing the door, a small piece of crumpled paper catches my eye near the bookcases. I walk over and bend down to pick it up. As I open it, I realize it is almost illegible. The only words I can make out is in a distinct red ink.

I bring the paper closer to my eyes to try to make out the words.

It reads, "*It will be, as it was destined to be.*"

I read it again, "*It will be, as it was destined to be.*"

So cryptic.

I fold the note in my desk drawer and go out to meet Eric, who is waiting outside for me. Today went nothing like

I thought it would. Nothing about this place is how I imagined it. The mix of feelings it stirs in me is unexpected. Carmine Moretti is nothing I expected him to be, but somehow, he is everything I wanted him to be.

227

Chapter 21

Carmine

"Are you sure you want to do this, man? This isn't exactly going along with the plan."

No fucking shit.

Alex's unease radiates through the phone, as it's starting to become contagious.

"What other choice do I have, if you saw my father down at the precinct today?"

Not that my father's presence at a police precinct is out of the ordinary. However, what is out of the ordinary is him talking to the cops and not evading them.

My hands tense in vexation as I clutch the phone to my ear, pure venom starting to boil in my veins. I make a fist, crashing it down on the backseat of the car, startling my driver, Rufus. I loosen my tie in the hopes that may help release this rage forming, but it's a useless attempt. I've been in too deep for far too long, I'm beyond saving.

The only thing that can calm me is between a Riccis legs.

"I know, man, but I still feel like bailing entirely on the gala is only going to raise suspicions, that's all," Alex warns.

"Well, seeing as how my father has, yet again, proven himself to be a spineless, untrustworthy coward, I don't see what other option we have," I retort.

I always knew my father was a backstabbing piece of shit. I've witnessed him wrong so many for his own foolish vendettas. The Marinos and Riccis always reigned supreme on that ever-growing list, but this, this feels low, even for him. Especially after ending my mother's life, stealing the direction I saw my own life going in. Now, he apparently views me as the enemy. So much so that he feels the need to warn the cops about me? He has always been a feeble man, but this, even for his vile self, is excessive. He has stolen everything from me, I will be damned if he steals my exit plan. *Not this time.*

"I already told Jake to meet me at the brownstone. I will give him what he needs to distribute. We don't need the gala, or any elaborate ruse this time. Just a straightforward exchange. I need to rid myself of this shit, ASAP."

"You really think having the drop at your place is the best idea?"

I can tell Alex isn't feeling too confident about this. I need to reassure him it will be fine. Better yet, I need to reassure myself it will all be fine. That I didn't keep my father alive for this long for it all to go up in flames before I put an end to him.

"Well, considering my father is becoming even more of a flight risk than we originally gave him credit for, what else do you suggest I do?" I ask Alex.

"Armando is an asshole, but he benefits from gala night

as much as you do, why would he compromise that?" Alex says, as we both try to brainstorm my father's motives.

"Who the fuck knows? Everything involving my father is a mess. I still say screw the gala tonight," I say, standing firm in my decision.

"Yea, but if you don't show at all, he is going to think I had something to do with warning you. Fuck, this is a mess," Alex mutters into the phone, the stress palpable in his tone. "I don't get why he is doing all this now," he says in genuine disbelief.

"Because I brought her back here, Alex. He doesn't trust my motives, so he is assembling a strong offense, in case I do what he fears," I remind him.

Ever since Sienna has come into the city, everything is both falling into place while simultaneously falling apart, myself included. I can't think straight when all I think about is her. All of this is for her, it's always been with her in mind, and now that she is here, the playful banter we have is consuming me. Making me grow impatient, not wanting to stick to the plan anymore, but instead, working my way inside of her, consuming her, claiming her as mine, once and for all.

"Yea, which is fucking risky in and of itself," Alex lectures.

"Listen, it's a risk I am willing to take. My father has now stolen my options from me."

"Yea, well, that's not the only trouble he is giving us."

"When he came down to the station, he requested to speak to a woman officer. That pain in the ass Vanessa was there, of course, so she jumped on that. Talking to one of the city's rumored crime bosses had her practically creaming her pants."

Of course, she did. This Vanessa is smart, and while I admire an intelligent woman, I don't need a detective quite literally snooping around.

"Ha."

"What the fuck is so funny?"

"Creaming her pants? You have such a hard-on for her, you know, if it wasn't for your wife, you'd have her in the back of the squad car every chance you got," I tease.

"Fuck you, man," he snaps back.

"Don't be mad at me because you can't fuck what you want."

"Yea, you are one to talk. How's your master plan going with Sienna?" I detect the venom in Alex's attempt at a joke.

"I'm working on it. We have this fun dynamic going on. She hates me, or so she thinks, but she will get over that soon enough. She is going to be joining me for dinner tonight," I say with pride.

"That's an even worse idea, Carmine." I swear I can feel Alex's eyes rolling through the phone.

"Don't worry, I can still play this out like I planned. I just need to rearrange some things, that's all. I will escape, and I will bring Father down before we disappear."

He may have brought me into this corrupt world, but I will see to it that when it is time for me to strike, I will make his death slow, agonizing, and dragged out. As he takes his last precious breaths, he will know what it feels like to be a decaying corpse, feeling helpless to stop the destruction that is on autopilot.

Watching my father bleed out will be the only mess he makes that will be worth the cleanup.

"Listen, I will try my best to make sure they don't come to your place, because once the inside surveillance gets wind that you aren't there, your apartment will be swarming with cops to see what you are up to."

"I didn't say it would be at my apartment. I said the brownstone," I say with a grin.

"Ah, good thinking. There will be no way to trace it back to you," he says, relieved.

"I know, that's the point."

Chapter 22

Sienna

I didn't think I could ever be as happy as I am right now to be amongst the masses of strangers that flood the streets. The crowded chaos of the smog-covered avenues that surround me feel like a breath of fresh air compared to whatever they put in the air at Marked Inc.

I try to collect myself as I make my way to the sidewalk, where Eric is waiting for me. He has the windows down, allowing the crisp, autumn air to make its way in the town car as he sits in the driver's seat. Seeing me approach the car in his peripheral, he lifts his head from his phone, tossing it on the passenger seat as he rises to attention. He opens the driver's side door and practically skips behind the car, almost tripping on the sidewalk to get to the back passenger door before I can.

"You know, I am perfectly capable of opening the door myself. I appreciate the gesture, but I don't think it's worth you falling for," I tease, not in the mood for this chauffeur role that Carmine so conveniently appointed him to.

Grabbing the top of the door, he guides it open wider for me to get in. "I know, but you can't blame a guy for trying." His words feel as though he is putting bait on a hook, waiting for me to bite.

I take my hand to his beard-covered cheek, looking him in the eyes. "Do me a favor, Eric, don't." I rub his cheek, warning him. Carmine's threat is still fresh in my mind.

"Don't …" he drags the word out like a question, waiting for what I am about to say next.

"Don't keep trying."

I release my hand from his face and scoot into the spacious backseat. Before Eric shuts the door, he looks at me, still stewing on my words.

"That's impossible, Sienna. Even if we aren't hooking up anymore, you are still my friend. I'll do whatever I can to protect you," he confesses as he slams the door.

Eric opens the driver door, letting in a draft as he shivers and rushes into the driver's seat.

I don't wait until he shuts the door to ask what he meant. "What do you mean, protect me? Eric, I am more than capable of taking care of myself," I blurt.

Shutting the door, he briefly looks into the rearview mirror before diverting his attention to the heat controls on the center console. He takes his time looking at the heat settings as my impatience mounts.

"I never said you weren't capable. Stop being so defensive," he responds, turning the heat dial on. Ironic, being that the entirety of his tone sounds extremely defensive.

I sit back in the seat and stare out the window when I see his hand grasp the headrest of the empty passenger seat. He twists his body, facing mine as he takes a deep breath.

"I shouldn't have to remind you of your lineage. You are Matteo Ricci's daughter. Just because he is dead doesn't mean that you are exempt from having a bullseye on your back," he says with a scowl.

In the time Eric and I have been friends, we have never discussed my father's "career." Living in New York with a last name like Ricci, running in the circles my family did, it was pretty much a given what my father's job entailed. Though, the way Eric just mentioned my father makes it unclear whether he is warning me or threatening me.

"I moved here to start over; I don't need you dredging up the past." I cross my arms, staring out the window and feeling heat surge through my face in anger.

He mumbles something under his breath before fixing his gaze back on mine through the rearview mirror, looking as if he is about to scold me. It's a fucking miracle we haven't crashed yet, given the bumper-to-bumper traffic and how little Eric has kept his eyes on the road.

"Last time I checked, starting over, as you so naively put it, wouldn't be coming back to the scene of the crime."

I lean closer to the back of his seat, locked in by my seatbelt. Frustrated, I unbuckle it, since we are currently just sitting in traffic. My heart is now pounding at his words.

"Fuck you. What, because of that tragedy, the whole city is now off limits to me?" My voice cracks as I feel a lump forming in my throat, trying to fight back tears.

"Don't cry," he alters his tone to sound like less of a jealous jerk and more like my friend. The friend I am missing right now, the friend I need him to be.

I take a deep breath to steady my tone. "I'm not crying, just do me a favor and don't talk to me the rest of the ride."

To my surprise, and much to my relief, Eric does as I say and doesn't speak to me. We make our way at what feels like a snail's pace back to the apartment. We are about a block away when Eric lowers the music he was playing.

"Listen, I didn't mean to upset you," he says, breaking the silence. "It's just ..." he stops himself.

Waiting for him to finish his sentence, I bob my head in anticipation, but silence remains.

"Fucking Christ, Eric, just spit it out."

He parks the car and I take his continued silence as my cue to get the fuck out. Ignoring the heat of his stare on me through the sliver of mirror, I grab my purse, about to open the handle when I hear the click of the doors locking.

Meeting his fiery stare, I try to unlock the door, but it's no use. He has his hand on the button, pressing it every time I try to drag the lock up.

"Open the Goddamn door!" I shout.

"Sorry, it's just that don't you find it a little odd that he asked you here on the anniversary of your parents' murder?"

I pause. Of course, it's a strange coincidence. But that's all it is, a coincidence. What, is the world supposed to stop every Halloween because that's the day my world ended? I'm not understanding what Eric is trying to get at.

"It's a coincidence, that's all," I brush him off, suddenly not sure if I am trying to convince him or myself. "Now let me out," I urge, as I notice a sadistic sneer begin to form on Eric's usually pleasant face.

For someone who is supposed to be warning me of some supposed danger, he suddenly looks like he is basking in whatever it is he is trying to insinuate.

"I don't know. I just don't think it's a coincidence that he also invited you to attend the exact gala they were killed at."

"Eric, what are you talking about?"

"Sienna," he hisses. "You don't remember?"

Fear and agitation are mingling in my stomach. I feel like I am going to be sick. "Yes, Eric, it was a gala in the city that my parents were killed at. It could have been any fucking gala. Now, let me out!" I demand.

"But it wasn't just any gala. It was the Annual Halloween Gala hosted by the Morettis," he says as he contorts his body once more, so he is facing me, looking as though he is basking in providing me with such information.

"How the fuck do you know that?" I press him, but I can tell he isn't going to flinch. For some reason, he wants me to work for this information.

"A little birdy told me," he sneers, before turning back around to face the windshield.

Despite wondering the same thing, since I first learned about the gala today, there is something in the way that Eric is warning me that I just am not buying. If his goal is to warn me, he is doing it in such a half-assed way that it makes me wonder if whatever he is trying to warn me of is just a punishment for not wanting to be with him.

Exasperated, and now even more anxious for what tonight has in store for me, I try unlocking the car door once more. Once again, he presses the lock button quicker than I can lift the lock on my own.

"As pleasant as this has been, I would love if you stopped being a fucking dickhole and let me out of this Goddamn car, ok? Thanks." My voice is sarcastic, but on the inside, I feel queasy. I just need fresh air and to get away from Eric.

Finally, I hear the click of the locks as they unlock. I grab my shit and scurry out of the car as Eric just sits there, wallowing in whatever the fuck has overtaken him. I don't care to ask him anything else, or even talk to him, for that matter.

I've always known Eric to be protective, but that, whatever the fuck that was just now in the car, has unveiled a completely different side of him to me. A side that makes me wonder if it was there all along and maybe I was too naïve to notice.

Almost to the lobby door, I hear a car door slam, followed by my name being shouted in a deep baritone. Knowing full well it is Eric, I quicken my pace, reaching for the heavy glass door.

"Sienna!" Eric calls out, but I ignore him. I open the door quickly, hoping it slams behind me and stops him from following me in.

I quicken my pace, though before I can hear the slam I so desperately was wishing for, I hear Eric run in, sounding out of breath.

"You forgot something!" he shouts, so loudly that everyone in the lobby looks my way.

I rotate my heels to face him. He is dangling the garment bag Elaine put the dress in for this evening.

"Thanks, have a good night." I go to snatch the dress out of his hands, but he doesn't let up.

He clicks his tongue, raising the garment bag just out of my reach.

"What the fuck, Eric?"

"You aren't getting rid of me that easily," he says as he

finally hands me the garment bag. "Take your time, I'll be waiting to take you to dinner. Boss' orders."

"Awesome, can't fucking wait," I say through a fake smile.

Relieved to escape Eric, for now at least, I head to the elevator. I look at the garment bag now draped over my forearm. A small lace ribbon catches my attention. Lifting it up, I notice there is a small gift bag attached to it. Before I look to see what is in the bag, I untie the ribbon that secures the handles with a note attached to it.

On the front of the note there is a picture of a large, golden moon in the background of a steep, darkened hill surrounded by a pumpkin patch. Admiring the detail of the watercolor design, I see a small arrow in the bottom corner. I flip it over, revealing a handwritten note.

Please, wear this tonight. Do not try to open, as nothing will be able to. Only I have the key.
Carmine Moretti

Chapter 23

Sienna

Seriously? *Don't try to open it, only I have the key?*

What kind of weird, poetic nonsense is that? Obviously, he knows nothing about me, because once I am told not to do something, it only fuels my fire to do so that much more. I have lived my entire life with people trying to tell me what to do, and the rebel deep within my soul has had enough. So, if he tells me not to try to open whatever is in this gift bag, then I guess the first order of business when I get up to the apartment is to try to open whatever I shouldn't be opening.

As soon as I enter the apartment, I toss my purse and the garment bag on the floor as I begin to tear at the bag, unintentionally ripping it. Curiosity swarms inside of me, wanting to know what tricks this unpredictable man has up his sleeve now.

The bag is so light; it feels like it is empty. I fish my hands inside, trying to feel for what it could be in it that adds barely any weight to the bag. Moving my hand inside, the feel of cold, delicate metal brushes up against my fingertips, unexpectedly causing a tingling sensation starting to work its way down my center. Desire begins to dance with my peaked curiosity, blurring lines that I shouldn't cross.

Gently grabbing hold of what feels to me like a thin chain, I carefully glide it out of the bag, revealing a beautiful, heart-shaped locket. There are intricate etchings all throughout the front and back on the jewelry making it look like an antique.

I scan to see where the latch is to open the locket. Two small tabs stick out on the side. I try to grasp them, but my fingers slip. Scanning the kitchen for something small enough to nudge the locket open, I see nothing. I try again with my fingers, but to no avail, they slip once more.

Defeated, I grab the garment bag from the floor, and with the locket in hand, I go to my room to get changed.

Standing in front of the mirror, I watch my reflection as I slip into the dress that was hand-selected for me. I scoff at the thought, but as I seal myself inside the dress as I bring the zipper upwards, I am in awe of the delicate fabric.

I do a side spin, admiring how fabric caresses my every curve. A flush of heat stirs in my middle, traveling down my warming front. I notice the same woodsy scent of cologne that Carmine wore in the office lingering ever so slightly on the fabric, making me wonder if he hand-delivered the dress to the car.

A tingling sensation overtakes my body as I am temporarily lost in the taboo reverie of my now boss' hands on the fabric that adorns my body. Taking in my silhouette once more, I feel proud of the woman who stares back at me. She has been through hell and deserves whatever this night has in store for her.

If Mama were still here, she would tell me to not be foolish, to act like a lady. The difference is, her definition and mine of what a lady is couldn't be more opposite. Mama preached that a true lady needed to always be the pinnacle of perfection. Standing in the background while society and men tell her what to feel, what to think, what to do. To me, however, a lady is to be whatever the fuck she wants to be. She can fuck whoever she wants to fuck and shouldn't care about the opinions of others.

I go to put on the gift from Carmine when I hear the front door to the apartment creak open. Startled, I toss the necklace in my purse and slowly inch toward my bedroom door. I place my ear on the wood, trying to hear what is happening on the other side. I hear shuffling and slamming of drawers. Then, I hear Nessa talking. Relieved it's her and not Eric, or even worse, an intruder, I relax and head to the kitchen to see her.

Head hung low; she scans the drawers of her desk frantically, not acknowledging me entering the kitchen.

"Where the fuck is it?" she mutters to herself, exasperated.

I walk closer to Nes to help her find whatever she is looking for. Before I can offer her any help, my heels click against the old wood, causing her to finally look up from whatever has her all frazzled.

She subtly scans me from head to toe, bringing her hands to her hips. "Well, you look nice." She seems surprised to see me so dressed up. Nes has known me long enough to know that I am a t-shirt and leggings girl, through and through.

"Thanks, I'm having dinner with someone." I ignore the judgment I'm detecting from her as she is still studying my dress, as if it's going to help her find what she was looking for just moments before.

"Dressed like that? Must be fancy."

"Yea, I guess. Carmine gave it to me."

"Wait a minute, Carmine who?" she asks, making it clear she already knows the answer to her own question. The look in her eyes has shifted from Nessa my friend to Nessa the cop.

Her arms move from her hips to crossing in front of her as she begins to pace. A habit she formed in college when she was trying to talk herself out of confronting the girl who stole her date at a party we went to. Except now, it looks like Carmine is the object of her anger.

"Are you talking about Carmine Moretti as in the sketchy CEO of Marked Inc., Carmine? Yea, he left that detail out last night at The Sandy Claws." Nessa says as she rolls her eyes, still pacing.

"Ok, first of all, I had no idea that was Carmine last night at the bar, and neither did you." I don't know why I feel like I need to defend myself, but again, cop Nessa is very different than my friend. Once she is onto something, that's it, she won't stop until every loose end is tied tightly in a bow of whatever design she deems appropriate.

Uncrossing her arms, she heads back to her desk, continuing her search as she talks.

"I know, neither of us did. But it wasn't sitting well with me that every time I kept asking his name, he wouldn't say it. So, I did a little digging, and sure enough, The Sandy Claws' Carmine is the same as Marked Inc.'s Carmine. I just don't understand, if he knew who you were last night, why didn't he say anything? He left that out on purpose, Sienna, and I want to know why."

"I don't know, maybe he is just eccentric," I deflect.

She looks at me, placing a hand on her hip. "Eccentric? Girl, please, Jack Sparrow is eccentric. This guy is a fucking sketchy chameleon."

She has a point.

"The hand-delivered letter summoning you to work for him, the private dinner. All of it. You grew up in this life, don't play naïve now. He wants something from you," she warns.

I know he wants something from me, but for some reason, I don't want Nessa to know that. I know she loves me like a sister, but that, coupled with her being a detective means she will no doubt insert herself into this, whatever this is with Carmine, and try to save me.

"You find what you were looking for yet?" I ask, trying to redirect the conversation.

"No, not yet," she huffs, sifting through the draws by her small desk off the kitchen before she stops to look at me with serious eyes that remind me more of my concerned friend than an interrogating cop. "You know about the Morettis, don't you?"

"Other than what I have learned today, honestly, no," I reply.

"Once I figured out who he was, I continued to do some digging. Apparently, the Morettis, specifically his father, Armando, have been on the department's radar for a long time. There have been several disappearances over the years that the Morettis have been connected to."

I raise my brow, confused. "Disappearances?"

"Yea, disappearances. I'm talking, untraceable, poof, gone out of nowhere, type of shit. It's like anything or anyone they come in contact with is at risk of disappearing without a fucking trace. Anyway, Armando volunteered some valuable insights today when he showed up at the precinct. Now that I am in the detective unit, I borrowed the flash drive with all the suspected Moretti case files, and I need to find it so I can compare it with what Armando told me today."

I shake my head, wondering why Carmine's father would volunteer information to the cops if they were suspected of so many disappearances.

"Why would he volunteer information pertaining to their business or about his son?" I ask.

"He mentioned he is concerned the gala may be a target of something, but he didn't elaborate beyond that. I want to find the flash drive because it can help me piece together things to look out for while I work security at the gala tonight."

I decide to leave out that I will be at the gala as Carmine's plus one, because I know she would try to stop me from going.

Nes' search is cut short when the radio holstered to her work belt begins to make a scratching sound.

"Shit." She rolls her eyes before taking the radio from her belt and pulling it up to her mouth. Pressing the button to talk, she clears her throat to speak. "Mendez, here."

"Vanessa, Chief is starting to ask where you are. Get your ass back here," the voice on the other line says tauntingly.

She takes a deep breath, hand off the talk button, she mutters, "Fucking prick," under her breath.

The radio makes that God-awful scratching sound once

more. "Yea, I copy Alex, 10-4," she replies into her radio. Holstering her work radio back onto her belt, she sighs as I see her turn off the volume.

"That's probably going to get me in trouble, but I don't give a fuck right now," she says with playful defiance.

She begins to head for the door, clearly giving up on finding her flash drive for the moment. "Sienna, listen to me. When someone like Carmine Moretti helps you, it's because he wants something from you."

I let out an exaggerated, playful sigh. "You sound just like your cousin."

Her face turns cold, concern washing over her usually golden skin. "Be careful with him, too. Something's off with him. He hasn't been acting right since you came to the city," she warns.

Before she heads for the door, she walks to me, placing her hand on my shoulder. Nes the cop is taking a backseat, while my friend moves back in, for the moment, at least.

"I have to go. Be careful, Sienna. I want you to text or call me if you need anything, please." She pauses for a second, as if contemplating the next words out of her mouth. "Don't be like your mama. If you smell trouble, runaway," she warns.

Nes, knows I'm nothing like my mother. Where mama sensed danger and stayed because she was afraid of the consequences. I see danger and often, run towards it and that is what scares Nes. And, if I'm being honest, that's what scares me, too.

Chapter 24

Carmine

Trying to calm the unease that is beginning to mount inside of me, I pace the perimeter of my study. I hate the anxious feeling I have, but between Sienna coming over this evening, my father's latest questionable behavior, and suspicions with the gala, my anxiety is at an all-time high.

I don't have fucking time to feel anxious. In fact, I don't have much time at all to do what I need to do this evening. I glance down at my watch to check the time. I arranged for Jake to arrive at the brownstone to pick up the latest batch of *fantasma* before Sienna arrives.

It's risky having product picked up from the brownstone, but lately, I don't feel like I have another choice. It does help that *fantasma* is unlike anything else being sold on the streets right now. Much like myself, *fantasma* is a product of deception. It has been specially formulated to be practically undetectable, which adds to the appeal. My clients can indulge in a clean high without the risk of failing a drug test. It's also highly addictive, which means it's highly profitable. In fact, *fantasma* has brought about the highest profit margin I have seen since I dove headfirst into the drug game.

My pacing halts when I hear footsteps in the hallway. I look up to see my housekeeper, Ella, standing timidly in the doorway. I was so preoccupied, lost in my own thoughts, I almost forgot that I asked her to come to the brownstone today to help me prepare for my dinner meeting with Ms. Ricci.

Aside from a handful of people, there are not many who come to the brownstone or even know about it. And no one, apart from myself and Alex, know about the previous owner.

"Mr. Moretti—" Ella begins.

I motion for her to enter the study. There is a subtle hesitation in her eyes before she obliges.

"I finished everything you asked of me, is there anything else you need me to do? I can stay to serve the meal if you prefer," she offers.

"That is quite alright, Ella. I thank you and I love how you set up in here." I gesture toward the bistro table I had her set up in the study. Black linens adorn the small, round table for two, with a crystal candelabra lit in the center.

She bows her head in almost a curtsy-like manner, taking in the compliment. "Ok, great, everything is prepped and ready to go in the kitchen for when you are ready."

"Excellent." I grab a wad of cash from my pocket and hand it to her. The way her face lights up with gratitude as the generous amount of money is transferred to her hands makes me smile. Part of me feels bad giving her what is essentially hush money to ensure she keeps quiet about the brownstone, especially to my father. However, I know Ella, a single mother of two, is appreciative of the payment.

My life has been in such a downward spiral that I almost forgot what it feels like to do good. Granted, this kind deed is technically considered bribery, but I'm no fucking saint. So, this is as good as it fucking gets.

"Don't forget what we discussed before you came here today," I remind her of our agreement to mention nothing of the brownstone, if asked.

"Of course, Mr. Moretti, I promise," she says as she secures the payment in her back pocket. She thanks me once more before she heads out of the study.

I inch closer to the pocket door, standing there until I hear Ella exit the brownstone. Once she is gone, I lock the door to the study as I maneuver my way to the dark wood built-ins that surround the fireplace.

Heading to the highest shelf located to the far left of the mantel, I reach for the black and gold spine of the decoy book I have placed in the middle of the shelf. My fingers are met with fine dust that has been collecting on it as I begin to pull the spine forward. The few times I have Ella come to the brownstone to clean, I give her strict instructions not to touch the bookcases in the study. I can't risk what lies behind these shelves being exposed...or anything else for that matter.

A cranking noise begins as I give a final tug to the decoy Poe book, causing the shelves to begin to shift, revealing a small, dark opening. I make my way into the tunneled darkness, feeling for the control panel on the wall. Once my hands find the panel, I press down on the first button I can feel, illuminating the control panel. I enter the passcode, which grants me access to my small stash room behind the steel door. As the door slides open a frigid blast of air hits my face. Flipping the light switch on, I see a small cloud form where my warm breath meets the cold air. The concrete walls and slate flooring do little to hold any warmth in.

I begin to assess the amount of *fantasma* I have packaged and ready to go as my phone vibrates with a text message from Jake saying he has arrived. I head to unlock the back door of the stash room to let Jake in.

We exchange a quick handshake and nod, wasting no time before grabbing the *fantasma* that needs to be transported. As we work, packing the product in the black duffel bag Jake brought with him, I take notice of how banged up he looks. Even in the dimly lit space, I notice the swelling on his face. Both of his eyes are puffy to the point of looking like they are only half open. He looks exactly as I imagined he would be considering him getting jumped just the night before on top of the last-minute alterations made by Christian. With the cops now sniffing around more than ever, I couldn't take any chances that he would be recognized. Jake didn't even blink when I told him to head up to Christian's floor earlier today.

This is the most product I have tried moving at a time, which I have done on purpose, because I know if anyone can disperse it, and quickly, it is Jake. He has been in a bit of a bind lately, so the money I am offering him to be my main distributor is worth his while and reassures me that he won't fuck it up.

I place the last bundle in the duffel bag and zip it shut. It's a tight squeeze but I am able to close the bag before handing it to Jake. "Alright, I think that's all of it." I stretch my hand out to his.

With a bag slung on each shoulder, weighing down his midsized frame, he sways forward a bit before grasping onto my hand. "I won't let you down, Boss."

"Very good." I nod, releasing his hand. I peer once more at my watch, confirming the time. Sienna will be arriving soon, so I need to hurry and lock this place up. "Keep me in the know, and should there be any surprises, you stick to the plan we discussed," I remind him.

Jake nods in agreement. With the weight of the duffels, he begins to walk carefully to the car he parked a few feet from the back door. I hear a grunt spill from his lips as he lugs the bags into the trunk. I know he has been through a lot today, considering his visit with Christian, and ordinarily, I would step in and help him. But the clock is quite literally ticking, I have mere minutes before I will be in a room alone with Sienna Ricci.

Anticipation begins to swirl in my gut as I lock up and reemerge through the small, dark opening back into the warmth of the study. I head directly to the pack of Parliaments on the desk, needing a rush of nicotine to my system to hopefully cancel out the angst running through me.

Cigarette in my mouth, I light it and begin to puff the bitterness into my system. The decoy book is still out of place, so I walk over to adjust it. My hand is re-coated in dust as I return the book to its fraudulent state.

The dust that has collected in this room reminds me of how long I have had to make this place my own. I have forced a lot of things to be able to sneak my way into her life.

I never wanted to be the enemy, but I eerily feel at home in this body that was designed to steal, torture, and kill. The fickle bitch of anxiety invades my subconscious, making me second guess my decision to bring her here for just a fleeting moment. Making me question if she will accept my lies once she learns the truth. There is so much I need to say to her, but even more than that, there is a debt that needs to be paid, and I will stop at nothing to take what is owed to me.

Chapter 25

Carmine

It's only been ten minutes since Jake left, and somehow, I am on cigarette number three and whiskey number two.

Killing time has never been a strong suit of mine. I usually use it as an excuse to smoke like a chimney or get loaded. Not like that is much of a deviation from usual day-to-day activities, but I'm exceptionally full of vices when there is time to spare.

Feeling restless, I twist my wrist toward me, lighting up my watch. The digital dial reads 7:00 p.m.

Excellent.

She should be walking through the door at any moment.

The ice in my drink taps against the glass as I return my wrist to my side, startling Nada as he rises from his dog bed. I need all the liquid courage I can get as I practically inhale what is left of my whiskey. Its sweet sting transports me into a somewhat relaxed state.

Nada's collar shakes as he prances over to me. Excitedly,

he jumps on his hind legs, which rival even my tall stature as his paws reach my shoulders.

"Down boy." I pet him as he pants in happiness. "We must prepare ourselves for our special guest tonight," I remind as I pet his short white fur once more before removing his paws from my shoulders.

The antique grandfather clock in the hallway just outside the study begins to chime, signaling the top of the hour. Just as the last chime echoes, leaving a distinct vibration through my eardrum, I hear the latch of the front door open. I put my whiskey glass down on the bar cart and place my hand on the pistol I have tucked in my belt, just in case. I assume it is Eric walking Sienna in, since I instructed him to bring her directly to my study once they arrived. However, I am always prepared in case the unexpected should occur.

My hands remain tight on the grip of my pistol as I listen close for confirmation of Eric and Sienna's arrival. A few seconds pass, until I hear a mixture of high heels tapping against the hardwood floor along with the distinctly sweet sound of Sienna's breathy tone.

Relief works its way through my body, knowing that she is approaching the study. I re-holster my pistol and head to the bar cart to take out one more glass. I set it aside so it's ready for when she is with me for a drink, alone and away from Eric.

I shift my attention to the door as I hear the clicking of Sienna's heels in the entrance in the study.

And *fuck*, is it a grand entrance that she makes.

I can't take my eyes off her as her curves sway their way over to where I stand. I'm speechless, absolutely entranced by her beauty. Her ink-covered skin glistens as the dress she wears highlights every perfect inch of her. She is an absolute vision of unapologetic sex appeal. She could wear a potato sack and I would want to fuck her raw in it.

Fuck. My mind begins to race thinking of how desperately I want to rip the black lace that adorns her curves off and onto the floor. I can feel the blood begin to rush down my dick, as I stare at her fantasizing about the depraved things that I want to do to her.

Oblivious to the scenes playing in my head, she makes her way closer, until she stops just inches in front of me, holding out her hand for me to shake. She is mouthing what is obviously a hello, though my eyes go right past her outstretched hand and veer down as the slit of her dress shifts slightly, revealing her thigh.

"Umm, hello." She snaps her fingers, visibly irritated with me. Her sassy attitude only intensifies my desire for her. The unintentional spell she has me under makes it difficult to control myself. In the office it was challenging, but I managed. However, here, alone with her, I can feel the little control I have dwindling.

"Good evening, Ms. Ricci," I say, snapping out of the daze she has put me in. "You look exquisite," I compliment her just as an obnoxious throat clearing distracts me.

"Thank you," she says, side-eyeing Eric, who is awkwardly standing in the doorway. I was so entranced by Sienna's entrance into the study that I totally forgot he was still standing there.

"Please, sit." I pull out a chair at the bistro table and wait for Sienna to park her luscious ass on it.

As Sienna sits down, I can feel Eric's jealous glare.

Vexed, I acknowledge him as I painfully peel my eyes off Sienna. I motion for Eric to enter the study. "Yes?" I ask.

Gritting his teeth, I can sense the rage he has toward me, but I also see the way he hides that around her. "Sorry, Mr. Moretti, I just wanted to know if you wanted me to bring out the appetizers yet?" he asks with a pathetically fake smile. He may be asking me, but his gaze is glued to Sienna.

How could I forget that I instructed Eric to stay and serve us this evening. A dick move, sure, but you know what they say, keep your friends close and your enemies closer. In this case, when you are certain your enemy wants to fuck the same person you do, you need to keep them extra close.

Without skipping a beat, Sienna rises from her seat and scoffs at Eric's question. "Seriously? You not only hired Eric as my babysitter, but now also as our personal waiter? Why, because of our history together?"

My tongue clicks as I wave my finger in the air. "The only thing I want from you and Eric is to be history."

"Excuse me?" Sienna asks, with a visible flush painting her cheeks.

"Yea, excuse me?" Eric chimes in.

Matching the fake smile Eric had just moments before, I flash him a stiff grin. "Do as I instructed you to do earlier. Get to it," I order him.

He is about to say something, when his eyes meet my clenched fists at my sides, stopping him in his tracks.

"You got it, Boss." He rolls his eyes, disappearing into the hallway.

Now that Eric is gone, for now at least, I can bring my attention back to where it belongs. On *mi reina*.

"Care for a drink?" I ask, trying to deflect the pissed off look she has on her face as she stands with her arms crossed.

Thrown off, she hesitates for a moment. "Sure, vodka tonic, if you have it, please."

"Of course, I do. I remembered." I grin. "Ms. Ricci, you may sit down."

"I'm ok, thanks," she says, keeping her arms crossed.

"Sienna, sit down," I say in a commanding tone that instantly catches her as well as myself off guard. I don't mean to be so venomous, but I have waited entirely too long for this exact moment to have anything ruin it. Including Sienna herself.

"Seriously?" Sienna says, angered by my abrupt command. I know she is not pleased with me right now, but this banter we have going on only makes the bulge in my pants grow, knocking at the seam of my pants, begging to be released.

"Eric willingly agreed to serve us," I try to reassure her before making my way over to the bar cart to fix her a drink. Though the shit-eating grin I have plastered on my face isn't convincing her.

She huffs a frustrated sigh before finally sitting down.

"Do you remember all your employees' go-to drinks?" she asks.

"No, just the ones that frequent The Sandy Claws," I say as the ice clanks against the empty glass I have for her before I reach for the bottle of vodka to add to it.

"I wouldn't call going somewhere once frequenting," she says. I look back at her and see her rolling her eyes. She looks more like she is fighting what she feels is brewing between us than being genuinely annoyed.

It's ok, mi reina, in due time, you will be giving in to me. Completely.

"Don't you want to, though?" I ask, pouring the vodka into her cup.

"Want to what?"

"Frequent The Sandy Claws. You seemed to take in the atmosphere, kind of like you are doing now," I point out.

She sweeps the smooth, jet-black hair that frames her face back behind her shoulder, as she begins to blush.

Fuck, she is immaculate.

"I've always been drawn to darker things, and this place—"

I cut her off. "Has a darkness about it?"

I hand her the glass and sit across from her at the table. She brings the glass to her lips before she answers, "Yes, there is something that feels beautiful and sad within these walls."

"Well, I'm glad you like my decor style. I like to think that here and at The Sandy Claws, I can be myself, not the version of me I must put on for appearances."

"Isn't that exhausting?" she asks with a level of sincerity that catches me off guard.

"Yes, it is," I say, simply. I don't even know where I want to go with this yet. The truth is, I have been keeping up appearances and leading a double life for as long as I can remember. Lies have consumed my life so much that at the end of the day, when I stare at myself in the mirror, I only see the demons I have unleashed and no longer the man who once had the stamina to defeat them.

"That was my whole life when my parents were alive. I miss them dearly, but I don't miss the act they had me put on. Who were they kidding, my father was as crooked as they come," she confesses.

Oh, I know, but he was nowhere near as bad as my father painted him out to be, I want to say, but I don't.

I must play this right. I want to come clean, but I can't just yet. I must see if she is even willing to listen to my plea for redemption before I lay everything out on the table.

"That sounds awful," I say, distracted with thinking of how exactly I want this evening to unfold.

Eric returns with our appetizers and quickly places each of the cocktail glasses on our plates, purposefully making no eye contact with us.

He leaves the study in a hurry as we begin to eat in silence, staring at each other in between bites.

Just as I am about to break the silence with some small talk, I notice a sliver of thigh peeking through the slit of her dress as she crosses her leg. My eyes feel like magnets, drawn to the pristine view of flesh that is displayed before me. I can't help but stare at the deliciously unique, inked stitching she has poking through the small section of thigh that is exposed.

"It's symbolic," she says, clearing her throat immediately snapping me out of my daze.

"Huh?" I ask, thrown off by her statement.

"The tattoo that you are eye fucking. It's supposed to be symbolic," she repeats.

Fuck, she is so bold. Not that I have any room to talk, I'm technically her boss, and the thoughts I have had for her are anything but employer-like.

"I wasn't—" I start to lie.

"Save it," she interrupts me.

Caught off guard by her abruptness, I clear my throat, ready to engage in whatever lesson she has for me. "Alright then, symbolism," I begin, motioning for her to continue talking.

"Yes, symbolism. Do you need me to provide a definition for you?" she asks, sarcastically.

"No, I think I am familiar with the term," I say, matching her sarcasm. "I was just curious how it pertains to the stitching you seem to have tattooed throughout your body."

"How do you know it's throughout my body?" she asks with enticing eyes.

"Lucky guess."

"What do you do when something is broken?" she asks, taking a shrimp from the cocktail glass in front of her as she slowly brings it to her mouth. She bats her eyelashes up at me, before beginning to nibble the shrimp with her teeth. Her cheeks then hollow as she sucks the remaining meat from the tail. Her mouth makes a subtle pop sound as she opens it slightly, releasing the now empty tail.

Fucking Christ. I feel my forehead begin to perspire as I tilt my head to loosen my tie. Whoever thought eating shrimp cocktail could be such a Goddamn aphrodisiac?

She drops the tail on the plate next to the cocktail glass before redirecting her gaze at me. Sweat continues to form on my forehead as I try to swipe it away discreetly, running my hand through the center of my hair.

Smiling, knowing exactly the spell she has me under. She widens her eyes at me, waiting for a reply.

Flustered, I answer her previous question, "Fix it."

"Exactly. Now if something soft, like a rag doll, for

instance, were broken you would take a needle with thread and sew it, right?"

"But rag dolls are relatively inexpensive. Wouldn't you just get rid of it for a new one?" I ask, trying to feed into this lesson of symbolism she has us in.

"Oh no, Mr. Moretti. Just because something is broken, doesn't mean it loses its value. It's just in need of repair. People, just like rag dolls, are capable of strength after destruction. In fact, the strength that comes from feeling as though you have been broken is often an underestimated power."

"Is that what you are, broken?"

She smiles, fully aware of what she is doing to me. I try to re-adjust in my seat. The blood rushing between my legs is starting to make my cock throb with the need to see what else she can do with that mouth of hers.

"Some could argue that. I mean, life hasn't exactly been kind to me. But I would rather push through that pain and fix myself than let it break or ruin me."

"Something tells me it would take a lot to ruin you, Ms. Ricci," I say with a grin, thinking of all the ways I'd love to fucking ruin her from the inside out.

"Wouldn't you like to know?" She meets my grin with one of her own before she shifts her weight to her elbows, resting them on the edge of the table. Her full breasts are begging to be let out from the way the sheer mesh of her dress holds them in place.

"Listen, Carmine, be straight with me, why am I here?"

"We are having dinner together. I thought that was obvious, given the plates in front of us." I let the sarcasm ooze off my lips. Sure, I know I'm being a dick, but seeing her gears begin to grind is just too much fun.

"No, I mean, why am I really here?" she demands, though there is still a hint of desire laced in her annoyance with me.

"I summoned, and you obeyed. So, I think the real question here, Sienna, is why did a smart woman such as yourself feel inclined to listen to a rumored madman like myself?"

"Madman?"

"Yes madman, I have heard the rumors about myself. I don't doubt that you have heard them."

"I know nothing about you. Trust me, it isn't for lack of trying, but for a man who has as much wealth and power as you have, it's like you just appeared out of thin air," she says, becoming increasingly exasperated.

"I have my reasons."

"Don't you think I should know what those reasons are?"

"Not yet. Where is that necklace that I told you to wear?" I ask, deflecting from this little line of questioning she has ensued.

Until I can wrap my hands around that pretty, little neck of hers, that chain will suffice as a reminder of me hanging around her.

Clearly flustered, she fumbles over her words just a bit. "Um, it's in my purse."

"Excellent, now, be a good girl and fetch it for me." I motion to her purse, and reluctantly, she rises from her chair to retrieve it.

I watch as she bends, admiring the way the fabric of the dress hugs her curves. Necklace in hand, she slips back into her seat, keeping the chain grasped in her palm. She doesn't say anything just yet. Instead, she sits, waiting for my next move.

"That's a good girl, *Sen*." I grin.

She hesitates, looking at me as if she has just seen a ghost. Maybe she has, maybe she hasn't. That's up to her to unravel. But tonight, I intend to unravel every inch of her. Making her wish that those stitched tattoos can keep her body intact once I am through fucking it senseless.

Chapter 26

Sienna

It's just a coincidence. An eerie, gut-wrenching coincidence is all.

I shake my head as I replay what Carmine just called me. *Sen.* I hate the effect that hearing that nickname has on me. Even after all this time, even after all the healing I thought I have done, I hear that name and I am somehow catapulted back to teenage, angsty and heartbroken Sienna. An era of my life I wish I could eradicate from my memory once and for all.

Carmine exaggeratedly clears his throat, waking me from the trance I have unintentionally pulled myself into. "Sienna are you with me?" he asks in a fervent tone that surprises me.

Still flustered from just moments before, I nod in response as I notice an eager grin begin to form on his face. His grin, although alluring, makes me feel nervous because I can't determine if its intention is in genuine glee or something more devious, he has waiting up his sleeve.

"Yes, sorry," I finally respond, as I nervously raise my hand to a piece of my hair I twirl. A habit I have always resorted to ever since I was a young girl, in moments of anxiety or uncertainty, and right now, I feel both.

His grin lessens with my response, clearly expecting more from me than my short reply.

"The necklace, Sienna," he reminds me.

"Yes, what about it?" I answer him, still playing with my lock of hair.

Dissatisfied once again with my answer, he leans his elbows on the table. His posture is slouched, but it doesn't make him any less intimidating or appealing. He rubs his open palms together, like he is contemplating what to say next.

"Give it to me," he orders.

His demand does something to me, it doesn't make me want to obey; it makes me want to challenge him. Not out of defiance, per se, but out of the thrill of learning what he will do to me if I don't comply with his commands.

I drop the strand of hair I have been toying with and shift in my seat, mirroring his hunched posture with my own. I meet his gaze as I rest my elbows on the table. It's not a large table, our half-bent arms are not that far from each other, and even in this otherwise plain position, I feel more than the heat radiating from the fireplace warming my core.

His eyes still peer into mine. I decided to raise the stakes a little, see how far I can push him before he cracks.

"Or what?" I ask, catching him off guard.

"What do you mean?" he retorts.

"What happens if I don't hand it to you?"

He takes his elbows off the table and repositions himself, leaning back on the chair. As he sits, he spreads his legs apart, forcing my eyes to follow his movements, imagining what he has contained beneath the linen of his pants.

"Ms. Ricci, I don't have time to play games."

That's rich coming from the master manipulator himself. He has been doing nothing but playing games since I met him. I've quickly come to realize that Carmine Moretti has this uncanny ability to simultaneously enrage me while also turning my center into a warm, open puddle.

"Is that so? See, I'm not sure you know this or not, but I'm not a fucking idiot," I begin, and just as I am about to continue, he begins to cackle. *This fucker.*

Irritated, I drop the stupid necklace onto the table. As I release it from my grip, the clasp hits the glass next to it, making a loud echo, which only fuels his obnoxious laughter.

"Something funny?"

He rubs his eyebrow as his laughter begins to dissipate. "You. You are fucking adorable," he says, and I can't tell if he is being serious or taunting me. Either way, it's only enraging me more.

He rises from his seat, walking closer to where I remain seated. "I never called you an idiot, those were your words. Now, please, the necklace," he reminds me once more, now snatching the necklace from where it landed on the table.

He lowers himself so his tall frame is hovering over mine from behind where I sit as he leans into my ear. "Allow me," he whispers, beginning to drape the locket around my neck.

The cool chain on my skin is a stark contrast to the warmth I feel in my center. The way his hands graze my skin causes my clit to throb with wanton need for him.

"That's more like it," he says, lowering his mouth to my ear once more.

Before I can respond, I hear the floorboards creak behind me in the direction of his desk.

I turn, still seated in the small bistro chair, and watch as he takes a seat at the chair of his desk.

"Please." He motions for me to join him, as he places an unlit cigarette in his mouth.

I rise from my seat and move to the chair in front of his desk.

Just as I sit, facing him once more, a cloud of smoke forms between us from his freshly lit cigarette.

I hate smoking. Papa smoked for years, and the smell eventually took over the entire house. It took months after Mama and Papa passed to get the smell of his Black & Milds out of the upholstery. But there is something oddly seductive about the way Carmine sits back in his chair, lighting his cigarette. Watching his lips pucker around the filter as he inhales the fumes, there is a calm that overtakes him. It's almost as if, as bad of a habit as it is, he does it to tame the beast inside of him. The brief relief it brings him and the way I can see his black eyes through the clouds of smoke ignites something in me, making me want to breathe in his smoke just to be closer to him.

His chiseled jaw tenses as his lips pucker around the shortening cigarette butt. I sit back in the chair in front of his desk, crossing my legs, in hopes that the slickness forming between them will disappear.

"So, what's so special about this locket, huh?" I nudge with genuine curiosity.

"Nothing, until its owner wears it," he says as smoke billows around his face.

"Me, being the owner?"

He takes another drag of his cigarette. "You are now. So ..." he begins.

"So," I repeat after him. "Why are we here and not at the gala?" I ask.

He leans back in his chair and tilts his head, staring at me. "Didn't feel it was necessary to show my face there this year, is all."

"Oh, that's it." I inch forward in my chair, locking my eyes on him. "Then, why did you mention how important tonight was for the company and have me wear this dress?"

He lets out a chuckle as he exhales the last of the cigarette before smashing it into the ashtray on his desk. "Tonight, is an important night for me and, well, the dress is one of a kind. Wouldn't you say, Sen?" he says, toying with me.

"Why do you keep calling me that?" I demand.

Unfazed by my anger, he reaches for another cigarette from the pack of Parliaments on his desk. He takes his time lighting it, while his gaze remains on me. "Isn't that a nickname for Sienna?"

"Yes, but no one calls me that anymore."

"Oh, really?" He perks up. "Care to elaborate?"

"Nothing, it was just someone I used to know called me Sen."

"Someone you used to know or someone you used to fuck?" he pries with palpable arrogance in his voice.

I hesitate, unsure of where this conversation is headed,

but certain it isn't in the direction of what is deemed appropriate employer-to-employee talk.

Before I can answer, I see Eric's scruffy beard in my peripheral.

"Not now, Eric. Close the door," he barks, as he lifts his hand, with his cigarette in it, toward the door.

I look to Eric, who has rage in his eyes. He peers at Carmine once more before obliging and shutting the pocket door to the study begrudgingly.

Carmine fixes his stare back at me. "As you were saying?" he motions for me to continue.

"Someone I used to know, is all," I answer, trying to think of something to say to derail this conversation from going where I fear it's headed.

"Did he fuck you like you deserve, this past love of yours?"

I blush. Despite fantasizing about Carmine from the night I unknowingly met him, this feels so personal. Too personal. He's my fucking boss. *What the fuck am I doing?*

"How is that any of your business?" I demand. This time, I rise from the chair in front of his desk. Once again, I have the perfect opportunity, the perfect reason to storm out ... but I don't. Instead, I shift my weight in my heels and stand there in front of his desk as if I am on display for him.

"It's a simple question, Sienna. Did he fuck you?"

I say nothing. I don't know how to answer him, but judging by the wetness I feel between my legs, my body is answering his question for me. No. Leo never fucked me like I wanted. He was good, but he didn't rail me like I craved. I always thought that made me dirty, that I wanted it rougher, harder, more passionate.

The striking differences between Leo and Carmine's physical appearances couldn't be more apparent. Even though the last time I saw Leo we were only teenagers, I don't even think his adolescent body would have been capable of morphing into the chiseled god that stands before me.

Leo had softer facial features, yet still had a rugged handsomeness to him. But Leo's handsome face doesn't hold a candle to the chiseled face of perfection that stands in front of me. Carmine's dark-as-night hair that is slightly slicked back in the middle only accentuates a face so perfect it makes me want to nestle it between my thighs, rendering him helpless.

Not to mention, their eyes couldn't be more opposite. I used to get lost in a daydreaming, love-struck kind of way in Leo's soft brown irises. But Carmine's dark eyes don't give me the opportunity to daydream. They are a haunting, pitch-black nightmare, waiting for me to peer into them so he can put me under his spell in a split second.

"Please, sit back down. I'm just trying to get a feel for the kind of woman you are, that's all," he says as he finishes his second cigarette.

I sit down, and as soon as the butt is put out, he walks his way over to the front of his desk. He leans his weight back, so he is half-sitting on the edge. His legs are staggered, and I try my hardest to look away from the noticeable and substantial bulge he has formed beneath his pinstriped pants.

His tall stature, even half-sitting in front of me, is overpowering. Trying to distract myself from gazing between his legs, I look up, and it's then I notice that he is playing with a chain with a strange, large key on it. He must have had it tucked under the collar of his shirt, because it's a distinctly large skeleton key. I would have noticed it when I first saw him.

I begin to study the key and notice the top is adorned with a winged bat. Next to the skeleton key on the chain is a *coqui* pendant that makes the hairs on my arms raise. It looks identical to the chain the woman from across the street, Miranda, has from back home. Another coincidence, likely, but how many coincidences can there possibly be before it becomes telling of something to come?

Suddenly, the note attached to the locket feels more ominous. What is that damn key to?

"You never answered my question. Did he fuck you like you deserve, or did he waste his time, tiptoeing like a boy around that perfect body of yours?"

I should kick him in the balls and fucking quit.

"Excuse me?"

Still half-sitting on the desk, he leans his upper body closer to me so that he is just hovering above me as he licks his lips. "A woman like you deserves to be devoured by a lover who takes their time appreciating every inch of you."

Fuck, I'm so wet. The way the words fall off his lips, practically moaning to devour me, is becoming too much to take. The pulse I have been experiencing on my clit is now beginning to throb violently with need.

I swallow, trying to distract myself from the slickness I feel trapped between my legs. "Is that why you called me here, Carmine? To devour me? I thought you needed me to work for you?"

"Don't act like you don't want me to devour you."

"Don't be arrogant," I say so my gaze is in line with his.

He lifts his hand, caressing my cheek before letting his thumb fall on my lip.

"I'm not arrogant, I'm confident," he says through a Devilish grin.

"Confident about what?" My voice is reduced to a whisper. It's like the need I feel for him is robbing me of the ability to speak at an audible level.

He rises from his seated position on his desk, his full height towering over me. He leans in, bringing his lips to my ear. "That you want to be fucked, praised and devoured like you deserve to be."

His words send a chill down my spine as desire begins to radiate all throughout my body.

My breathing increases and the only words I am able to muster are, "Please, Carmine, no more games."

His arm outstretches toward me as I stare at the same skull and floral tattoo that stole my attention last night at The Sandy Claws. He gently guides me to the armchair I was just sitting in, forcing me back down.

He begins to unbutton his pinstriped jacket as I ask him, "What are you doing?"

Draping his jacket on the desk, he lowers to his knees right in front of me. "Considering that I invited you as my dinner guest, and seeing that we finished our appetizers, I feel this insatiable need to satisfy this hunger I feel building inside of me," he says as he brings both ink-drenched hands to my thighs, giving them a squeeze.

"Go tell Eric to get the rest of the food then, since you rudely turned him away," I say, trying to distract myself from the need that is brewing inside of me.

"No need. The only thing I have on the menu for this

evening is feasting on your pussy like it's my last fucking meal."

As soon as the words leave his lips, I feel my willpower dwindle. He begins to take the fabric that drapes at my heels, rolling it up slowly, exposing my throbbing wet center.

"Carmine," I sigh.

"You said no more games. So, I will tell you exactly what I am going to do to you. I am going to rip this pretty little dress off you so I can spread your thighs apart, burying my head in-between them. I want you to suffocate me, as I devour you," he says with a ravenous smirk. "I have been waiting so fucking long to see the way your pussy glistens for me."

I feel myself getting wetter the more he expresses his desire for me, but the way he emphasizes how long he has waited for this moment confuses me. As much as I want nothing more than to constrict his air as he is buried between my sex, I instinctively feel my hand reach for his, stopping him from adjusting the last of my dress up and away from my slit.

"Are you sure we haven't met before?" I ask in desperation.

"Enough, Ms. Ricci," he snaps.

Ignoring the aggravation, I have stirred inside of him I continue. "You said you have been waiting for so long, that implies you either know me or ..." I stop. That feeling again that he wants something from me comes creeping back in. I can't forget that I am a Ricci. Riccis were hated by just as many people as they were respected by. His name sounds familiar, but I still can't place him. Suddenly, the desire I have for him begins to mix with fear and I don't know which one I should give into first. I want to run but running would mean that I would be away from him. I'm not sure I want to be.

He pushes my hand off his so he can get back to what he has planned for me. "I promise you, Ms. Ricci, I brought you here for a reason. We will get to that after. So, tell me where you want it."

"Want what?" I ask, feeling my cheeks begin to flush.

"Where do you want to come when I devour you? On this chair or the near the fire?" he asks, darting his eyes in the direction of the roaring flames contained in the fireplace.

His forward desire to please me makes the ability to form coherent words escape me. I don't know how to answer him. I've never had a man be so direct in his pursuit to please me. I thought men like him only existed in romance novels, yet here he is, a living, breathing, ink-covered god wanting to —*begging* to—taste me.

"I'm waiting." He grins.

I don't respond. Instead, I rise from the chair and make my way over to the fireplace. It's warmth on my skin mixed with the warmth I feel radiating in between my legs renders me speechless. I lay myself down on the rug in front of the crackling flames as I move the thigh slit of my dress over. Spreading my thighs wide, I reveal my slick ache for him as he follows me like a predator out for its prey onto the rug.

"Very well," he says as he kneels before me, spreading my legs apart even wider.

Within a split second, his tongue is catching the puddle that has been running down my inner thigh.

I arch my back and let out a moan that I didn't even know I was capable of as he grips my hips and begins devouring me with the ravenous warmth of his tongue. He passes his tongue up and down my slit, before lifting his head slightly. I look down at him and we lock eyes.

He goes to speak between teasing kisses on my inner thigh, "I have all night, *mi reina*. I want you to take your time, revel in me fucking you with my tongue."

Chapter 27

Carmine

Now that I have her beneath my tongue, I don't think I can live another day without the ecstasy she supplies my depraved soul. Her moans unleash a primal desire inside of me unlike anything I have ever experienced. It's simply not enough to taste her, I need more of her.

I need all of her.

Nothing has ever satiated my desires the way her sweet tang does as it invades my taste buds. I am coming to the realization as I am consuming her wet center that no one other than her will ever fill the void that has haunted me all this time. A fate I've quickly accepted and only hope in time she will come around to with some convincing.

I take my time working my tongue between her thighs, paying close attention to the way she bucks her hips each time I lick and gently suck on her clit. With each pass of my tongue around her sweet spot, I feel her tremble beneath the warmth of my mouth, making me increase the intensity as I devour her. I have fantasized for so long about having her surrender her inhibitions to me that, in this moment, with her glistening in my face, I feel like I am about to burst. Just the sight of her arousal is making my cock ache to be inside of her.

"Like that, don't stop," she begs as she grabs hold of the small throw rug that she lies on top of, trying to brace herself against the pleasure coursing through her.

Just as she goes to grip the shag of the rug, I bring one hand up and over top hers, pinning her wrist down against the hardwood floor above the fabric she tried to grab hold of. She is too lost in my tongue on her to notice the floorboards in the hallway creaking with, undoubtedly, Eric trying to eavesdrop through the closed pocket doors of my study.

I almost feel bad for the guy. How torturous it must feel to be so close to the one you desire to only have them lost in ecstasy at the hands or mouth of someone else. I sneer to myself at the thought because *almost* is the keyword. I almost feel bad, but I don't, because being so close yet so far from the one I need to be *mi reina* has been my dull reality for far too long.

Being this close to her is intoxicating. Now, I know why addicts crave the high of the drugs I sell, because once you have a high that numbs the pain and propels you into pure bliss, you don't care about anything else. She is my drug; she is my bliss.

My fingers dig into her wrist as if they are magnets being pulled toward her delicate skin. Desperation for her takes over, and the way she moans in response to my unyielding hold on her only increases my need to dive into her more.

With one hand still latched onto her wrist, I work my free hand inside of her while my mouth continues consuming her. Her soaked walls clamp down on my fingers as I slide them into her while sucking on her swollen clit.

I continue alternating between fucking her with my tongue and fingers as I feel her walls expand and contract as her release is near. She begins to arch her back, pushing my head deeper in between her legs. Her free hand clenches my hair as her orgasm reaches a crescendo. She forces my face down with such intensity that my lungs begin to ache as I am starved for air, buried in this bliss that is her arousal. The lack of oxygen only makes me want her more. Air is over-rated, anyway. If I die buried between her thighs, then I will die a happy man.

Her hips thrash as she continues her spasming against my face.

I gently kiss her clit once more, making her flinch slightly beneath my mouth, still sensitive from her release. I'll let her rest for now, because I can already tell my hunger for her will never be fully satiated. I could eat her sweet pussy for every fucking meal of my life, and it still wouldn't be enough.

She finally releases me from her grasp as I also undo the taut hold I have on her wrist, already missing the warmth of being perched between her legs. My hand trails her smooth skin as I rise to my knees. She lifts to a seated position on the floor and surprises me by taking my hand that was just inside of her, capturing it between her delicate palms.

With both hands, she raises my large, calloused hand that is still damp from her. The light of the fire roars behind us, illuminating her arousal still fresh on my fingers.

Her thick, dark lashes flutter as she glances down, admiring the slick reminder of where my hand just traveled moments before. A smile forms from the sweet depths of her mouth before she looks up, locking her seductive gaze on me. Slowly, she brings my wet fingers close to her full lips, causing an immediate pulse to begin traveling through my length.

My heart races as my cock stiffens even more than I thought possible as I watch the ink on my fingers disappear into her mouth. Her cheeks hollow as she begins to suck on them, bringing my digits deep against the back of her throat.

Fuck. What this woman does to me should be illegal. She teases me a few moments more before slowly releasing my fingers from her mouth. Licking her lips as if she just had a tasty meal. I notice her chest rise, taking in a deep breath, as if she is preparing herself for something. Perhaps, a confession?

And here I was thinking I was the only one of the two of us harboring secrets.

"He made love to me," she blurts out.

Jealousy trickles in at the mere mention of another man after I just fucked her like that with my tongue. Perhaps one orgasm wasn't enough, maybe *mi reina* needs more of me to convince her that, in my presence, I am the only source of pleasure she needs.

"He made love to me ... to answer your question from before," she repeats herself as she walks closer to the shelves on the fireplace.

Her bare, delectable ass is in my direct view as she readjusts the fabric of her dress. Bringing it back down over her curves, sadly covering her flesh once more. Like a pathetic puppy, I stand to follow her, wherever she is going, I need to be there. I'm like an addict for her.

Shit. I pick up my pace, trying to not let my anxiety show as she begins scanning the books and other things that line the rich wood shelves.

I step just behind her as she slowly moves one foot in front of the other with a raised hand tracing the spines of the books before her. I notice her squint to make out some of the titles, playing it off like she is just observing, but I know with her being a writer that books are more than just decorations to adorn a shelf. They are her escape, her reality, and her refuge.

I find it adorable as she tries to decipher what my collection says about me. But still, I need to play this safe, one curious gesture toward something she isn't supposed to see could derail this evening in an instant. So, I remain close and follow her, not like I am complaining.

Still studying the dozens of book titles before her, I clear my throat, trying to bring the conversation back to what she started just before.

"You know, if you weren't so Goddamn sexy, *mi reina,* I'd be more enraged that you mention another man after I just had you weeping in pleasure on my taste buds," I say, regrettably. As the words leave my lips, I feel an increase of blood rush down my shaft.

Her face flushes, startled from the intense desire dripping off my words. She bats those beautiful, full lashes at me like she did when my fingers were practically playing with the back of her throat. Though, this time, she looks at me with an adorable curiosity.

"Reina, huh?" she asks, biting down on her bottom lip.

"It means queen in Spanish."

"I know what it means," she says, unimpressed with my deflection technique. That or the nickname. "My mama was

Puerto Rican," she continues, this time, looking back at the bookshelf next to where she left off. "Spanish was her and my Titi Lana's first language. Although, she didn't teach me much outside of how to say the basics."

"So was mine," I blurt.

She turns to me with a sadness in her beautiful brown eyes. The past tense of my words clearly rattles an emotion in her. An emotion that I know, sadly, she tries to work past daily, though the pain remains. No amount of time or vices or anything could ever take away the pain that grief plagues us with.

Maybe now she will see that we have more in common than the ink that covers our skin and the chemistry that we cannot deny. We are two motherless beings, whose mothers were stolen from us too soon. Both from an island that would be the perfect escape from the forever hostile environment that is our reality.

"I'm sorry for your loss," she says, reaching for my forearm. The sincerity in her touch pings at my heart, flooding me with the first moment in a long time that I have allowed myself to feel something other than calculated rage and scheming.

"I'm sorry for your loss as well." I want to tell her how truly sorry I am. How I know the answers to the questions that have haunted her all these years. That I am the descendent of a real-life boogeyman, a fat, soulless corpse who walks around killing because he is afraid the more people know of his weak character, the less powerful he will be. But I don't offer that information to her yet, I don't want to scare her off.

"Thank you," she says. She looks as if she is going to say

more, but she hesitates, leaving her mouth open as she physically contemplates what to say next. "Sadly, I am no stranger to loss."

"Is that so?" I press, wanting to know what other losses have scarred her heart.

It's then that she moves her hand to her hair, bringing the fallen piece that covers her face in place behind her ear, where I see the beautiful stitching tattoos that decorate her clavicle are also found on her inner elbow. How I missed that before, I don't know. Then again, she might have me beat in the tattoo department. She is arguably just as covered as I am, if not more.

I don't know why I am pressing her, when I already know all there is to know about Sienna Ricci. I know of the deaths and disappearances that haunt her. I already know who she is about to speak of. Though in my quest to know every mundane and intimate detail of what makes the woman before me so beautiful, even in her brokenness, I want to hear it anyway.

"That guy you were prying about before. He is just another tragic loss in the life of Sienna Ricci," she says, throwing up her hands with a not-so-convincing chuckle. Her sarcasm isn't lost on me. I know that pains her just as much as losing her parents. But I want to know if losing him is something she can get over. I don't want that standing in the way of what is mine to take.

She stops, scanning the shelves between our words and, as if she is bracing herself for a conversation she clearly does not want to have, she seats herself on the emerald loveseat in front of the fireplace. She crosses her leg over the other and the slit in her dress shifts, revealing a sliver of her thigh, immediately stealing my attention.

Trying to break myself from the pull my eyes feel toward her flesh, I adjust my stance and try to see what she is willing to tell me. "How did you lose him?"

"Kind of how most losses happen. One day here, the next day gone," she scoffs again, trying to hide herself in sarcasm. I find this defense mechanism to be more adorable than I know she is trying to make it come off.

"What do you mean, gone?" I again press her. I'm playing a dangerous game right now. I know I'm pushing her buttons, because she clearly is not amused with the topic of conversation, but I can't help myself. She just looks so fucking exquisite when she is flustered.

She stares at me as if in disbelief of my prying. What can I say? She should realize by now that I am a boundary-pusher, nothing about me or the life I lead is conventional. However, it is not lost on me that in any other context, especially with me being her boss, it would be inappropriate. But when it comes to the plans I have for her, it's important I know where her loyalties lie, and more importantly, where her heart is.

"Gone, as in, no longer here." I can tell she wants to end the conversation, but I'm starting to get what I want out of her, so I continue to press her.

"So, he is dead then, I'm assuming?"

"Whether he still roams this Earth is an irrelevant detail. He is dead to me," the bitterness is evident in her voice. Legs still crossed, she begins bouncing her leg, fidgeting just slightly.

Her anger and hurt make me want to comfort her, but I

don't. This is the emotional response I was hoping to drum up in her, to see if she would even be willing to do what I need her to.

"Well, if he is alive, he is a cowardly fool for leaving a woman like you," I say, buttering her up, though I mean every word. "And if he is in fact dead, well then, he must be rotting in a perpetual Hell that is existing without you by his side."

"Is that so?" she says, with her interest piqued.

"Anyone who has had the privilege of being inside of you who then leaves, whether by self-will or forced by God, will experience the most torturous pain one could ever fathom."

"Ha, well, I don't believe in God."

"Good, because if you did, he wouldn't be able to save you from what I have planned for you, Ms. Ricci."

"Is that so?" I can tell by the way she smirks that she thinks I'm kidding. She wishes.

"What's so funny? Don't be rude, do share," I say as I meet her grin with a more devious one of my own.

"Nothing, it's just that something tells me, if it were you back then and not him, I might have been the one who didn't survive."

Probably. Little does she know that her survival was solely based on the death that happened the night her little lover boy vanished.

"Is that so?" I ask, wanting to know more of why she thinks she can't survive at my hands.

She continues, as if she is lost in her own thought process, aside from our conversation, "I'll tell you what, though. Death, as inevitably wicked a concept as it is, has made me stronger. It has made me realize that I can walk through fire and come out still intact. Different, sure, but intact, nonetheless. It has taught me that life is more fleeting than it is precious. In those fleeting moments is when we decide what we want to do with the time we are given."

"And what do you want?" I pry, wanting to get at whatever has been boiling beneath her surface, begging to be let out.

"Right now ..." she trails off, suddenly hesitating, as if I didn't already notice the desire in her eyes.

"Go ahead, *mi reina*," I urge her to continue.

She sighs, as if mentally surrendering to me before she parts her lips to speak. "I want answers, but I'm not stupid. You aren't going to give those to me, not yet anyway. But the answers I seek have somehow become less about you and more about me."

"How so?" I ask, wanting her to spill her guts to me before giving me the opportunity I so desperately need to rearrange hers.

"I don't know who you are or why you called me here. I should care, but I don't." She pauses, and I can sense the hesitation in her voice. She takes a deep breath in this time, giving off an aura of liberation instead of angst. "I want you to breathe me in like the smoke that filters into your mouth daily. Except, when you exhale, take the pain that has fractured my soul away with it," she blurts, suddenly seeming relieved.

Oh, how I want nothing more.

Before I can muster up a response to her poetic lust, my attention is pulled when the familiar squeak of the hardwood presents itself before a dreaded knock at the door.

I have been so lost in Sienna's presence that I keep

forgetting Eric is still fucking here. At first, it was just to toy with him, let him see that what he once had is his no longer. But I am sure Sienna's moans that echoed through the brownstone confirmed that already.

"Yes, Eric?" I answer.

Eric mumbles through the door. Irritated, I interrupt him.

"Open the door when you need to speak to me, Mr. Mendez," I peck at him.

He slides open the pocket door with an irritation that matches mine. Except, while my eyes are peering at his, waiting to hear what it is that he needed to interrupt us for, I can't help but notice his eyes immediately look at how the warm glow of the fire illuminates Sienna's beauty.

Breaking him out of the trance Sienna unintentionally has him in, I snap, "Mr. Mendez, what is it?"

He waits for a second, as if he didn't think this whole scenario through before interrupting us. Shaking his head, he snaps out of it, directing his gaze to mine. "You have a phone call."

I'm perplexed because I didn't hear the house phone ring. Truthfully, it barely ever rings, because not many people know of the brownstone, and landlines, really, in today's age? It's just a backup, one that I am regretting as of this moment.

It's then that I search my pants pocket for my cell phone. I grasp it, immediately putting my businessman hat back on. I have been so swept up in the plans I have for Sienna I almost forgot the actual work that needs to be done.

I hit the side button of my cell phone, which illuminates the lock screen, displaying five missed calls from Alex. Shit.

He must be pissed. I then turn my phone to the side and realize that I had my phone on silent by accident.

"Very well, thank you," I say, backing down from the anger I feel toward him.

He nods but still hangs in the doorway. I look back at Sienna, who is looking down at her hands, which she can't stop fidgeting with.

"Please, make yourself at home, I will be right back." I head toward the doorway that Eric still stands in, waiting. For what he is waiting for, I don't know, but I am no longer in need of him this evening. I will see to it that Ms. Ricci gets to where she needs to be this evening myself.

I walk past him as he turns, still there in the doorway, but with his attention fixed on me when I say, "You can come back in two hours to pick up Ms. Ricci. Your services are no longer needed inside the brownstone for Ms. Ricci, I will take care of her."

Chapter 28

Sienna

The heat radiating from the fireplace behind me is nothing compared to the inferno that I feel brewing inside, as made evident by my flushed cheeks. Anger swirls inside of me as I can literally feel the judgment oozing from Eric's reprimanding glare. His eyes are locked on me as he remains just outside the door, even though Carmine dismissed him before running off to see whoever called him. Eric's glare doesn't dissipate, instead, it only intensifies as he stands there, waiting for me to say something.

Another moment passes in this strange stare-off we find ourselves in.

"I'm fine, Eric," I say. Not exactly riveting and arguably vague, but it's something. I, of course, don't tell him that I am, in fact, more than fine, but I think he can put two and two together from the guttural sounds of pleasure that echoed off the rich, wood-bordered walls in Carmine's brownstone.

Just the thought of the way Carmine had me in his

mouth makes me grin as I feel a slight pulse resurface between my legs.

"I gathered that," he scoffs. "Just don't say I didn't warn you," he threatens.

"Warn me of what?" I ask as I cross my arms.

"Him. He wants something from you," he says before rolling his eyes and heading out.

Finally, alone, or at least, for the time being, I head to the loveseat that is stationed in front of the fireplace.

Sitting on the rich emerald loveseat, I lean back into the soft, velvety fabric. I close my eyes and bring my fingertips to my temples, trying to process this evening. I had a feeling that something would transpire between Carmine and me.

There is an undeniable physical chemistry between us, I felt it the moment my hand lingered in his last night at The Sandy Claws. The physicality of our interaction, however, doesn't bother me as much as him being my fucking boss. Fuck. That definitely complicates things.

I open my eyes, adjusting my posture as I decide to look around the room instead of stew on the boundary, I demolished the moment I agreed to this evening with Carmine. My eye is drawn to the grand fireplace and ornate built-ins that surround it. They are stained in a rich walnut, each with a unique, pointed arch top, creating a moody yet serene ambiance. Atop of each of the pointed arches are ornate scrolls worked into the wood trim, with what appears to be a gargoyle design laced into the woodwork.

I scan the shelves over some more from the loveseat, while I wait for Carmine. Curiosity and impatience begin to take hold of me with each passing moment. I rise from my seat, and just as I am about to head toward the bookcases, I hear what sounds like a thud come from the hallway. I turn, looking over my shoulder, expecting to see Carmine in the open doorway, but he is not there. No one is.

I turn my attention back to the bookcase and decide that while I wait for Carmine to return, there is no harm in indulging my curiosity a bit.

You can tell a lot about a person by the contents of their personal book collection, and I am dying to know what Carmine's shelves say about him.

There are six full bookcases by the fireplace alone, not including the two slender ones near the entrance of the study, just past where the pocket door slides open. He must enjoy reading, or at the bare minimum, enjoy being surrounded by books. Either way, a man who submerses himself in this many books intrigues my bookworm heart.

As I examine the shelves, I am met with an array of non-fiction books. Expected, but boring. I take in the mix of eclectic décor and more books. Most of what I see are business books, along with some biographies, but nothing that I would want to curl up and read. I almost give up perusing, when I spot a collection of what seems to be some romance novels on the far-left bookcase. Unexpected, but a nice surprise. He must be reading something and taking notes, for the way he worked me before. *I support it.*

Just as I am about to head back to my seat, my eye catches a black velvet box on the shelf just above his small collection of romance books. The box is decent in size, not too big but large enough that it stands out amongst the sea of the books that surround it. Even in the dimly lit den, among the dark wood shelves that encompass the room, my eye can't unsee this damn box.

I tiptoe closer to the box to inspect it more, but the shelf is just out of my reach. I look over my shoulder to see if Carmine is back yet, on the off chance he wouldn't have made his presence known upon arrival.

Once I confirm the coast is clear, I walk to the bistro table where Carmine and I ate our appetizers in the study and quietly lift one of the chairs so I can use it to give me a boost. Placing the chair in front of the bookcase, I hike up my dress and step up, so I am now eye-level with the black box.

Now that I am closer, I see that it's made of the same material as the velvet loveseat. I run my hand on it, the soft texture sends an unexpected chill down my spine, and for some reason, in response to the chill, I decide to turn over the box.

Not sure what I am expecting to find or why I need to scrutinize this box anymore, I do it anyway. Nothing about this night makes sense already, so might as well stay on brand and keep snooping.

I take both hands and slowly turn the box to get a look at the back on the off chance that it is different than the seemingly plain front. The soft texture of the box glides without making a sound on the wood shelf as I rotate its position.

To my surprise, the back of the box is different. Centered in the middle is a bronze keyhole in a shape that looks like an elongated skeleton. I would say it's probably made for an antique skeleton key, but the shape of where the key should be inserted to open the box looks nothing like any opening for a skeleton key that I have ever seen.

I squint at the locked box, as if that has any power to open it. Suddenly, I hear footsteps, accompanied by a bell-like sound. *Shit.*

I turn and am immediately met with the rumble of his seductive baritone filling the room. "Looking for this?" Carmine taunts as he reaches underneath his shirt, unveiling a long chain with a large fucking skeleton key attached to it. *Double shit.*

I feel a lump form in my throat as my stomach feels like it is sinking. And here I was worried about crossing a boundary with Carmine. Now, I not only have crossed one boundary, I tacked on another one: snooping around.

Before I could open my mouth to defend myself, he brings his index finger to his pursed lips, motioning for me to be quiet. The fierce look in his eyes has my heart beating so fast, I swear I can hear the blood swishing in my ears.

"I told you to make yourself at home, not snoop through my shit," he growls. His gaze shifts to the box that I clearly moved from its original position for a moment before diverting his attention back to me.

He continues, "Just like the locket I gifted you, I told you that I had the key. It also applies to that box you were trying to sneak into," he says, cryptically, as he reaches in the pocket of his striped suit jacket for a smoke.

As he lights up, it's then I look down and realize the jingle noise I heard when he entered the room belongs to the collar of the most unique-looking pit bull I have ever seen. He is albino, with beautiful, big, light eyes. The dog wags his tail as if he was waiting for me to notice him and prances over to me. An adorably welcome distraction, I kneel to pet him, hoping Carmine will move on from this.

"Don't think because Nada likes you that you'll get off the hook that easily," he says as he exhales dramatically.

Still petting Nada, I look up at Carmine, whose towering presence makes my bent knees feel even weaker.

"Sorry, I just—" I begin before he cuts me off.

"You just what?" he asks, with a tense jaw.

I pet Nada once more as he wags his tail and heads to the dog bed right by the fireplace that I somehow missed before. I follow Nada's prancing, trying to formulate the proper excuse as to why I was snooping around.

"You just what?" he repeats.

"Well, I was trying to tell you, but you interrupted me, for starters," I say, expecting him to have some smart-ass remark in return.

He bites down so that his teeth show, aligning in an awkward straight line. Sighing to let the smoke out of his mouth, he says, "Well, you have the floor now, Ms. Ricci, I'm dying to hear this."

Yea, me too.

I try to come up with some legitimate excuse as to why I was snooping, but I can't think of a damn thing. So, screw it.

"I don't have a good answer other than the box just spoke to me. I'm not going to waste your time with some bullshit excuse other than I was just fucking curious, and I'm sorry," I say bluntly. *Honesty is the best policy, right?*

"Good, it should," he says as a grin escapes his mouth, softening his tense jawline.

I roll my eyes and cross my arms, shifting my weight to one leg, as my one hip juts outward.

"It should?"

"Yes. Except, you need this to open it," he says, dangling the chain around his neck.

Men like Carmine Moretti don't crack easily. They

spend their lives crafting the perfect lie, which makes chipping away at it a slow, torturous process. Still, I am stubborn, so I take a stab at trying to chip away at his elusive, strikingly handsome persona.

"If it's supposed to call me, as you say, then why can't I open it?" I ask.

"Because," he answers plainly.

"That's it? Just because?"

"Be patient, *mi reina*. When I'm ready, I will show you the box. Until then, it stays untouched, do you understand?"

I shift my weight to my other hip, arms still crossed, starting to feel pure exasperation at the fact that he thinks he can just toy with me like this.

"Or what?" I say, tired of the games.

"Or I will find another use for this key around my neck," he says with a seductive smirk. He begins to rub the long skeleton key between his fingers in a suggestive way that somehow, even with the fury I feel toward him, makes my clit throb with need.

The need for him to move his hands from that key and onto me make my ability to maintain the thin line we are skating on futile. My stance relaxes as I approach him, wanting to get lost in his scent. "Is that supposed to make me want to behave?"

He licks his lips, tightly grabbing the long key that hangs from around his neck.

"I hope not." He grins.

Chapter 29

Carmine

That was close, *too fucking close.*

I knew bringing her here would be risky. I should have known that having my skeletons out in broad daylight was reckless. It's no surprise that the box, the books, all of this would call to her. She is the product of secrets, so why wouldn't she be attracted to mine?

The key that can unlock everything she so desperately wants to know is in my hand, but I don't want to unveil that just yet. I'm far more interested in what I can unlock from her this evening.

"So, are we done here?" she says with a look that contradicts the words that just came out of her mouth.

With you? Never, mi reina.

I look at the clock centered on the mantle. The gala started well over an hour ago, we could still go. Although, judging from the phone conversation I just had with Alex, I think it'd be best we hang back ... for safety reasons.

Wouldn't want history to repeat itself, being Halloween and all.

"Where do you go off to?" I hear her ask, snapping me out of my momentary fog.

A simple question with a complex answer. I head to fix us another drink, to divert the conversation. "Drink?" I ask.

She hesitates, not expecting my diversion. "Sure," she says, but I can tell by the look in her eyes that I am not off the hook just yet.

I begin to make our drinks when I feel her right behind me. "You didn't answer my question. Where do you go off to?" she asks again, this time cornering me, both literally and figuratively. Her warm vanilla scent permeates my nostrils as I finish pouring the vodka into her glass.

"If you're referring to me taking that phone call before, I do run multiple businesses, which I am neglecting at this moment to have you here," I internally cringe at my response to her. It is not her fault I can't fucking concentrate for shit when she is around. It's also not her fault that we are here tonight, of all nights, but it's safer for the both of us to be away from whatever Armando may or may not be up to.

I can tell she is not satisfied with my answer as she lets out an adorably frustrated sigh. She isn't going to let this go, then again, how could I blame her? I've simultaneously given her everything she could ask for and nothing she can tangibly grasp, or understand, for that matter.

"No," she starts, again. "I mean, where do you go when you drift off like you were just doing before? You have this intense, almost hypnotized look on your face. As if you are recalling something painful, yet you seem to take pleasure in the act of reminiscing."

"I'm a busy man, Ms. Ricci, I work late nights and rise early, and I zone out occasionally. I wouldn't read into it." She isn't buying it, once something is on Sienna's radar, that's it. A trait I admire, except for when I am trying to avoid her questions.

Before she can ask me another thing, I interrupt her thought process to help ease her off my trail. "It's just a busy night, with it being the gala and all."

Hoping that would help shift the conversation, I am surprised to see the look of utter annoyance on her face as she dives into her next line of questioning. "So, why are we here if it's so pertinent to have you attend the gala?"

"Truthfully, I didn't feel like it, it's terribly dull having to talk it up and schmooze with people I don't give a fuck about," I lie. I'm not about to tell her that our attendance there has the potential to be disastrous given what Alex has briefed me on.

Gala night has always been smoke and mirrors. Make appearances, mingle a little, while the bread and butter of our business works its way into the underbelly of the building. I made sure to be an integral part of the design process of the building. It was important to have escape routes, hidden doors, that kind of thing, so that our operation can run smoothly.

"If I'm being honest, I'm relieved you didn't have me attend the gala. Social situations like that are not my jam."

"Interesting you say that, because when I was on the phone earlier with my cousin, Alex, he said a woman named, Lana, I believe it was, was asking about you."

I study her face, waiting for a reaction. She stays surprisingly stoic, a constant surprise this one.

"I have a Titi Lana, but I doubt she would be at the gala, unless she has a new guy I don't know about who invited her."

"Could be, Alex didn't say," I answer as I take a gulp of my whiskey.

"Alex?" she thinks for a second, trailing off her words. "That is the guy from The Sandy Claws that works with Vanessa, right?"

Yes, Vanessa, don't remind me.

During our brief phone conversation, Alex updated me on a conversation he had with Vanessa earlier. Apparently, my father felt it important to disclose the possibility of shady dealings happening at the gala tonight. He said gala night has been notoriously plagued with tragedy and he feared tonight would be no different. Rich, coming from him since the majority of said tragic events on or around gala night happened because of him.

"Yes, he is my cousin," I answer her question, hoping that will be enough to exit this topic. "Interesting, didn't know you had family in law enforcement," she says, sounding surprised.

"Well, I guess we shouldn't do anything illegal, wouldn't want to get locked up," I joke.

Sienna looks at the clock on the mantel. "It's getting late," she says slowly, as if she is carefully choosing every syllable that comes out of her mouth. "I'm sure you'll want to make at least a quick appearance at the gala."

"I don't need to be there if I don't want to, it's the perk of being in charge." I grin mischievously.

Summoning her here under the guise of "working" for me was a mistake, because the lack of legitimate work I have for her will only fuel her suspicions more. And with making such a big to-do about it being gala night, and here we are not at the gala, her suspicions are going to grow until she forces me to surrender to her questions.

If it were up to me, I wouldn't have her work another day in her life. Not because I'm some misogynistic asshole. That's my father's title, not mine. I would rather have her spending her days fueling her passions and sharing her endless talents that this world is in desperate need of.

She takes the last sip of her drink and slowly walks it over to the bar cart. I can't help but stare at the way her ass jiggles slightly with each step she takes. Arousal rushes over me once more as I yank on the chain around my neck, as if that can relieve me of the desire trying to reemerge.

I was so busy trying to deflect our conversation that I forgot how naughty a certain someone was being. I almost forgot what she tried to do when I caught her snooping around. *Almost.*

Moving away from the bar cart, she makes her way back to the bistro table as she sits down. She begins to fumble her hands inside her bag, looking as if she is ready to leave.

"Where do you think you are going?" I ask in a devious tone.

She runs her hand through her thick onyx hair "I don't know, you tell me," she says with a sarcastic, lust-filled look in her smoky eyes.

"Sienna," I begin. "You wanted to unlock the box, but how about something else, instead?"

I can tell her interest is piqued by the delicious look smeared on her face.

"What can I unlock?" she asks in lustful anticipation. Her breath quickens.

I know she carries wounds that her soul has been trying to stitch together, but in time, she will see why I brought her here. But first, I am going to devour her with my tongue and key. Half pleasure, half punishment. Can't let her think snooping around is tolerated, though it's really just an excuse to get closer to her once more.

"It's not a question of what you can unlock, it's a question of what you want me to unlock for you," I answer.

Chapter 30

Sienna

As soon as the words leak out of his sadistic mouth, I feel an unfamiliar sensation begin to take hold of me. My heart feels like it is going to burst out of my chest, though it's unclear if it's from nerves or from the unhinged desire I feel creeping into my dampened center.

The need I feel in my subconscious is steering me down a dangerous path, with all routes leading to him. I must reach for whatever logic still lingers inside of my brain to resist the storm he is stirring inside me. If I don't leave now, my fate will be sealed, and I will be lost into the dark abyss that is him.

With my heartbeat drumming inside my chest, I abruptly rise from my chair, causing it to let out an ear-piercing screech against the hardwood floor as it falls behind me. The storm he has created inside me has me working on a two-sided adrenaline, both fueling my desire for him while giving me the power to attempt to resist him. I use the concoction of adrenaline as my cue to leave if it isn't already too late for me. Nothing good can come from his callous ways, just like nothing righteous can come from how my body will react to his depraved intentions for me.

My vision tunnels to my leather tote bag. "I think I am going to head out now," I declare, though not as confidently as I intended. It's like my body and mind are in a war, toying with me, dangling this man in front of me.

To my surprise, he says nothing. He doesn't fight me or try to convince me to stay. I don't know whether I should feel disappointed or relieved. Either way, I take it, and with both hands grasping the leather strap now slung over my shoulder, I head to the open doors. Expecting him to follow me, I turn back, spotting him standing by the fire, holding the ominous chain draped around his neck in one hand with Nada perched at his side.

We lock eyes just as a devious expression takes over his face. I ignore it, saying nothing and just as I am about to take another step, a whooshing sound penetrates my eardrums. Before I can process where the noise is coming from, the pocket door that stands just mere inches in front of me zooms past me, slamming shut. Followed by the sound of wood doors crashing closed, the image of a skeleton surrounded by florals flashes before my eyes.

I lower my gaze to see Carmine's hand locking the door. I see the fury he feels inside in the veins that are now raised throughout his hands. Exhilaration begins knocking at my chest as the familiar pulse of arousal continues beating between my now slick thighs.

The flash of ink escapes my peripheral as I am spun around, viciously. My purse drops from my trembling shoulder but doesn't fall to the ground as Carmine's hands are gripped tight on my wrist. He moves his hand for a second to let the bag thud against the floor before returning his hand to my wrist with an even firmer grip.

He leans into my ear, and before he can mutter even a syllable, the heat from his mouth sends shock waves throughout my body. "Don't kid yourself, *mi reina*, you can try to run all you want, but you can't hide from me. If I don't find you first, your soul will remind you that right here, right now, is where you belong ... with me." He clicks his tongue as his stern tone radiates through me.

He wraps his massive hands around both my wrists, handcuffing my hands together. He had me in such a daze I didn't realize that all this time I had one wrist free, I could have fought him off, but I didn't. It's like my body wouldn't allow me to.

Cuffing my wrists in his palm, he walks me back as his eyes pierce me with his ravenous expression. The chain around his neck swings as he takes one ferocious step after another. We continue to glide across the room, until my back hits the wall, making a *thud* sound. He raises my hands above my head, still clasped together by his grip, pinning me against the wall.

He leans into me, towering over my frame as I look up to his dark eyes. The scent of lingering tobacco mixed with his cologne invades my senses, as does the vibration of his baritone in my ear. "I know you recognize a part of yourself here in the dark corners of this room, don't you, Sienna?" His whispers send goosebumps all over my body.

I nod, unable to formulate a quick-witted response or any attempt at denying that his vague statement rings with truth. There is something about this room, about him, even about that fucking box that feels as familiar as it does mysterious.

In the short twenty-four hours I have known Carmine, it's obvious that he finds a sick pleasure in hypnotizing my body into submitting to his wicked ways. Everything is a riddle to him, a game of dangling snippets of truth in front of my face, making me grasp for hidden clues that only lead to more dead ends. It's like everything he does is with the intention of getting beneath my skin. Whether it is to pleasure me or irk me, he clearly gets off on getting a reaction out of me.

He leans in closer, this time it's close enough for me to feel his hardened length beneath his pants rub against me.

"Admit it, you don't want to leave. You'd rather indulge your curiosity and play a game with me." As the words melt off his tongue, he extends it and moves his tongue to the base of my neck, and in one swift motion, licks up my neck, melting me beneath the heat of his mouth.

I don't want to leave, because somehow, in some fucked up way, I feel like I am supposed to be here. The gala, Halloween, all of it seems too coincidental. I think about what this night has meant for so long, Mama's and Papa's murder, losing Leo, all of it, and I feel like Carmine knows who is responsible. I can feel it. He harbors secrets that belong to me, and I want to know them. Just as I want to know him, because maybe sharing the pain I have tried to run away from these last few years will somehow hurt less.

He releases my arms and reaches for the chain with the key around his neck.

The quiet yet calculated way he moves makes everything in me come to life. There is something within him, a beast, perhaps, that he tries to tame in almost every interaction I have had with him. A monster like that should scare me. But if monsters look like him, the only thing I should be afraid of is how much my demons want to come out and play with his.

I watch as he slips off his chain, burying it in his palm. He doesn't let go of it as he slowly unbuttons his pinstriped jacket. He walks to a garment hanger near the mantle and places the jacket on there before making his way back to me.

He has on a half-buttoned-up white shirt that does a terrible job of concealing the ink splattered across his skin. Murals of black and grey are painted all over his muscular body. I don't know where to rest my eye first as he begins to undo the remaining buttons of the shirt, until he takes it off, revealing a white undershirt that hugs the muscles of his torso.

He waltzes over to me, chain in hand, as I stand there in a trance still, with my back against the door. He brings his free hand to my neck, squeezing it just enough to make me gasp, but not too much that I don't enjoy the pressure of his grip.

His teeth gently nibble on my ear before he licks his lips to speak again.

"You and I have something in common. You see, when tragedy plagues your life, it brings with it a cloud of darkness that follows you wherever you go. You can try to run from it or ..." he stops for a moment, taking a deep breath in. It looks as if he is trying to tame the literal beast that is trying to work its way out of him. "You can take the power that the dark cloud gives you and make it work for you instead of against you. We share a common enemy. An enemy that has created a dark, ominous cloud over both of our lives. Now, the question is, do you want to go on living life broken or take the revenge that is rightfully yours?"

I squirm under his grip on my neck before he decides to let me go. I gasp for air, but just as my lungs try to expand to take in a breath, he crashes his mouth into mine, stealing my opportunity for new air to enter my lungs. Just as I lose myself in the bliss that is his mouth on mine, he stops abruptly, leaving me with a throbbing ache that nothing except him can fix.

I let out a flustered sigh, needing him back against my body, when he kneels before me. He inches forward slightly on his knees, and as he lifts his hands, he secures me firmly against the wall. With a deviously handsome glance, he stares up at me before grasping for my thigh, bringing it over his shoulder, now exposing my arousal to him.

He grins as if in approval at the way my sex is already slick as I wait for him to begin whatever he has planned for me.

Still glancing at the sight of my arousal, he licks his lips. "Who knew all this talk of revenge could get a woman going the way it has you?"

"You clearly don't know as much as you think you do about me, because the thought of making my enemies suffer makes me wetter than you ever could," I challenge him.

A delicious smirk falls from his lips at the boldness of my words that even shocks me.

"Is that a challenge?" he whispers, hovering his breath just above my slit. The simple act of his hushed words lingering over where I want him the most sends chills throughout my body. "If I have to keep you here all night, making you come over and over again until you can barely fucking walk, I will; just to prove you wrong."

He shifts his mouth to my inner thigh, as he bites down on my flesh so passionately it causes me to wince. Pain and pleasure radiate as his lips tease me. He continues this torturous dance on my inner thigh before lifting his head from in between my legs.

"Now, be a good girl and let me begin what I have been wanting to do since the moment my tongue left your pussy earlier."

As soon as he finishes his sentence there, his mouth is again diving into me. The way his tongue devours me makes my whole-body quake. I feel as though I am suspended in mid-air with a pleasure I have never experienced before him.

Lost in pleasurable bliss, I feel an odd sensation begin to form in my center. Through the wetness of my slit and the warmth of his mouth, I feel something cold. Jagged, almost. I peer down to see where this feeling is coming from, but I am unable to see anything other than Carmine's mouth suctioned onto my clit. Whatever he is doing feels equal parts uncomfortable and intoxicating.

I try to keep my eyes on him, but with each stroke of his tongue, I find myself shutting my eyes, leaning into this bizarre sensation. Then, I feel what I think to be metal go deeper inside me. I look down once more at Carmine working in between my legs when I see it.

The long skeleton key from his chain is now tucked between his thumb and forefingers as he methodically fucks me with it. The metal of the key feels cold as he glides it in and out of me. Its rigid texture against my wet walls feels better than I could have imagined. As if his mouth didn't feel good enough already, this strange thrill is bringing me to the brink of a release I don't know the rest of my body is ready for.

"What are you doing?" I exclaim between moans as he picks up speed, both with the key and his mouth.

He lifts his mouth from my dripping center, as his finger and key remain inside me, going in and out as he watches, momentarily, before looking up at me to respond, "You tried to unlock my secrets, so I am unlocking you."

I glance over to the box that remains on the shelf. This can't seriously be all over that damn box, can it?

He follows my gaze, and I feel the key dig deeper inside me. I squeal, though, it is more out of pleasure than out of pain as he clicks his tongue.

"Eyes on me," he reprimands me before bringing his mouth back to my clit.

If this is what he considers a punishment, him sliding a naturally ribbed object into me so I am on the brink of an orgasm, then I will gladly be punished by this man any day.

"That's a good girl," he praises between licks. "Now, I am going to finish you off with the only thing that will open that box you were eyeing," he says as he continues to glide the key into me, this time bringing his thumb to my clit. The mix of his flesh and the metal is making me want to burst immediately.

"So, when you want answers, you can think about how I made you come with the key that holds the answers your soul desires," he says, ominously, as he feverishly working the key inside of me as he moves his thumb to my aching center.

I want to know what the hell he is talking about, but I can't take it anymore. As he continues to move the key in and out of me, I feel the ridge on the end of the key scratch my walls slightly as I clamp down on it, as I come.

He leaves the cold jagged piece of metal inside of me as I revel in the aftershock of pleasure, he just gave my body. He twists the key once more before taking it out of me.

"You are absolutely delicious, *Sen,*" he says, admiring its dampened gleam

As he rises to his feet, I take his hand that the key is in, tossing it to the floor, disinterested in the secrets he has or the games he plays. The euphoric high from the release he just gave me, while undeniably amazing, was not enough. I realize that in this moment, I feel the unfamiliar sensation of addiction begin to strum up in my core.

Suddenly, the need for answers and logic dissipates, and in this moment, I want him, more of him than I'm sure he is willing to give me. But I will settle for the pleasure he brings my body for now.

I pull him in closer to me by the loops on his pants, his tall frame now towering over me. Our lips meet again, this time with a passion that gives the heat radiating from the fire-place a run for its money.

We make our way in front of the fire as he lays me on the floor, pinning me down once more, but this time with both hands as he works his mouth on my neck. As he kisses me, I feel a desperate desire to see what he is working with, so I wiggle myself free from his grasp. I begin to unbutton his pants, needing his length in my greedy hands.

While I work on freeing his length from his pants, he rises to his knees and leans over to the bottom shelf of the bookcase closest to us. He futzes around, searching for something, and I look up to see he is grabbing a condom.

He brings the condom wrapper to his mouth, about to open it when I pant, "It's okay, I'm on the pill, and I'm clean."

He doesn't respond, but I know he hears me, because he tosses the unopened wrapper to the floor. He then finishes unbuttoning his pants, sliding them down, along with his boxers, revealing his impressive, already hardened length.

I bite my bottom lip, admiring his thick, long shaft as I notice the length of him has an intentional pattern to it. At first, it looks to be a piercing, but there is nothing that protrudes through. As I look closer, I see that the almost ribbed-like texture seems to be coming from beneath the skin of his shaft.

A Devilish grin forms as he notices my eyes studying his length. He hovers over me as I lay there in torturous anticipation.

"I want to feel you dripping on my cock, *mi reina*," he says as he begins kissing my neck before traveling down to my collarbone. "Can you do that for me, pretty girl?"

I nod, then realizing I am still in my dress, but before I can sit up to try to take it off, the distinct sound of fabric ripping hits my ear.

His strong hands tear at the mesh fabric on the top of my dress, and like a ravenous beast, he doesn't stop. He keeps tearing the fabric, until I am left in literal shreds, aching more than ever for him to be inside me.

"Stop teasing me," I beg as I reach for his thick shaft, running my hand from the base to the tip. "You have me here, now fuck me," I pant in desperate need for him to take this ache I feel away from me.

As if he didn't seem ravenous already, somehow, hearing

me vocalize the need for him to fuck me sends him into a fury.

"Be careful what you wish for," he warns, gripping my hips with both his hands before raising me and flipping me around so I am on all fours before him.

He slams his length inside of me, causing me to flinch as I adjust to how deeply he penetrates me. Once he is fully inside, my walls accommodate his length, willingly. I don't know what is more impressive, the size of his length or the texture of it. As he moves at a feverish pace, I begin dripping, feeling the strategically placed grooves that are scattered throughout his length working me.

I let out a moan as he grabs my hair that is draped over my face, blocking my vision. He yanks my hair, wrapping it around his fist as he lifts my upper body while still inside of me so that he can kiss my neck as he ravishes my insides. He continues like this for a few more thrusts and then he releases the hand on my hip that his watch is on. He directs his attention to it, beginning to swipe, while maintaining his skillful pace inside of me, working me with his ribbed shaft. Confused, I try to turn from the tight grip he still has on my hair to look up at him.

"Don't worry, *mi reina*, this won't hurt ... that much." He clicks his tongue as he swipes something on his watch. Before I can process what he is referring to, I feel an intense rattling sensation inside of me. His thrusts intensify, as does the rhythm of whatever is vibrating. The unique texture of him not only massages my insides, but it also begins to shake me internally. His thrusts pick up pace, now matching the tempo of the vibration that is taking over my walls.

"Carmine," I moan.

He lets go of my hair as he immediately brings his hand over to my clit. Between the circular motions of his fingers on my clit mixed with his skillful plunges inside me with this indescribable beat of his dick, it's just too much. It's too good. I yelp an unrecognizable sound of pleasure, one I didn't even know I was capable of, as I am close to finishing.

His digits glide around my sweet spot as they are now slicked with immense arousal. "That's it, *mi reina*, surrender to me," he grunts, continuing to work me into oblivion. "Give in to me."

The sensation of him inside me feels like a darkness is claiming me. Taking my soul with each thrust. I lose track of time as I lose the will to hold in the climax beginning to mount in me. I give into it, surrendering my body to him and as my release begins, capturing his length within my walls.

As I finish, he brings his watch back up into view, feverishly swiping the screen, making the vibrating cease. Instead, I am met with the equally pleasurable natural pulsing of his length as he pours his venom in me.

He is still inside of me as we both are lost in a heated, post-orgasm bliss, when a loud crash comes from what sounds like upstairs. Nada begins aggressively barking in response to whatever the commotion is. Carmine pulls out of me, with his dick still glistening from our combined arousal. He slips on his pants with a troubled look on his face. Grabbing the pistol, he had hidden behind a painting near the window, he tosses his white shirt and jacket from the floor in my direction.

"Here, put these on and shut the door behind me. Do not leave this room until Eric comes in to get you. He should be waiting outside to bring you home. I will go get him. Do you understand me?" he urges.

I nod, trying to process what the fuck just happened. I have questions, like what is that magic that is his vibrating dick? What is that noise? All of it. I don't want this to end yet. I guess I'll find out after.

Pistol in hand, he slides open the door before looking back at me once more. "Told you it wouldn't hurt," he hisses with a smug expression as he vanishes into the dark hallway.

I shut the doors behind him and wait for Eric to come get me. I let out a sigh of relief, feeling safe...for now.

Chapter 31

Carmine

Leading with my pistol, I leave Sienna in the study as I quickly make my way to the front door of the brownstone. I turn the knob, expecting to have to walk at least a couple of feet to meet Eric at the town car, but just as the door swings open, I am startled as I see him already standing there just outside the door.

"Eric." I nod as I lower my pistol to my side, though I don't holster it just yet.

I still am uncertain about him. I don't like the way he slithers like a snake, trying to insert himself in places he doesn't belong. His moves feel as calculated as his words feel hollow.

His aura is deceptive, his presence is a nuisance. He is a snake in the garden, and I should know, takes one to recognize another.

"Mr. Moretti." He nods back as he takes his hands out of his pockets to take out the earbuds in each ear.

"Sienna is getting dressed. Go inside and meet her in the

study. See to it she gets home safe," I sneer. Petty comment, yes, but if I must keep my potential enemy close, I might as well have a little fun reminding him of what he can no longer have.

Even under all that poorly manicured facial hair, I can see his jaw clench in response to my low blow.

Expecting him to follow, I half turn my back to him to head back inside, but he just stands there, with a dumbfounded look on his face.

Frustration begins to seep into my veins. I don't have time for this. I need to get Sienna out of the brownstone and figure out what the fuck made that noise upstairs.

"Today, Eric," I remind him, as I motion for him to follow me with the hand holding my pistol.

He stares at the shiny metal, the streetlamps outside the brownstone reflecting on the barrel. A subtle, friendly reminder that he should do what he is fucking told.

"You got it, Boss," he says, snapping out of his trance. Finally, he follows me back inside. I walk slightly ahead of him, but not so far ahead that I can't keep him within my line of vision. He takes his cell phone out of one pocket and begins rapid texting, his thumbs moving a mile a minute, but his eyes aren't looking at the screen. Instead, they are fixed on me.

We make it to the study; the doors are still shut as I instructed Sienna to keep them.

"She's inside the study. When I head up the stairs, I want you to take her home, immediately," I order.

An unwelcome grin forms on his face, feeling out of context from how our interactions usually go. Not to mention, I'm instructing him to take Sienna home, so what he could possibly find amusing in this scenario is equally as baffling to me as it is maddening.

"Now, Eric," I demand, not hiding my vexation.

"You got it, Boss," he says condescendingly.

He glances down at the pistol in my hand as he inches toward the pocket door to let himself into the study. Just as I think he is finally obeying my orders, he stops, and again, I am met with a condescending look.

"You know, Mr. Moretti, old houses like this, no matter how nice you fix them up, they always seem to have issues." He now steps away from the door and steps to me. "You can fix the exterior of something all you want, but if the interior is decaying, you got yourself a problem."

I really am growing tired of this motherfucker.

"I don't have time for riddles, Eric. If there is something you need to say, then fucking say it."

I begin to walk down the hallway to finally head upstairs to see what the fuck that strange noise was. I am not two steps up when I hear Eric once more. "That noise was probably a leaky pipe, is all," he says as he finally disappears into the study to retrieve Sienna before I can reply.

As I walk up the stairs, trying to keep my weight on the center of each step, which are adorned with a black and white baroque pattern runner to soften the usual creaking sounds, I realize something.

I never told Eric what I was checking upstairs. So, how would he know I am inspecting a sound? Better yet, how could he have heard it if he was outside with an earbud in each ear?

Chapter 32

Sienna

I hear the faint murmurs of Carmine and Eric exchanging words in the hallway. I can't make out exactly what they are saying, but knowing the two of them, I'm sure it's some petty cock measuring contest.

The fire that once roared in the fireplace is slowly dwindling. So, as I wait for Carmine and Eric to stop verbally sparring, I scan to see if Carmine has a poker of some sort to help move around the logs to resurrect the blaze. The stupid box stands out at me once more. I debate grabbing it to sneak a peek, but dismiss the thought, because as much as I enjoyed the "punishment" Carmine had for me, something tells me I won't get off easy a second time.

Grabbing the wrought iron poker, I bend slightly to start moving the logs around. The warmth of the fire radiating on my face is a welcome contrast to the slight chill I feel from the lack of pants or panties beneath my current ensemble.

A cool breeze nips at my ass as I hear the door slide open. *Great, Eric.*

He clears his throat, signaling that he is about to enter the room. I play with the logs and embers once more before setting the iron piece down, turning to face Eric for my walk of shame.

"Nice outfit, Sienna," he says sarcastically. "Black and white stripes suit you." He is trying to make me feel embarrassed, and if he were, perhaps, kinder to me, like the friend I used to have before sex made things complicated, maybe I'd be more embarrassed. But now? I'm just over it.

"Ready to go?" I ask, petting Nada goodbye before reaching for my purse.

Eric looks over his shoulder to the hallway before scanning the study. He looks nervous. A shift from his sarcastic demeanor he presented not just a few moments before.

He reaches for the car keys, dangling them. "Yea, just take the keys and head to the car. It's parked out front. I'll be right there."

Confused as to why he would need to hang around in Carmine's brownstone any longer than necessary, I decide to push his buttons a bit. See if I can figure out why he has already looked over his shoulder twice in less than two minutes, rocking slightly on the heels of his dirty, checkered grey Vans.

"That's okay, I'll wait to walk out with you."

He hesitates, clearly not expecting my response. He rubs his hand through his beard, taking in a deep breath.

"No, I said I'll be right there," he says once more, except this time, he isn't even looking at me. Instead, he has his attention directed at his phone as he swipes to message someone.

Bored of this standoff Eric and I have found ourselves in,

I decide to give up and just head to the car. As much as I am loving the scent of Carmine that his clothes are drenched in permeating my senses, a glass of merlot and a bubble bath are calling my name right now to end this eventful evening.

"Alright, Eric," I finally oblige as I go to walk through the dark hall and to the front door. I look back to see if Eric decided to follow me out, but all I see is an empty hallway and the dim light coming from the study, as I exit the brownstone.

I press the button of the key fob, unlocking the car, and slip into the backseat. Not even two minutes later, Eric scurries out of the brownstone and, at first glance, it looks like he is talking to himself. I inch toward the car window to see what he is doing, when I notice the white earbuds in his ear. Whoever he is talking to has him a bit more animated than usual. I also can't help but notice how tense he looks.

Curious as to who the hell he is talking to, I try to discreetly lower the window just a crack to hear what is going on. Despite the noisy cars that pass by and the groups of trick-or-treaters still making their rounds, I am close enough to make out some of what Eric is saying.

"I have to drive her back. Just be quick," I hear him mutter as he approaches the car. He looks up and at the back passenger window. I panic, even though I know he can't see me with the tinted windows, but the cracked window, well, that he can see clearly. I wait until he walks in front of the car to get in to raise the window on the off chance he didn't notice.

I settle back in the seat with my heart racing, but I try to play it cool. He opens the door and slams it shut, not saying a word to me. I look forward and see his Beetlejuice tattoo as he reaches for the radio, turning on some 80's rock station. He looks in the rearview mirror and catches me looking at him. Instead of saying anything, he raises the volume slightly. I can see his mouth still moving. So, clearly, whatever conversation he is having, he doesn't want me to hear. He moves his lips a few moments more before ripping the earbuds out of his ears, throwing them onto the empty passenger seat.

I jolt forward as Eric slams on the gas, driving us into the busy city streets. I'm relieved he is in no mood to talk, because truthfully, neither am I.

As I cross my legs, I feel the dampness between them still, which makes me feel cold. I turn the knob on the back-seat heat to warm me, when I see my phone light up with three missed messages, all from Nessa.

"We need to talk."
"Don't ignore me, I know you are at his place."
"When will you be home? Girl, we need to talk."

I need to text her back and let her know I am on my way home. I love how protective of a friend Nessa has always been, it's one of her best traits. Her fierce loyalty and protective nature, it's what makes her such a good cop. Well, now, detective. However, now that she knows I not only work for Carmine, but I spent time alone with him, she is going to be extra protective.

I text Nes back, letting her know that I will be home soon, and that Eric is driving me back. I toss my phone back in my purse so I can just close my eyes and ground myself a bit more before getting home.

I feel the car swerve, waking me from my attempted rest, when I try to see what the hell Eric is doing. I see he has one hand on the wheel and the other is down, texting feverishly.

"Hey! Quit it, you're going to get us killed!" I shout over the music.

He doesn't respond, but he throws his phone down on the floor of the car in anger.

I roll my eyes and sit back in my seat, not knowing what has gotten into him tonight.

We finally pull up to the apartment and I am crawling in my skin to get out of this damn car. I barely allow the car to come to a complete stop before I am trying to open the door handle. But the second I go to lift the handle, the music stops, as the locks click. Unable to lift the lock, I move forward in my seat and tap Eric on the shoulder. "Let me out, Eric, I'm tired and I want to go home."

He doesn't say anything, and still, the door remains locked. I move the handle back and forth in anger, even though I know it's useless, it won't open until he unlocks it.

"Let me out, now," I demand.

He reaches his hand to the back headrest of the passenger seat to adjust his gaze on me.

"Eric, stop, you are scaring me," I plead.

"You should be scared, but not of me," he says, unconvincingly.

"And how is that? You are acting like an irrational, jealous—"

He cuts me off. "Jealous what, Sienna? I would choose my words wisely if I were you," he warns.

Throwing my hands up in the air, wanting to just forfeit this conversation with him, I settle myself back in my seat and wait for whenever the fuck he decides to open the damn door. He can't keep me hostage here all night. *I hope.*

He sighs in disappointment, as if he was looking forward to whatever smart-ass remark, he thought I had for him. Ordinarily, I thrive on back-and-forth banter like this, but now, I am just tired. I'm also freezing because Carmine's suit, while comfortable, does absolutely nothing to keep me warm.

"Just be careful," he warns, bringing down his intense tone a bit.

"I will be, now let me out, please. It's getting late," I urge him.

Still, the car doors remain locked.

"I said be careful," he grits through his teeth.

"I heard you. Now, let me the fuck out. This isn't funny, Eric."

A sinister chuckle vibrates from his throat. "No one ever said it was funny. A man like Mr. Moretti has more skeletons in his closet than a graveyard has dead bodies. I suggest you heed my warning, or I fear the joke will be on you."

An ironic warning coming from Eric, who is keeping me in this damn car for his sick amusement, while vaguely threatening me with his riddles.

"Whatever, Eric, unlock this damn car, now."

The lock clicks, finally, as he unlocks the car. I grab my purse to hustle out of the backseat as he warns me one last time, in case I didn't hear him already, with the numerous warnings he gave me while holding me captive.

I slam the car door shut and cross my arms, trying to bundle myself more in Carmine's jacket. Eric doesn't drive away yet, and I can feel his glare on me, but I don't care. I hurry into the lobby of the apartment to warm up.

As I wait for the elevator to come down, I briefly ponder Eric's warnings. I know there is some truth to them. I'm not stupid. I know there are demons Carmine tries to hold at bay, but I'm okay with that. What Eric doesn't realize is my bigger concern is trying to figure out if Carmine's demons want to end me or play with the ones I have tried to suppress for so long.

Chapter 33

Carmine

Adrenaline fills my chest as it travels to my ears, robbing me temporarily of my hearing. I continue up the stairs to see where that noise came from. It was such a loud thud, almost like someone dropped something heavy or stomped their foot. Trying to rack my brain for what could have made such a sound, I lead the way with my pistol, just in case.

With bated breath, I begin to scan the hallway before investigating each room. The upstairs of the brownstone, although ornate, is small. There's just a rectangular landing that leads to my bedroom, the bathroom, and a small utility room.

So far, the landing looks untouched, not that there is anything to the landing, aside from the glistening oak wood floor. Each door to the three rooms upstairs looks just as I remember leaving it. All ajar, so nothing peculiar there. I walk through the doorway to my bedroom first and flick on the light switch swiftly with the tip of my gun. I stand on the threshold and examine my still-made bed. Not even an imprint on it.

Back out onto the center landing, I make my way to the bathroom, remembering Eric mentioning something about a leaky pipe. In all the years I have lived here, I have never had any issue with the plumbing in the upstairs bathroom, despite the age of this place.

The bathroom is small, with a large white clawfoot tub that I upgraded to shortly after moving in, taking up most of the space. The first thing I do in the bathroom is quickly open the curtain, thinking if someone were hiding, that would be an obvious hiding spot. But as I move the thick, white curtain, nothing is there but an empty tub. I then inspect the exposed plumbing of the tub and there are no leaks. The only other possibility of a leak would be from the sink. I open the vanity doors and with my empty hand, feel under the sink, and just as I suspected, it is completely fucking dry. Not a drip, fucking nothing.

Despite the coast being clear, relief is the furthest thing from what I am feeling right now. A suspicious rage begins to take over as I grip my pistol tighter before making my way back downstairs to the study. The supposed leak, the loud bang suddenly feels more like a distraction technique than impending danger.

I rush down the stairs to make sure the study and what lays behind it are still intact. I'm inches from the entrance of the study in the hallway when I feel a breeze hit my legs, first traveling up my spine. I walk closer, pushing the door all the way open to see the bookcase intact, thankfully, but the window is open. The curtains flail in the October wind. I go to close the window, rattling my brain as to what is going on, when I see it.

It can't be.

I walk closer in a panic. The study still feels chilly from the wind that blew in prior to me shutting the window, but my body is encompassed in sweat. The thought of intruders trying to kill me in my own home is more comforting than what my eyes are witnessing right now. I can't fucking believe it. It's gone.

The box.

Fucking Christ.

The box is fucking gone.

Well, tonight just got a hell of a lot more interesting. Now, I need to check on The Sandy Claws and make sure none of my other secrets are being exposed. It looks like my list of enemies just got longer.

I take my usual seat at The Sandy Claws, relieved that, despite it being Halloween night, the crowd is back to usual. Slow and somber, just as I like it. It's almost bar close, so most people have already cleared out. Only a few regulars and some cliché costume-clad patrons remain.

I light a Parliament, feeling like I can finally take a deep breath and attempt to relax. Tonight, did not go as I anticipated, but fuck, was it worth it.

I still need to be filled in on how the gala went without me. I'm sure Father will chew my ear off, lecturing me for my lack of attendance, but being in Sienna's company is worth my father's wrath. *Always.*

Now that I have gotten my fix of her, I'm afraid nothing and no one can stop me from feeding my addiction. No one will do but her; *it's always been her.*

Fuck, just thinking of this evening with her at the brownstone resurrects a part of myself I almost forgot even existed. I wasn't made to worship an invisible God in a pretend palace in the sky. I was made to worship her. Every fucking delicious inch of her. Her body is a conquest I will never tire of. The way I made her surrender her inhibitions only feeds my desire for her.

She's worth any trouble that may head my way. Now with this box missing, and the likely possibility of an intruder or thief at the brownstone, it looks like trouble has come for me, trying to ruin my plans for her and I.

As I exhale the smoke from my cigarette, I spy an unexpected guest heading my way. Dressed in an all-black, fitted pants suit, Vanessa practically storms through the velvet entryway curtains. Her eyes are a metaphorical gun aimed right at me. *Joy.*

I motion over to José, who is solo behind the bar, to bring me a drink.

"What can I get you, Boss, the usual?"

"Please." I say to him as I take a long drag, letting the smoke fill my lungs once more, preparing myself for whatever Vanessa needs to speak to me about.

She stops right in front of the table I am sitting at, widening her stance with both hands on her hips. She is trying so hard to stay composed, but the anger coursing through her petite frame is speaking loud and clear. Beautiful and angry, a lethal combination in a woman.

"Ah, Vanessa, right? How can I help you this evening?" I ask, taking a quick drag, blowing it where she stands.

She wafts the smoke away. "Didn't anyone tell you how bad those things are for you? Not to mention, illegal to smoke indoors ... as I mentioned to you last night." She rolls her eyes.

"Unfortunately, the worse things are for me, the more I am inclined to partake in them," I confess. "Please, do sit." I motion for her to join me even though I know whatever she is here for is likely not good. However, I must play my cards right and if playing nice with Sienna's cop friend is what it takes, then so fucking be it.

She hesitates before finally taking a seat across from me. She sits strategically, moving the jacket of her suit back so her Glock is front and center.

"Anyway," she says, flustered. But as she is about to begin whatever spiel she has for me; I catch Jose's attention once more.

"Yea, Boss," he says, slinging a rag over his shoulder

"Make that two whiskeys, one for my friend here, along with mine."

"I will have nothing, thanks, that's not why I came here," she says, trying to refocus.

"If you didn't come to a bar—*my bar*—to drink, what did you come here for?" I press her.

"Listen, Mr. Moretti, I'm going to cut right to the chase. What do you want with Sienna?" she asks bluntly.

"I don't know what you are talking about. I hired her to work for me, that's all."

"Let's call a spade a spade here. You didn't just hire her,

you sought her out. There is a difference. Now, I want to know why that is."

I lean back in my chair. "Is there now? I mean, technically, don't all employers seek employees?"

"Don't play games with me, Carmine, if that's even who you really are." She squints her eyes in suspicion, studying me for a moment.

"You look a bit flustered, are you sure you don't want that drink?"

"Listen, your charming bad boy act may work on most of the girls in here, but it isn't going to work on me, and it certainly isn't going to work on Sienna." She sneers.

Seemed to work just fine on her a few hours ago.

My cock hardens momentarily at the thought of Sienna's moans replaying in my mind. Nothing brings me more pleasure than pleasing her.

"Sienna has been through enough in her life, she doesn't need you to involve her in whatever messy shit you have got yourself caught up in," she warns.

"Oh, darling, no one knows the pain Sienna has gone through in her life more than I do. She is everything I plan on saving, including myself," I blurt, feeling anger suddenly take over.

"She warned me you talk in riddles."

"She talks about me, huh?" I try to bring the intensity down in my voice, instead opting for my usual sarcastic, condescending tone.

"I just want to know how and why Sienna fits into all this. If your father goes through with the deal, that we will potentially make with him, you could stand to lose everything. Your freedom, your reputation, The Sandy Claws, Marked Inc., all of it gone. So, why bring Sienna into this?"

"And what deal is this?" I ask in genuine curiosity.

"Well, I can't disclose that information to you, Mr. Moretti."

"Doesn't surprise me, the man is a coward. He would make a deal with a tree if he thought it could get him out of trouble. He is what we call a rat in our line of work."

"Interesting," she says, raising a brow.

"How so?" I reply, not sure if I follow.

"The dynamic, or lack thereof, between you and your father is interesting at the very least."

"What's not to get? It's a tale as old as time. Father brings son into the world, makes him a sacrifice to absolve him of his own sins, while he gets all the glory and freedom."

Vanessa just stares at me with a blank expression. I guess she wasn't expecting a crash course in mine and my father's fucked up history.

"Poetic, huh? A father's love so great that he wishes suffering on his son in exchange for his salvation. My father has a God complex, he thinks he is untouchable when, really, he is just a fool."

"Clearly, you and your father have some unresolved issues," she says, shrugging in discomfort.

You don't even know the half of it.

Vanessa thinks that me learning of my father's betrayal will break me. Luckily for me, my father broke me years ago. Her words are meant to scare me, but instead, they ignite my desire for revenge.

I need to end this conversation. Vanessa is starting to chip away at the facade I have worked so hard to build. This isn't a time for vulnerability, this is a time for battle. I need to end my father and absolve myself of his wickedness once and for all. Freeing myself, freeing *mi reina*.

I put out my cigarette and immediately grab for another one. As I light the tip, I see Vanessa's agitation begin to build with me.

"You know, since you know so much about my family, why don't we talk about your cousin, Eric?"

"What about him?" she asks, her jaw tensing as she clearly doesn't want to discuss him.

"As I am sure you know, he works for me."

She nods. "Unfortunately," she says as she rolls her eyes.

"I know that he has a history with Sienna. Do you think he would let that get in the way of his ability to work for me?"

Shaking her head, as if I am throwing her off guard, which was the intention of my conversational detour, she responds, "I'm sorry, I'm not seeing what changing the subject to my cousin has to do with anything."

"Answer my question, Vanessa," I demand.

"Fuck that, you didn't answer mine. Why Sienna? What the fuck gives?" she shouts, standing up and making the chair skid across the floor.

I don't let her antics affect me. I chug my whiskey and glance over to José, who has been eyeing Vanessa and me this whole time. He is like a trained and loyal pit bull, ready to attack if I need it. I gesture to him to stand down. Vanessa and her badge do not scare me.

Clearing my throat, I respond to her. "My father isn't who he appears to be. He paints himself a saint when he is as wicked as they come. He has destroyed any semblance of normalcy or hope that I could have ever had in life. He thinks he can write the story of my life however he sees fit. He may have conjured up a story for you, but I have control of its ending."

Vanessa looks confused, as I intended her to be. I speak cryptically on purpose; it is to get people stuck in their head and distracted from whatever it is they want from me. It's like a conman's magical power. Works every time.

I get up from the table and turn to Vanessa before I head to the back room.

"And to answer your question of why. It's always been about her, that's why."

She and I are simply meant to fucking be.

Chapter 34

Carmine

10 YEARS AGO

"Snap out of it, already. I'm tired of you acting like a prissy bitch," my father mocks as I sit at the kitchen table, wondering what the hell I did to deserve a man like him to be my father.

"She's lucky she is even alive to experience grief. That's her punishment," he says with a smug chuckle I would like nothing more than to smack off his face.

"Her punishment for what? Being born into a family she had no fucking say in?" I ask, curious as to why my father builds these vendettas that he has against everyone.

He grabs a smoke, laughing at my question, only fueling my rage. I know more than anyone what it means to be born into a family that drags you down. My father drags down everyone in his midst.

"Just because you have a hard-on for her doesn't mean you can save her. She doesn't even know you exist, so don't be a fucking creep. You'll get over her once you let another broad get under you. That's how it works." My father sneers.

Clearly, heart-to-heart interactions are not his forte. Most interactions that require him to have one iota of compassion are beyond him

"Oh, that's how it works, huh?" I roll my eyes, tired of my father's disregard for, well, everyone and everything.

"Listen, don't be a fucking smart-ass. I'm your father, I'm telling you that's how it works. Plenty more pussy where that hoe came from. You can't trust women, keep them at a distance, but close enough to suck you off when needed."

Wow, what fucking riveting, heartfelt advice, Father.

I get in his face, seething with anger. How dare he talk about her like that, after what he did to her.

"You don't get to talk about her like that." I spit in his face, unintentionally, but I don't regret it either.

"Oh yea, what are you going to do about it? You don't exist to her," he reminds me, only fueling my anger.

He continues. "One day, Son, you will thank me. When this empire I have built is yours, you will sit back and thank your old man for teaching you difficult life lessons."

I roll my eyes and laugh.

"Something amusing you?" he asks, irritated at my demeanor.

"Difficult lessons? You haven't taught me anything, you have created almost every difficult situation that I have ever been in."

This man is a literal walking, breathing cancer, he sucks the life out of anyone in his presence. The longer I am in his presence, the more I feel myself slowly withering away from who I need to be.

"How so?" he asks, with a confused look on his face.

God, this man is so dense, it's pathetic.

"I'm not playing games with you, Father. You are a disaster, and you leave a bloody trail everywhere you go, expecting the clean-up crew to pick up after you."

"Yep, damn right, and it makes me a better man," he says with pride, not realizing how delusional he is.

"That's rich, coming from the man who slaughtered my mother because she had a bigger set of balls than you could ever have."

Rage is filling his fat mug, making him turn fire engine red. "Don't you dare disrespect me in my house!" he roars

He cuts me off. "You know why I did what I did. She didn't want to uphold her end of the bargain."

"Bargain? How could any situation that results in being stuck with you be a bargain?"

"Listen, Carmine, marrying a made man means you take a back seat as a woman, you stand there and look pretty, you do as you are fucking told. She couldn't do that. Even worse, she didn't want you to fulfill your birthright, to become a king in our world. Being a made man is a privilege, your mother just couldn't see that. So, I did what had to be done," he says with such a false sense of pride it disgusts me.

"This was never meant for me. It was supposed to be—"

He cuts me off. Pain masked as rage takes over his trembling voice. "Don't you dare speak his name in this house."

"Why? You had two sons, why can't we fucking talk about him?" I provoke him.

"Because I fucking said so, now quit it," he seethes between gritted teeth.

"Or what? You set our family on fire, all because you couldn't accept what happened. I'm tired of being punished by you."

"You don't need her," he tries to warn.

"You don't know anything about me or what I need."

"I know that you need to watch how the fuck you talk to me," he reprimands.

"Ha, you fool," I begin. Father goes to interrupt me, but I charge him, pinning him against the wall with my forearm against his throat, cutting off his air.

"You don't know what you started by trying to mold me into your protégé. The student will surpass the teacher, when you least expect it, and Sienna Ricci will be the least of your fucking worries, you piece of scum," I warn him, meaning every fucking word.

I release my forearm from his throat as Father gasps for air. Not so tough now.

"What the fuck is that supposed to mean?" he says, trying to regain a full breath.

"It means that you can't mess with fate. Our bodies may be apart, but our souls are marked, promised to each other."

"Yea, well, good luck with that. You are fucking nuts. Sienna never loved you; she loves Leo. You are no one to her."

I walk up to him and tense my jaw. "Leo is nothing compared to me."

"How's that?"

"Because he left her. Once I find her, I will replace him. I will consume her, and you won't be alive to stop me."

It's the souls that are meant to be ...

Chapter 35

Sienna

As I stare out the window, taking in the bustling city scape that lay outside the glass, I soak up the last of the fall ambiance that dresses the surrounding streets. In just a few days' time, these same streets will be covered in frosted greenery and twinkling lights, retiring their frightful décor until next year. It's as though the second the calendar reads November 1st, the switch from spooky to jolly is flipped, and everyone moves on like nothing ever happened.

I've tried edging forward like the rest of society on this day, but my heart has never allowed me. If only flipping the switch on my demons were that easy. My soul feels free on Halloween, it's the rest of the year that I must hold back and pretend the darkness isn't where I want to stay. So, while Christmas lights will be strung in the days to come, whatever light exists within me remains dim, succumbing to the shadows that keep their hold on me.

It is amongst those same shadows that consume me

where the remnants of grief lay dormant, sadistically waiting to torment me.

Grief is a tricky thing. It can be suppressed enough that eventually functioning day to day becomes possible, but the affliction it brings to the heart can never be escaped. Most associate grief with the first few weeks of excruciating pain after losing someone. But it is much more than a period of time we spend mourning the absence of our loved ones' lives. It's everlasting, unpredictable, and it shows up when you least expect it.

It can present itself in the nostalgia we feel when we are struck with the realization that life is no longer as it once was. Situations change; sometimes for the better, and sometimes situations become more complex, forcing us to grieve what once was and who we once were.

Grief comes and goes. In it we unfold parts of ourselves that we perhaps would have never met if they weren't touched by the ominous hand of affliction that casts a shadow on everyone in one way or another.

This reflection of grief often comes to me the day after Halloween, which has always felt so strange to me. Jack-o'-lanterns still adorn the fronts of people's homes, costumes are thrown about the floor from the night before, the leaves are drenched in autumn's best hues as they grace the ground. Yet, everything changes.

Often, I find myself grieving a time in my life when things didn't feel so heavy or confusing, for that matter. I miss the times in my life where existing didn't mean having to live with things continually changing or abandoning me.

This year, however, feels different. The grief is still there, but it is mixed with guilt. Last night was the first Halloween in years that I didn't sit around and sulk in my painful memories. Carmine was a welcomed distraction from all that has plagued me for so long. Although, Nes would disagree.

I was so relieved to not have to deal with her last night after Eric dropped me off. I didn't feel like dealing with the shitstorm that would have been her questioning me as to why I felt the need to be alone with Carmine last night.

It's not that Nessa's apprehension toward Carmine is unwarranted. It's just that I don't think he is as bad as she thinks he is. I mean, he's no saint, that's for sure, but in the little time that I've known him, I feel this justification in his darkness. It's like, every move he makes, even the sinful ones, are for a greater purpose.

Maybe Carmine is right about darkness. It gives you pain and sorrow, but his focus on the power it gives you, well, that resonated with me. Thinking back to his dark gaze last night, I felt as though I could feel grief in his eyes, but his body moved in strength, *in power*.

Perhaps, my perspective could be associated with being the daughter of a deceased criminal, but there is something good in Carmine, buried beneath his sinister persona. Either way, Nessa would never understand that sometimes, those who are perceived as bad are maybe more misunderstood than they are evil. Evil takes many forms, and oftentimes what shines is false and what is naturally dim is doing nothing but living its own truth.

I sip my coffee, still peering out the window, when I hear Nes open her bedroom door. I turn to greet her as she makes her way into our small, galley-style kitchen.

"Hey, Nes," I say to greet her, instantly regretting where I left the clothes Carmine sent me home in. I folded them and put them next to the coffee machine so I wouldn't forget to return them today, but there is no way she isn't going to notice or make a comment once she sees them.

She heads over to the coffee to grab a cup and I notice that her police vest is overtop her white sweater, which is odd. Not that she doesn't usually wear her vest, but it's typically concealed beneath her clothing.

"Hey," she greets back when her eye catches Carmine's folded jacket and shirt on the counter. She glances up at me with discerning eyes before redirecting her focus to the coffee machine, grabbing a mug from the cabinet above it to pour herself a cup.

"How was work last night?" I ask, trying to make small talk.

She pours her coffee before responding to me. "Be careful today. I know you are meeting with Carmine," she warns.

"Well, considering that I work for him, meeting with him is kind of expected," I joke, expecting at least a half-grin from her, but she remains closed-lipped, with a look of concern on her face. "You sound like Eric. Seriously, chill. I am perfectly capable of taking care of myself," I remind her, trying to brush off the agitation. I feel that everyone keeps treating me like I am some delicate, naïve girl instead of a grown woman who can discern things for herself.

"So, the late-night meetings at his place are also part of this expectation?" she presses, with a smidge of judgment laced in her tone.

"It was nothing." I blush.

"Right, that's why you have a freshly fucked glow still smeared all over your face," she points out.

I already know where this conversation is headed and I'm just not in the mood for it. I know Nes is only looking out for me, but I can deal with Carmine myself. I look down at my coffee mug, which is halfway full, and decide to pour the rest in a to-go Thermos to avoid whatever else she wants to lecture me about this morning.

"Excuse me, I need to get in the cabinet, I'm going to be late for work." I try to move past her, but she stays blocking my way. "Nes, seriously, move."

She steps aside, and I quickly grab the first Thermos I see. I bring it to my mug to pour the coffee so I can get the fuck out of here.

"I have to get going. I want to make sure I have enough time to grab a cab to make it into work on time," I say, trying to make as graceful an exit as possible.

"No need, Eric texted me already that he is downstairs," she says, staring at her phone.

That's weird, I wasn't made aware of Eric picking me up today again. I really hope this is not a permanent thing with Eric driving me around. Especially after how weird he was acting last night.

I go to the entry table, grabbing my keys. "You know, Nes, given how much you despise Carmine, doesn't it bother you that Eric works for him also?" I ask with genuine curiosity. It surprises me how nonchalant Nessa is about Eric working at Marked Inc.

"Honestly, yes. It bothers me a shit-ton, but this is the longest time Eric has been clean and out of jail. Why that is exactly, given Carmine's exceedingly sketchy persona, I don't know ... yet."

It's then I realize that in the time I had been hooking

up with Eric, I never even bothered to ask about anything in his life. Let alone allow a conversation to go deep enough to know that he had been in jail. And in all the years I have been friends with Nessa, she never brought it up. Maybe it's because she was embarrassed, or because she always wanted Eric and me to end up together, so she figured it would ruin his chances with me. Not that a little jail time would have deterred me from pursuing Eric if I wanted to.

All my father's friends and colleagues were always in and out of the system. It made me view crime as normal, made me ignore the things that most in society deem unacceptable.

I don't even know how to respond to that, so I don't.

"Alright, I'll see you later." I'm about to head out the door when Nessa runs up to me, grabbing my shoulder to get my attention.

I turn around, surprised by her intensity. It's not like this apartment is big, there was no need to run. She could have caught up to me or gotten my attention by taking just a few steps.

"Yes?" I look at her noticing the concerned look back on her naturally beautiful face.

"Please, if nothing else, just be alert," she warns.

"Nes ..." I begin, pouting my lip as I take my free hand to her shoulder. "I can handle myself, I'm a Ricci, remember?" I bring her in for a hug to reassure her I know how to handle a man like Carmine. I spent my life surrounded by plenty of men like him. Granted, none of them were so eager to please me or looked like an inked-out, chiseled god, but that's beside the point.

"That's what concerns me," she says as we move from our embrace.

"What? That I am a Ricci?" I ask.

"Yes." The relief our embrace gave her dissipates immediately, and a pressing look washes over her face.

My brow lowers as I shake my head, trying to unravel her warning. "Nes, what are you getting at?"

She doesn't respond, but instead, moves to the small safe she keeps underneath her desk adjacent to the galley kitchen.

She bends to turn the dial to unlock it, and when she stands up, she has a small black revolver cupped in her hands.

Not that I am unfamiliar with guns but seeing her about to hand me one immediately snaps me out of my daze. "Vanessa, what the fuck?"

"I can lose my badge for this, but I want you to bring this with you today."

"To work? Are you fucking crazy? Why do I need to bring a gun to work?"

"If what I suspect is correct about Mr. Moretti, this is the least of your worries. Just take it, you know how to use it." Vanessa hands me the revolver. I look to her as she nods her head in approval. I unzip the front pocket of my purse and slip the revolver inside of it before heading to the door.

It has been years since I last shot one of these. Papa used to take me out to the range whenever he felt a moment of guilt that he wasn't home enough. Since I was an only child and not a son, Papa's idea of bonding was mostly centered around things that he wanted to do. It didn't bother me. I felt like when I was with my father, I could be myself. A woman, not a prim and proper lady, like my mother so desperately wished I would be.

I walk out of the apartment lobby to find Eric already sitting in the driver's seat of the town car. I'm relieved he doesn't come to the door to open it for me. After that interaction with Nessa this morning, and whatever was up with him last night, I am in no mood for forced pleasantries.

"Good morning," I greet him as I slide into the back seat.

"Morning, Sienna. Mr. Moretti informed me of a different meeting location today," he states as he looks to his side view before merging into the bustling avenue.

"Another location?" I ask, but Eric ignores my question.

My stomach drops as nausea begins to creep in, thinking of what this other location could be. Then, I grip my purse, remembering the little gift Nessa gave me this morning, which eases my anxiety.

I wonder if she had an inkling of where I would be working today and that's why she gave me her gun. I should be more concerned, but I know Nes, she is my best friend, she wouldn't feed me to the lions. She gave me the gun to protect myself, from what exactly, I don't know, but I will not go down without a fight, that's for damn sure.

I am here for a reason. In this city, in this moment, broken, stitched together by a needle and thread, but here, nonetheless. I was spared that night for a purpose, and now, I want to find out who is responsible for the situation I find myself in.

Chapter 36

Carmine

The morning light pours into the barren warehouse, bringing with it a welcome glow, highlighting my father's bound and gagged body on the metal chair he is still passed out on. I know I gave him a hefty amount of sleeping pills to be able to drag and secure him in place, but I was expecting him to be awake by now. Impatience begins to take over as I starc at my watch, trying to time this morning's pre-work endeavor, making sure I have ample time before Ms. Ricci arrives. I can't wait to hear her high heels tap the concrete floor of this warehouse as she witnesses the gift of my well-curated act of vengeance.

My shoes make an exaggerated crunching sound as I step on the plastic tarp I have laid beneath where my father remains bound to the chair. The crunching noise continues as I circle around him. He should be awake by now. Fucking Christ, this man can't even arrive to his death sentence properly.

After the discovery of the missing box last night, as well

as my little chat with Vanessa at The Sandy Claws, I called daddy dearest here under the guise of having a drink to discuss business at the warehouse. Naturally, he obliged my request, foolishly thinking I wanted some father-son bonding time. I scoff at the thought because I have zero desire to spend any quality time together.

He hates me just as much as I hate him. Though, for whatever reason, he accepted my invitation, giving me the opportunity to confront him about my mounting suspicions against him.

To my surprise, he showed up to the warehouse solo. A rare sighting, seeing as he always has his minions in tow. He is naïve to think that I wanted legitimate time with him. However, I am thankful because it granted me the opportunity to do what I have craved to do for so long, even sooner. Eliminate him from the space he takes up on Earth.

Before I could get to that part; I did what any loving son would do. I slipped him one too many crushed-up sleeping pills in his whiskey and waited until his pudgy system finally passed out. I then laid out this obnoxiously loud, yet effective, tarp and began the process of lugging his fat ass onto the chair and tied him up like a piece of meat about to be roasted.

Painfully aware that I am running out of time, and immensely eager to do what I have wanted to do since the day my father killed what little good was left in me, I kick his shin, trying to nudge him awake. His large calf feels like kicking fucking steel. If it weren't for the black dress shoes I chose to wear today, my foot would be throbbing. Still, he doesn't move, so I lift my leg once more, with more force in my kick.

A whimper falls from his lips, as he begins to wake up. Groggy still, his eyes remain closed as his large frame begins to wiggle slightly before coming fully to and realizing there are restraints on him.

"Oh, Father ..." I tease. "Wake up."

He wiggles his wrist once as he begins to come to, before jolting forward. Taking in his surroundings, his eyes widen as he tries to take a deep breath in. He begins to choke on the handkerchief I have stuffed in his mouth, and a devious chuckle escapes me as I revel in the bastard choking on his own air.

Ah, I suppose I should play the role of the loving son and save my father from his choking spell. It's only right. He should be able to speak his piece before I take away his ability to do so ... *forever.*

I rip the fabric from his mouth. Disgusted with the damp feel of the cloth, I throw it to the ground, where it falls on the tarp. I shake my hand in disgust as he gasps and chokes some more.

He looks at me with pleading eyes, finally realizing where he is. "Son, please, what is this?"

I take a smoke from the pack in my suit pocket and take my time dangling the lighter in my hand, slowly flicking it and bringing it to the tip of my cigarette. I inhale as I inch myself right in front of him, letting my height tower over him. Looking down at him, I exhale, allowing the smoke to billow all over him. He begins to cough and squirm some more, now rocking the metal chair, making an awful echo throughout the warehouse of crinkling tarp and metal hitting cement flooring.

"Please, do be considerate. This warehouse makes every little move you make echo," I taunt.

"Son, what is this?" he demands, anger trembling in his voice, as he regains more consciousness. I don't answer. Instead, I take another drag of the cigarette and let it hang out of my mouth as I raise my fist, crashing it into his pudgy face. He lets out a pitiful wail as I continue to pound my fists against the flesh on his face, causing his once-olive skin tone to become a shade of murky crimson.

His wails increase in volume with each hit, making me thankful for the warehouse's secluded location. His threshold for pain has never been as high as mine. Can't blame him, he is a cold-hearted prick who didn't have to live through losing all that I have.

I show no mercy by giving him a break between swings. As soon as I am done with one punch, I immediately go into the next. Just warming up for the finale, *his final act*.

When I decide he is banged up enough—for now—I finally let up. But not for his sake. No, my cigarette is dwindling down to the filter, and I wouldn't want to risk burning my lips. Oh no. These lips must stay in pristine condition. How else would I be able to taste every delicious morsel of *mi reina's* body?

He grunts as he tries to move both hands, trying to loosen the restraints. I notice one of the ties is beginning to come undone, so I take the dwindling butt out of my mouth bringing it to his hand.

I dig the tip into his flesh, twisting it for good measure as he roars in pain.

Now that I have him distracted in his increased anguish,

I run to my tool bag on the other side of the tarp and grab the nail gun.

My father's moaning ceases as he sees the nail gun in my hand, as I walk back to where he is restrained. He mutters something in Italian, as he tries to further loosen that pesky restraint that won't cooperate.

I click my tongue as I quicken my pace, raising the nail gun in the air.

"Son!" he attempts to yell, reeling from the pain as I bring my hand down, crashing the gun into his hand. Pressing the trigger, the quick and precise swish of the machine sends a large metal nail into his arm, pinning it to the metal armrest of the chair.

"Just for good measure," I say as I swiftly bring the nail gun to the other arm, repeating the same motion. Muffled screams and inaudible attempts at words drip from my father's mouth as the blood oozes from his flesh upon impact. I bring the nail gun down, admiring the pain I have inflicted on this sorry sack of shit.

His head hangs as he wallows in the agony that is surging throughout his body.

Glancing down at my watch, I see that I am ahead of schedule somehow.

"You know, Father, today has me feeling rather exhilarated since everything I have desired is finally coming to fruition," I say, condescendingly as ever to my father, whose head is still hung low. "Because of that, I'm feeling generous. I will give you a few moments to recoup so you have your energy to do what you've refused to do ... answer to me." I walk over and kick his shin. "Then, we will pick up where we left off."

I use the time to put away the nail gun and tidy up a bit before I approach him once more. As soon as his time is up and my feet crunch closer to him on the tarp, he begins to come to.

"Son, forgive me!" he cries out once more, the desperation and pain intermingling in his tone.

I hate when he calls me son, he is nothing but a sperm donor to me, and a treacherous one at that.

"It's a little late for forgiveness." I circle around him in the chair as he is trying to flinch his way out of the restraints. "Besides, what should I forgive you for, exactly? So many sins on one man's conscience. Forgive *me* for not being able to keep up," I say. He is so desperate for me to release him that he doesn't pick up on my sarcasm. Instead, he clings on to my words intended to mock him, once more pleading for mercy.

I chuckle, running my now throbbing hand through my semi-slicked back hair. The mixture of sweat and blood isn't enough to keep the single strand of my black hair from getting in my face. I shake my head, attempting to move it, trying to collect my thoughts. I have waited so long for this moment, to look him in the eye, to speak my piece.

"Please, Son, I beg you."

Ignoring his plea, I walk back to my little bag of tricks and sift through my options, trying to choose the next contender to inflict lasting pain on him.

"Please, Son, I beg of you. You can't do this," he pleads once more.

Clicking my tongue with my back turned to him, I raise one hand, signaling him to give up his pitiful begging.

"You know, Armando, a supposed wise man once told

me that Moretti men do not beg, and they certainly do not stoop so low as to beg for forgiveness." I stop for a moment, sorting through my bag before continuing my spiel for him. "I believe it was the same man who also said that Moretti men show no mercy, no matter what. Truly wise words, wouldn't you say?" I smirk, as I settle on my tool of choice for ending the motherfucker. A wooden bat wrapped in spiked chains, with nails poking out.

Bat in hand, I rise and redirect my attention to him. "Do you know who is responsible for ingraining in me such poignant words?" I jest.

He shakes his head, shocked that I would use his own motto against him. The look of betrayal on his face I must admit is pure bliss.

"I said that, but I certainly think that being your father, I am an exception to the rule."

"Are you though?" I ask, as I begin to walk toward him.

I admire the sharp metal nails scattered throughout the wood. Lifting the bat in the air, I swing it to practice. Fantasizing about how exhilarating it will feel to have this wreck his flesh.

I have never been much of a baseball guy; football has always been more of my thing. Though if baseball games were played with deadly bats such as the one that my fist is clenched around, then shit, sign me up to go see them Yankees play.

I begin to zone out with each swing, becoming giddy knowing that, today, I will inflict earth-shattering pain on him, kind of like the pain he has caused me. But luckily for him, the pain I will inflict on him is physical.

What he did to me, the internal pain he caused me ...

The kind that eats at your heart, chipping away at your soul, draining the life from your being, scarring your insides until you are nothing but a walking corpse? No, that kind of pain is everlasting. That's the kind of pain that I have been forced to live with. It's the kind of pain that has exposed the darkness that laid dormant in me for so long. It has never healed, and fuck, is it hungry for revenge.

I swing the bat once more, still in my daze, when I notice his mouth moving.

"Please!" he shouts, bringing my focus back to him. "I would never betray you."

My grip tightens on the end of the bat. "You are despicable. Even on the cusp of death, you still can't bring yourself to admit all your wrongdoings."

"Oh please, you act like you are a saint." Even swollen from the blows to his face, he still conjures up enough strength to be a delusional wise ass.

"The difference between you and me is that I never claimed to be a saint. I'm far from it. I don't deny my demons, I accept them, and in turn, they allow me to live my life freely. Unlike you, who can't accept your demons, so you punish others for your own downfalls."

"You can't be seriously punishing me for what I did to her parents? We were at war. I did what anyone in my position would have done."

Funny how he forgets the war he started in our family that happened long before what he did to the Ricci family.

"It's about many things. I'll get to your feeble vendetta with the Riccis in a moment. But why don't we start from the beginning?" I say as I swing the bat once more in the air, this time just a tad closer, making him flinch in fear. "Let's start with what you did to my mother, because you couldn't accept the death of your sweet golden boy, Car—"

My father freezes. This is the first time I have mentioned my brother's name to my father ever. He has stopped me every time, and for some reason, I obliged his request to not mention him, but I am fed up with biting my tongue. The death of my brother catapulted my life into a tailspin I have yet to recover from.

"How dare you!" he shouts, interrupting me.

"Yes, how dare I confront my father about the rampage he went on, lashing out at my mother for the death of her son? How rude of me. I'm sorry, Father, the truth too much for you to bear?"

He says nothing.

"Try carrying the burdens of your actions for the last decade-plus of my life. You couldn't accept what happened, so you ruined our lives and continued your rampage, hurting anyone that got close to us," I remind him, the anger scorching through me.

Clearly, I've struck a nerve because he tosses in the chair. Once again rocking the metal legs against the cold flooring, grinding my nerves.

"Son, the Riccis were no good—" he begins.

I swing the bat down to my side and use it as if it were a devious cane. I walk toward him, clicking my tongue.

"Focus, Father. I said I will get to the Riccis in a minute. But I am talking about our family, or what was of it, that is. You never respected my mother. You taunted her for your own shortcomings, and you could never accept that she left with your only remaining son. So, you waited, and when the time suited you, you killed her for leaving you. And what did that give me? A gaping hole in my heart and no fucking mother, that's what!" I roar.

"I had no choice, Son," he says in a pitiful tone.

I scoff at his despicable excuses. "No choice, huh? Tell me how you had no fucking choice when you drove to her sister's house and shot her, mid-fucking day. Only to drive off like a fucking coward."

"I had no choice; she knew too much. Then, she started associating with the Marinos and the Riccis, and I worked too hard to have some bitch take down my empire."

Unbelievable. I crash my fist into his jaw, hearing the cartilage click as he yelps in pain.

"You want to talk about choice? I had no fucking choice when you forced me to become the heir to your corrupt throne!" I shout.

"It was your eighteenth birthday, Carmine, it's tradition. To initiate the first-born sons into the family business."

"Except, I wasn't your first-born son." I begin say as my voice cracks.

"You act like you don't love this life. I made you into the man that stands before me today, you can't let bygones be bygones?"

Bygones be bygones. He is a bigger idiot than I even gave him credit for.

I spit at his feet. "You didn't answer my question from before, which of your sins should I forgive today? So many to choose from. Ah, yes ..."

"Carmine, please," he begs

"Don't call me that, you pathetic swine." I spit at him once more. "Do you think the death of my mother is forgivable? Then, threatening me that if I didn't go comply to your twisted demands, you would kill *her* instead?"

He interrupts me, "Sienna was nothing to you."

"Seriously? That's all you took away from what I just said. No remorse for ending your former love's life? Or ruining mine? No, the only thing you focus on, yet once again, is this foolish feud with the Riccis."

"You shouldn't speak of things you know nothing of, Carmine," he insists.

"I told you to stop calling me that," I order.

"Carmine is your God-given name." he says.

"Don't bring God into this, he isn't going to save you from my wrath."

I lift the spiked bat up and quickly scan the number of nails on it. "Shit," I exclaim with a false look of concern on my face, which gives my father a brief glimmer of hope, as if I'd let him out of this.

"What, Son?" he pleads.

"Oh, nothing, it's just that I suddenly realize I don't have enough nails on this damn bat," I say with increased sarcasm. I look to my father, who is finally realizing that he is responsible for this monster he sees before him.

His fat face turns a ghostly white as I retreat once more to my tool bag to add just a few more nails to my bat. He watches in stunned silence as I retrieve some long, extra sharp nails that I carefully hammer into the wood.

I continue hammering the extra nails as I address him again. "I know that you feud because you are weak, and it is in your rash bouts of weakness that you actually did yourself a grave disservice."

"How's that?" he whimpers.

"In your endless moments of weakness, you gave me the ammo I need to take everything from you, as you have done to me. An eye for an eye, so to speak. I can sit here and rattle off the endless grievances against you. You have stolen from me, killed parts of me, and now, just when I thought you couldn't disappointment me more, I find out that you are talking to the cops." I crouch so that my eyes are in line with his. "It couldn't be that Mr. Armando Moretti, the strong and ruthless mobster, is in fact, a rat, is he?" I ask, coyly.

He tries once more to lift from his restraints, but instead, the nails cut at his flesh more, causing him to yelp in pain as his blood begins to drip right where I want it to: the tarp, so that clean-up will be easier.

He takes a deep breath, trying as hard as he can to work through the pain coursing through his pathetic body. "Son, it's not what you think." He doesn't sound convincing.

"Ah, is that so? And why should I believe you?"

"I am many things, as you so obnoxiously pointed out"— he scoffs briefly before refocusing on his words—"but a rat I am not. If anything, it has been in my stepping back from the company and observing with fresh eyes, if you will, that I see the possibility of not one, but two potential rats in our midst."

Perhaps it's the adrenaline coursing through my veins as I stand the one in control, with a bat of death in my hand, but my father seems to almost be telling me the truth. Not that it would change the outcome of what I have planned for him today, but I'd be lying if I said my interest isn't piqued.

Before I press him further on his so-called observations, I decide to have a little fun with the bat in hand. Satisfied with the number of nails I have in the bat, I rise and approach my father, swinging the bat once more. Except this time, it is not a practice round.

Raising the bat with a vengeful fury, I channel all the rage I have inside as I crash down on his right thigh. He lets out an inaudible screech, which sounds like music to my ears, just as drips of crimson immediately begin to spew out of his leg, dripping onto the tarp.

Before I remove the bat from his flesh, I dig it in deeper, causing him to wince.

"I'll help you in a minute, Father," I say with a sadistic grin. "Now, what is this about not one, but two potential rats?"

Grimacing in undeniable pain, he moves his head slightly, nodding in agreement. I press the bat in just a tad deeper, as he yelps in pain.

"Fucking Christ!" he roars.

"You are going to have to do better than that if you want this bat out of your leg." I click my tongue sarcastically. "I'm having a hard time believing this, coming from a man who has been seen talking to the cops."

He hangs his head, and I'm not sure if it's in defeat or in pure exhaustion. I'm about to shake him to speak when he finally opens his trap.

"Let me guess, your fucking cousin told you that." He tries to roll his eyes, but the swelling prevents them from giving the dramatic effect he was going for. "He doesn't know what he is talking about."

Pressing down once more, I dig the nails into his thigh before removing it. The sound of screaming and ripping flesh penetrate my eardrum, echoing amongst the cold concrete of the warehouse. Blood drips from the bat, as particles of torn skin adorn it. I admire the carnage before addressing his stupidity.

"Unlike you, Alex has my undying trust. But it's not only Alex who warned me that you were trying to rat. Another officer did, as well."

He shakes his head. "Let me go, damn it, and I will explain," he pleads, rocking the chair once more, annoying the ever-living shit out of me.

I throw the bat down and rush him, pushing his heavy body to the ground, with him still nailed to the chair.

Through gritted teeth, I get in his face. "No. You are going to fucking tell me right where you lay." I spit at him, my saliva mixing with the blood that drips down his face. . "Now, hurry the fuck up before I bury you."

Reluctantly, he continues. "Son, you have been so fucking wrapped up in getting that fucking bitch to notice you that you have been unaware what's been going on around you. Same goes for that fuckface of a cousin you have." He stops, taking in a shallow breath before he continues spewing out his fucking bullshit. "You should be thanking me."

A deep chuckle roars from my gut, as I stand up and indulge myself in this much needed laugh. My father remains stuck to the chair I threw on the ground, looking up at me in confusion.

"What the fuck is so funny?" he mumbles.

"You." I let out another laugh before I steady my breath. "You are fucking deranged. Why the fuck should I be thanking you of all people?"

I wait for him to say some bullshit that will undoubtedly make my blood boil.

"I have noticed weird shit happening ever since you started fucking Lizzie. Nothing too egregious, but enough to make me wonder. Then, I noticed the same shit was happening to some of our previous colleagues. What I found extremely interesting is once you went behind my fucking back and brought that Ricci bitch into our establishment, even more suspicious things started happening. Twice as fast," he warns.

Aside from the jump that happened the other night when Jake was in the middle of a transport, my father is right about one thing: a lot of suspicious shit has happened lately. The box is missing, and there is money missing from our accounts. I discovered that gem once I received the finalized reports from Felipe after our meeting. A lot is off, but I still can't eliminate my father from the list of suspects.

"Ok, so if what you are saying is true, which sounds like a hell of a lot of speculation, why would you start talking to the cops?"

"To derail them from looking at Marked Inc., Carmine! If I put the heat on a possible duo that is committing crimes against us and other businesses alike, we give the cops what they want, while they give us what we need."

I take mental note of the emphasis he put on the idea of a duo being behind all this mayhem in our already chaotic underground. Once again, I can't tell if he is telling the truth. Maybe there is a duo, which he is a part of. Which wouldn't surprise me. But on the off chance that what he is saying is accurate, he is going to have to do a hell of a lot better than this drawn-out spiel.

"And what is that?"

I watch as his weakening body takes a deep breath in. He

lifts his heavy head slightly before slowly opening his trap once more. "We need to deflect from ourselves, you fucking fool," he seethes. "Fuck, I failed you more than I thought I did by not killing your mother sooner. The little time she had to raise you on her own, she poisoned your ability to fucking use your brain."

Rage overtakes me as I feel my cheeks flush with the heat of my anger. Even when he should be pleading for his life, he doesn't display an ounce of remorse. Not that him showing any contrition would change what I have in store for him. I'm not God, I'm not looking to turn the other cheek or redeem the unredeemable.

"Neither your mother nor your stupid fucking Titi did you any favors, and not to mention your taste in women. Sienna Ricci," he scoffs before gagging on the blood dripping down his face. "Well, she is the worst combination of her treacherous parents."

I wind up with the bat, and with all my might, take a vicious swing, crashing down on his leg. He yelps in pain as I yank it from his bloodied skin. I raise it above my head, ready to strike again.

I feel my heart begin to race, as blood begins to feel like it is swishing in my ears from adrenaline. "Stop it, you don't know her," I yell.

"Neither do you," he says, trying to steady his breath, working through the pain. "Any woman who makes a man turn on his blood is a worthless bitch. She never loved you; she doesn't even know you, Carmine. It was Leo she loved, not you, you fucking fool."

Just the mention of Leo makes my blood boil. That lucky bastard, he had what I need ... *her*.

"I took no oath of loyalty to you. I only complied this long out of convenience, giving me time to avenge the blood you have on your hands."

I swing again, not waiting for a reply.

"It wasn't me," he whimpers.

But it's too late, I ignore his plead. I continue to raise the bat, ready to crash it into his body, reducing him to nothing but bloody remnants.

"Save it," I say before I swing again, the rage building, my swings each faster than the last. With each blow to his body, the nails scratch and make a loud clinking sound.

Swing.

"You thought I would just forgive you!" I roar at him, not expecting a response. There is no way he could even muster up the strength to answer me, that is, if he is even still alive.

Swing.

I swing once more, but it's useless. He lies there, a bloodied, unrecognizable mess. Broken, crimson colored flesh spewing everywhere, leaving me breathless, tired, and dignified. I have dreamed of this moment for so long, the moment my fucking useless father would die at my hands. Now, I am just one step closer to my escape, or rather, *our escape.*

So close, mi reina, so close.

I toss the bat into the middle of the bloodied tarp, landing next to what once was Armando Moretti's plump body, which is now an unrecognizable lump of dead flesh. But it's not the thud of my nail-covered bat landing in the pool of blood that takes hold of my attention. I tense as the familiar sound of heels click on the cement floor. I'm not expecting Sienna to be here yet. I glance at my watch. I still have a good hour before she should be arriving.

I resist the urge to look at who is coming my way, though the echo is only intensified by this hollow warehouse, taking hold of my eardrums.

Panic grips me, stealing me from what should be such a blissful moment of exacted revenge. It's not that I don't want her to know what I have done, but seeing me like this—covered in blood, standing in glee over the corpse of my father—well, that may be a level of darkness that my little rag doll might not be prepared to embrace. *Yet.*

The distinct sound of high-heeled footsteps continues to echo. I turn around, running my blood-splattered hair out of my face to get a better look at who is coming.

Just as the hair escapes my eyes, I am met with a familiar face. One I was not expecting.

Shit.

The clicking stops just before the edge of the tarp.

"Hello, Carmine. Long time no see ..."

Chapter 37

Sienna

I remember the first time Papa showed me how to use a gun. Mama begged him not to, she hated guns and saw no need for a girl to be in possession of one. However, my father couldn't have disagreed with her more. He was adamant that if nothing else, I knew how to use a gun properly. I never questioned him because, even at a young age, I knew that what he was showing me would someday come in handy.

Most of my friend's fathers emphasized self-defense classes or carrying pepper spray, while my father emphasized violence under the guise of protection. I knew my father was preparing me for a potential war.

He knew the constant threat of danger that lurked amongst us. Given our family name, he felt it important to not fill my head with silly fairytales. I swear, the cynical realism my father poured into me from a young age must be where I got my strong love for all things spooky. When you learn that more of life happens in the shadows than in the light, you tend to flock to what lives in the darkness more.

Now, as I drive outside the city limits to whatever undisclosed location Carmine told Eric to take me to, I am especially thankful for that first lesson at the ripe age of twelve. Because today feels like the day I was meant to prepare for.

Eric turns down an unmarked street and through a dense patch of hanging trees, a long gravel road reveals itself. I peer out the window to try to determine where the hell we are, but all I see ahead in the distance is what looks to be an abandoned building made of half-decaying brick. As we drive closer on the bumpy gravel, it appears to be an old warehouse.

Wonderful.

The car makes an abrupt stop as Eric parks it, but he doesn't get out right away. He reaches for his phone, not realizing there is not even one bar of service in whatever hellhole we drove up to.

"Shit, alright, Boss said to give him a shout when we got here, but I have no service," he says.

"Yeah, me neither. Guess that's common when you drive away from civilization," I say, getting myself out of the car.

Eric shrugs before he runs around to meet me, more antsy than usual.

"You good, Eric?" I ask, but before he can answer, we both are distracted by what appears to be two people shouting. I grab my purse and feel for the pistol still in the front pocket, debating if I need to reach for it now.

There is an altercation going on inside between a man and woman, from the sounds of it. I look at Eric and we both head inside toward whatever quarrel is going on.

The door to the warehouse is wide open, making the echoing of the voices sound even louder. As we make our way into the huge, two-story open space, I first see a woman with her back facing Eric and me.

"I told you I wanted to be the one to handle it. I wanted him to feel just an ounce of the pain he has caused!" the woman shouts.

It's then that I notice, smack in the middle of the large open space, a curtained-off area. My eye first scans the tops of the curtains, which are hung by what looks to be a metal frame. The material of the thick curtains looks just like The Sandy Claws. My eyes travel down the tall curtains, and I notice red liquid pooling out onto what looks to be a large plastic tarp. My stomach turns at the sight, knowing that Carmine must behind the drawn curtains, doing God knows what.

I walk closer, curiosity overcoming me. The woman mumbles something to herself, clearly aware of mine and Eric's presence. Then, as she turns around to face us, my stomach drops.

"Titi Lana?" I ask, confused, as she stands there with pleading eyes.

It can't be. What the hell is she doing here?

I am ashamed of the amount of jealousy that is intertwined with that question. There has to be a logical reason why she is here alone with Carmine, arguing in an empty warehouse in the middle of nowhere. I sound more naïve than rational, trying to calm myself from the unexpected envy filling my body more with each passing moment.

I notice there are tears in her hazel eyes. "Titi, what the hell are you doing here?" I say as I run up to hug her. We stand there, locked in an embrace, as I feel the tears roll down her always perfectly made-up face.

"I'm sorry, honey, I was going to tell you. I swear it, I just needed to—" she interrupts herself, wiping away the remainder of her tears as she clears her throat to regroup. "He just beat me to it."

I shake my head, "Beat you to what?" I ask.

She takes in a deep breath but does not answer my question.

"Titi, beat you to what? What the hell is going on?" I press once more.

She still doesn't answer my question.

"Did he hurt you?" I ask, bringing my hands back to her forearms, slightly shaking her so she can answer me.

Finally, she comes to, snapping out of the daze she was in, "No, he didn't. He just prevented me from hurting who I came here to hurt," she says as she peers back at the curtained-off area, looking agitated.

"Hurt who? Titi you are scaring me," I say, with apprehension in my eyes.

Before she can say anything, I hear the curtain rings cling against the metal rod as the row of velour fabric begins to become smaller. My eyes leave Lana's face as I process the man emerging from the curtains. Carmine opens the curtain, revealing himself.

He looks like he has gone through war. He is without his signature black pinstripe suit, instead, in a once white undershirt covered in crimson. Blood splattered on his face, his forearms, hands, everywhere. Not an inch of him, aside from his eyes, is not covered in blood.

Through the sea of red, I notice the veins in his forearms are bulging, pronounced, as if he just got done working out.

Even stained in blood which should be concerning, I can't look away.

He walks toward Lana and I and, of course, he has a cigarette hanging from his mouth. Somehow, his ink-filled arms, now glistening from the death that is splattered all over them, create a throbbing in my center. I try to look away, but it's too late. The throbbing is now mixed with the wetness forming, making me wanton for him. *Fuck, I'm so messed up.*

He takes a long drag of his cigarette as he looks to me, like he and I are the only ones in the room.

"Ms. Ricci, I do hope you are prepared for what I have planned for you today," he says. His ability to be so nonchalant amongst the confusion and chaos that surrounds us is truly remarkable.

I turn to Titi Lana, but before I can say anything to her, she reaches for my hand glancing at Carmine once more. "Please, call me later, we need to catch up," she says to me.

You think?

Carmine directs his gaze to Eric, blowing his smoke in his direction "See Ms. Diaz out of here, Eric."

Eric nods and walks up to greet Titi Lana, but she looks to Carmine instead. She flips her elegantly draped, wavy brown hair before inching closer to him. "I will see myself out the same way I came in, Mr. Moretti." She looks back toward Eric, scanning him up and down. "I don't trust him," she mumbles but her statement is loud and clear.

Eric hears her also and awkwardly backs away. "It's no problem, Boss, I have to head back to the office, anyway. There is some unfinished business I need to take care of," he says, ominously.

I'm curious what Eric needs to get done at the office,

considering he is an intern and Carmine doesn't seem to utilize him for any work other than errands or driving me around. I look at Carmine, who nods, half paying attention, as his intense stare melts me.

As Carmine brings his arm up, puckering on his cigarette, I see crimson droplets bead down to the floor. Whatever was the cause of the blood drenching his skin is beyond that curtain, and as concerned as I should be, I hate to admit that intrigue takes over.

Eric nods goodbye to us all before scurrying out of the warehouse. The door slams, echoing through the empty warehouse.

Lana moves a moment later and she whispers something to Carmine before coming back to give me a hug.

I watch Carmine's eager eyes, studying me as I interact with Titi Lana and say goodbye to her. Through puffs of smoke, I see an unexpected yet adorable grin form around his mouth.

"I love you, Sienna, call me when you leave. I'll explain everything," she says before tapping her heels in the opposite direction of the entrance Eric and I came in.

The fact that I am alone with Carmine in this environment solidifies all my fears about him, and then some. I don't know whether to walk toward him or run away. So, instead, I stand frozen, hoping that my mind will take over, because my body melts under his wicked flame.

"Ms. Ricci, follow me this way." He motions for me to come closer as his body starts turning toward the bloodied, curtained island in the middle of this otherwise pristinely clean, yet empty, warehouse.

"I made a little mess, hope you don't mind helping me

clean up," he says nonchalantly, as he begins to peel the curtain back further.

Before I can process who lays undoubtedly dead behind the curtain, my eye goes to the dark red splatters all over the tarp, causing my heartbeat to pick up. My heart is beating so loudly that my ears feel full.

I stand there, just staring, and then he slips his equally red-covered hand in front of my gaze, reaching it out for me to grab. I look up, and then, the quickening of my heart beating dulls. Instead of racing anxious, sickening thoughts, I am met with an eerie calm. A calm that eradicates my fear, and it is then that I see him.

I truly see Carmine. Not his flesh but his soul. Before me lies death. Skeletal, raw death. It's the kind of metaphorical death that makes me know that, in this moment, this is the end. The end of what I knew before him, the end of living a life, waiting for a soul as fucked up as mine to mend my wounds and accept my scars. Taking on the burden of living life broken, not alone, but together.

I squeeze his skeleton-inked hand, finally moving my eyes to the scene behind the curtain. Even with the blood that surrounds us, with the distinct stench of metallic death that penetrates these exposed brick walls, my hand in his, we proceed forward in silence. There, lies evident a new form of understanding between us. The beginning of something I never saw coming, the start of something my soul has been knocking at my chest to let in. *Him.*

Chapter 38

Carmine

With her hand in mine, I feel her tighten her grip as her boots crunch on the blood-drenched tarp. She tries to move methodically as to not get any blood on her shoes, but with the amount that is seeping from what is left of my father, it's almost impossible at this point. Not to mention, the hand that she is holding onto for dear life is stained with blood that has already transferred onto her skin.

As we walk past what remains of Armando Moretti, she stays quiet. No quick-witted comments, no reaching for her phone to attempt to call Vanessa, no screams, nothing. Not like she could make a call even if she wanted to, as there isn't a cell tower to be found for miles. It's one of the many reasons I love bringing my kills here, nowhere to escape and nowhere to call for help.

I wait for her to process what she has just seen as I bring her to the back brick wall, away from my father's latest and, more importantly, final mess. She lets go of my hand and stands there, just staring at my father.

I leave her there as I continue to walk, lighting another cigarette. I lean my back against the rough wall, with my arms crossed, waiting for her. I have waited what feels like a lifetime for her. What's a few more minutes?

She finally begins to walk toward me, her heels leaving the plastic tarp, now hitting the concrete floor louder with each step. I feel the blood rush to my groin as I am met with an angry scowl on that beautiful face of hers.

How fun.

She walks closer to me, and her perfume immediately overpowers the smell of the nicotine that spills out of my mouth. She steps closer until her cleavage rubs against my bent elbow with cigarette in hand. She takes it from my fingers and brings it to her mouth, puckering, careful not to smear her lipstick on it. I stand there, breathing her in. She is a fucking vision and as always, an unpredictable one.

For someone who detests smoking, she sure seems comfortable, inhaling the smoke without coughing, as if she were a seasoned smoker. She blows the smoke in my face and the mixture of the nicotine and her mouth in such close proximity to me is truly intoxicating.

God, I want her so fucking bad.

"Why?" she asks bluntly between taking puffs of smoke into her perfect mouth. She tilts her head back, pointing toward my father.

I hesitate. There's so much to unravel; a simple answer won't suffice. I can't help but smirk instead of answering her. I can tell she is trying so hard not to unload her anger on me.

"Mi reina, those are bad for you," I tease, deflecting her question as she puckers her lips around my cigarette, taking another drag.

She releases the smoke that collects in her mouth, blowing it towards my eyes, causing me to blink as it burns my pupils.

"Don't be a fucking hypocrite. You're bad for me, yet here I am," she says with her arm up, taking in the almost empty warehouse. I look past her, taking mental note of the cleanup I have to do.

I decide to go back to her initial question for me. I love seeing her feisty side, but even I know that I am on thin ice with her.

"Why what, *mi reina*?" I hiss, taking back my cigarette, locking my eyes on hers.

"Should we start with why you killed your father and fucking dragged me here to be an accessory to murder?" She takes a deep breath, ready to rattle off a laundry list of questions she has for me. "Or the fact that my Titi was here, and that you know her? I don't know, Carmine, how about fucking all of it," she exclaims. "You have some explaining to do."

"Calm down, Lucille Ball," I tease again.

"This isn't the time for jokes about one of my favorite shows." She shakes her head, flustered. She stomps her heel in anger. "Stop avoiding my questions. I'm tired of playing your games," she says, unconvincingly. But I know her father trained her well. There is a high possibility she is armed, and if I don't play my cards right, I could be the next corpse in this warehouse.

A devious expression crosses my face. I can't help myself. I'm a glutton for punishment and seeing her fired up is the ultimate aphrodisiac.

"You didn't seem tired of the games we played last night,

Sen."

"I told you to stop calling me that." She stomps her foot once more, however, this time she takes the remaining cigarette butt from my hand, tossing it on the ground as she does.

"No, you didn't; you asked me why I called you that. You never told me to stop," I challenge her.

"You are so frustrating! Stop patronizing me." She goes to turn away, but I refuse to let her escape.

Before she can even take one step away from me, my hands grip her arm, pulling her into me. I lower my eyes to hers as my jaw tenses. "Have I struck a nerve? You know, for someone who is complaining about games, you seem to have no issue with them when the games involve you coming more times than you can keep track of," I remind her.

She tries to break free from my grip, rolling her eyes, but her attempts at unclenching my fist are not convincing. "You are sexy, and you wanted to fuck me. I have needs, too, you know. But that ends now," she lies.

Still in my grasp, we stand another moment with our eyes intensely locked. I only break eye contact when I feel her hardened nipple graze my arm. *My little, horny queen.*

"Like what you see?" I tease, as my eyes draw attention to her stiffened nipples.

"Unfortunately," she scoffs.

"In time, you will learn that I hold a priceless fortune with your name on it."

She ignores me. "Just tell me why you called me here," she says, trying to be stern, but it feels like she is begging.

"I summoned you because I wanted you—"

She cuts me off. "No, we have been over that, and your

answers as to why I am at Marked Inc. did jack shit in helping me figure out your intent. Why am I here? In this creepy-ass warehouse, where you killed your father? Watch what you say next, because your lies aren't going to cut it," she says angrily, fighting back tears.

Lost in the beauty that is her dampened eyes, I loosen my grip on her arm. She doesn't waste a fucking second once free from my hold, as she fumbles for her purse on the ground. The familiar click of a pistol cocked and loaded penetrates my eardrums as she stealthily rises from her crouched position.

Walking toward me, she aims the gun in my direction. Tears swell in her eyes, though her stance remains strong. Even with her sights on me, ready to shoot at any moment, she looks devastatingly beautiful.

"Why, Carmine?!" she asks again, her voice slightly trembling. But her stance is solid; her arm hasn't flinched once, despite the emotion swarming through her at the moment.

"I know your talent," I blurt.

"How? How the fuck do you know my talent, huh? You don't fucking know me! What are you, some kind of sick stalker who seduces women before you bring them here, in the middle of fucking nowhere, to kill them?!" she shouts, gun still pointed in my direction.

"I'm not a stalker, Sienna." I sigh, reaching for another cigarette, but the pack is empty.

"Then, what are you and why the fuck am I here? I don't want to be involved in this!" she shouts. "And how is it you know so much about me?"

"I know that your father was a shark in the drug game. I

know, despite his tough persona, he was a loyal man, but he was loyal to a fault. That fault landed him in a coffin, along with your mother," I half answer her questions, trying to figure out how much I want to disclose to her as she has a loaded gun pointed at me.

I continue, "I know that you miss them more than you let on. I know that your head is your safe place, because in your head live the stories you have always wanted to tell, the stories you need to tell. I know that you are the most exquisite woman I have ever laid eyes on. I know that your pain has made you the strong goddess I see standing before me. I know you, Sienna Ricci, better than I think you know yourself."

I feel this odd mixture of tears starting to pool in my eyes just as blood rushes to my dick so violently that it is practically begging to be unleashed.

I fucking know you, Sienna.

I have fucking always known you.

I expect her to question my unfiltered confession, but she doesn't.

Waiting for her to speak is intolerable. I need her to say something, fucking anything. She can tell me to go to Hell for all I care, tell me to go fuck off. I don't care, I just need her to say something.

She drops the gun and steps back from me for a second. "Was he a bad man?" she asks. Her demeanor is calmer than before. Perhaps my erratic, semi-confession eased her. It has the opposite effect on me right now. I feel as though I am on the verge of losing all fucking control.

"Who? My father?" I ask, feeling thrown off my game.

"Yes, I assume it is his blood that is staining your, and

well, my hands now," she says, looking down at the blood that covers her delicate hands.

"Yes, he was."

"So, he deserved it, then?" she asks, staring back at his bloodied corpse.

"Yes, he did ..."

"Why did he deserve it? I mean, you aren't exactly a saint. Hell, neither am I, or any of us, really. What gives you the power or the right to make that decision? A decision that costs you your father."

"Because he stole something very important to me, as he did you."

"What did he do that was worth having his blood on your hands?"

"He killed my mother," I confess. I hate saying those words, even to this day. They sting just as much as they did from the moment it happened.

I walk over to her, grabbing her chin with my hand. "And he killed your parents for the ties they had to my mother."

"Oh my God." She gasps. "Ties? Wait, my Mama and Papa? It was him?!" she exclaims in instant disgust for my father and breaks down crying. Sad, beautiful, justified tears.

I go to embrace her, wanting to take away the emerging pain she is feeling. But as I go to touch her, she flinches, moving away from me instead of leaning into me, like I want her to. Like she should.

"Sienna, there is a lot you don't know," I say in a begging tone.

She looks at me and sniffles back her tears before clearing her throat.

"Fucking clearly."

Chapter 39

Sienna

This is what I wanted ... right? *Answers.*

I spin around and away from him to think. Although, thinking or processing the information I just heard feels impossible when all I can see is blood. So much blood everywhere. I bring my hands to my temples, as if massaging them can work a magic spell and give me the words to say, the clarity I need, the right thing to do.

Ha, the right thing.

The right thing would be to run ... fast. Away from this man, away from this warehouse, to somewhere—anywhere—that has even one bar of service. To get help, to call Nessa, or the local police station, wherever we are.

But I don't want to do the right thing. At least, not by society's standards of what is right. Because if what Carmine is telling me is true, that the man who is responsible for half of the DNA in his body is, in fact, the killer of his mother and my parents, then who am I to punish him.

My chin is still in his hands, his scent, his overpowering

presence, *his darkness* begins to work something inside of me like an all-consuming incubus.

"He stole your happiness. He needed to pay the price," he declares as he breaks loose from the grip he has on me and heads to what looks like a tool bag made of leather.

I'm looking back at him, standing there in the crimson of our shared enemy, when I notice his eyes. Once harsh black pits, they seem lighter, if that's even possible. Still ebony, but instead of being pitch-black, they resemble dusk. It's like exacting this revenge lifted a weight off his depraved, aching soul. But the thing with eyes is that they speak for us, often when we are unable to speak for ourselves. And it's now in his silence that his eyes scream something from the depth of his soul that he wants me to know.

"Tell me something, Carmine," I say as I begin to circle the crime scene that he has now, by default, involved me in. "I know your father wronged you. He did the unthinkable— he took your mother from you. But why include his trans- gressions against my parents in your vendetta?"

He doesn't say anything. Instead, he seemingly ignores my valid question and walks over to the large, black leather bag on the tarp that is in the middle of a pool of blood. He begins searching intently for something, while still leaving my question untouched.

Vexed, I break the silence. "I asked you a question."

Still futzing in that god-forsaken bag, he does not answer. I swear, through his peripheral vision, he must be able to see the pure anger I am feeling toward him now, because he begins to smile.

Done with these games and craving answers, I charge toward him, grabbing his thick arms and moving him away from his tool bag. But he is built like a rock. My attempt is futile and only makes him laugh more, sending pure rage into my veins. He then grabs me, and in one stealthy swoop, pins me to the ground, with a devious smirk just inches from my face.

"Answer me, now!" I demand, trying to free myself from his body on top of mine, but he doesn't let up.

He brings his lips just inches from mine as my anger somehow turns into a heated arousal. Cool and collected, he shoots me a grin once more before finally parting his lips. "You know, when someone does you a favor, I believe the proper thing to do would be to extend a thank you."

He gets up and walks toward the brick wall to the far corner of the warehouse, with what looks like an incinerator near it.

I sit up and speak, even though it's to his back. "Right, thank you for committing a gruesome murder that you now have involved me in." My voice echoes, drenched in sarcasm.

I stand to follow him, continuing to talk. At this point, I don't care if he responds, I just want him to listen and hear what I have to say. Hopefully, I can instill some logic into the man. "In case you have forgotten, Carmine, my best friend is a cop, who, oh yea, works with your fucking cousin. Do you seriously think this can be swept under the rug?" I ask, continuing to make my way toward him as he is busy conducting sick, twisted business as usual, messing with what is definitely an incinerator, now that I have a closer view.

"Do you really think this is my first kill?" he asks with a confidence that makes it clear to me that, no, it is not.

"I don't know," I lie. I can tell already by the way he

moves around in this place that he has been here many times, to more than likely do what he is doing now—kill.

He grabs another tarp from a small shelf he has near the incinerator and begins unfolding it as he continues.

"My cousin not only knows but condones my uncanny ability to swiftly rid this world of the detestable, and again, Sienna, I did this partly for you," he almost lectures as he begins to unfold the tarp. "This little, self-righteous, good girl act you have going on, while fucking delicious, is truthfully not you." He sneers.

I shake my head. "This is unbelievable, and here I am thinking you wanted me for my intellect, but now it's for some crazy vendetta you have that I'm not even sure I believe you about, by the way. Was fucking me also part of that plan?"

"Don't act like I forced you. You were wet for me like I was hard for you the second we locked eyes on each other. Our physical connection is a bonus on top of what already lays the foundation," he says, laying the fresh tarp down.

"Well, you better check your foundation, because it's cracked."

The mix of emotions I feel when I am in Carmine's presence is maddening. I still don't understand how I fit into this mess. None of this makes sense. My head is spinning with questions I need to know the answers to.

"And while we are at it? Why the fuck was my Titi Lana here?" I ask, still trying to figure out what she meant by *"he beat me to it."*

"I wasn't expecting her to be here, but she was determined."

"Determined?" I press.

"To drain the life out of that monster, watch him bleed, and rid him from this world. Now, which one do you want to start writing first, a parting letter or obituary?"

Wait, what?

I have never felt so confused in my life. A parting letter? Obituary? Fucking, Titi Lana potentially killing someone? What the fuck is my life right now?

"You do realize you're insane, right? I just met you. Why would I help you bury your father?" I say, shaking my head in disbelief at this situation.

"Have you, though?" he asks in a devious tone.

"Have I, what?" I ask, confused.

"Just met me. You can't honestly think a banter and connection like ours just happens overnight, do you?" There is a familiar gleam in his eye, as he is clearly toying with me.

I sigh, exasperated from the never-ending circles he talks in. "You're hot and I have been single for far too long, and I gladly accepted your physical invitation. Stop making it into something it's not."

"How about you take your own advice? You're making this into something you know it's not. He is the reason you buried your father and your mother, isn't that enough?" he roars.

"No, it isn't. I'm not going to lose my freedom for your revenge party. Sorry, you have the wrong girl."

"No, I don't. I have exactly the woman I need standing by my side," he says with an eerie confidence.

I shake my head at him. I hate this mess he has inserted me into. On the one hand, if he is telling the truth, and he killed his father as some sort of revenge for the death of my father ... It's honorable, but also sick, because I am no one to him, whereas that's his fucking father. He is clearly unstable; desirable, but unstable.

"This is too much. I'm not going down with you for this. No fucking thank you."

I go to walk away, when he grabs my wrist, twisting it so I have no choice but to turn and face him. Just one touch from him, even when it's filled with angst, sends a warmth to my pussy that I can't fight. I'm not even sure I would want to fight it, even if I could. I hate that he has this effect on me. He is no good; he is trouble. Yet here I am, constantly feeding into his delusions.

He yanks me and throws me against the wall, the exposed brick scraping my shoulder. I squirm, and part of me wants to run while part of me shamefully wishes he threw me against the wall to shove into me with the growing bulge I feel forming.

"I have waited entirely too long for this moment. I have plotted, planned, I have waited too long for you. To avenge your parents' deaths. To avenge what he took from us. You need to listen to me," he declares in a seductively breathy baritone.

"Us? Carmine, there is no us. I don't know what the fuck you are talking about. You are fucking crazy!" I yell. I swallow hard, the warmth growing more and more by the second. Every venomous, confusing word that comes out of his mouth intensifies my sick desire for him.

"Yes, Sen."

"You're a creep," I lie to him. While he is creepy, he is the kind that makes you want to run to him for a thrill, not run away from a scare.

"Admit it, you like when I call you Sen. It brings you

back to a time when things were less complicated." He smiles, making me melt inside, but I refuse to let him know that.

"Well, if my life is complicated now, it's because of you, Carmine." I try to loosen myself from his grip once more. His grip becomes tighter, but not out of anger. It's like he is holding on to me for dear life, not wanting to let go. Like he doesn't want to lose me.

"Admit it, you like this banter we have. You like that I hunted you down, that I brought you here. I have waited lifetimes for you. A soul as crushed and fucked up as mine. A soul to mend, to bend, to never break but stitch back together. I couldn't find you in my youth, but now that I have finally found you, you are fucking mine."

I look at him, and I don't know why, but desire is clouding my judgment. His eyes look sincere, his body yearning like mine. Maybe he is telling the truth? Maybe he stalked me to give me the gift of revenge.

And while it's a sweet, yet sick gesture, it is a gesture, nonetheless. I think of Mama and how she longed to have Papa notice her, to make her the center of his universe. He provided her all the things money could, but that was never enough. Mama longed for him to desire her. To love her enough that if someone wronged her, he would kill for her if need be. Not for his pride, but for her glory.

Carmine is flawed, like me, but his intentions are pure. Not in the traditional sense of pure, but pure enough to me. He feels a sense of loyalty to me; he feels like he owes me for the sins of his father. Maybe it's the fucked-up lifestyle I come from that ruined me, but this murderous gesture of his, if I am being honest with myself, I find endearing.

I'm so fucked.

He stands there, waiting for me to say something. My silence, while I am trapped in my head, must be confusing him.

"Sienna, are you there?"

"Sorry, do you have a sink here?" I ask, trying to snap out of the daze I have been placed in.

"Um, yes, why?" he asks, confused.

"Because I would prefer you not to have his blood on you when you fuck me."

Chapter 40

Carmine

Desire radiates throughout my body from hearing her explicit need for me to fuck her here, in this warehouse. Most would see the splatter of a fresh kill all over my skin as a deterrent, yet she remains here, with her pussy purring for me. If it weren't for her request, I wouldn't even bother to wash the blood off my skin. What poetic justice it would be to be balls deep in her with the blood of our enemy still damp on my flesh.

The thought of taking her on the cold, concrete floor brings arousal to my body. I want to savor her, worship every part of her curves. I want to flood her body with my venomous seed as she drowns in me, marking her as mine. It's been less than twelve hours since I have had her, and already, I am a fiend for my next fix.

As I head toward the sink to oblige her request, reality violently whips me in the face as the literal stench of death slowly begins to permeate my nostrils. Fucking Christ. Even in death, my father's presence haunts me. I don't have much time. I must begin working on disposing of him before his rotten scent fills this place.

I'm about to turn the handle of the faucet when suddenly, she stops me with her delicate hand.

"Wait," she commands, stopping both her and me in her tracks. She grabs my right arm that is covered in blood, which stains her skin on contact. She doesn't even flinch. Instead, she grips my forearm tighter and forces me to face her.

As if I need convincing. She could get me to do anything. I will obey willingly.

"Yes," I purr, waiting for her to speak whatever has so abruptly come to her mind.

Her grip remains clasped firmly on my forearm. She is silent, but her body is screaming.

Unsure of what her next move is, I wait for her to speak. Instead of opening her mouth, she lets go of my forearm and reaches into my pants. My cock awakens from the heat of her hand so close.

"This is all so fucked up," she blurts in a hushed tone as she begins stroking my length.

"I thought you wanted me to wash up first," I remind her playfully.

She quiets me with a kiss before continuing. "Everything about this place, this past week, about you, tells me I should run," she confesses. The apprehension in her voice is ripe. She wants to move on, but she can't. I know the feeling because that is what she does to me. I couldn't move on from the idea of her, even if I tried. She implanted herself in my brain long ago. Without realizing it, she has made me a monster on a mission to save her and destroy anyone or anything that gets in our way.

"So, why don't you, then?"

"I can't. There is something about you that makes me feel at home. It's like I recognize a part of myself in you," she confesses as she slowly continues to stroke my length.

"What is it about me that made you care enough to lump me into your reasons for killing your father?" she asks. "You clearly have had issues with your father prior to me being in the picture. Don't use me as an excuse to justify your kill."

You are not an excuse. You are the reason, mi reina.

"I feel a sense of responsibility for you, Sienna," I confess.

"Because of what your father did to my parents?"

"That's a part of it."

She squints her eyes at me in deep thought, trying to unravel the mess I have just spewed in front of her. "Care to elaborate on the other part?"

"Not right now, with my cock in your hand. I'd rather play first, talk later," I say with a grin. Just as the words leave my lips, she lets go of my length, leaving me with a painful, longing ache.

"You're not responsible for me. I don't know what you think you owe me, or whatever sick fucking scheme you have concocted in that fucked up head of yours, but I can take care of myself. I've accepted that my parents are dead. I don't need either of our lives to end in jail because of your vendettas." She lets out a frustrated grunt before turning to storm out.

Not so fast, mi reina.

I run and grab her arm. She winces at how strong my

hands are grasping her. There is desperation in my grip, but I can't let her go. What if she tells Vanessa what I did before I can talk to Alex to deflect the situation? I can't risk that. I have risked everything for her. I can't risk her running now. Not when we are so close to what I have dreamed of for entirely too long.

"Let go of me now, Carmine!" she shouts.

"No, Sienna, I can't."

"You can't or you don't want to?"

"Both." I grit my teeth.

"You're fucking crazy."

"No crazier than you."

"What the fuck is that supposed to mean?"

"Tell me you don't feel it," I press.

"Feel what? Your freakishly large hands, probably leaving bruises on my skin?"

I grip just a bit tighter, my calluses scratching her soft skin. "Don't act like you didn't love what these hands did to you the other night. And don't act like you don't appreciate what these hands have done for you," I say, looking at the corpse I have yet to deal with.

"You are crazy. Let go of me," she says, as tears begin to form in her angry eyes.

It's ironic how her mouth shouts in anger to let her go, but her skin magnetizes to my touch. She pushes, I pull. We are stuck, *marked*.

"If wanting to undo the wrongs that have been done to you, while pleasing you makes me crazy, then yes, I am fucking crazy. Certifiably insane."

She begins to cry.

I continue, "But you cannot, for one second, tell me that

even in this blood-filled, fucked-up warehouse, you don't feel it."

"Feel fucking what, Carmine?" she shouts, with tears streaming down her perfect face.

I let go of her, and instead of running, she turns toward me with clenched fists pounding at my chest. There is relief in her anger. There is release in her tears.

"Do you feel it, Sienna? Less broken?" I interrupt her rage and take hold of both her hands as she collapses on my chest.

"Yes," she admits.

"Like the scars you wear on your heart, all the open wounds that needed healing, can finally be stitched back together?"

"What is your fucking point?" she says in my chest through muffled tears.

"I knew from the moment I learned what my father did to your parents, and ultimately did to you, that I would forever be marked to you."

"Marked?" she lifts her head, confused.

"Indebted, responsible." *Obsessed.*

I know she feels it. She stares at me with an intoxicating mix of fear and desire.

I continue, "I know you have faced heartbreak on so many levels. Let me take that from you. Let me help you hurt less."

A subtle smirk forms along her lips, her demeanor morphing in front of my eyes. Her desire is overpowering her fear. My words are igniting a flame I know she has buried deep.

"So, that's it, huh? You think you and your magical, vibrating dick are all that is needed to heal me?"

Ha, she liked that improvement.

"What are you, God, thinking you can absolve me of all my sins and hurt, is that it?" she asks, trying to maintain her anger, when I can see her beginning to melt for me.

I click my tongue. She can't help herself. Forever feisty and testing the boundaries, both hers and mine.

"God and I don't belong in the same sentence together. My form of healing may hurt you," I warn.

"I know," she answers, surprisingly, before calming her breath, as if she is finally accepting her fate. "When I'm with you, you break apart everything I thought I knew. You numb my pain, eradicate my fears, and feed my soul something I never knew I needed. You make me feel—"

"Whole?" I interrupt her.

"No. Just less broken. Like my demons are allowed to dance freely," she declares, with a wicked air that suits her more than she realizes.

"Is that what you want, Sienna, for your demons to dance freely?" I ask as I stand before her, wanting to peel back every layer of darkness within her that is begging to be unleashed.

"I want your demons to fuck my demons, so I can forget all the pain that has haunted me," she once more declares as she surrenders her darkness to mine.

"Your wish is my command, *mi reina.*"

Little does she know that my demons will haunt her for the rest of her days.

Chapter 41

Sienna

Stale cigarette smoke mixed with the distinct aroma of metallic death lingers on his skin as he ferociously grabs my face. The blood that stains his skin looks like ichor, glistening on his brawny, inked physique, intensifying my yearning for him. At first, the thought of him on me with death still damp on his skin seemed off-putting, but now, he could literally drown me in the distinct, crimson liquid and I wouldn't put up a fight.

His tongue crashes into my ready mouth. With each kiss, I feel like my will to resist him is dwindling. The need I have for him is beyond anything I can comprehend. I suspend all inhibition when I am in his presence.

I release my tongue from his and gently bite his lower lip as I rest my hand on his growing bulge. He lets out a low moan that sends a longing throb down my center. I kiss him, then bite his lip again, slowly dragging it out just a bit before releasing it and making my way down his neck.

"*Fuck,*" he says, reveling in my kisses. It turns me on

hearing his moans in response to my mouth. I continue to trail my kisses down his neck as he takes his hand, slipping it down my pants.

"Fuck, you are wet," he says as he begins working two fingers in and out of me. "You like that, *mi reina?*" he asks as he brings his thumb up to my clit as he still works his fingers in me.

"Yes," I moan, barely able to respond as he smirks, taking pleasure in working his hands faster through my slit.

"I want you to soak my fucking hand," he says as he lays me on the cement. He cups his hand under my head, so it doesn't hit the hard, cold floor. A simple gesture that makes me even wetter, knowing that my comfort and pleasure are a priority to him. He slides my pants off and spreads my legs wider, so he has better access to where I am dripping for him.

The way he works his thumb over my clit as he pleases me makes me go wild. I feel the beginning of my release build as he takes his other hand to the bottom of my shirt. Still working one hand inside me, he skillfully uses his other to take off my blouse, reducing me to just my black lace bra. He reaches his hand to the back clasps, and in one motion, undoes the back, releasing my aroused nipples to him.

Bringing his lips to my breast, he kisses the soft flesh before concentrating his tongue on the barbell that is pierced through my nipple. The flicks of his tongue matched with the quickened pace he is maintaining between my legs begins to take over my body, leaving me aching for release. His warm, wet tongue on my breast is enough to make me come right then. After a few more flicks of his tongue, he makes his way down to my center, which is wet and swollen for him.

"You are glistening," he says as he teases me with the tip of his tongue.

"You're teasing me," I say with desperation in my voice.

He lifts his head, purposefully placing his face inches from my throbbing pussy, as he breathily says, "I'm not teasing, I'm just getting started. Now, be a good girl and shut that pretty mouth of yours so I can taste you."

Before I can even respond, he is back at my center. My legs instinctively spread wider as he cups my ass while sucking on my clit with such a hunger that I squeal in uncontrollable pleasure. I can tell my moans are turning him on because he makes an animalistic growl that subtly vibrates my pussy, much like that dick of his from last night.

"Fuck, I could eat you all day," he says in between ravenous swipes of his tongue.

Shit, and I would let him, too.

"Sit up and watch me devour you. I want you to watch me make you come the way *mi reina* should."

Fuck, I love how he calls me a queen, his *reina*. I feel more like the Queen of the Damned, but for him, I will gladly take on whatever name he calls me.

I do as he says, bringing myself up onto my elbows, and the sight of this beautiful man swallowing me whole is just too much. I can't contain my orgasm any longer. As he is sucking on my sex, he looks up at me with mischievous eyes, like he knew that I would instantly come watching him. His gaze locked on me as he hovers by my clit sends a fierce rush of pleasure through me that makes my body shake uncontrollably as I reach orgasm.

"Ah, yes," I let out.

He gets up from his position nestled between my legs

without breaking eye contact. He looks hungry, determined, and in this moment, I am intent on doing anything he wants me to. He presses me back down to the ground, more forcefully than before this time. I don't mind. I just need him inside of me.

I glance down at his hard and ready length, appreciating the subtle ridge-like texture beneath the skin of his shaft.

He hovers over me, immediately plunging into me. I squirm as he first enters me, just as I did last night, needing to accommodate his girth once more. Despite Carmine being the biggest I have been with, not to mention the most uniquely textured, I immediately mold to his size as he moves in and out of me. As he thrusts on top of me, his bat chain slightly swings by my face, and I notice he still has his bloodied undershirt on. I kiss him as I go to lift his shirt off him, when he tenses, thrusting harder. I try to get his shirt off again. I need to see every inch of him while he is in me. I want to be swimming in his inked, murderous flesh, crimson, and all, I don't care. But again, he tenses, this time pulling out of me.

"What are you doing? I need you back in me," I plead.

"I need you to behave and let me fuck you," he says blankly.

Confused and full of lust, I go to kiss him, uncertain of what I did to make him so upset. I try to lift his shirt up again, and he stops me with urgency in his eyes.

"What the fuck is your deal?" I say, becoming infuriated.

"I just want to fuck you; I don't need you seeing my scars!" he roars.

"I don't care about your scars," I say, confused as to why he would think I'd care about that.

"Well, I do," he says cryptically.

I can't with this man. No one makes me so full of lust and irritation all within the same breath as he does.

"You know what, Carmine? Forget it," I say, angrily.

He laughs. "Oh, you're not in the mood, huh? Your soaking wet slit says otherwise, *mi reina*." He sticks his fingers back in me.

I try to get up when he grabs me and pulls me back down to him. He kneels behind me, taking my throat with both irresistibly strong hands. He leans over, hovering over my back as he angrily whispers in my ear, "No, I won't forget it," he roars, entering me again.

I moan the second his length meets me once more.

"I can never forget a single moment with you," he confesses between pumps into me.

Thrust.

"Ever."

Thrust.

"I could fuck you for a lifetime."

Thrust.

"Now, take it like a good girl."

I can hear my wetness growing as he slaps against me, each thrust making me feel more alive. I arch my back as he collects my hair that was draping over my back, yanking it so I move upright toward his breath.

"I have missed this," he whispers in my ear as he starts pounding into me faster. As our bodies dance together, surrendering to the lust that has overcome us, I am made aware that this has been predestined. Predetermined by Carmine himself. He has longed for this, waited, plotted for this.

He has killed for this.

Killed for me.

Whatever this is. Whatever it is that he is hiding from me, whatever it is that he thinks he needs from me scares me, but not enough to run away. His intentions may be more sinister than I had realized, but he has unlocked something in me.

Before I can respond to him, he is thrusting into me with such a level of intensity that it is as though he is solidifying a pact, we have made with the Devil himself. I can feel him start to pulse as he fills me. It's then, I realize, maybe I was meant for this life. Danger doesn't deter me. The unknown doesn't scare me if I'm with him, whoever he really is. Not knowing every inch of his corrupt soul is what scares me.

Chapter 42

Carmine

The view of Sienna on all fours, surrendering her body to me, is the only view I want to indulge my eyes in for the rest of my days. Her curves are a hill I would die climbing, gasping for air, wrapping myself in her sultry imperfections. How long I have waited to have her close enough and willing to be in my now wicked presence. It's a surreal reality that I will stop at nothing to maintain. *Absolutely nothing.*

I have spent the better part of eternity fantasizing about the curves that were just crashing against my skin, giving me a euphoric high only a goddess like herself can give. Every moment I am in her presence, she makes my dead soul come to life.

My hands still dig into her hips as I finish spilling my venom into her. As the poison leaves my body, my grip tightens as every drop of my release flows inside of her, staining her soul.

I finally pull out of her, as much as it kills me. A mischievous grin forms as I take note of her glistening, damp reminder all over my cock. I feel power surge to my ego, seeing that, despite our unorthodox relationship, I make her drip for me like she does. The way I make her moan when she bursts in pleasure for me is something that fucker Leo was never able to do. Or Eric, for that matter. That, I am certain of.

No foolish ex from her adolescence or pathetic attempt in her present can ever come close to doing to her body what I have. What I was made to do to her. I am emerging from my dead conscience, a new and rising king on a quest. Fucking her senseless is a part of that, while still executing my plan for revenge and redemption at her feet.

I know she is confused, even conflicted, about me. I don't blame her. I have left her with many questions and few answers. It doesn't take a rocket scientist to see that this doesn't make sense, that we don't make sense. But that's the thing with chemistry. It doesn't have to make sense to make it feel good.

I watch her with hungry eyes as she gathers her clothes from the floor.

"Couldn't get enough of me from last night?" she jokingly asks as she slips back into her clothes.

"You are incredible, you know that?" I ask her, but it's really a statement.

"I know I am, but why do you think so?" she praises herself confidently, just as she should.

"Well, for one, you fuck like a goddess, and it amazes me how you haven't run yet." I smirk.

"Why, do you want me to run?" she teases.

"No, never again." The words slip from my mouth, and I instantly feel my insides churning, trying to grasp the words to take back. I look up to Sienna, trying to read her, hoping my careless slip goes over her head. She squints her eyes at me, clearly hanging on to every syllable I just said. *Fuck.* I know that look, that's not good. I need to think fast.

Sienna licks her lips slightly before opening her mouth. My palms are clammy. I debate interrupting her with anything, a kiss, another lie. Anything to distract her.

"Again?" She emphasizes the word.

"I didn't mean to say that," I lie.

"Yes, you did. I know your type."

No, you don't.

"You say what you mean, you mean what you say, no matter how you choose to say it. You may sprinkle truths here and there, afraid if you engage with your feelings too much that your tough exterior will crumble. I may need to dig deep, but the truth is there."

There she is, my quick-witted minx.

"I just meant that I enjoy this, whatever this is, and I don't want—" I begin, but I'm surprised by her direct demeanor as she cuts me off.

"To run away like she did, whoever she is?" she asks.

Mi reina, *there is no one except you.* No one could ever take hold of my heart or cock the way she has. She does things to me that she doesn't even know of. If that makes me crazy, so fucking be it. I will gladly lay my psychotic freak flag at her feet. Because that's what she makes me: fucking crazy.

"I was going to say I don't want to scare you off, I need you here," I say, not too sure of how convincing I sound.

"Here, as in glued to your dick, or in the office. Since

we're being honest and all," she says in her deliciously sarcastic tone.

"Well, if you are so keen on being honest, I think you should stop trying to pin me as the sleazy boss, when you have been more than a willing participant," I snap. This is typical of me. I become defensive when I feel the walls that I have worked so meticulously at building are threatened.

"Don't paint me as the office slut, Mr. Moretti. Society may say it's wrong what we are doing, but society is stupid, because they will paint you a triumphant hero, while they paint me a whore."

"I'm anything but a hero, Ms. Ricci."

"And I am anything but a whore, Mr. Moretti."

"I never said you were," I remind her.

She rolls her eyes. "You clearly needed someone to fuck and fill the void you have been left with, and I can relate. Maybe we are both so broken that that's why this works," she snaps.

There is pain in her voice. Her sexy facade is just a disguise she wears to mask the pain she has carried all this time. I know this because I, too, wear the same disguise. Daily. For too fucking long.

We are two souls torn in two, trying to repair the damage with intimacy. But little does she know that her betrayer and healer are one and the same.

"It seems we have more in common than we thought, Ms. Ricci."

This song and dance we continue to play is tempting, making me harder than it should, but time is literally ticking, as is Sienna's patience with my games. Her shoulders tense, as if she is rehearsing all the ways she can tell me off in her head. I want all the time in the world with her, but I have a business to run, movers to keep moving, *bodies to bury*.

"Well, seeing as how you clearly didn't need my assistance in this creepy warehouse, I'm going to see if Eric can swing back and bring me to the office," she says, reaching for his phone.

"There is no service here," I remind her.

"Fuck," she exclaims, tapping her heel in frustration.

"Don't fret, Ms. Ricci. I already radioed my driver Rufus who is waiting outside to bring you back to the office."

I head to the small window toward the front of the warehouse to confirm that it is Rufus here to bring Sienna back to the office. I see Rufus' grey hair from the driver's seat.

Turning to Sienna, who looks absolutely exquisite, with her post-sex flush on her cheeks, I say, "I will see you out, so we can both carry on with our day."

Once again, I come off much colder than I intended it to. It's been so long since I have had to play this role that sometimes I forget what it feels like to not be a cold, ruthless, soulless killer. I want to apologize, correct my tone, but I opt not to. Instead, I sink into this role I have sadly perfected.

I walk Sienna to the creaky door, and as I open it, she takes the knob from my hand and clicks her heels past me, not giving me time to speak. I want to pull her in close and kiss her, but Rufus is already parked and waiting for her.

"Thank you, Ms. Ricci, I expect you will finish the work I gave you for today that's already on your desk before our dinner meeting!" I shout at her back as she walks away, giving me a perfect view of her plump ass.

"I already have plans, sorry," she shouts back, as she continues to strut away from me.

That's what you think, mi reina.

Her hips sway exaggeratedly, as if she is putting on a show for me. I can tell she's annoyed with me, but that's ok, I can live with that. I'd rather have her angry where I can see her than broken where I can't fix her.

Sienna stops as she opens the car door and nods to me, trying to mask her annoyance and gets into the car. I nod to Rufus as I instantly make my way back to the warehouse to radio Alex.

I hit the button to the direct line with Alex. I always hit the button for our initial line three times and wait. He will signal once if he is able to talk, twice if he is not. I wait, and after he hits the signal once, I switch over to our other line.

"Dude, what the actual fuck is going on?" Alex says the second I turn the channel.

"Sorry, I got caught up."

"Yea, well, now isn't the time to get caught up, as you like to put it," Alex lectures me, speaking in a hushed tone.

"Ok, there is something else I am clearly missing, Alex. What's going on?"

"What's going on is that Lana called me and told you what you did. We talked about this. Having Lana involved was crucial to the success of this," he reminds me.

"I decided that his blood is worth having on my hands. Why have her take the rap for it? He was my father, after all," I say.

"Yes, but she was more than willing to end him. And given her relationship with Christian, he would have her fixed up and new in no time, making her untraceable."

I laugh. "You're sounding more like a criminal than a cop right now."

"I'm very much still a cop, who is trying to help the lesser of two evils, one being my cousin, who is more like a fucking brother," he says, breaking his previously hushed tone.

"Christian will work his magic, whether she has bloody hands or not. I needed to end him, to close the chapter that has remained unwritten, haunting mine and Sienna's lives," I seethe.

"Next time you want to veer from the plan, consult me first. There is only so much I can do to help you. Vanessa was supposed to meet with your father today, and she's going to know something is up when he doesn't show." He doesn't hide his disappointment in his voice.

It's not that he isn't used to my impulsive behavior, he just always worries that one of these days I will be too impulsive, and he won't be able to save me from it.

"We'll be gone by the time she puts anything together," I remind him.

"Remember, the '*we*' you are referring to won't happen if you are in jail. I'm a cop, not a magician. There is no guarantee that if Vanessa pieces together what you did, I will be able to save you from her," he says, taking in a deep, stress-filled breath.

"I'm not asking you to. Now, head over to the old warehouse. I have the bastards corpse to dispose of," I say casually.

"Yea, I know. Lana filled me in. I'll be over in twenty," he says, immediately turning the radio channel off as it fades to irritating static.

I feel a sudden strange ache coming from my ribcage. I must have pulled something, either in the struggle with my father or when I was entangled with Sienna. It's an interesting life I lead, killing and fucking, all within one hour. As I rub my rib to try to relieve the ache, I remember the intentional scar my flesh holds there. I immediately feel an ache in my chest. A memory repressed for so long that its reemergence feels more crushing than comforting.

As I remove my hand from my rib, I hear my calluses scuff against the fabric of my shirt. Reminding me, yet again, of what could have been mine. I lift my hand, sliding a black glove onto it, then switching hands, doing the same to the other. I grab my toolbox as I begin to clean up.

I think back to the ache I felt just moments before I reentered the area that's pooling in blood. A king is nothing without his queen. I remind myself as I pick up the saw. She is worth the bloodshed, the betrayals, the sorrow.

I'm doing this for her.
I'm doing this for us.

Chapter 43

Sienna

Heat radiates on my cheeks as I slam the car door. Frustration kills any ounce of lust I felt just moments before. I stare out the tinted window at the most infuriatingly intoxicating man I have ever had the displeasure of meeting.

Every time he summons me under the guise of work, it doesn't take long for our undeniable desire for each other to take hold.

There is still time for me to abandon ship. It's only been two full days that I have been in the city. There are plenty of other fish *and* employers in the sea, right? Who am I kidding? If only it were that easy. Carmine Moretti isn't just any man; he is an incubus. He haunts my dreams, invades my reality, and leaves me constantly desiring more of him. I moved to the city with the naïve hope that I would be able to start over and escape my past, yet I feel like I'm running into an even more fucked-up version of it. He knows it, too. Every time he stares at me, with those chillingly beautiful onyx eyes, and grins that deliciously evil grin, he knows I won't run. He fucking counts on it. He is quicksand, and I am trapped, drowning in him.

I remember talking to Mama once about the concept of soulmates. This was shortly after I first met Leo. We were young and carefree, but in his presence, there was a deep familiarity, one that felt like home. I made the mistake of trying to open up to Mama about it and I can still hear her laugh buried deep in my psyche.

"Hija, *soulmate implies that our souls know what is best for us, but it's not our souls that determine our love, it's God. You are young still, pray to God that he will show you what is best for you. Don't be fooled by the enemy trying to confuse you with your own instincts,*" she said.

I scoff as I recall her words. Religion robbed her of the ability to step outside of herself for just a moment to consider that there could be more than the doctrine that has been ingrained in us from birth.

That specific conversation has replayed in my head for years. It has consumed me, even admittedly over the grief I feel for my parents at times. That's the thing with unresolved anger; it festers and boils over the good things, tainting everything. All my memories of her are of a mother who didn't know how to give motherly advice. I know she loved me, but all she ever did was preach to me about a god that dictates our personalities, our morality, our everything here on Earth. Shaming us if we do not conform, without giving tangible proof that our conformity to his rules will make it better when our life here ends. All the hollow preaching robbed me of the ability to think for myself, and worse, made me feel guilty for much of my life for attempting to do so.

Maybe that is why I am in the fucked-up position I find

myself in now. Maybe I am fucked up, or maybe I am the product of being steered so far in one direction that I have grabbed the wheel and derailed myself off a cliff of logic or reason. I am what happens when you are pushed too far to conform.

As we continue to drive in silence, I am immediately grateful that Carmine's driver, Rufus, isn't one for small talk. Finally, a peaceful ride without having to deal with Eric's antics. I go to call Titi Lana to find out more about what she had to tell me from the warehouse, but instead, I decide that can wait. I just want to fade into the silence, because I know a storm is on the horizon. I can feel it.

I exit the elevator and head in the direction of my office. The office I have spent minimal time in since I started working at Marked Inc. Who knows how long I will even spend there today, because Carmine, as usual, gave me no real directives, other than that file folder I already have.

As soon as the elevator doors open, I spot Lizzie at her desk. She looks up from whatever she was doing and rises from her seat. I pick up my pace, but she scurries in front of my door, blocking my entrance to it.

"Don't get used to it." She sneers, with her arm stretched in the doorway.

"Oh, hi, Lizzie, how are you?" I say sarcastically, trying to bring attention to her—as usual—rude demeanor.

"The attention," she says, dramatically bobbing her neck as she speaks, which makes her bright auburn hair bounce obnoxiously.

"The attention? What are you getting at, Lizzie? Just speak your mind." I have no time for this.

"I see the way he looks at you." There is a sadness that radiates through her bitchy attitude.

There is so much I can say to her in my defense, but it would only be like throwing salt on her still-healing wounds. So, I refrain. Judging by the broken tone of her voice, it's clear that whatever was between them must have been ended on his account. That, or it was possibly one-sided.

"I don't know what you are talking about," I lie. I feel for Lizzie, but at the same time, I feel foolish. I shouldn't be surprised that I'm not the first employee he has fucked.

Lizzie looks flustered, as though she wasn't prepared for how passionate she is getting talking about this. "You're not fooling me, Sienna, just be careful. The only thing that hurts more than his touch is when he renders you useless and moves on to his next conquest," she warns.

I look at Lizzie, who went from angry to oddly sincere. It was her way of extending an olive branch, I guess.

Thankfully, a phone call comes in, diverting Lizzie's attention back to her desk, allowing me to head to my office and get on with my day. First thing I want to do is finally call Titi Lana so she can fill me in on what the hell she was doing at the warehouse today.

But my focus is stolen as soon as I open the door to my office. My stomach drops when I see the black box from Carmine's brownstone. The box that he snapped at me for attempting to unlock before he opened me up to another world of pleasure I never knew existed.

Confused as to why this is in my office, I walk toward the box in the center of my desk, where I see an envelope. What makes me feel unsettled before I open the box or the note attached is that Carmine was so adamant about me not opening it last night that I doubt he would just leave it here on my desk, like nothing happened. Who left it here? Better yet, who stole it?

I open the envelope and unfold the note that is inside. With a trembling hand, I begin to read the handwritten note.

"The sins his father committed against you don't hold a candle to what he stole from you. His father killed your parents, but he killed someone else you used to hold dear."

I fall to the floor by my desk with the note in hand. I was so eager to read what was in the envelope that I didn't notice there was something else inside. My heart races as I see what appears to be the back of a polaroid picture now on the floor next to me. Hands trembling, I reach for the polaroid and slowly begin to flip it over.

A guttural screech escapes my mouth as I drop the picture. It now lies face up in front of me, and I bring both my hands to my mouth. Trying to hold in the nausea I feel forming in the pit of my stomach. Staring at me, is a picture of Leo and me. Not just any picture, but the picture I had hanging in my room before I left for the city.

It is then I come to the disturbing realization that I have not only fucked the enemy, but Leo's killer.

Chapter 44

Carmine

12 YEARS AGO

Darkness.

I try to open my swollen, aching eyes, but all I see is the bleak, pitch-black abyss ridding me of the ability to process where I am. I feel myself slipping into the ruinous role I was predestined for.

I am pulled from my racing thoughts by the press of cold steel against my wounded body. Once the realization that the cold, sharp point of the scalpel is slicing my flesh, panic sets in. As the scalpel slices through what feels like my temple, I go numb as each cut goes deeper, as if it is about to reduce me to a skeletal form.

I should be fully sedated, but I guess that is an insignificant detail when forced against your own will. My limbs and torso are strapped to the table, I couldn't move even if I wanted to. Whatever they gave me is strong enough to make my body feel heavy, like quicksand is encapsulating me, increasing with each passing second.

I feel numb, yet fully aware, slowly fading into what I can only assume is my body's response to the trauma I have just endured. And now here I am, about to endure more trauma from the man I should look up to more than anyone in this world. He is showing me his scars, while giving me more. Each sting of physical pain is only solidifying my twisted fate.

I want to scream, but the pain is so intense that screaming for help seems useless. I try to wiggle my limbs, but the restraints are so tight I am barely able to move. Another cold slice penetrates my skin, and then more darkness somehow takes over until there is nothing, until I am nothing.

I drift off, not sure if I am dreaming or if I am finally leaving my earthly form and on to whatever realm lurks beyond this earth. I don't believe in Heaven or Hell, so maybe I will become dust. Particles blown about in air and quickly forgotten.

Time passes. How much, I am unaware.

I wake up sometime later and open my eyes, still seeing nothing. Everything is dark.

I go to move my arms, but they are still restrained, even tighter than before. My body feels like it was run over by a truck. I try to take a deep breath and collect my thoughts. My mind is racing almost as fast as my heart.

I try to access what the hell is covering my face, but with my hands restricted, I can't move them to feel what I assume is some sort of gauze.

Since I have no other options, other than laying here, wherever here is, alone with my restricted body and endless thoughts, I try to process what the hell happened. I'm trying to piece together the violence I witnessed, the evil I had no choice but to succumb to.

Suddenly, the silence of wherever I am is broken. Muffled sounds, which I can only assume belong to the monsters who dragged me here, fill the room. I try to focus on what is being said, but I can't make out a sound. My head is pounding, and with my ears covered, it is hard to find the concentration I need to distinguish the sounds happening all around me.

I feel something touch my arm. I can't even flinch like I want to—my restraints are too tight.

"This is Carmine." The familiar voice permeates my ears as the wraps around my face are loosened just enough that I have gained some of my hearing back.

"Son, I am proud of you. What a monumental moment this is. That girl will have no fucking idea what hit her. But I will tell you what, you fucking hit her where it hurts, you stole the last thing that she loved. Now, because of you, she will spend the rest of her days a walking corpse. Dead on the inside, paying for what her parents did to us."

Panic sets it. I don't let him know I heard every word he just said.

What the fuck did I do?

Chapter 45

Carmine

"Now that this is behind us, you should probably go see her. She misses you," Alex reminds me as he helps me lug the last of the bloody tarp into the incinerator. I have spoken to my aunt, Alex's mother, throughout the years, but I haven't been able to go see her in person.

We slam the door of the incinerator shut in unison and step back to admire the flames hard at work, burning a lifetime of backstabbing, cowardly antics. Reducing painful memories to ash. There is justice within the flames. There is immediate relief in my father's absence from this Earth. No longer must I share any space with the man who created me. Now, I can only hope that our sins don't lead us down a similar path and that we don't meet again in Hell. I'll let fate run its course and hope for the best, I suppose.

We stand a few moments more just staring, taking in the finality of my father's monstrous life, when I turn to Alex to pick up the conversation he started. "Funny, didn't think she missed me, since she never mentions it in our business correspondences," I point out as Alex hands me a fresh pack of Parliaments that I snatch from his hand.

"Don't be like that, Carmine. You know why she acts like that. She *has* to," Alex says, defending his mother as he lights up next to me.

"We *all* have had to do a lot to survive him." I nod in the incinerator's direction.

I don't regret killing my father. It had to happen, and what better man for the job than his own flesh and blood, who he betrayed time and time again? Despite it needing to happen, it doesn't make it any easier. Especially when the man staring back at me in the mirror is arguably just as monstrous as he is. Maybe worse. Every day I live a lie. I deceive to survive. Sometimes, I believe that I belong in that incinerator. But then again, if I burn, she remains without me. I did this for Sienna; it was the only way we could be together *for good.*

With my father out of the picture, our family war is null and void. Sienna and I can be together without the threat of war breaking out between opposing families once more. All that is left to do is to convince her that I am the one she needs, the one she craves. I will spend the rest of my life fulfilling every desire she has. I will infiltrate her heart, if I haven't already. I will wake her soul and feed her bittersweet *nightmares.*

"Yea, I guess I should stop by and see her before I leave," I concede.

"She didn't forget about you," Alex says, trying to tame the anger he sees boiling at my surface.

"I would fucking hope not. How could she forget feeding me to the lions?" I shudder at what I had to give up in order to be the one who stands here today, alive. What she allowed to happen to me. I know it technically worked out for the best, but still, it doesn't hurt any fucking less.

"Oh, cut the shit. You know damn well that you don't give a fuck about any of that. I would call you a selfish fuck, but that would require you giving a shit about yourself or anything other than her. God, that fucking girl is going to lead to your demise, if she hasn't already," he says as he takes a smoke from the fresh pack I just opened.

We both light up a cigarette and stand watching the flames burn what's left of Armando Moretti. The crackling sound they make, along with the rattling of the ancient incinerator, echoes in the warehouse. It is music to my fucking ears.

We wait until the job is done, and as we go to lock up the warehouse, Alex puts his hand on my shoulder. His face looks concerned. "Just be certain, that's all, before you leave with her. Because once you leave, that's it," he warns.

"Alex, I've been sure since the moment I met her."

"How did you know that quickly? Shit, I didn't even know with April until we were hooking up a couple months, and even then, she pressured me into settling down. No regrets now, of course, but man, isn't it difficult to be sure of anyone?"

"I'm sure of no one and nothing other than what my soul tells me. My soul has been knocking at my rib cage, roaring to let it free, let it rejoin its other half. She is what my soul has always desired. I won't stop until Sienna Ricci is mine and no one else's."

"Well, I guess, if you change your mind, Christian can

work his magic once more and you can be off starting some-where new *again* ..." he trails off.

"Where we will be, Christian's services will not be needed. I have too many bad memories tied to his blade. I lost too much the day his scalpel tore my flesh. I won't make that mistake again."

Alex finally stops with his attempts to have me come to my senses. Deep down, he knows that I mean it when I say I will stop at nothing to have Sienna Ricci. *All of her.*

Tonight, I will confess my sins to her in the hope that she will grant me the redemption that only she can give me.

But first, I decide to stop at The Sandy Claws for a drink before I prepare for Sienna's arrival at the brownstone tonight. She didn't want to be my dinner guest tonight, but I worked my charm to convince her to stop by for a drink, at least.

I'm about to take a sip of my freshly poured whiskey when I spot a familiar face, Vanessa. *Fuck.*

Alex was right to warn me about her. I knew it would only be a matter of time before she started sniffing around, looking for my father. But hours later, after one missed meet-ing? That I was not expecting. Already sitting down, with my half full glass of whiskey, I swirl the liquid around the glass with laser focus, waiting for her to begin her question-ing. Judging by the intensity of her stride and the stern look on her face, she isn't here for pleasure, she's here for me.

She stops right in front of the table I am sitting at, taking her hands out of the pockets of her long trench coat, placing them on the back of the empty chair in front of me.

"Ah, Vanessa, to what do I owe the pleasure?" I say through a forced smile.

"I came here looking for your father. I was supposed to meet him today and he didn't show up," she says, subtly scanning the small crowd in the bar.

"Have you met my father? A gothic, grunge bar isn't really his scene," I snap back.

"Yea, well, he is your father, and this is your place, so wouldn't any loving father come for a drink to support his son's business?" she says with palpable sarcasm.

I let out a genuine chuckle, nearly spitting out my damn whiskey. "He was anything but loving. Cut the good cop shit. What do you want?"

"Past tense, interesting," she notes.

"Don't get your panties wet, Mrs. Officer, it was a simple mis-wording." I clear my throat. I realize how much of a dick I am coming off as, and truthfully, it's just too fun not to be sometimes. "He *is* anything but loving, satisfied?"

"Hardly." She is unimpressed by my antics.

"Yea, well, you aren't Sienna, now are you?" I mumble as I signal to José to bring me another whiskey, *quickly*.

"I don't know what the fuck your obsession is with Sienna, but I'm not here to discuss her with you," she says, flustered. I can tell that she truly is here on business, which makes her seethe inside that she can't interrogate me the way she wants to about Sienna. I know she will, but first, she must check off the actual cop questions.

"Then do tell, what are you here for?" I ask with genuine

curiosity. I need to get a feel for what she knows; or thinks she knows, that is.

"I was supposed to meet your father today and he never showed. I tried calling him and it went straight to voicemail. Just wanted to see if you have heard from him today."

Just him pleading for his pathetic life.

"Can't say I have." I shrug off her questions, acting as disinterested in the topic of my father as I truly am.

"That's strange, considering he is your father and business partner."

"Was my business partner. Do forgive me for the past tense, but in this case, it is appropriate, seeing that he sold his shares to me not too long ago," I say with ripe condescension.

She rolls her eyes. "Sorry, I just assumed—" she begins before I cut her off.

"Your assumptions mislead you, Vanessa. Now, if you don't mind, I have an evening meeting I need to prepare for," I say as I bring my whiskey glass to my lips, slamming the amber liquid down. José must have been eyeing me from the bar because the second I lower the glass to the table; he comes over asking if I want another. I decline, as I am ready to end this impromptu meeting with Vanessa.

I rise to put my jacket on, signaling to her that I am done here. "Good evening, Ms. Mendez." I nod as I begin to walk past her. I'm not even halfway to the door when I hear Vanessa shift her stance, so she is facing my back. The chair skids just slightly, and her hands are on me, grabbing my attention.

"Oh, Mr. Moretti, one more thing," she begins.

I take a deep breath as I turn back to face her. There is a vindictive gleam in her eyes.

"I have a meeting with another associate of yours coming up. If they don't show up, it will only further confirm my suspicions. I wouldn't do anything impulsive if I were you," she warns.

I just give her a nod.

"I'll be in touch. I know where to find you," she says as I walk away.

"Whatever you say," I mumble, out of her reach as I walk through the curtain entry doors. I head back into the cool autumn air, heading to where Rufus is parked and waiting to bring me back to the brownstone.

Vanessa does not scare me. What does scare me, however, is who the fuck is trying to talk to her, aside from my father. If there truly is another rat in our midst, then it's going to be a fucking problem. I don't have time for another snake in the garden.

I phone Alex on the way to the brownstone. "So, your girlfriend was at the Sandy Claws," I joke.

"Very funny, fuckface. If you're referring to Vanessa, yes, I know. She made a huge stink, as I knew she would, when Armando didn't show to their meeting."

"Yea, well, that's insignificant to me. She can't prove anything. However, she did mention that there is someone else that's talking to her. Know anything about that?" I ask.

"Fuck would I know?" Alex asks.

"Well, look into it, because if I go down, so do you, cop or not. You are in this for life."

"You are like a brother to me. I will look into it," he says with genuine love. It's true, Alex has always been more like an older brother to me than a cousin. I have never doubted his loyalty to me.

"Good. Alright, well, I have to go. Sienna is coming over soon," I say as I unlock the front door to the brownstone.

"You finally going to admit what the fuck you did to her?" he asks.

"Depends how the night goes."

Chapter 46

Sienna

"Did you know?" I ask Titi Lana, afraid of the answer I am about to hear. I lay on my bed, just staring at the ceiling, wishing this was just a bad nightmare.

"Yes, honey," Lana confesses with a sadness in her voice.

I drop the phone and stare at the picture of Leo still in my hand. I hear Titi Lana ask into the phone if I am there. I don't pick the phone up yet, I feel paralyzed with reemerging grief.

I take a deep breath and reach for the phone. The sadness and anger I feel simultaneously mixes in my gut, making me feel as though I am going to be sick.

"That's it? Don't you think you owe me a better explanation than just a simple yes?" I don't bother hiding my anger. At this point, I am seething. I feel so betrayed.

"I don't know where to start, Sienna. The Riccis go back a long way with the Morettis, there is a lot of bad blood there," she says with a sigh

My head is spinning. I knew my family had secrets, but this, this feels like too much to comprehend in a day. How could any bad ties have anything to do with Leo? I search my brain of all the years I knew him, trying to think of anything that could have hinted there was something wrong.

"How does Leo fit into that, though?" I ask, genuinely confused.

Lana takes a deep breath. "Like I said, there is a lot of bad blood between the families. Leo was caught in the crossfire," she finally says.

"Of what, Carmine's wrath?" I snap as warm tears begin to pool in my eyes, and then uncontrollably spew down my face.

I feel nauseous, this is all too much. I suddenly realize this job wasn't given to me because I deserved it, it was given to me because I needed to be here. I'm a puzzle piece in Carmine's sick game. He's been watching me, waiting for me, fucking playing me. My parents' deaths didn't excuse me from the made life, they just catapulted me into it.

"I think it's best that you calm down and talk to Carmine about this. He will be able to explain things better than I can to you." The calmness in her voice turns my tears into rage.

I somehow doubt that he can explain anything to me that will put my mind at ease. This man has had twisted motives with me from the start. Not to mention, he has a literal box of secrets he has been hiding in his home. A box that I am going to make him own up to, whether he wants to or not.

Lana continues to talk, trying to ease my mind, but it's not working. My brain is moving a mile a minute, thinking of all I have learned today. "It's a fucked-up tradition in made men's families. Carmine's mother leaving made it complicated." Lana stops. "I've already said too much. Listen, call me later once you talk to him. I love you, Sienna." She hangs up. Not with a warning, like everyone else has given me about being careful around Carmine. Just a generic goodbye, as if my world hasn't just caved in on me ... again.

I hang up the phone and stare in my closet to find something to wear tonight for another evening meeting at Carmine's. I sift through the crowded hangers until I find the sexiest dress I own. A black, form-fitting, off-the-shoulder dress that hugs my curves with a slit on the thigh, much like the one Carmine tore off me last night. Except, tonight, I am not dressed to impress; I'm dressed to kill. Kill him for what he stole from me.

I want to make sure I have him groveling at my feet, begging for his life with a hard dick when I put the barrel to his head. I will seduce him and get one last blast of pleasure before I end him. *I need to end him.* There is no other way. How can I go on fucking the man who killed my Leo? Carmine stole the last good thing I had in my life and now I will make him pay for it.

All these years, I have been tormented by grief for the man I loved, not knowing what happened to him. Not knowing the reason why he left me so unexpectedly, only to find out I am screwing his killer, who also happens to be my boss?

I should have known better that something like this would happen. My father had unsettled disputes. I will be plagued by my family name for the rest of my days. I've always felt that way, but today, this... Well, it solidifies that feeling.

It was foolish of me to think running off to the city would

resolve any of my issues. Instead, I ran to the lap of a murderer, an irresistible one at that.

That's what the most messed up part is. I barely know this man, yet, when I'm with him, I want him inside me. I feel this mind-altering experience when I am entangled in his ink-drenched skin. Just the flashback of his muscles gripping me as he ate me to orgasm makes me twinge inside.

I look at myself in the mirror before I head out. I barely recognize the woman that stares back at me as I slip my pistol into the lace garter. It was a gift from Titi Lana on my eighteenth birthday. I remember the day she gave it to me; she told me that every woman who runs in our family's circles needs to have three weapons on her at all times: her brains, her looks, and a gun discreetly holstered, where her prey will likely fall. And given the fact that Carmine has made himself at home between my legs, killing him after he's done there will be as poetic as his end will get.

He will pay for this.

I walk to Eric waiting outside the town car and roll my eyes at his predictability.

"You are early," he says, peering down at the garter that just slightly peaks out of from my dress. It shows just enough to be seductive, but not enough to give away what I have stowed away in it.

"Cut the shit, Eric, I'm not in the mood," I say as I head to the driver's side door.

Eric scurries to follow me. "Oh, no need, Mr. Moretti

specifically instructed me—" he warns as he sees me about to open the driver's door.

I cut him off. "I don't give a fuck what Mr. Moretti has instructed you to do," I warn as I take the pistol from my garter. "I said I will drive tonight, now get in," I instruct, pointing him to the passenger seat with the pistol in my hand.

Eric is calm; the fear I anticipated on his face is not there. He seems oddly unfazed by the weapon in my hand.

I glance at my watch. Eric got to the apartment early, which bodes well for me, because it gives me the opportunity to arrive before Carmine is expecting me. I need to catch him off guard. I'm so tired of this controlling prick planning every single encounter.

"I really don't mind driving," his voice trembles slightly, but he is surprisingly calm for me pointing a gun at him.

I cock the pistol. "Don't make me repeat myself. You know who my father was, right?"

"Yes," he concedes.

"Exactly, so, unfortunately for you, little encounters like this are in my DNA. So, don't try a fucking thing. I won't hesitate to shoot your dick off," I warn as he hands me the keys.

I hold the pistol in my right hand the entire time just in case Eric tries anything. I probably should be worried about the level of exhilaration I feel right now, gun in hand, on the way to seduce my kill.

"Should I call Mr. Moretti and let him know we are on our way?" Eric asks.

"No, that's fine. I'm dressed to kill tonight. I don't want

to spoil the surprise for him," I say with a determined grin on my face.

We pull up to Carmine's brownstone and that nauseous feeling I had when Lana told me about Carmine and Leo begins to surface again. This all feels incredibly unfair. I finally make it to the city, have this cushy job that literally affords me all the time in the word to write what I want to write on the side, given the lack of legitimate work given at said job. I meet a rockstar in the sack who worships my pussy unlike any man I have ever met, and now, I have to fucking kill him.

I throw the car in park and turn to Eric.

"I've got it from here, but thank you for helping me in your own fucked up way," I say, giving him a kiss on the cheek, pistol still aimed toward his dick.

"Oh, you are more than welcome, Sienna. What are friends for, right?" Eric says in an ominous tone.

I secure my pistol back in my garter and grab my tote bag from the backseat.

"Leave," I remind Eric as I make my way to the front door of the brownstone.

Eric slowly drives off as he peers at the front door. He knows what I plan on doing after I get my answers. I think I made my intentions with Carmine this evening clear. I just don't need Eric parked out when the shots are fired. I need time to clean up the mess.

I go to ring the doorbell, but I notice there isn't one. A detail I hadn't noticed before since Eric let me in last time. There is an old, gold knocker in the shape of a bat centered on the door. I try not to smile, but there is something unexpectedly sweet about Carmine's ode to gothic architecture.

Shit, Sienna, focus.

I lift the knocker and am startled by how quickly Carmine answers the door. As we both stand in the front of the brownstone, I notice he seems genuinely surprised at my early arrival. Good. I want him to feel thrown off. It will make what I came here to do that much easier.

I look past his stunned expression and instead take in his broad, strong shoulders adorned with black and grey ink that peak through his tank top. There is ink splashed all over his body that it is difficult to decipher where one tattoo ends, and another begins.

"Ah, Sienna, I wasn't expecting you yet," he says as he outstretches his arm on the wood trim that surrounds the doorway.

Once again distracted by the murals of ink on his skin, I swallow hard trying to remind myself of what I came here to do.

"I know. I figured I would take you up on that offer for a drink sooner than we discussed. I'm feeling rather thirsty this evening," I say flirtatiously.

He grins, immediately picking up on the vibe I am throwing his way.

"Sounds good to me, please come in" he says motioning for me to enter.

I walk through the doorway and stand in the dimly lit foyer as he locks the door behind us. Following his lead, we make our way in silence to the study toward the back of the brownstone.

"I'll make you a drink to enjoy while I finish getting dressed" he says about to head to the bar cart when I reach my hand out, stopping him.

"What's the point?" I say as I bring my index finger to the exposed skin on his forearm. I know I'm putting the charm on heavy with the intention of getting him going, but as my skin is touching his, I feel the effects start to work their way through my center instead.

He looks at me with a ravenous grin. This is going to be a lot harder than I anticipated. "Very well, Ms. Ricci. What will you be drinking this evening?"

"I'll have a Manhattan."

He nods, surprised that I deviated from my usual drink order. Honestly, I wasn't even in the mood for a Manhattan, whiskey is not my favorite but it's the first drink that came to mind. It's like my subconscious wanted me to honor Leo in some weird way, considering that I came here with the intention of confronting his killer. Leo's Titi Rose always made herself a Manhattan to relax in the evening and she would make him one from time to time. Manhattans became his favorite drink because compared to the cheap Coors we would drink at parties; it was a welcomed change. Tonight, honoring him with his once favorite drink feels fitting.

"Manhattan, interesting choice. You continue to surprise me," Carmine says, and for some reason, he looks uneasy.

"I guess I'm full of surprises; what can I say? Truth be told, I'm not much of a whiskey drinker, but it was a good friend of mine's go-to drink."

"I see," he says with palpable apprehension.

He hands me the drink. "I will be right back." I walk toward him, grabbing the loops on his pants. "Like I said, what's the point in getting dressed?" I repeat myself.

Anger surges through his perfectly sculpted face as he

takes my hand, spinning me around and forcing my freshly made drink to the floor. In a swift rush, he pins me against the bookcase, forcing multiple books to fall from its shelves. Still pinning down my hand, he takes his hand and works his way between my legs. Panic sets in, not wanting him to see my gun, but thankfully his hand travels to my other thigh.

"Someone is horny tonight," he says as he curls two fingers inside of me, working them in and out at a slow torturous pace.

As his rough hands enter me, I feel myself starting to drip onto his fingers.

"Now, tell me, what's a pretty girl like you doing with this?"

Before I could even answer him, he pulls the gun from my garter as he moves his fingers faster. He brings the gun to my temple as he continues to fiercely fuck me with his fingers.

"What's the matter, Sen? Suddenly speechless, *mi reina?*"

The way "queen" in Spanish rolls off his tongue as he whispers it in my ear is enough to bring me to release at this very moment.

"Stop calling me that," I say in between panting.

"What, Sen or *reina?*" he grunts.

"Both, I don't know, just stop." I say flustered, as anger and arousal battle each other inside of me.

"Why?" he presses. "Say it!" he demands once more.

"Because he called me that." I admit, feeling a tinge of defeat knocking at my heart.

"Who called you that?" he roars, as he continues to press

me for answers that I don't want to give him. This is a sick game he is playing; I should give into the anger I feel and stop him. Though the way his fingers feel inside of me is clouding my judgement.

Before I can answer, he continues working my center as he brings me to an explosive end. My walls tighten around his fingers as the aftershock of my release courses through my body.

"That's it, *mi reina,*" he says, taking his now drenched fingers out of me. "I love when you come undone for me."

Fuck, he has me so frazzled. I need to get that gun back. I'm not leaving here until I get what I need from him ...*revenge.*

He releases me from his grip, my pistol still in his hands. Panic begins to take over as I try to think how I can get the gun back.

Oblivious to the way I am racking my brain with how I am going to kill this fucking bastard; he moves back over to the bar cart to pour himself a drink.

"You know, they say you can tell a lot about a person by what they drink. Seems your friend, the Manhattan drinker, tried too hard," he says with an irritating, cocky attitude.

"How do you figure?" I reply, eyes still fixed on my gun.

"Manhattans, although popular, are a pretentious drink for wannabe whiskey drinkers. If you want whiskey, just be a fucking man about it. Drink it straight."

"But it stings more that way," I say, trying to steady the beating I feel in my chest.

"That's the point. The sting is meant to distract us from the pain we feel," he says as he places the pistol on the bar cart, now walking toward me.

If I wasn't on a mission to kill this man, I would welcome his vulnerability, but right now, I need to find a way to get the pistol back and maintain the upper hand. Then Titi Lana's words hit me like a ton of bricks.

The three weapons. Brains, looks, sex.

I walk toward him and bring my lips to his. Pulling him in for a kiss. God, even his whiskey-flavored lips fucking do it for me. I brush my hand over his growing bulge. Atta *boy.*

I begin to kiss his neck before I kneel in front of him. I look up at his overwhelming physique hovering over me, feeling like I am kneeling to a dark king, a wicked god. Pleasure returns to my middle and my nipples peak as the simple act of kneeling at his feet is bringing me an unexpected level of pleasure.

"Let me return the favor," I say with a hungry grin as I begin to unbutton his pants. I glance over to the bar cart to my left, figuring that I have a small window of time after I suck him off that I can run to grab it.

I realize this is the first time in all our trysts that I am going down on him. I may be using oral as a distraction technique, but I'd be lying if I said I wasn't looking forward to having his salty venom drip down my throat.

Taking the base of his thick, pearled length, I guide it into my mouth, making it hit the back of my throat. Which immediately makes him groan. I work his shaft with my thumb, rubbing his bulging vein as my mouth glides up and down.

As I am working him with my mouth, I glance up, wanting to take him in as he's enjoying it. I speed up the pace, trying to make him come quicker. I have a small window to kill the man whose dick is currently hitting the back of my throat.

I feel his fist tighten against my hair as he is about to explode in my mouth.

My opportunity is approaching.

Chapter 47

Carmine

I tug her onyx locks wrapped around my hand as her warm mouth glides up and down my cock, picking up speed. Keeping my hand firm against the nape of her neck, she takes all of me in her mouth, like the good fucking girl she is. As her lips glide up and down my length, her lipstick begins to smear, painting my shaft with a seductive hue of mauve pigment. Looking up at me with her siren eyes, she swirls her tongue, massaging the bulging vein at the base of my cock, which begins to send me over the edge. I feel release start to build up as I am getting ready to pour my venom inside of her.

"Like that, *mi reina?*" I ask as she lets out a slight purr. I can tell my arousal is increasing hers.

"You like taking my cock in your mouth, my dirty girl?"

"Mhm," she replies.

"If you keep purring like that, you're going to make me explode."

She slips me out of her mouth, and I feel a sudden desperation overtake me. No, don't tease me, not now.

"Then do it. I want you to pour your poison down my throat," she says to me with her hand still wrapped around my shaft.

"If that's what you want, *mi reina*."

"That's just the beginning of what I want from you," she says deviously, as she readjusts herself, this time picking up the speed she as she brings my length in toward the back of her throat.

I close my eyes, getting lost in the ecstasy that is her mouth. I tilt my head back, pouring my release inside of her. Like the good girl she is, she doesn't waste a fucking drop of my venomous seed. My eyes are still closed as I revel in my post-orgasm high when I feel it ... a shift.

A literal shift, Sienna is stealthy, because no sooner than she swallows the last drop of me does she bolt toward the bar cart. My pants still at my ankles, I chase after her, toward the pistol that her eyes are locked on. She reaches for the pistol as I jump behind her, forcing us both to the floor. I roll on top of her, trying to pin her down.

We lock eyes as both of our hands are on the grip of the gun.

"Give it to me, you bastard!" she yells, trying to fight me off.

"My cock or the pistol?" I sneer.

She spits at me. Her salty saliva stings my pupils as I shake my head to wipe away her spit. I grip her wrist tighter, forcing her hands to drop the gun. I kick the pistol away, keeping my hands on her wrists.

Fuck.

She is sexy when she's angry.

She takes a deep breath, trying to squirm her wrist from my grip, but she should know better. I have no intention of letting her go.

"You are an evil bastard, you know that?" she says, spitting once more in my face.

"Suddenly decided you'd rather spit than swallow?" I tease.

"What do you want from me, huh? You fucking lured me here. For what? To hire me, seduce me, and then know what it feels like to fuck your kill's ex?"

I look at her, confused. My tone shifts, because I suddenly feel like everything I suffered for, everything I waited for, is going to be lost.

"You don't know shit!" I yell. I am coming off angrier than I am. Inside, I am dying with nerves, but I can't let her see that.

"You're psychotic!" she screams. "Let go of me, you fucking bastard."

"That's rich, coming from the woman who begged to have me fuck her mouth, all the while she has been sitting on this supposed information," I remind her.

She tries to let go of my grip, but I won't let her go. Not now, not ever again.

"I'm over you and your games," she seethes.

"The games have only just begun." I flash her a wicked grin, tightening my grip on her.

"Give it to me," she demands.

"Mmm, such a pretty sight, seeing you beg for me. How long I have waited for you to beg for it, *for me.*"

"I know you killed him, it had to be you!" she says with tears beginning to form in her eyes.

"Killed who? I gather you have figured out what I really do for a living. Let's try to narrow it down. Who I killed today? Last week? Last year?" I say, evading her obvious question. I know who she is referring to. I was going to tell her, but not like this. Fuck, none of this is going the way I thought it would.

"Think farther back than that, you sick son of a bitch!" she yells with tears in her eyes.

I release her, genuinely wanting to hear what she thinks she knows. "Ok, who, then?" I ask, already knowing the answer.

"Leo!" she yells. There is such pain drenched in the volume of her voice.

Fuck. My stomach drops. This isn't going to end well.

"You killed the one good thing in my fucking life!" She shouts.

She doesn't fight back her tears. She is sobbing. What would be an otherwise ugly sob if it came from anyone but her. But with her, nothing is ugly. Her feelings are valid, raw, *real*. Unlike me. Everything about me up until this point has been fake, a farce. A sad fucking attempt to mask the pain I carry, the secrets that define me, the past that I have tried to escape.

I want to wipe her tears away. I want to take her right here, right now, but not when she is like this.

"Nothing about you makes sense. Nothing has made any fucking sense since the moment you hunted me down and brought me here to this," she says, looking around. Hands up in the air, as if she is admitting defeat.

Not yet, mi reina, we are so close.

"So, what is it? Do you get some sick pleasure out of stalking ex-girlfriends of the men you murder?" She is sobbing as she walks toward me and starts pounding my chest in anger. I stand there, taking every blow of her fist, every tear splashing in my direction. I take it because I deserve it. I unintentionally caused her a pain I never intended for her or me. I was only trying to save her.

I continue to stand there as she is pounding her fists into me until she finally collapses into my chest. I stand there stiff, not wanting to make a single move that will throw her off.

"What, are you fucking dead? Say something, you fucking prick! You owe me at least that," she mumbles into my chest, her voice muffled from her tears.

"I owe you much more than what my words can attempt to explain," I finally say.

"You are a fucking soulless bastard, just like your father, my father, every man in my fucking life. Every man, except for him," she says, wiping away her tears.

"Who, Leo?" I ask, looking down at her, grabbing hold of her chin.

She steps back, loosening my hold on her perfect fucking face. "Don't you dare say his name, you don't get that right!" She slaps my face. *I deserved that.*

"Take the pistol. Go ahead, finish what you came here to do," I say in defeat.

She looks at me, confused. "What? You're not even going to try to defend yourself, explain yourself, anything?"

"You didn't come here for explanations; you came here for vengeance. That look in your eyes, Sienna, I know that look all too well. That is the look of a lover so scorned, so broken that having the blood of the person who stole the one in your life that made you feel less broken, even for a split fucking second, is worth whatever consequence may come of it."

She stands there, not expecting my bluntness, perhaps, because she is momentarily frozen. I, too, feel frozen, stuck in a position I never wanted to be in ... *her enemy*. I wanted to be her refuge, her safe space, her lover, her greatest conquest. Yet, somehow, we ended up here in this bleak, cold, fucked up place.

"So, go ahead, Ms. Ricci, try to shoot me," I say, with my hands up in the air.

"I'm a good shot. Be careful what you wish for," she tries to steady her voice through her tears as she reaches for the pistol.

"I do not doubt that the daughter of Matteo Ricci is a good shot. The only thing I doubt is that you'll be able to pull the trigger."

"You are contradicting yourself."

"Having the ability to do something and actually doing it are two different things. Ms. Ricci."

"I'm going to kill you Carmine Moretti. Shut the fuck up," she says as she slaps my face again.

I stand stoic.

"You are fucking unbelievable, say something, feel something! Goddamn it. Killing you almost seems pointless! Feel something, you fucking piece of shit."

"Why? because I am already dead inside?" I ask her.

"Well ... yes. I figured you would beg for your life, something, anything. But clearly, you don't give a fuck about anything or have an ounce of remorse."

"If you wanted to kill me, you would have done it already."

"No, I am waiting," she says.

"For what?" I ask, curious as to what she could possibly be waiting for when her opportunity is ripe.

I watch as she walks to her purse. She bends down, a fucking magnificent sight. She picks up something and remains bent, facing the pocket doors that remain half shut.

Her grip still firmly on the gun, she turns around with whatever she just took out of her purse. I am so lost in watching her that I almost miss what she is holding. I study her eyes, still damp from emotion, as she peers down at her hands. I then follow her gaze. Immediate horror fills my soul when I see what she is holding.

I realize then that only one of us is going to make it out of this room as we entered it.

Rest In Peace, Carmine Moretti.

Chapter 48

Sienna

I thought this moment would feel more liberating, but the more I gaze into his eyes, I'm not so sure. I feel more conflict and less consolation than I was anticipating.

I've waited so long for this moment; to finally have answers, to be granted the gift of closure. But is closure a gift when you realize that the one that can close that painful chapter is the one who caused it in the first place? Even worse, the closure they can provide is nothing compared to the hole they will leave when they are absent from your life.

Carmine is the reason I have suffered the worst heartache I have ever experienced, aside from my parents passing. He is the reason Leo is gone, yet here I am, standing with the box that holds the answers he has the key to, and suddenly, I don't want to go through with what I set out to do.

There is so much of him that reminds me of myself and that scares me. Nothing about him is good, except for how he makes me feel. Maybe that is enough. Maybe I am not any better than he is. Maybe we are a match made in Heaven or Hell, who even knows anymore what is real.

I feel like I don't know anything anymore.

As much as I don't want to see the contents of this box, I need to. I have to. For Leo.

"You stole that?" he accuses. He starts to inch toward me like a lion moving in toward its prey. Methodically planning the opportune moment to pounce.

Not this time, buddy.

"It was a gift," I say, tightening my grip on the box with my gun still visibly planted underneath it.

"It's not a gift if it was stolen," he says, inching closer again.

I move the box away from the direction he is walking toward me.

"I don't know who left it on my desk, but it is the gift I needed to end this torturous chapter in my life." I take a deep breath. "To end you." I let the finality of my words drip slowly off my tongue. Despite the inner turmoil I have suddenly been plagued with, I need to let him know that there is no way out of what he has done to me.

He takes yet another step closer to me, causing my heart to beat so fast that I swear I can hear it echo against my chest.

"I don't know who took that and gave it to you, but this is not how I wanted you to—"

I cut him off. "What, find out that you killed my boyfriend?"

He shakes his head. "Sienna, you don't know what you are talking about. You have absolutely no fucking idea what I have gone through."

I step to him, and with both hands, I shove the box into

his chest. "What you have gone through? Oh, please, whatever you think you have gone through has been nothing compared to the hell I have had to live all these years," I say, pushing the box into his chest harder. "Now, open it!" I demand.

He takes the box from my grip, looking at me with pleading eyes.

I stand there, staring at him. Waiting for him to refuse, to argue, to say something. But he says nothing. Instead, he heads to the bookcase and places the box on the shelf next to what I immediately recognize as a collection of Poe's poems. I recognize the binding because I have the same exact edition in my collection. It's one of my favorite books that I re-read often.

He turns to me, as if oblivious to the situation at hand. "Do you like Poe, Ms. Ricci?" he asks.

Thrown off guard, as I am in almost all encounters with Carmine, I shake my head, trying to process my response. "Umm, yes, of course, I like Poe," I reply, confused. "He is the only one of the classics that made my English lit degree tolerable," I confess.

"No surprise there. You strike me as the dark romantic type. Much like myself."

I shake my head, becoming increasingly agitated. Typical Carmine, always playing games. Too bad I refuse to let him win. Oh no, not this time.

Pistol still in my hand, I move to the bookcase that he is leaning against, aiming it right at him.

"Open the fucking box right now," I demand

"Or what? You are going to shoot me?" He shrugs, without an ounce of fear in him.

"Yes!" I shout back

He clicks his tongue. "No, you are not. You would have done it already." His tone is more of a reprimand, which sends my blood boiling. My finger is shaking on the trigger, but just as I am about to pull it, he begins to speak.

"... this maiden she lived with no other thought," he begins to recite from memory.

Is this whack job seriously reciting Edgar Allan Poe right now? And not just any Poe work, but "Annabel Lee", to be exact. *My favorite poem.*

"... than to love and be loved by me," he continues to quote.

My heart flutters so fast that I feel lightheaded. I lower the gun and bring my hand to my temple, rubbing it in disbelief of all this man keeps putting me through.

"Carmine, stop it!" I beg.

He stops reciting the poem and brings his hands to the chain on his neck. Ah, fuck, that key. I try to stare away from it. I have pleasurable memories tied to a key that I don't think many people can say they have.

"You have a choice; either I unlock it or you do," he says as he rubs the top of the skeleton key with his thumb, eyeing the box he placed on the shelf.

"I want you to unlock it," I demand

He nods in satisfaction with my response. "As you wish."

He stands there with the key in hand, but neither of us move. I feel every emotion possible at this moment, though my anxiety is starting to take over, making me increasingly angry.

"Carmine, the box," I urge him

"I was a child and she was a child, in this kingdom by the sea ..."

There he goes again reciting Poe. I can't take this anymore. He has stolen everything from me, and now, I feel him stealing my Goddamn sanity, or whatever remnants are left of it.

I charge him, gun in hand, and strike him to the ground. He maintains his firm grip on the key, quite literally holding onto it for dear life. As we tumble, entwined, the gun thuds against the floor, skidding away from us. I try to crawl toward it, but he flips me over, pinning me to the ground.

I squirm under his grip; his eyes are pinned on me just as much as his hands.

"Is this why you dragged me here, to torture me?" I yell, with tears flooding my eyes as he remains fastening me to the ground, overpowering me.

He says nothing as I continue to yell at him.

"Do you get some sick satisfaction knowing that you have fucked what he used to? Knowing that you killed the person I once loved"

I stop.

Once.

I said once. Not love, as in the present.

I said the person I once loved. Past tense.

The truth stings as it whips me in the face. A part of me will always love Leo, but knowing he was killed, as tragic a reality as it is, is the closure I need. Fighting this man, killing this man, won't bring Leo back. And it certainly won't bring me back. Nothing I do can resurrect the girl I once was, and as I look into Carmine's dark irises, I realize maybe I'm not supposed to.

"No, *mi reina*, I brought you here not to torture but to unravel you," he declares, with an odd sense of pride. "You have tried to stitch your broken pieces for so long, but what makes you so uniquely beautiful is the pain you carry, because it has turned into the strength you wear so eloquently."

His words are as oddly poetic as they are cryptic. I squirm once more under his grip as he continues his speech. "You asked why I summoned you here. The answer feels complex, but it's simple, really. I needed to provide you with a new foundation of truth. Perhaps it is one you didn't think you needed, but it is one you deserve."

Well, shit, this sounds a whole lot like a fancy, drawn-out version of torture to me, but even his evil truths are aphrodisiacs, it seems.

"And what foundation is that?" I say, holding back the burning tears I feel beginning to collect, waiting to be released.

"On me. Where you are meant to rest in peace."

"You're going to kill me?" I ask, my voice trembling.

"I'm not going to kill you. I'm going to resurrect your soul, so you can feel alive again and free from the shackles of grief that have bound themselves to you." His words sound sadistic, but the passion that he exudes feels anything but.

"I have lived too long, feeling as if I am dead, and something tells me, Sienna, that you have done the same," he continues.

I shake my head. "Just give me the key," I say, trying to snap myself out of the trance he has me in.

"I'm not your enemy," he says, almost sounding convincing enough for me to believe him. But I don't, *I think.*

"How can you say that? You're a murderer!" I shout.

"I killed for you."

"Don't you dare pin your kills on me. Every kill you have made is on you, because of you," I seethe.

"I had to kill Leo," he begins, but that is when my hearing dimmed.

Had to kill Leo.

His mouth continues to move as I replay that sentence repeatedly in my head. The confession I have been waiting for. The confession that makes my world come crashing down all over again.

I finally come to, snapping out of the fog his confession has me in as I catch the last of what he is saying.

"The only way that I was able to preserve your life was to end his. It was the only way I could save you. It was the only option I had to save us."

I can't believe what he is trying to tell me right now. What, did he seriously believe that killing Leo was the best way to separate us, so he could have me for himself?

"There is no us, you sick fuck! Now, give me the fucking key!" I shout, my voice still trembling, but the anger is taking over.

"I've waited so long to say this to you, Sienna." He clears his throat, about to speak whatever he thinks his piece is. I'm fully expecting him to begin reciting Poe again, but as he begins speaking, it's not Poe he is reciting, it's my poem.

"Fractured we remain, scarred by our past and wary of the future," he begins to recite.

My heart is racing. How does he know that poem? No one, aside from Leo and Eddie that day at the tattoo shop, ever laid eyes on it.

"Carmine, what are you doing?" I ask, but he ignores me and continues.

"Together we sit waiting to be mended from a pain that feels like it's beyond repair."

"Stop it, you are scaring me," I plead. The emotions this is bringing up in me make me feel sick. Though, as I look at him reciting my poem, there appears to be a weight lifted off his shoulders.

"One side mine, one side yours."

"You're fucking sick, Carmine, stop!" I plead, fighting back the tears.

"I hold the needle, you hold the thread ... Oh, how I have missed you my beautiful, *Sen,*" he interrupts himself.

"Stop!" I shout. I can't take this anymore.

"You should be the one to open it, but before you do," he stops himself and begins to take off the undershirt he is wearing.

What the fuck is he doing?

I look down at his usually confident, strong hands, which are now trembling. His vulnerability in this fucking bizarre moment we have found ourselves in is like a magnet. I can't help but be drawn to him.

I rise and stand in front of him, waiting. For what exactly, I'm not sure. But this moment, through the bewilderment and betrayal I feel, something tells me to stop and hear him out. To see what it is that has him quivering.

My gaze locks in on the tattoo on his hand. I watch as his fingers begin to bend as they grasp the fabric of his undershirt. He slowly begins to raise the fabric, revealing his torso. The muscular definition that comprises his arms continues through his abdomen, as does the mural of ink that adorns the rest of his body.

My eyes scan his flesh as the white of the shirt disappears, leaving me with a feast of muscle and black ink to rest my sights on. I'm not sure why he is taking off his shirt so dramatically, but as he turns, I suddenly become dizzy. Déjà vu, nausea, desire, grief all begin to invade my system. I feel like the room is spinning, yet I am grounded in the vision before me.

It can't be.

I squint to make sure I am not hallucinating.

But there it is.

My heartbeat quickens, and my limbs feel heavy. I move closer to him, to confirm that this isn't a dream, that this isn't a nightmare.

A shiver works its way through my spine, as I lift my hands outward and closer to his skin.

There it is, buried in a sea of ink and scars. I run my trembling digits over the distinct jagged scar on his ribcage that runs through an intricate black and grey design of a locket.

A half locket with the face of a rag doll.

My breathing quickens as I see in cursive lettering, right beneath the locket, the word "siempre." *Always.*

I say the word beneath the tattoo out loud as he takes my hand in his.

"I had it added shortly after that day, just like in the painting that Eddie's—"

I look up at him. "Leo?" I whisper in absolute disbelief of the words that are coming out of my mouth. "It can't be true, can it?" I ask, my whole body shaking in disbelief.

"It's the only truth I have left, Sen. Please, open it." He motions to the box. "Everything you need to know has been waiting for you in that box. It's been in there since the last time we went to the cemetery."

"How do I know—" I begin to ask before he cuts me off.

"If it's me?" he interrupts. "Ask your soul. It has recognized mine since the second you saw me on Devil's Night," he says with tears in his eyes, which somehow, as he is speaking, lessen in their onyx tone.

He begins to recite the last two lines of the poem I wrote, the one that inspired our locket tattoo, all those years ago. "*I am the needle; you are the thread. Together, we weave a wicked love story from the dead.*"

"Oh my God."

He grabs my face, cupping it in his large palms.

"God has nothing to do with it," he says as he presses a kiss on my lips. "God, if such a concept truly exists, could never drum up enough creativity to give you to me, and he certainly couldn't keep me from you. No imaginary concept in the sky could ever be responsible for the way I make you scream my name, or the things I would do to your body for the rest of my days. Nothing, not even death, can separate my soul from yours. This is real, Sen. Can't you see, *mi reina*, you and me, we are simply meant to be."

Chapter 49

Carmine

Mi reina.

The cause for my demise.

The reason for my triumph.

The only one that can evoke love from my bleak, damned soul.

For far too long, I have felt dead inside. Haunted by visions of pain and carnage, reducing me to a shell of the man I once was. But with her, the shadows that consume my life have a home. With her, my darkness no longer needs to hide, but instead, it can play ... with hers.

We were robbed of our beginning, without explanation. Now, only we can write our ending, no matter how fucked up a tale it may be to get there.

She remains speechless as my grip stays on her delicate face. Her tears stream down her cheek, splashing against my fingers, as I wait for her to say something, anything.

I hate that I betrayed her, but I will do whatever I have

to, so she knows all that I have done has always been for us to exist again.

When my mother was alive, she used to call it "dying unto oneself." She meant it in the more religious sense, to deny oneself their desires and urges to honor God. I did something similar, except, in my version, I denied who I was —killed him—so I could blend into the world my father forced me into. So I could live to see her. My desire has always been her, and my urges have been to kill anyone and anything that stands in the way of that. *Myself included.*

I have fantasized about this for so long that I don't know what I will do if she runs. My soul simply could not survive another parting. I would rather her shoot me in a fit of rage than live another second of this wicked life without her. *Without us.*

Letting go of her chin, I walk to grab the box, hoping that its contents will help explain what I know my words alone cannot.

As I reach for the box I am startled as I feel the warmth of her trembling touch on my bare ribcage. Without a warning, she lifts my right hand up to expose my side of the locket we share, etched on my flesh. She traces her over the healed artwork that rests beneath the scar I wear from my father's wrath years before. No amount of surrounding ink or wounds to my flesh could ever take away from the sentimental shine of our locket.

The feel of her fingers on my skin eases my worries. She continues moving her delicate fingers overtop my ink, feeling the validation she needs and deserves, while I wait. As delicious as her touch feels, in this moment, I crave her voice.

I know she must have questions, lots of them. How could

she not? It's not every day that you learn your boyfriend, who disappeared without a trace, suddenly reemerged as a blood-thirsty criminal, who will literally burn the fucking world to the Goddamn ground to get you back. That, and I look nothing like I used to. Shit, I'm nothing like I used to be.

I lose track of how many minutes pass as we stand here in silence. Once she finally drops her hand from my torso, I use it as my opportunity to give her the box.

"Here, it's yours, as am I, *mi reina*," I say, handing her the black box with the same elongated skeleton key that I brought her to the brink of ecstasy with just yesterday.

"Thank you," she says, finally breaking the silence with beautifully glossy eyes from the tears she has cried.

She seats herself in front of the fire, on the floor which creaks as I kneel to join her. We sit together as she inserts the key, twisting it once to finally unlock what I have kept from her all this time.

Bittersweet memories come crashing at us both as she sifts through its contents. Pictures of us, cards from anniver-saries, everything I could hold on to before I saw her again, it is all in the box.

"Oh my God, Mama's earring. I knew I had to have left it in your car when we drove to the cemetery," she cutely exclaims, as if the pictures of us, the tattoos, all of it weren't enough evidence.

Then, she pulls out the note I wrote her just before I had her summoned to the city. When I needed a therapeutic release before I could get to her.

"What's this?" she asks, beginning to unfold the note.

"A letter I wrote you," I say, suddenly feeling a flush strike my cheeks. Now I know how she felt in the cemetery all those years ago. The vulnerability of having your written thoughts read by another is a fucking trip.

With the paper still in hand, she places the box on the floor as she lifts herself, bringing her lips to mine.

"Read it to me ... out loud," she sweetly demands, handing me the words I wrote for her. A deliciously devious smirk escapes from her mouth and she nudges me. "Payback's a bitch huh?" she jokes, referring to that night I read her poem out loud.

"For you, *mi reina*, anything," I say, playfully obliging her request. It's the truth, there isn't a thing in this life, or any life that may exist after, that I wouldn't do for her. Limitations do not exist when it comes to what I would sacrifice for my rag doll.

My heart thumps in my chest as I clear my throat. But it's not my nerves I feel that cause my heart to skip a beat, it's the feeling of absolution I feel in this moment beside her.

Mi Reina,

Life without you is purgatory. My heart a ticking time bomb, locked in a holding cell with bated breath, anticipating the moment my tattered hands will have the privilege of touching your flesh. Life with you will be like a game of Russian roulette: unpredictable and impulsive. Together, we will live on the edge of greatness that our broken souls know nothing of but crave immensely. Through pain, grief, flames, and dust, it's plain to see that you and I are meant to be.

El que tiene las respuestas

"Fuck," I blurt, suddenly exasperated as I finish reading.

The man I am claiming to be looks nothing like who she associates with the name that used to be mine. My soul is the same, but my body looks nothing like what she is used to me looking like.

"What happened to you?" she asks, bringing her soft hand to my face. She moves the stray strand of hair that covers my eyes out of my way.

"My father," I begin.

"Your father?" she asks, confused.

I take a deep breath, finally willing to admit the fucked-up lineage I come from. "My older brother died when I was young. He was my father's pride and joy. He never wanted kids, he just wanted one son to be able to pass the family business on to. Carmine was that."

"Carmine?" she asks.

"Yea, that was my brother's name. He died in a car accident. Except, he wasn't driving. He got plowed by a drunk driver when he was outside playing one day, and my father blamed my mother. He blamed her because he wasn't home," I scoff in disbelief at my father's antics now and then. "Funny thing is, he was never home. He didn't give a fuck about anyone but himself, but with Carmine dead, the original plan of my brother taking over on his eighteenth birthday was out the door. So, the fucker waited until my eighteenth birthday to claim what he felt was his, or some fucking bullshit like that."

"Fuck," she says, taking a deep breath, processing what I just told her.

"Yea, you're telling me. He was such a worthless piece of shit. He took out all his rage on my mother, to the point where she knew the only way that I would have a chance at happiness was for her to leave him and escape to my Titi's house."

"Oh my God, Titi Rose," Sienna says, slowly putting the pieces of the puzzle together.

"Yes. Rose Cruz was my mom's sister. My father was furious that my mother left him. He threatened to kill her, and once your father learned just how much of a piece of scum mine was and cut business ties with him, he followed through with his threat.

Rose raised me as her own, since her son, my cousin, Alex, had grown out of the house already. We knew it would only be a matter of time before he came for me, just like he did my mother," I say as a chill begins to creep down my spine, going down this fucked up memory lane that is my family tree.

Sienna shakes her head. "Wait, I'm confused."

"If you weren't confused, then that would make you more devious than I give you credit for." I grin. "My Titi Rose had enough of my father's bullshit. He was responsible for the deaths of all the people she loved. My father killed my Uncle Victor after a business deal went bad. He killed my mother for escaping his wrath, and he killed your parents for not wanting to associate with him and his shitty business practices anymore. Titi Rose wanted him dead and knew that if she called him and said he could have me on my eighteenth birthday to help carry out the family business, I could infiltrate the business and eventually end him." The relief that comes from finally talking to someone other than Rose or Alex about this is exhilarating.

"Wait, but how does that explain how or why you look the way you do?"

"Ha, you can also thank my father for that. The night we went to the tattoo shop, my father was infuriated to find out his only living son, who he never gave a fuck about, was dating a Ricci. He had Christian work his magic on me by reconstructing my face to look like someone you would never believe is me. It was his way of taunting me with what he thought would be the end of us." I shake my head at just the thought of my father thinking he could separate Sienna and me permanently.

She takes in a deep breath. "Well, the joke is on him because you are immaculate."

"Guess you can say I was derived from an immaculate

conception," I say, not being able to pass up the joke she set me up for.

She smiles at my joke, before her face falls to a serious state once more. "I have waited so long for this; something I didn't even know was a fucking possibility. I thought you left me, ran off with someone, or were dead. I hated you for so long," she confesses, and I can sense a trace of guilt in her voice. But she shouldn't feel guilty. I don't blame her for how she feels.

I grab hold of her face once more, bringing her into me. "It's my fault you are like this."

Sadness and anger blend. "No, you don't get to take credit for the woman I am. Heartbreak made me stronger. I pulled myself up from devastation, and it wasn't you or God or anyone else, for that fucking matter. I saw my way out of the flames. You can't take credit for that," she says, breaking from my grasp as she rises and walks closer to the fireplace.

"I would never try to take credit for the woman that stands before me. You have grown on your own. Morphed into a masterpiece of strength and beauty all your own. I just ask that you let me know this Sienna 2.0," I say, following behind her.

"What song was playing the night we went to the cemetery?" she blurts out, clearly not listening to what I just told her.

Our song.

She turns to me, finger pointed at me. I know she is still processing all of this, but fucking Christ, does she look intoxicating when she is angry. "You owe me this. If you even are who you say you are. I need to be certain, answer my question so I can know if you are the monster that I see or the man that I know."

"Sen, *mi* beautiful *reina*, I am both the monster you see before you and the man that you know, that owns your heart like you do mine. Leo was weak; Carmine is strong. He was my father's creation, but I have survived in this new role. I have fucking thrived in it."

"Please, cut the poetics and answer my question. I need to be certain," she demands once more.

She is right. I owe her that much. And she isn't running; that is a good sign. It's because, deep down, I know she knows, souls don't lie when they find their mate. The soul leads and the body and the mind simply follow the soul's command. Our souls have been branded to each other. *Marked.*

I pull her close to me with an intensity that even surprises myself. I cup her face in my hand, while my other hand is firmly against her hips. I guess it's the kind of intensity that would be expected when in the presence of the person who owns your soul. And she, Sienna Ricci, owns my damned soul, every irredeemable, depraved, hollow part of it.

I still don't answer her. Instead, I move over the speakers on the bookshelf. I still have my old iPod. A dinosaur in today's technological world. I keep artifacts like that often because they bring me back to a simpler time, a time when it was just her and me. I can sense her impatience as she lets out a frustrated sigh. With the iPod in hand, I swipe to our playlist and hit play on our song. As soon as the guitar starts, I hear sobbing, pure sobbing.

I don't know whose sobs are whose, hers or mine, but together, we are beautifully broken, trying to sew the pieces together of our shattered past. A shattered past we never asked for. Before I can turn around, I feel her wet tears on my neck as she kisses it.

"Hello, there, the angel from my nightmare," the Blink 182 song "Miss You" swoons over the speaker. We don't say a word, there is no need to. This is our song, a somber tale of our angsty youth. Which now feels like the anthem of our love story.

Despite the ignorance of our youth, we always knew that we were destined for each other, even when no one believed we would last. But fate is a tricky thing; you can try to run from it, but you can't escape it. A marked soul will always find its way home to the one it finds true solace in. My soul has always ached for her, my heart has always had her name etched into it. Love was merely a foolish concept until the day Sienna Ricci walked into my life. Now, I wish the word love could even begin to portray the way I feel for her.

Tears streaming down from both of our faces, we intertwine our bodies and somehow make it in a swift motion from standing to panting on the floor. Clothes go flying as tears continue to fall. Fierce, intense kiss after kiss, we lock eyes on each other and there is nothing else in this world that matters.

"Leo, my Leo," she cries out between kisses.

"Sen, my beautiful Sen." I kiss her cheek, reveling in the salt that is her tears. There is not a part of this woman I don't love, not a part of her I don't want to know. Her happiness, sadness, anger, revenge, brokenness are hers just as much as they are mine. Every good, bad, and mundane part of her is living breathing art.

With the music still playing in the background, she

straddles me as she grinds against my growing length. In a matter of seconds, she guides me into her. The warm embers from the fireplace illuminate her every curve as she bounces with more intensity on top of my dick.

The sound of the crackling fire mixed with her wetness as she rides me is like music to my ears. I look over to the antique mirror across from us. I begin kissing her neck as I stare at our intertwined reflection. It is then I see the pieces of the locket fall into place. My right rib tattoo joins her left rib tattoo. As our bodies collide, the pieces of the locket tattoo join. An insanely poetic way to fuck *mi reina*.

She flashes a seductive grin as she begins to pick up the speed as she rides me. As if, this didn't feel good enough already, she lifts both her delicate hands to her breasts as she starts playing with the barbells that pierce through her nipples. She licks her full lips and then says the most intoxicating words I have ever heard. *Her poetry.*

Out from her mouth pours the words that inspired our tattoo. The words that I have replayed in my mind every single fucking day, to help me make it through the depravity that has engulfed my being.

The heathens, the heretics, the lost souls, who pick up the pieces he so conveniently has forgotten. Our hearts, both broken into pieces, can be joined together like a locket. To make what is broken, whole. To make what is full of doubt, full of peace. One side mine, one side yours.

Hearing her recite her poetry while I'm deep inside her

is a religious experience. An experience I will never forget and hope to experience for the entirety of my days.

She pushes me down, so I lay flat on the floor as she grinds on top of me, working her hips, riding me to a state of bliss. I don't take my eyes off her, not for a second.

"Carmine," she pleads in pleasurable bliss.

"You can call me Leo if you want," I whisper.

She lowers herself on top of me, her hair brushing up against my face as she goes to whisper in my ear, "Leo never fucked me like you do. Now bend me over and claim me, Carmine Moretti. I'm yours"

"Is that what you want, mi reina, to be claimed?"

As she shifts her body so that she is on all fours with her ass presenting to me, she looks back at me. "I want to be, marked."

She arches her back up ever so slightly as I grab her neck, squeezing it as she purrs.

"That's a good girl," I hiss.

I thrust into her, loving the slap her plump ass makes against me. "Yes, Carmine, yes," she squeals.

I can't blame her for still calling me Carmine. Leo was dead to her. Carmine found her. Leo let her go and Carmine will never be so foolish.

"Where do you want it?" I ask as I continue to pump closer to my release.

She angles her head back, peering her eyes upward toward me. "All over me. I want to drown in you," she replies as she quickly releases her sex from my length. She flips around, kneeling in front of me, tilting her head back and sticking her chest out as I paint her with my venom. Marking her as mine, and I'll be fucking damned if ever lose her again.

Chapter 50

Sienna

It's him. Well, the new and improved him.

A more chiseled, sinister version of the boy I used to know. But that's the thing, we aren't kids anymore. We have grown into versions of ourselves that twelve or thirteen years ago we never would have seen coming. Life has handed us a fucked-up deck of cards and we are dealing them our way, however we see fit.

I'll admit, I feel less guilt now knowing that the mysterious man, who has been consuming my mind and ravishing my body every chance he can get, is who my heart has always longed for. This new version of him makes my heart and body feel things the old him never could.

As I clean his cum off my chest, I look at him slipping his pants back on, admiring the way his broad, muscular back tapers into a V shape. The name Leo doesn't fit the man that stands before me. The man who stands before me is ominous, mysterious, bold. All the things that Leo wasn't, but back then, I wouldn't have appreciated those traits as much as I do now.

As I begin to get dressed, I can't help but shake the feeling that something bad is about to happen. I can't explain it, but it feels as though we are on the cusp of a war of some sort. It's an ominous feeling, like the one I got the day Mama and Papa were murdered, and the day Leo disappeared.

There have been numerous times in my life when I have felt as though there is danger, lurking in the wind. This vibe that I am getting makes me feel like this is just the beginning. Of what, I'm not sure, but something is coming, I can feel it.

"What's on your mind, *mi reina?*" he asks, taking notice of the perplexed look on my face as I try to sift through what exactly has me feeling this way.

"Why do I feel like things are about to get worse?" I ask.

"Because they probably will," he says with an eerie, honest calm.

"Wow, that's reassuring." I try to laugh it off, but I truly can't shake this feeling in the pit of my stomach.

"I'm sorry, I don't mean to come off blunt, but that's something I have learned quickly in this life our parents have dragged us into," he begins. He takes a brief pause, pulling out a cigarette from his back pocket. He runs the filter across his lips, wetting it slightly before lighting the end. He closes his eyes and takes an exaggerated inhale. He pauses briefly before exhaling the smoke out slowly, along with a grunted sigh. His eyes still closed, as if he is about to unleash more truths my way.

I brace myself for whatever may come out of his mouth now as he redirects his stern gaze my way. Puckering his lips around his Parliament once more, he takes in a brief puff of smoke before allowing it to hang from his mouth as he begins to talk.

"The night it happened, changed me. A war was declared that I had no choice but to immerse myself in. The night my father stole me, he forced this life upon me and with that I have fallen into the familial role of having a long list of enemies. So, sadly mi reina, the threat of danger quite literally lurks around every corner. It's best you live each day expecting the worst to happen, so on the off chance it doesn't you can revel in feeling safe...even if momentarily."

He exhales smoke and offers me the moistened cigarette. I reach for his half-finished cigarette, bringing it to my lips, as I nod for him to continue.

"I remember that night like it happened yesterday. I still don't know what was worse, the physical pain or the emotional turmoil. I learned weeks later, once the bandages came off, that my face was no longer mine and my name, along with my entire life, changed as the dominoes began to fall," he says, shaking his head, as if still in disbelief.

I take a quick drag before handing him back what remains of our shared Parliament. He takes the last of it, inhaling deeply, before he walks the butt over to the ashtray on his desk.

"It's ironic how the job Christian was forced to do on me is now crucial to the success of Marked Inc. Aside from the drugs, we are pros at lying, concealing the truth, concealing identities. It's all part of the dark magic that is the company."

I walk over to him and trail my index finger down the length of his forearm. My fingers slowly crawl down to the bulge still present between his legs.

"Was this one of the alterations you had done?" I can't

help but grin, thinking of the newfound experience that is his length inside of me.

He lets out a laugh. "Ha, oh, that?" He looks down suggestively at my hand lingering over his length. "No, I had that done somewhere else. I figured you would enjoy that improvement."

I lick my lips. "Oh, yea, I've never been with anyone who is pierced down there." I suddenly blush.

He leans in for a kiss, letting his thumb linger over my bottom lips.

"Pearled, *mi reina*, not pierced." He chuckles. "Anyway," he begins as he releases me and paces his study.

"Vanessa told me about people, suspected criminals mostly, literally disappearing into thin air," I say bringing the conversation back. Now it all makes sense. Why the Moretti family has been getting away with so much over the years. They are literally untraceable by design.

"Trust me when I tell you, most have not disappeared. I mean, yes, some, are dead now, but that is beside the point," he says nonchalantly. "But most are still here roaming these crowded New York streets with their masks on. Think of it like an episode of *The Twilight Zone*, mobsters getting a new face on every time the feds are on their ass. Camouflage of the flesh," he jokes.

"So, what made you finally track me down and bring me here to the city?" I ask.

"Your Titi Lana," he begins, grabbing hold of my hand. "After my father had your parents killed at the gala, Lana formed an alliance, if you will, with my Titi Rose. My Titi started taking over the family business after her husband, Victor, was killed by my sleazebag father."

"Titi Lana?" I ask in disbelief.

"Yes, Lana has been working closely with Titi Rose, well, you may now know her as Miranda …" he trails off.

"Wait. Creepy Miranda?"

He laughs. "Yes, creepy Miranda." He refocuses the conversation. "Lana and Rose—or creepy Miranda, as you put it—have been a huge driving force in the underground drug running I have been doing. The goal has been to save as much of it for our escape as possible."

"Escape? Carmine, what the fuck are you talking about?"

"Sienna, I am a criminal. A criminal that cops like your friend, Vanessa, can make their career off bringing down. It's only a matter of time before Vanessa becomes more suspicious and Alex won't be able to protect me anymore," he says, squeezing my hand.

Before I can respond, a loud thud comes from outside the study. It sounds like it came from the hallway.

"Are you expecting anyone?" I ask him.

He puts his finger over his lips, motioning me to be silent as he grabs his gun and quietly inches toward the door.

"Hide," he whispers.

I hear his warning, but I choose to ignore it.

"Hide, Sienna, now," he repeats, this time in a more commanding voice.

"No." I stand my ground.

"No? Really, this isn't a time for stubbornness, Sienna." He tosses his cigarette on the floor and gives it a tap with his foot to put out the glowing embers.

"I'm not being stubborn. I can protect myself. I don't need you sacrificing anything else for me," I whisper.

Unamused, Carmine rolls his eyes. "There is no

convincing you, huh?" A sweet smile escapes his face before redirecting his attention to the sound from the hallway.

"Nope, so don't try."

I've lost you once. I'm not losing you again.

Suddenly, the noise stops. Carmine looks at me apprehensively, and then both doors to the study slide open as Eric enters with a vicious look in his eyes.

"Eric, what are you doing here?" Carmine roars. He brings his hand to the pistol holstered at his side. He senses it, as do I. Something is off.

"Sorry, Boss, this couldn't wait. I was supposed to meet with your father today, but Lizzie informed me he hasn't been around?" Eric says, unconvincingly.

Carmine lowers his brow, hand still at his side, ready to retrieve his pistol if need be. "Since when does Lizzie concern herself with my father's affairs?" Carmine questions.

"Since she became my girl and has been looking out for me," Eric says, as if that would make either of us flinch.

A sarcastic chuckle spews out of Carmine's mouth. "Ah, I hate to disappoint you, Eric, but if you came here to flaunt your newfound relationship with Lizzie, I could give a rat's ass who she fucking spreads her legs for. So, cut the shit and tell me what you are really doing here."

Eric shrugs his shoulders before throwing up his hands. "Alright, Boss, you got me. I didn't only come here to tell you how good of a fuck Lizzie is. I also came here to tell you that this little reunion you are having with Sienna—well, that ends tonight," he says with a sadistic look.

"Oh, yea, and why is that?" Carmine steps to Eric, puffing out his chest. Both of them are muscular and tall, but holy shit does Carmine tower over Eric, in both size and intimidation factor.

"Because we are going to fucking kill you both," Eric says, laughing.

Rage overcomes Carmine as he charges Eric. Eric ducks and tries running toward the fireplace, but Carmine is too fast and grabs him, slamming him by the collar against the bookcase. Books come crashing down as the bar cart vibrates from the force of their scuffle.

Carmine takes his clenched fist and crashes it into Eric's smug face, which only makes him laugh, fueling Carmine's anger more. Blood begins to trickle down into Eric's thick beard as Carmine doesn't relent, continuing to pound his fist into his face.

"What the fuck do you mean, *we?* Who is the fucking we?" Carmine demands between punches.

Suddenly, the sound of heels clicking down the hallway steals all our attention.

"Her and me," Eric mumbles, wiping the blood from his lip.

Lizzie appears in the doorway wearing a long, tan trench coat, with a matching hat that is serving some serious Carmen Sandiego vibes.

"Good evening," she says, giving me a vindictive glare first before directing her attention to Carmine and Eric.

Carmine releases his grip on Eric as he walks in Lizzie's direction.

"What the fuck are you doing here," he seethes.

"Oh, Carmine, don't pretend that I am a stranger in front of your girlfriend. I have serviced you plenty of times after work in this very study."

I internally cringe at Lizzie's comment. She looks at me instead of Carmine, as if waiting for a reaction from me. She can wait all day. I am not giving her shit.

"What are you and numb nuts doing here?" Carmine demands.

"Seeing things through is all," she says with a smirk. But I notice through her forced smile she keeps side-eyeing Eric. I then decide to divert my attention to Eric in case he has any tricks up his sleeve.

"What the fuck does that mean?" Carmine asks, unimpressed with how they are dragging whatever this is out.

"It means," Eric interrupts, "you are an ungrateful son of a bitch. You don't deserve any of the opulence or power you have. And you certainly don't deserve her."

Carmine's jaw tenses as he is still facing Lizzie, with his back turned to Eric.

"You are right, Eric. I certainly don't deserve her, yet she has chosen me over you, and she will continue to choose me over you in this life and the next."

Eric shakes his head, clearly pissed off. He goes to open his mouth, but Carmine, back still turned to him, cuts him off.

"Is that why you did it?" Carmine asks.

"Did what?" Eric asks.

Finally, Carmine turns to face Eric, as Lizzie and I watch whatever battle needs to happen between them.

Carmine begins to pace, walking in a circle around Eric, a tactic that is already throwing Eric off his game.

"Ah, let's see, where do I begin?" Carmine asks rhetorically, before he lays into Eric. "Stole from me. And I don't mean just the box from the brownstone. Although we will address that in a second."

With Carmine still circling him, Eric tilts his head to catch Carmine's glare on him.

"I don't know what you are talking about," he says, almost convincingly.

Carmine stops his pacing and charges Eric, pinning him against the bookcase once more. "Stop playing fucking stupid. I know you are the rat. I know you stole from one of my runners. I know it was you, and then to top it off, you stole something from the brownstone."

Grabbing Eric by the collar once more, Carmine twists his clenched fist upward, slowly cutting off his airway, causing him to cough.

"I know it was you. Admit it." Carmine spits in his face before releasing his grip on him.

Gasping for air, Eric collapses on the floor.

"I stole the box, but you are wrong about all that other shit," he says, trying to defend himself.

Shaking his head, Carmine grabs the gun from his side and cocks it back, aiming it at Eric. "Are you calling me a liar, Mr. Mendez?"

Wiping more of the blood that has been dripping from his nose off his mouth, Eric shrugs. "That's exactly what I am calling you."

My eyes widen. As soon as the words leave Eric's lips, Carmine presses the trigger, reducing him to a lifeless lump on the floor.

Lizzie lets out a shriek as she runs to Eric's side. The crimson that pools from his body begins to stain her coat.

She kisses the top of Eric's head and whispers something before she rises.

"Sienna, Sienna, Sienna. That's all you ever thought about. You never gave a fuck about anyone else but her. Well, it's your downfall, Carmine, because when you go to jail, your girlfriend won't be alive to miss you anymore," she threatens.

My stomach turns with her threat, because women like Lizzie, the scorned kind, fulfill their promises and relish in their threats.

Unfazed, Carmine reloads his gun. "Oh please, you didn't give a fuck about him. What, are you going to kill me because I offed your flavor of the week? Get the fuck over yourself, Lizzie," he snaps.

"I know you killed your father," she says rather plainly.

"I don't know what the fuck you are talking about," Carmine denies.

"I set up cameras in the warehouse. I knew it was a matter of time before you killed him for all he put you through. Too bad he didn't rat you out to the cops." Lizzie sneers.

"Impossible. I know it was him and Eric," Carmine says, trying to wrap his head around this mindfuck of a conversation as much as I am.

"Oh no, that is where you are wrong, Car. It's very fucking possible," Lizzie says with pride.

Holy shit, the rat was Lizzie.

Piecing it all together, Carmine outstretches his arm, pointing his gun to her. "Lizzie, really? How could you?"

"How could I, Carmine? How could you? The fucking

both of you. You both just live life breaking people's hearts because you couldn't accept that the two of you were over!" she shouts, ripe with pain. "I still have access to your computer. The second I saw you researching the island, I knew you were trying to slip away unscathed. Not this time," Lizzie threatens.

I hear Carmine shout something as Lizzie runs at him with her gun in hand. She hits him with such force that it knocks his gun out of his grasp. He grabs for her hand that the gun is in, constricting her movement as they scuffle.

I don't know if it was panic, adrenaline, or both that determined my next move, but the thought of losing him again was not an option I was willing to risk. I grab Carmine's gun from the floor and carefully take off my heels so I can sneak up on them.

Lizzie breaks free from Carmine's hold on her, and just as she is about to aim her gun at him, I creep up behind her and tap her on the shoulder.

As soon as her shiny auburn hair wafts my way, I pull the trigger without hesitation.

Carmine looks up at me in a grateful shock. "Sienna, why did you do that?"

I ignore his question and pick up one of the books that fell when Carmine had Eric pinned against the bookcase earlier.

Carmine meets me at the bookcase. "Sienna, why did you do that?" he asks. "I could have handled her."

I grab his face in my palm, and on my tiptoes, I rest my mouth inches from his.

"Oh please. An unarmed person against an armed one, you do the math. There is a higher probability of the Jets winning the Super Bowl," I tease him before resting my lips on his.

His tongue swirls in my open mouth as he twists me against the bookcase. Traveling his lips to my ear, he whispers, "I would never let anything happen that would take me away from you again, you know that."

I pull away from him, locking my eyes onto his. "I know, but you know what?" I ask as he nods for me to continue. "The best thing you could have ever done to me was shatter my world, because it was then I realized I could survive broken. I just can't live without you."

He smiles. "You never have to again."

"Good." I look at Carmine to quote the most appropriate Poe work I can think of, as I place the book back on the shelf. "In the words of Poe himself—'I was never really insane except upon occasions when my heart was touched.'"

"So, have I touched your heart, Sen?"

"You own it," I remind him.

Chapter 51

Carmine

I glance down at the pool of crimson that has begun to seep into the grooves of the weathered wood floor.

Without me having to say a word to direct her, she begins to roll the drenched rug away so we can begin the clean-up process.

As she finishes rolling the rug up and stares at Lizzie's and Eric's lifeless bodies, she suddenly slams her palm to her forehead. "Shit," she exclaims.

I go to comfort her. "I know this is a lot to absorb." I motion to the blood that surrounds us. It's a reminder of how I will kill anything and anyone that stands between her and me.

I've done it before, and I will continue to do it. Eliminating anyone that dares threaten us again and judging from how *mi reina* swept in on today's action, I think it's safe to say she feels the same.

She shakes her head. "No, no, it's not that. Although, yes,

this is a fucking mess we have found ourselves in," she agrees. "It's that I forgot I was supposed to meet Vanessa for drinks today," she says as she heads for her purse to grab her phone.

"What time?" I ask as she retrieves her phone from her bag.

"In a little over an hour, shit," she says, suddenly looking nervous.

"We just have to hurry and move them to the warehouse, then I will take over," I say, trying to reassure her.

"Ah, God, that creepy-ass warehouse ..."

"Yes, that warehouse. The same one I fucked you in by the last tarp I blooded. Oh, *mi reina,* don't act like you are above the depravity."

"I never said I was. It's just that when I am with you, it's like I have this darkness that comes to the surface," she confesses, making her even more exquisite to me.

"Does it scare you?" I press, curious as to how admitting that darkness exists within her makes her feel.

"No, because when I am with you, I feel like myself. Like everything I was told is wrong isn't, because out of all the people in my life that supposedly care or love me, you have been the only person who I feel like I can be myself around."

"Then it's not darkness, *mi reina,* it's your truth, our truth."

"You're right, fuck 'em," she says as a wave of relief takes hold of her.

"Fuck 'em."

~

Sienna and I work together in silence, moving in perfect unison. I hand her the tarp; she hands me the rope. Working like a well-oiled machine, a very fucked up machine, but an efficient one, nonetheless. I guess that's what happens when you are a product of this crime lifestyle. There is no escaping it. We were destined to have blood on our hands, because it has been poured into our DNA.

Once Eric and Lizzie are wrapped and ready for transfer, I text Alex to meet us at the brownstone. Sienna wraps her arms around me from behind and whispers in my ear, sending a familiar chill down my spine that only she is capable of.

"Are you sure we need Alex for this? Shouldn't we just keep this between us?" she asks, kissing my cheek.

"If we want to keep this between us, having Alex involved is crucial."

I call Alex, and he arrives at the brownstone within minutes. When he meets us in the study, his brow furrows at the rolled-up tarps and now dried blood on both of our clothes.

He hesitates, unsure of how to proceed in front of Sienna. "Um, Car, you want me to drive Ms. Ricci home first?"

"No need. She will be accompanying us," I say as I reach for her luscious hips, dragging her in close to me.

Alex looks surprised, but he obliges. He remains quiet as we lug the bodies into the car and for the remainder of the drive to the warehouse. I can only imagine what is going through his head right now. We have never had company during any of our disposals.

The memory of me taking Sienna in that barren warehouse is making the blood rush to my length. I smirk, indulging myself in the memory of getting lost in her curves once more when I look over to her, noticing she suddenly seems frazzled.

"What is it, Sen?" I ask, rubbing her arm.

She stares at her phone, scrolling through what looks like numerous text messages.

"It's Vanessa, she left me a voicemail and a whole bunch of texts asking if I'm with you," she says, looking nervous.

"Fuck, we need to hurry," I say, trying to reassure her. Vanessa has no idea about the warehouse. At least, I don't think. So, we shouldn't have to worry about her showing up there."

"Guess we are going to have to wait to fuck again at the scene of the crime," she jokes with playful eyes.

Ha, my little minx. Great minds think alike.

"Technically, it's where we are hiding said crime," I tease.

We exchange a smile that is worth more than any words could possibly convey. Her presence brings a calm to the chaos that has embedded itself in my life. Though, somehow, with our hands interlocked as they are, all I can see is the finish line. The quick approach to exiting this life that has held us captive, dictating who we should be and with whom we need to be with..

As Alex turns down the long stretch of bumpy road that leads to the warehouse, he looks in the rearview mirror to grab hold of my attention.

"Carmine, doing this quick would be in your best interest. Vanessa has been blowing up my phone this whole drive, until I lost service," he warns.

Fuck, this woman is relentless.

Chapter 52

Sienna

"Alright, I can take over," Carmine suggests as we finish lugging both Eric and Lizzie's bodies to the front of the warehouse, so they can be disposed of properly in the incinerator.

"No, this is my mess just as much as it is yours. I want to help," I say, as I grab the hair tie from my wrist and begin putting my hair into a ponytail. I always wear my hair down, except when I am exercising and cleaning. But now, I guess I can add disposing of bodies to that list.

Carmine clears his throat. "Sienna, please."

"Stop it, I can handle it," I say with a confidence that surprises even myself.

I'm so sick of the men in my life treating me like some delicate flower. If I was capable enough to aid in killing them, then I'm more than capable enough to aid in their disposal.

I know this isn't his first kill. God knows how many he has sent to the incinerator, so it doesn't surprise me that he assumes I will sit this one out. He may be used to working alone, but now, we will work in all regards as a team.

He hesitates. "Yes, but—"

"Yes, but nothing," I cut him off. "I want to help. Let me just text Vanessa back first."

I go to grab my phone, but he swipes it out of my hand.

"What the fuck, Carmine?" I shout, my voice echoing amongst the warehouse walls.

"*Mi amor*, there is no service here, remember? Where we are going you aren't going to need that," he reminds me as he tosses my phone on the ground.

"Unless we are going to the grave, where could we possibly be going that doesn't require a cell phone?" I ask, but he isn't listening.

Instead, he walks to the front of the warehouse. I watch as he slowly opens the door as a loud creak echoes filling the stillness that surrounds us.

Facing away from me, I see him lean over to hug someone, revealing a woman's manicured red nails embracing his back. He whispers something to the woman he is hugging. He stands up and moves from the doorway, revealing a familiar face.

Creepy Miranda.

She flashes a warm smile. Honestly, the only smile I think I have ever seen from her—as either Rose or Miranda— as she begins to head toward me.

"Hello, Sienna," she greets me with her hand extended, waiting for me to shake it.

I stand there, still trying to process everything I have learned today and everything that has transpired since.

Finally, my hand meets hers as I try to think of something to say. "Hello ..." I stall, suddenly realizing I don't know what to call her.

She releases my hand and directs her attention to the incinerator. "I see you two have wasted no time in getting reacquainted. I trust that you have filled Ms. Ricci in on the next steps?"

I look at her, confused. "Next steps?" I ask, almost not wanting to know the answer.

"Yes, dear, the way for you both to make it out of here. You have too much blood on your hands, as does my dear nephew." She darts her eyes to Carmine for a second before redirecting her gaze to me. "Truthfully, Plan B is probably what is best for you both—"

Carmine interrupts. "I haven't told her about that yet." He looks at Rose, signaling his annoyance with her revealing what he hasn't yet.

She clicks her tongue, shaking her head as she walks to the incinerator to turn it on. The motor begins to rumble stealing all our attention.

"Well, now isn't the time for dallying, Carmine, we discussed this. Alex has stalled enough with her cop friend. You are running out of time," Rose says in a stern tone. "Remember, boy, you wanted this. You wanted her. This is the only way you get to keep her. This is the only way out," she reminds him, sounding ominous.

Where the fuck are we going now?

"Goddamn it, I know, would you give us a fucking minute," Carmine roars as he reaches for my hand.

Unfazed by his outburst, she agrees. "Fine, just make it quick. We need to clean up this mess and get you both out of here," she says, directing her attention back to the incinerator.

"*Mi reina,* do you trust me?" he asks, stroking my hand in his with his thumb.

"I shouldn't," I tease.

He squeezes my hand slightly, the vulnerability that briefly entered his voice now is overtaken by his stern tone. "I'm serious, do you trust me?" he asks again, this time with an intensity that makes my heart skip a beat.

"Yes, I do. Beyond all logic and reason, I do," I admit. My answer brings a smile to his face, softening his intensity just a bit.

"Good." He unclasps his hand from mind, bringing his calloused palm to my cheek. "What if I told you that we could go someplace where we wouldn't have to worry about all this? Start anew, start over together."

"That sounds amazing, but how?"

He looks over my shoulder, out the large window of the warehouse that is behind us. There is a bright light that begins to peer through the glass, reflecting off the steel columns that hold up the structure. I turn to see where the light is coming from as I hear a whooshing sound of what sound like a helicopter. It's difficult to see clearly, but from the way the trees outside are rustling about, and the noise that accompanies their movement, my assumption appears to be correct.

"Your cousin is ready for you both," Rose shouts, sounding out of breath, as she begins lugging one of the wrapped bodies toward the incinerator.

Panic begins to set in as I realize that the helicopter is for us. I'm not afraid of going to whatever undisclosed destination Carmine has in mind, although knowing him, maybe I should be a little scared. It's the realization of leaving without being able to say goodbye to Vanessa and Titi Lana, or even tell them where we are going, that makes me feel sick.

"Wait, I have to say goodbye." I head to pick up my phone, but it's useless, even if there was service, the screen is shattered from Carmine chucking it on the concrete.

Carmine lowers his hand to where I am crouched down on the floor. "Leave it, Sienna." He gestures to my broken phone. "Lana knows. She will take care of updating Vanessa when she can, and in time they will be able to visit," he reassures me as I shift my weight to his hand to stand back up.

"Visit us where?" I ask.

Rose slams the door to the incinerator closed and its loud sound steals my attention. She walks over to me, opening her arms for an unexpected hug. She squeezes me before stepping back to take my face into her hands.

"Sienna, I know your life has been riddled with heartbreak. Just know that only you are in charge of writing your happily ever after. You are strong, you can and will do amazing things. Take care of my boy, he has waited what feels like a lifetime for you." She smiles before dropping her sentimental demeanor and bringing back her usual intense one.

She gives Carmine a hug and then motions us to the back door of the warehouse. "Now, go, both of you!" she commands.

Carmine takes hold of my hand as we hurry our pace to the back doors. As soon as he presses his weight into the bar that opens the door, the sound of the helicopter is almost deafening.

As we approach the door to the helicopter, Carmine steps ahead of me to open the door. My eyes are met with Alex in the pilot seat, along with Nada who is sitting next to me excitedly wagging his tail.

"After you, *mi reina*."

"Carmine, where are we going?" I ask with my foot on the first step leading into the cramped quarters.

"To live out our beautiful nightmare," he says with a devastatingly beautiful smile.

Once seated, Alex wastes no time taking off to wherever we are headed.

Carmine rests his hand on my lap as my head falls on his shoulder.

"So, can we live like Jack and Sally if we want?" I tease, quoting our song.

He kisses the top of my head. "And we'll have Halloween on Christmas, except this time, there will be no end, I'm never letting you go."

Chapter 53

Sienna

I look out the small window of the cramped helicopter to distract myself from the questions beginning to swirl inside my head.

"Where are we going?" My voice cracks slightly in anticipation.

"I told you, but first, we have to make a pit stop," he says with a grin. His eyes practically beam with excitement at whatever he has planned.

Releasing my hand, he reaches for a cigarette. He flicks his lighter, letting the embers crackle on the end as he takes his first drag. Smoke billows from his mouth, filling the small space.

I'm about to make a smart-ass comment saying as much as I love him, I would prefer not to inhale his secondhand smoke. But even I know that is a lie. I would suck the cancerous smoke from his mouth without hesitation, and foolishly if the tables were turned, he would do the same for me. We've killed together, so what's a slow, smoke-filled death together in comparison?

I lose track of time, lost in my thoughts and before I know it, I feel the 'copter begin to descend. Still not sure of where we are going, I look out the window once more, and confusion smacks my tired brain when I see what appear to be tombstones. As our descent continues and the smog begins to separate, I realize my eyes are not deceiving me, we are surrounded by the distinct slate of gravestones.

"Where are we?" I ask already knowing the answer; however, I'm confused as to why this is our pit stop.

"Oh, come on, don't act so surprised. Since when have you shied away from a little carnage, my macabre queen," he says with a smile that makes my heart flutter with anxious arousal.

Once we land, Alex leaps from his seat and outside the still running 'copter to let us out.

Carmine takes one last drag from his vanishing cigarette and tosses the butt out of the door, while Alex motions for us to come out.

Carmine grabs hold of my hand, bringing me closer to him. His eager lips make their way up to my ear. "Are you ready, *mi reina?*" he whispers in his seductive baritone.

"I guess," I reply in a breathy tone, still reeling from the effect he has on my body.

"Come on, we have to pay our respects," he states with a mischievous grin.

He leads me out of the helicopter and motions something to Alex. He nods to Carmine and says, "I'll take Nada for a ride with me, be back then". Carmine waves to him as he shuts the door.

The propellers begin to swoosh loudly as Alex takes off. I wait until the noise lessens to address Carmine again.

"Pay our respects? Who died?" I ask. But he still does not answer me.

Instead, he guides me deeper into the sea of tombstones that encompass whatever cemetery we are in. Still waiting for Carmine to reveal what he has up his sleeve, I follow him, accepting his silence in the hopes that I haven't made a colossal mistake by fleeing with him.

I should know better. As if any moment with him could ever be a mistake. Any hellish moments I experience in his presence are arguably bliss compared to moments I was robbed of his presence.

We continue to walk, losing the light the helicopter gave off as Alex soars above us. Tonight, is exceptionally dark, making the night sky appear vaster than it already is. Not a star in sight, just a velvet, black ocean of endless sky adorned with a luminous full moon. The leaves swirl and crunch as the combination of the November wind and the propellers dance together. My hair releases itself from being tucked behind my ears, and as I go to move it back in place, Carmine suddenly stops. That's when I see *it*.

My heart begins to race with curious excitement as I take in the two beautifully ornate tombstones that are in front of me. I let go of Carmine's hand and continue to inch forward, admiring the details of the chiseled stone. My eyes are immediately drawn to the baroque scrolls that line the arch top of the slate. The scrolls etched into the stone match, except for one detail. One has a hummingbird, and the other has a flower. It looks like a hibiscus. Not that I know my flowers—I have a black thumb. I only recognize the flower because it matches a tattoo that I have. It was one of the tattoos I got shortly after Leo left. It is a hibiscus, the flower of Puerto Rico. Just like the flower that was in the painting from the tattoo shop all those years ago.

I take my hand and glide my fingers across the detailed art.

"Carmine, this is beautiful," I declare.

"You like, *mi reina?*"

"They are beautiful, but why are you showing me this?" I ask, stating the obvious. Not that I don't love cemeteries. Carmine, of all people, knows my affection for them, but still I'm not sure why he is showing me this.

"I wanted to see if you approved."

"Approve of what?" I ask with urgency.

"Where we will lay to rest."

I freeze. Suddenly, the cemetery has gone from creepy and possibly erotic to unnervingly surreal.

Did he just say what I think he said? Did I seriously endure the Hell I have for these many years to be reunited to only meet my demise at his hands? Fucking Christ, his hands. Even in this momentary panic, I can't stop staring at the way his strong hands grab for yet another cigarette. How can he make things that are so detestable somehow alluring? How does he always know how to lure me to where he knows I want to be?

My mind is racing, though my legs remain planted to the ground. I want to run, but I can't.

"Did you bring me here just to kill me?" I can barely muster up the words.

He doesn't answer right away. As he lets the plumes of

smoke mask his gorgeous face, he releases a brief smirk before answering me. Whatever he brought me for, whatever he has up his sleeve, he is getting a sick enjoyment out of it.

"Relax," he says, seemingly unfazed by his own odd demeanor.

"Umm, easy for you to say. You aren't the one who is being surprised with matching grave plots," I say sarcastically. Sarcasm has always been my shield, especially when I am uncertain. And this, whatever this is, has me feeling very uncertain.

"I didn't bring you here to kill you, Sienna. Just the opposite." He pauses.

"Care to elaborate?"

"Do you remember that day we got our locket tattoo?"

How could I forget? It was the day my heart broke, and I simultaneously found myself. I embarked on a now twelve-year-long obsession with the therapeutic art of needle to flesh. It was the moment I thought I lost my love but gained strength within myself that I did not know existed.

"Yes," I reply, simply.

"Do you remember the story of Alida and Taroo? The hummingbird and the flower?"

"Yes. I can't believe you remember. You seemed to be zoned out when Eddie was telling the story."

He reaches for my hips, pulling me into him. "I wasn't zoned out. I was trying to figure out how to get us here. To this moment." His grip remains strong with one hand as his other extends to emphasize our considerably morbid yet beautiful surroundings.

"What, to our funeral?" I half joke.

"To where we can finally let go of what was expected of us and be just that, us."

I was so distracted by him whisking us away in the helicopter that I didn't notice holds brought with him a small leather bag. He releases my hand and opens the bag, taking out something I can't quite make out in the dim moonlight. As he tosses the bag, I still don't pay attention or try to attempt to see exactly what he has in his hands. In this moment, all I see is him. He's all I have ever wanted; in whatever form he graces me with.

Inching closer to me, he continues. "One day, when I am reduced to nothing but bones beneath the dirt, my spirit will attach itself to yours. I will haunt your heart, as you have haunted mine, so you never forget that we belong to each other. In life, in death, and every concept in between. We have been marked, and you, *mi reina*, are the fate I accept with every fiber of my fractured being. You are my flower, and I am your hummingbird. Nothing can tear me away from you, not again. I have killed every obstacle that stood in our way, including my old self, to be here, where I stand with you right now. Where I will stand, always, because like the hummingbird and the flower, like the skeleton and the rag doll, you and I are meant to be."

Hearing Carmine's declaration of his love for me brings me back to that day years ago at Oogie's. The ticking of the grim reaper clock is almost audible in my mind as I teleport my memories back to that day. I can still remember every detail of the scythe on the clock and its engraving that read "memento mori."

Remember, you must die.

Before I can respond, he raises his other hand upward to reveal what I had almost forgotten he retrieved from his bag. Suddenly, a round, pale mask emerges. He stretches back the elastic from the mask, bringing it to his face. The moon shines on his now masked face, revealing pitch-black eyes with a devious, stitched grin against an all-white mask.

The darkness of night makes his internal darkness glow that much brighter. Most would run in the presence of such raw honesty, but I could never run from him. Only to him. Here, in this place, surrounded by the reminder that this life is fleeting, I feel nothing but my fate seeping in.

My fate is him. My king in life and death. And I, his queen. *His reina.*

"What do you say?" he says, holding out his hand for me to take. Instead, I lie down on the ground in front of the tombstones that eerily have our names etched in them. As I lean back on the ground, he drops to his knees, following my lead.

As I lay here with his weight on top of me, a man who I ironically thought was dead, I realize there is another kind of death aside from when our bodies leave this earth. There is death of expectation. The loss of what we think our life will be and what it instead becomes.

I never expected *this*. I never expected to have lost so much in my life yet gain even more than I could have ever fathomed. I never expected him to save my heart from the pain that he unknowingly caused. Yet, in his presence, I am met with the end of what I thought would be my fate and the living, breathing reminder of what is to come.

"What do you want?" he urges.

"For you to fuck me one last time as Sienna Ricci."

"And who will you be after, *mi reina?*"

"Whoever I want to be."

He is the needle. I am the thread. Together, we will weave a beautiful nightmare from the dead.

Epilogue

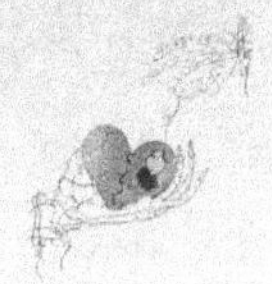

Sienna

Three Years Later...Halloween.

A warm breeze filters through the open window in my home office, letting in the crisp, autumn-drenched air. The sound of leaves rippling in the wind as they fall from the trees is mixed with the distinct chirping of the *coquis* that echo in the distance. It's a sound that I have grown to love the longer we have lived here. Autumns are warmer here on the island than back home in New York. But the beauty of this island feels more like home than anywhere else.

This year marks three years since we have made the island our home. Carmine inherited land from his mother that he spent years dedicating to building an off-the-grid escape for us. Our own slice of Heaven on Earth, our beautiful gothic oasis.

I lean back in my velvet chair, admiring the scenery

outside my window as Carmine shifts his weight from where he is positioned under my desk.

"Please, for me," he begs as he lifts his head from in between my legs.

I roll my office chair back, allowing him to come up for air. It's no wonder that he spent so much time picking out the perfect desk for me to write at, because he spends enough time underneath it while I write.

I look down at him, kneeling before me. I will never tire of how he makes my heart skip a beat when I am in his presence. "It's not finished yet. I don't want to read it to you until it is perfect."

Still on his knees, he leans toward me, bringing his hands to my knees as he lifts himself slightly, coming closer to my face. He licks his lips before bringing them to my neck for a kiss. He knows that is my weakness. He won't stop seducing me until he gets what he wants. Persistent man.

He trails his tongue down my neck until his lips are at my collarbone. I jump, as the cool sensation of his breath hits my skin as he sinks his teeth gently into my flesh.

"That's what you said about your last two books, and they are both best sellers," he reminds me in -between nibbles.

I still can't believe I am finally an author. Granted, it would have been nice to write under my given name, but with the business Carmine is in and the disastrous trail we left behind, a clean slate was needed. More importantly, an untraceable one.

"I know but—"

He interrupts me, bringing his finger to my lips to quiet the doubt-filled words he already knows I am going to say.

I kiss his fingers that are draped over my mouth, which brings a wickedly beautiful smile to his lips. He moves his hand down, pulling my chin into his grasp. "How many times do I have to tell you, if you wrote it, then it's perfect. You write from your soul, and your soul is worth sharing. Every deep, passionate, dark, intimate part."

I roll my eyes and smile at him. His persistence, to drown in all parts of me, physically, emotionally, creatively, all of it, is just so him.

"Ah, fine, but it's not finished yet, I'll just pick a random paragraph."

"Perfect, now, let me get back to what you so rudely interrupted before the girls wake up from their nap," he says with a ravenous smirk.

He grabs hold of my wrist as he goes to kneel back down in front of me.

"Ouch, be careful," I remind him, as I dart my eyes in the direction of the fresh ink on my wrist. With apologetic eyes, he gently kisses it, realizing he unintentionally scratched my latest tattoo. *Our* latest tattoo. It was an early anniversary present to each other. He got a hummingbird, and I got a hibiscus, both in the shape of a locket.

As he nestles himself once more between my legs, I glance at the monitor from the twins' nursery to make sure they are still asleep. I turn down the volume, keeping the monitor in sight in case one of them wakes up. Not that we don't have enough help if one of the girls does wake up. Titi Lana and Vanessa are here visiting for the week, to celebrate with us since Halloween is a busy time for our family. Not only is it our anniversary and Carmine's birthday, it's also the twins' birthday.

As I begin to read to him, the heat from his mouth on my slit slips me into a pleasurable oblivion.

"Go ahead, pretty girl, don't let me interrupt you." He continues to move his warm tongue up and down my center, teasing me until I continue reading.

It used to be me reciting Poe while he fucked me with his tongue, but now that he is married to an author, he requests my work instead. An unusual, yet ego-boosting kink he has acquired. Personally, I'd rather hear any of Poe's countless masterpieces read aloud any day of the week, over having to hear my own voice reciting my work. But he insists, so I gladly oblige him.

I settle on a random paragraph to read him from my latest work in progress. Concentrating is difficult as he dives into me with his tongue, but my eyes lock find a random paragraph and I begin reading it quickly before I come undone.

"Death came for me, swiftly in the night. I knew my fate was just around the corner, though its arrival was something I still didn't anticipate. Death sunk its teeth into me, not by bullet, blade, or illness. Death came in the form of a man who stole everything away from me that I thought I wanted and in return gave me a gift I didn't know I needed. A second chance, freedom, unconditional love. Death, sweet muerte, seeped itself into my bloodstream and in me now flows the crimson of a woman who can finally survive his skeletal grip."

He dives deeper in between my legs before I finish reading, and I squeeze my thighs around his neck as I release on his face.

"Delicious as always, S. Schelectro," he praises. *I love*

when he calls me that. He helped me come up with my pen name, given our mutual love for all things Halloween and how so much of our lives have centered around it, we found it fitting.

"And perfect timing," I say as I look at the monitor and see both girls waking up.

He stands up before kissing me on the forehead. "You stay and write, *mi amor*. I'll take care of the girls." He is about to walk to the door when he stops, turning back to face me.

"I almost forgot ..." He motions to a wrapped present that I didn't notice before in the corner of the room, by the gathered, tied-back curtains. He retrieves it, crinkling the wrapping paper as he hands it to me.

"Happy Anniversary, *mi reina*." He kisses me, handing me the gift just as the girls begin to stir in their nursery.

"Come on, boy." He claps his hands, waking up Nada, who has been sleeping on his bed in my office. He slowly wakes up, shaking his collar, before he trots over to Carmine.

Eagerly, I tear away at the gift wrap in anticipation as to what he got for our anniversary. We said no gifts, especially since he had Eddie fly out to do our tattoos for us yesterday. It has become an anniversary tradition for Carmine to fly Eddie out to tattoo us and to spend some time on the island.

I rip at the last bit of wrapping paper and my heart stops.

Tears begin to fill in my eyes as I stare at the painting that made my heart skip a beat all those years ago. The one hanging in Oogie's, that Eddie's wife, Maria, had painted. I run my hands over the canvas, admiring the simplicity of the painting. The hummingbird on its flower. *The lover finding their home in their soulmate.*

I look over to the monitor as I hear the twins cooing. Carmine begins getting both of the girls out of their cribs as he clears his throat.

He looks to the camera in their room, staring at me as I watch him on the monitor.

"I am the hummingbird; you are my beautiful flower. In life and death. *Siempre.* Happy Anniversary, *mi reina.* Thank you for igniting a fire in my soul, one that I would be nothing without."

I put the canvas down on my desk and reach for the monitor. Carmine's eyes are still on me, as he now holds both of our girls in his arms. I press the intercom button to speak.

"Happy Anniversary, *mi amor.*"

Carmine smiles before inching closer to the camera of the monitor. "I love you, *mi reina.* I have always and will always love you. Even when my body someday turns to ash, I will haunt your heart, so you will always have a piece of me with you." He declares through the speaker.

Tears begin to form in my eyes as I press the button to speak. "There is no one I'd rather be haunted by ... I am the needle ..." I begin.

"You are the thread ..." he replies.

"Together, we weave our love story from the dead," we say in unison through the intercom.

Now that I am a mom, I often think of how Mama would feel seeing me choose the life she despised and not only living it but raising our daughters in it.

It's funny how, even as adults, our parents' approval still weighs on us, even if they are buried beneath the ground. It's a burden our conscience carries, especially if we have veered off the path our parents set forth for us.

I'm not sure where Mama and Papa's souls rest now. I'm still not sold on the concept of Heaven or Hell. It all feels so subjective to reality. All I know is I don't want Carmine and me to waste our years on this Earth worrying about how to conform our souls in the off chance that there is a palace in the sky. I don't want to raise our daughters to be slaves to that delusional conformity, either.

One day, when my time comes, and I reach the end of the road, I will take my chances to see if mine or Mama's beliefs were correct. All I know is that I have already lived life without Carmine, and it felt like Hell on Earth. Now that I have him, *all of him*, the idea of Heaven does not feel like it's in the sky, but instead, it is right here. It is right now. Heaven, if such a concept exists, is in the moments that I have with Carmine and our little family.

Here, on *La Casa De La Espiral*, we have stitched together our own perfect ending.

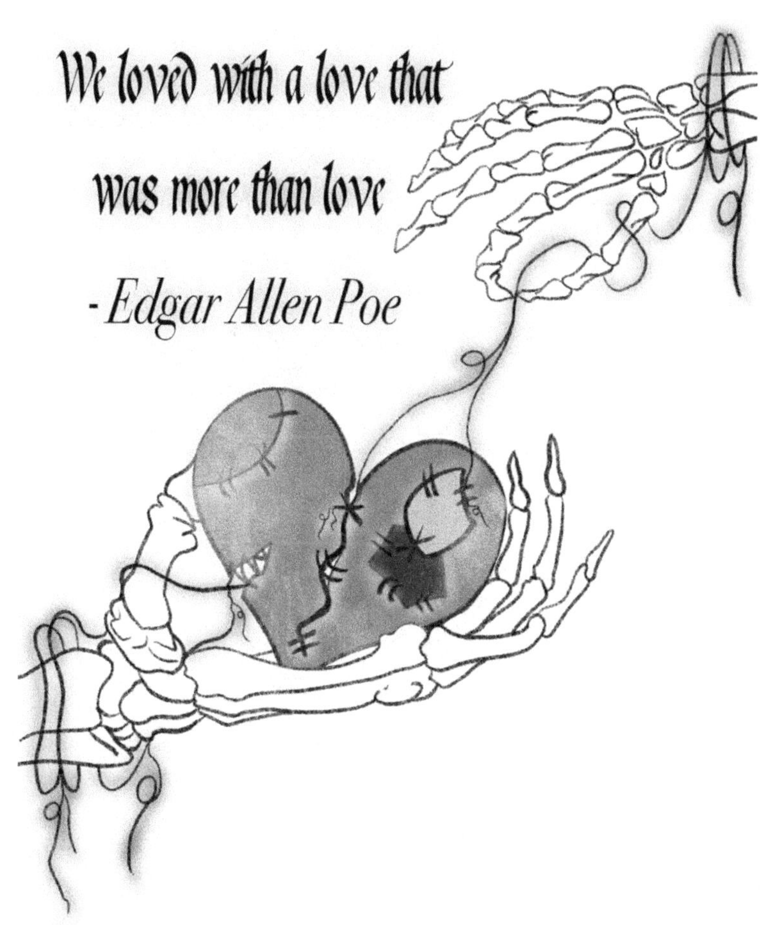

We loved with a love that
was more than love
- Edgar Allen Poe

Thank you for reading!

Thank you for taking a chance and reading my debut novel! I hope you enjoyed Carmine and Sienna's story as much as I enjoyed being the vessel to share it!

If you did enjoy Skulls and Stitches it would mean so much to me if you would consider taking the time to leave a review. Reviews play such an integral part in authors success (especially as an indie author) so that would mean the world to me!

Leave a review on Goodreads!

Leave a review on Amazon!

Afterword

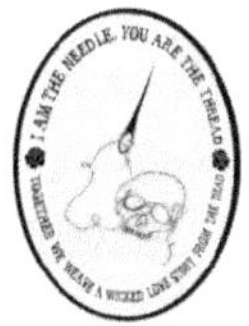

If you follow me on Instagram, or "Booksta", as most of us prefer referring to it as, then you will already know that I LOVE all things spooky. The Nightmare Before Christmas has remained one of my favorite movies even to this day.

The dynamic between Jack and Sally always resonated with me. So when I finally allowed myself to give into my life-long dream of becoming an author, I knew I had to write something that spoke to their relationship, and so Skulls and Stitches was born.

As long as I can remember I thought in story form. From a young age I would process my surroundings in my inner voice. Envisioning how to transform my surroundings into words that felt just as alive on paper as they did in my mind.

For fun I would write short stories, poems, anything that came to mind. I always scribbled my thoughts out onto paper, hoping one day I would gain the courage to set my words free out into the world.

When I was ten years old, I did a "What I Want To Be" when I grow up project and I said a writer.

I kept that dream dormant for over twenty years until I reached rock bottom in my life. Questioning the faith that was put on me from a young age, dealing with a health crisis in my family and being dealt with a deck of cards that made me feel broken. I escaped the chaos on my life through reading and writing again. Just like Sienna, words written and words read truly are my favorite forms of therapy.

I don't know if my life would be the same if I didn't rediscover my love for reading and indulge my dreams by setting pen to paper.

Like my dedication to my daughters said. If there is a dream in your heart, if there is something you feel you are destined to do or be, love yourself enough to follow that path. It may not be the popular path and chances are it won't be easy but it will be worth it. Life is too short to be anything but your true self. Believe in yourself, believe that you deserve to write your own happy ending and fight like hell to make it happen.

I can't thank you enough for reading my debut novel. I have poured my heart and soul into this book, while also following two very stubborn characters leads, Sienna and Carmine. I hope you loved their story as much I loved being the vessel for them to tell it to the world.

Acknowledgments

To my husband, Douglas.

Much like Sienna and Carmine, we knew from the very beginning that we were meant to be together. We had a magnetic pull to each other that defied explanation and now all these years later, it was that very connection that has laid the foundation for our relationship. We have been through so many highs and lows over the years, throughout it all we have only become stronger as a couple.

You remain the best decision I have ever made. Our love story has been worth every ounce of pain, every obstacle, every moment good or bad, because together we are at home. We knew it then and we know it now.

Thank you for being my biggest supporter, always encouraging me to chase my dreams and for loving me even on my darkest days. You will forever be the Jack to my Sally, just like our matching locket tattoos. I love you, *siempre*.

To my daughters,

In being your mother, I have learned so much about myself.

One day, when you think back to those moments when your mama was jotting random thoughts down or staying up until late at night with her laptop, I hope you realize my why.

The two of you inspired me to follow my dreams so I can be the living proof you need to follow yours and never give up.

There is nothing more that I want in this world than to raise my children to be strong, independent people. I want you to chase after your dreams, set goals and live your authentic truth, whatever that may be.

I love you both so much.

To my parents,

Thank you for always encouraging me to write even when I doubted myself. Thank you for providing me with an upbringing that helped mold me into the woman I am today and for loving me unconditionally. Your love and support always means so much to me and I hope that I make you both proud. I'm thankful for you both. (Especially thankful to you dad for instilling in me a love of all things spooky, you created a Halloween loving monster!)

Vera,

Thank you for always being like a second mom to me. For supporting me, encouraging me and loving me as your own. The same goes to you, Fil. I hit the jackpot having in-laws like you both! Also, thank you for all the free advertising you do for me spreading the word about Skulls and Stitches !

Jenny,

Now we have an adult version of our favorite childhood movie! Thank you for always encouraging me to follow my dreams, I love you leetle!

Stevi,

Thank you for making the process of editing my first book such an amazing one. You have made me a better writer and for that I am so grateful. You have such a talent for helping writers express themselves while refining their work to be the best it can be. Skulls and Stitches wouldn't be what it is without you and I am so excited to begin work on book #2.

Sophia,

My fellow skeleton loving, Libra. I knew from the moment I saw your work that you HAD to make the cover for Skulls and Stitches! What started as a working relationship quickly blossomed into a friendship and I am so thankful for you. You are so damn talented and I can't wait to see what you will come up with for my future books!

Beta Readers / ARC Readers,

Your excitement and interest in my work feels surreal. Your feedback, praise, all of it means so much to me. Thank you for embarking on this journey with me !

Bookstagram Peeps/friends,

The internet sucks. There I said it. It can be a black hole of nonsense. However the book community, well that has become a safe haven that I am so glad I stumbled upon.

To my younger self,

You did it. You dreamed, you set goals, you pushed through your self doubt and YOU made it happen.

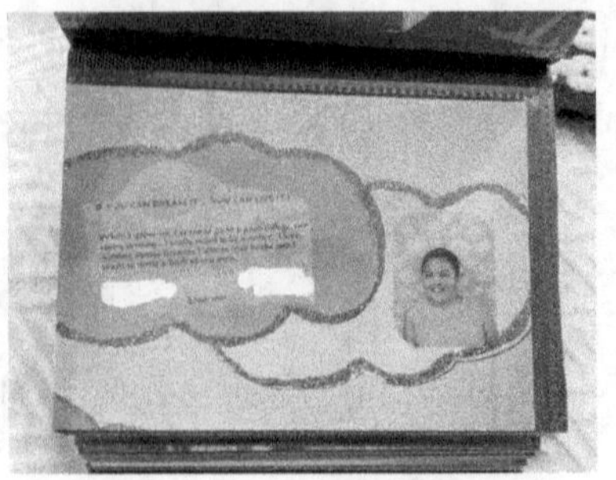

About the Author

N.J. is a life long lover of all things spooky and Halloween which she draws inspiration from in her writing. She wishes she could live in a world where Octobers never end. Sarcasm is her love language and it's a rarity to find her without a coffee in hand or wearing all black. With a BA in English Lit, she decided to put her degree to use and release the stories collecting in her head out into the world. She enjoys spending time with her husband and two daughters, getting lost in a good (preferably spicy) book, adding to her tattoo collection, listening to oos alt. rock and dreaming of the next morally grey villain she can write about!

Connect with N.J.!
  Instagram: @njweeks.books
  Website: njweeksbooks.com

www.ingramcontent.com/pod-product-compliance
Lightning Source LLC
Chambersburg PA
CBHW060600300726
48975CB00005B/1397